Western Skies

Western Skies

by

Larry Northway

aventine press

Published by Aventine Press
55 East Emerson St.
Chula Vista CA 91911
www.aventinepress.com

ISBN: 978-1-59330-967-1

Printed in the United States of America

Table of Contents

Chapter 1

New Beginnings

It was a warm, actually hot, morning in May, 1866. The Montrose family slowly approached Tucson. The family was composed of Carl, his eldest son Mag (short for Magdol) aged 16, and Desmond, called Des, aged 12. There were also two younger boys. Edwin, called Ed, was 6 and his brother Ali, for Alistair, was 7.

There was no mother in the household, she had died when Ed was born on the family plantation, called Oakside, in Virginia. She extracted a promise from Carl on her deathbed. "Make sure you get these boys out of the south before there is a war." Carl had kept his promise, sold Oakside, and liquidated all his other assets. The family relocated to Chicago and lived in one of the downtown hotels. Carl invested the money in real estate and munitions, and he did quite well for himself during the Civil War. In fact, he became a millionaire many times over.

Carl, however, was not satisfied with life as it was in Chicago. He didn't feel he belonged in the smoke-filled board rooms with the other investors, and he was not happy with how his sons were growing up. Mag loved the social life of the city and was quite popular. He gloried in the attention of all the admiring young ladies but seemed content to leave a string of broken hearts in his wake, not really caring about any of them. Carl wasn't positive, but he expected Mag had let himself be caught by one of them a time or two. Mag liked being rich and loved the privilege that came with their status. He was a bright boy, but not willing to put in the effort to develop that intellect. In short, he was spoiled.

Des was also bright, but not eager to bring attention to that fact. He preferred to blend into the woodwork and never wanted to bring notice to himself. Carl was afraid he would never make anything of himself, not because he couldn't, but because he wouldn't. He had not yet caught the social bug from Mag. He was a bit awkward and shy in social settings, but he was not unpleasant, he would never think of being unpleasant. It would never cross his mind. He did as he was told, without protest or complaint. Carl was not sure what was under that demeanor.

Ed and Ali were both young and as yet untried, and unspoiled. They were lively and rambunctious; and he was glad to say at times they had a bit of the devil. Ed had never had a mother to spoil him, and Carl suspected he longed for a bit of that. Ali had had a bit of a mother's care, but he hardly remembered it. They both were independent and could easily amuse themselves although not always in the most appropriate endeavors. They both, however, were pleasant children, eager for approval from their father.

Carl decided that for the sake of his children he should provide them with an environment that tested them a bit, to make the most of them. He corresponded with a banker in Arizona and purchased a ranch near Tucson, the Ranchero Grande. He tied up his affairs, liquidated some assets, and they all took a train to St. Louis where he purchased a wagon with a team, and a horse for each of them, as well as all the assorted requirements for a trip west. They set off across the prairie for Arizona. After several little adventures and misadventures, they had reached this point. The tired travellers were entering a very hot and very dusty small western city, glad to have finally got somewhere at last, driving a tired worn wagon with five horses attached to it and trailing along. The three younger boys were semi dozing in the back, while Carl and Mag sat on the seat.

As he drove down the street, Carl saw his target. There was a livery stable across from a bank and beside a slightly worn hotel. These were all the items he required at the moment. He pulled to a stop in front of the livery stable and leapt down. He said to Mag, "Be right back, keep them all here."

Carl entered the stable and found a boy sleeping at a desk. He shook his shoulder lightly and the boy leapt to his feet, fists raised, "Don't touch me, never touch me."

"Easy kid, I just want some help. I have a team of four tired horses and a wagon outside, and five saddle horses. Can you look after all of them, water and feed the horses, give them all a good grooming? It will only be one night; we leave in the morning. I think we will stay at the hotel across the street. How much? I'll pay up front."

"Six bits a horse and I will bring the wagon inside for the night. You can put the saddle horses in the corral to the side and I will look after the team first." Carl paid him and the two walked outside where the boys were gathered by the wagon. "The biggun is Mag, the middleun Des, and the two smallest Ed and Ali. Boys, put the saddle horses in the corral, after you have taken the saddles off, you can leave them in the wagon. Then grab your bags and we will stay in the hotel across the street."

Mag said, "You know our names, what's yours?"

"Name's Chuck," he mumbled.

After the horses were in the corral, Carl and the boys crossed the street to the hotel and he approached the desk, "I'm Carl Montrose, and these are my sons, we need a room for the night with two beds, one night."

"Hey, I'm Rafe. The room will be a buck for the five of you, number 22, top front. There is a room up there for baths, hot water. The girl is upstairs, pay her 25 cents each for the water and towels."

Carl led the boys up the stairs and into the room. Mag said, "I'm sleeping with dad, you three in the other bed. I am tired of the little ones kicking me all night."

"Okay guys, here are 4 quarters for baths, you all could use one. I have to go next door to the bank, but I won't be long, and then we will go down for supper." After Carl left, the three younger ones argued over who should go for a bath first. Mag said, "You guys fight it out and I will go first. He grabbed a towel and a clean pair of pants and crossed the hall to where a girl was sitting in a chair by a door.   "Hey, I'm Mag, here's a quarter for the water, the bath."

"I'm Louise, the tub is in here. There are two taps, one cold, but it ain't that cold, tank on the roof, and one hot, right from the boiler. Mix it how you like it, and I'll get you a couple bigger towels. The ones in the room are a mite small."

Mag started the water and started removing his clothes, hanging them on the hooks provided. He was six foot one, dark hair and eyes, and muscular; the envy of many a girl. He stood there, naked, waiting for the tub to fill. Just then the door opened and Louise entered, "Here's your …" then she stopped. Mag approached her and reached behind her to close the door and flip the latch to lock it. "I have been bouncing around in a wagon with three brothers and my dad for weeks, not a girl in sight. As you can see, I need a girl. Want to help me out?" He leaned against her so she could feel his need.

"Why should I? I don't know you, and you don't care about me."

"This isn't about caring, it's just about enjoying ourselves. You had offers from anyone better than me lately? Trust me, you will enjoy it. I know what I am doing." He sank to the floor, pulling at her to join him. She allowed herself to be drawn down and let him remove her clothing. After he was done, Louise rose and said, as she put her clothes back on, "You were right, you do know what you are doing, too bad you didn't love me." Then, she slipped out the door. Mag slipped into the bath, which was still warm, and quickly washed. He was thinking to himself, "That was nice, she was eager, felt good."

Mag returned to the room and the two little ones were still arguing. Des left for his bath. He tossed Louise a quarter, and she handed him a towel. Des ran his water and had a luxurious bath, thoroughly enjoying himself.

Next door, at the bank, Carl introduced himself to the bank manager, Lionel Deeds. He turned over a letter of credit from one of his Chicago banks, and said, "That's for four hundred thousand. Take out the rest of the money for the ranch, the fifty, and deposit the rest. You are now my banker, I guess. Tell me about the current situation at the ranch."

"Ranchero Grande, it's called. The last owner, Jackson, has left, and I am supposed to send the rest of his money to him. Sixty thousand acres, about seven or eight hundred cattle, a crew of cowboys, maybe ten, house staff, five or six, and the usual people you find around the big haciendas. They have been told of your imminent arrival."

"Okay, keep your eyes open for sales of contingent lands, any side of mine. Now, I have some hungry boys to feed." When he returned to the room, the youngest two were still arguing over who should go for a bath next. Carl grabbed them both by the scruffs of their necks and marched them down the hall to the tub room. He pushed them through the door and reached for a couple of quarters to give Louise, then he entered and turned on the water. "Now, get in there. You have fifteen minutes. If you are not clean when I come back, I will take that brush there and scrub you clean. Now get to it." As he left the room and went back down the hall he was grinning. He entered the room and looked at the other two.

"At least you two are clean, but Mag, why do you look like that cat who just ate the canary?" he asked suspiciously.

"No reason dad, I am just glad we are almost there."

Fifteen minutes later Carl returned to the tub room. He felt the boy's hair and looked behind their ears. "Okay, I guess," he said dubiously. They breathed a sigh of relief. "Now, here's a towel, get up out of that tub and back to the room."

"Daad, in these towels? Down the hall?"

"It's only ten feet, and you are clean, defeats the purpose if I let you put these dirty clothes on. Now let's go, I'm hungry."

As they were eating, Carl said, "After dinner, we will go find a store and get you guys whatever you need. This might be the last chance for a while."

Dinner was plain, but wholesome, and filling. Dessert tasted home made, apple pie, and the little ones had seconds. Afterwards, they strolled down the street and entered Peters' Dry Goods. Carl sent the boys to hunt up pants and shirts, and a new jacket for the nights that were cool in the desert. Since he wasn't sure what was at the ranch, he gave the owners a list of dry goods, like flour, sugar, tea, molasses, coffee, and the myriad of other items required for a modern household. Items that were not worth carrying cross country. He told them they would pick it all up in the morning. There would be several barrels so they would have time to get it all ready. He chatted amiably to the Peters as the boys gathered their purchases, and Mrs. Peters tallied the total as the items were placed on the counter. The boys snuck in a few toys here and there, which Carl did not object to; and Des snuck in a few books, again with no objection. Finally, they were done, and the total was arrived at.

"A hundred twelve dollars," said Mr. Peters. "I am afraid I don't know you, so I can't run an account for you." Carl handed over twelve hundred dollars and said, "Here, put the rest on an account as a credit balance. We will be living a bit outside of town, and if any of the kids come in for something, I want them to be able to get it, no question. We Montroses will be around for a while."

The Peters saw their best sale of the month leave then looked down at the fist full of money they had, somewhat awed. As they walked back towards the hotel, Carl saw a gunsmith and dragged the kids in. The sign over the door simply said, "Sam's."

"You Sam? We want some guns, holstered pistols and rifles, the best you have." Sam showed them the new Colts that took shells and had interchangeable cylinders. He also had a rifle that held ten shells and ejected spent shells at the pull of a lever. Carl said, "Okay, three dozen of the rifles,

50 000 rounds for them. Pistols, three sets of double holsters for us three, a dozen single holsters and pistols, 100 000 rounds, and two dozen of the cylinders. A dozen shotguns, 5000 rounds. I want something small enough for the little guys too." Sam produced a couple of two shot Derringers. "Okay then, and a thousand rounds for them too. They have to do some target practice. We'll let you take the night to get it all together and we will pick it up in the morning on the way out, but I will pay you now." Then, they completed their journey to the hotel. Mag was a bit troubled and whispered to his father, "Why the artillery?"

"Mag, don't want to scare you, but there are Indians out here, Apache, and they are pure evil. I have bought the guns. If you ever have to use them, don't hesitate. Pure evil."

The other boys were trailing behind and discussing the guns too.

"We're six and seven and he bought us guns. What's wrong with him?"

"And we all will learn to use the rifles too."

"I dunno guys, and he expects me to wear two on my hip. God almighty."

Back at the hotel, they got rid of their packages and went down to the dining room for coffee and a night time snack, then the family retired. There was a brief altercation where Carl separated two kicking boys and put one on either side. "If I get kicked someone will get spanked," he said simply.

Chapter 2

First Sight of Home

They were up by 6:30 the next morning, and went in search of breakfast, which they found in the dining room. Rafe took their order. Carl and Mag ordered scrambled eggs and sausages with coffee, and the three younger all had flapjacks and milk, double orders. When they were done, they went upstairs and gathered their belongings then headed over to the livery stable. The door of the stable stood open with the team already hitched to the wagon. The horses in the corral all had their saddles and were standing there quietly. Carl handed his bag to Mag and said, "Here, get our stuff stowed in the wagon and our horses tied to the back. I'll be right back, just want to say bye to the Baxters."

As Carl went towards the back of the stable, he heard the swish of a whip and someone crying out in pain, then he heard a voice say, "You are a stupid lazy boy, lazy." Then another swish and cry. Carl strode in and grabbed the upraised arm saying, "When I walk in on something like this, I might think there was a lazy youngster getting what was due, but I have seen Chuck here work and know that is not true, so then I have to think perhaps the problem is with you. Now, drop the whip and I will let go of your arm." The whip was dropped, and the arm released. "Chuck, am I right in assuming this is where you live, here in the stable?"

Chuck nodded his head. "Okay Chuck, gather your stuff up and put it with ours in the wagon. You just got a new job. You work for the Ranchero Grande, you can look after our horses."

"Now, Baxter, is there something you want to say?"

"I never wanted this, the stable, the boy, I only got into it because of my brother, and then he died and left it all for me to deal with," he said miserably.

"Then this might be your lucky day Baxter. Come with me." As they passed the wagon and the boys, Carl said, "Boys, Chuck is with us now, Mag take them all, and the wagon, down to the general store and load our stuff. Wait for me there, I won't be long," then he led Chuck's uncle across the street to the bank, where he had seen Deeds enter earlier. "Deeds, you can do me a service today, can we borrow your office for fifteen minutes?"

When they were sitting, Carl said, "Can I have a sheet of paper and a pen?" Then he spent a couple of minutes writing. He looked up and said, "Baxter, when I found you whuppin that boy I had two choices, turn the whip on you or just make you go away. You are lucky I chose the latter. I will buy the stable and I will take responsibility for the boy. Then, for a while at least, all your problems are gone, but I am sure you will find some new ones. For them, you can't blame a poor 12-year-old boy. Sign this, irrevocable, makes me Chuck's guardian, and then give it to Mr. Deeds here to witness, in case for some reason you try to change your mind in the future, you can't. Now Baxter, how much property comes with the stable, and is anything owing on it?"

"About two acres, free and clear."

"Okay Baxter, I want the stable and the land, not any livestock, you can sell it or turn it loose. I will pay you $1800.00 for the land and the stable. The deal will close at noon today. Mr. Deeds, can you write that up for us so we both can sign?" After the papers were signed and witnessed, and a copy given to each of them, Carl said, "You come back here then, and Mr. Deeds here will have your money. You better get busy Baxter, you have to clear those animals out, but you can be on your way by noon."

The two watched Baxter scoot away and then Carl said, "Start another account for me, call it land development. Take 50 000 from the main account, put it in the new account, and then take his money from that. After he collects his money, send a man over to lock and seal the stable, just to keep the drunks out. Get the property surveyed, do what you have to with the title and get the taxes sent here to you and you pay them, and all costs, from the land account. For each property you look after for me, I will pay you personally one hundred dollars a year, from that land account. Next time I come to town you can give me the survey and a set of the keys. Mr. Deeds, one of my weaknesses is owning properties. When I come to town next have a list for me of what is available and I am sure we will add to the portfolio, and everyone I add that you tend to, earns you another hundred a year. We straight Deeds?"

"Yes Mr. Montrose, we are straight, and sir, we all knew what he was doing to Chuck and no one had the gall to do anything about it. Welcome to Tucson."

Carl caught up with his family at the general store. He glanced in the wagon and saw most of the goods were loaded. He also saw a pitifully small pile of Chuck's belongings in the corner. He beckoned Chuck inside and called over Gillian and Stu Peters. "We have had a new addition to our group. Remember all the stuff the boys got yesterday, get Chuck here the same, here's another hundred for the account, get him his stuff and charge it all to the account later. A few minutes later Chuck was pushed out the door, a new hat on his head and carrying a big pile of clothing. Carl waved at the Peters as he headed to the door. On the way he grabbed a container of the rock candy and held it up saying, "Charge it to the account" and then he was gone. Gillian and Stu smiled at each other. They had made as much profit in one day as they had in the last month. Carl Montrose was already their best customer, and over the next few years, their best friend.

Carl climbed up on the wagon seat beside Mag. The kids were in the back and all the horses tied to the rear of the wagon, so they followed along. "To the gunsmith Mag, here have a piece of candy," then he took one himself and handed the jar to the boys in the back with a warning, "There should be enough there for a week, if you all try to eat it all today someone is gonna be sick tonight."

At the gunsmith, Jeffers was ready and the guns were quickly loaded on the wagon. He said, "I was short one of the rifles, but I will order it and you can pick it up next time you come to town."

"That's okay Sam, but we have one more new addition." He beckoned Chuck forward and when he was standing beside him, Carl said, "Fit this one out too, Colts, double holsters. I think we have enough bullets already." That took about five minutes and then they were on the road.

As they creaked and rattled along, Mag softly said, "Okay Dad, what's the story on the new kid?"

"When I went in, his uncle was whipping him with a buggy whip, calling him lazy. You saw how hard that kid worked. And he lived there in the stable, like a dog. So I bought the stable to get rid of the uncle and as a part of the deal had him make the kid my ward."

Mag was grinning at his father, "Dad, you are soft hearted, no matter what the others think, you couldn't let that pass could you?"

Carl said, "Yes I am soft hearted, but there are limits and you have pushed me right to the edge a couple of times."

When they were about an hour out of town, Carl yelled back, "You guys make yourself useful, break out some of those rifles and load them. It will be starting to get dark by the time we get there. Hand Mag and I a set of the holsters, after you load them of course."

They stopped and had lunch by a stream, some stew from cans warmed over a fire. Chuck ate with gusto and Carl had a thought. "Chuck, I guess you missed breakfast today, here, have a can of peaches." He then handed a couple open cans of peaches to the others to share. After lunch, Des came over and sat beside Chuck. He had a pair of overalls with something wrapped in it. "Chuck, don't take this the wrong way, but you used to live in a stable, now you don't. Frankly, you need a bath. Let's go along the stream a bit and find one of these pools in the rocks where the water is a bit warmer. I have some soap and a towel here along with a pair of your overalls."

At first, Chuck was offended, but then he realized, Des was only trying to help. They went along the bank and they found a suitable pool. Des said, "Go ahead, I'll turn my back. I brought a rifle to guard against bears or whatever the hell they have out here. There must be something that will try to eat us."

Chuck laughed, "There's only two things you have to worry about out here, and neither will try to eat you, although you might druther they did. Rattlers and Apache, that's all you have to worry about." Chuck quickly stripped off his old overalls, and sat in the pool of water. It was warm from the sun and having a bath was quite pleasant, apart from the soap in your eyes thing when you washed your hair.

Back at the wagon, Mag and Carl watched them go and Carl said, "That was a good idea, to have Des do it. Des has a kind gentle manner. We wouldn't want to offend Chuck."

"No Dad, we wouldn't, after all he was doing the best he could, given his circumstances."

"I think someone else is a little soft hearted too, if he dared to admit it," said Carl.

"Yeah, maybe, can you imagine the life that kid had, being whipped and having to live in a stable, not even being fed properly. Dad, you ride us a bit, but you would never do any of that."

At the pool, Chuck had finished bathing and had dried himself then put on his new overalls, and a pair of sox and boots, then as he looked around, he said, "Des, did you bring a shirt?"

Des turned to him, "Did I forget a shirt? Sorry. Just do up one of the straps on your overalls."

"Can't. Too embarrassed," Chuck reached for his old shirt and Des yelled out, "Stop. After all that trouble to get you clean you are not putting that shirt back on. What is the problem? It is just us guys, no girls, nothing to be ashamed of."

"It's not that, it's this," Chuck turned so Des could see his back, and the scars and welts that covered it. Des touched the back lightly.

"Chuck, you don't have anything to be embarrassed about, this was done to you, not by you. No one will think any less of you. Someday they all will see it, but here, you can wear my shirt, it was clean this morning, and I can get another one when we get back to the wagon."

"You'd do that for me? Give me your shirt?" Chuck said as Des undid his overall straps and stripped off his shirt then held it out to him.

"Sure, that what brothers do for each other, anything."

Chuck was looking at him with a strange expression on his face and Des said, "What? You didn't realize that. When Dad took you, it was not just a job, you are part of the family now. We are brothers. Now put that shirt on so we can get back. The more time we are out here alone, the more chance of meeting a rattler or its human brother."

The boys left Chuck's clothes by the river and returned to the campsite. Carl watched them walk up and wondered to himself what had happened to Des' shirt but he didn't ask. Sometimes, with boys, it was better not to ask questions. You never knew where the answers might lead. They got back on the road and no mention was made of Chuck's new condition. Des rummaged in a pack and came up with a shirt. It was a hot day and they all were semi dozing, except Mag, who was driving. He crested a hill and a scene of horror opened out before him. He stopped the team.

In a shaky voice he said, "Dad, Dad, wake up, look."

Carl roused and looked down the hill. There was a wagon on its side, and the contents were strewn over the road. The initial impression was of some type of accident, but then he saw the bodies tied to the wagon wheels and the ones on the grass beside the road. Carl yelled to the back, "Boys, get those rifles out and lever a round into the chambers, and get down!! You may have to use those guns at any moment." He motioned Mag to go down the hill, "Slowly" and told him to stop a dozen or so feet from the wreckage. "Guns at the ready boys, but stay in the wagon, in shelter."

He and Mag approached. They came to the four bodies on the ground first. There was a woman, a daughter they assumed about fifteen or so, and two twin girls about ten. One of the little girls still held a teddy bear. They all had their dresses thrown up towards their heads and their underclothing down around their ankles. It was evident they had been raped, repeatedly, and forcefully, likely until they died as there were no bullet wounds or slit throats to account for their deaths.

Tied to the wheels on the wagons, it was clear the males had not had easier deaths. Their shirts were ripped open to leave them bare chested and their pants and underclothing were down around their ankles. The faces and chests were covered in tiny little slits, deep enough to hurt and bleed, but not one of them deep enough to have caused death.

Mag said, "What's that, in their mouths?"

"Son, that's their penis. The Apache cut it off and put it there as a sign of disrespect. They don't do that to other warriors."

"Dad, do they do that before they die or after?"

"Mag, they do it before, probably at the first when they start. They want the victim to feel the most pain for the longest time. The blood loss from that is likely what killed them."

"Oh God Dad, I'm gonna be sick," He turned away and leaned against the wagon, vomiting repeatedly. Carl put a hand on his shoulder when he stopped and said, "We can't leave them like this. Go back to the wagon and get the boys out with the shovels. Have them dig five graves on the other side of the wagon. The twins should go in together. I'll cut the men down and make everyone decent and then we will bury them." As Mag supervised the others, Carl prepared the bodies. He found blankets in the wagon to wrap each of them. Then he looked for something to identify the family. He found a bible and a box of papers. They were from Indiana heading for California. Names were Sherman, Herbert and Gladys, son Peter, daughter Elizabeth, and twin girls Meg and Jenny. Such a horrific way for a family to end, he thought.

When the graves were ready, he and Mag moved the bodies. None of them was very heavy. Carl read from the family bible over them, Corinthians seemed appropriate, and the graves were filled in. Carl found an empty jar and scribbled a note detailing what had been found, when, and by whom, and asking that whoever found the jar, take it to the sheriff in the nearest town. He left the jar by a crude cross Mag erected over the graves. Then they carried on.

The boys in the back were silent, even though they had been spared much of the horror. Mag was quiet too, then he grimly said, "If that ever happens to us, we have to see to them first, and then to each other. We can not let them do that to us."

Carl simply said, "Yes."

Finally, about dusk, they stopped at a fork in the road. There was a sign with an arrow. In fact, two arrows. One pointed to the right and said, "Richville 127 miles." The other pointed left and said, "El Ranchero Grande 3 miles."

As they drove up the drive, they noticed a beautiful sunset in the west. There were many cacti, and many of them almost looked as if they were praying to the setting sun. The hacienda became visible. It looked almost like a fortress, high earthen walls, small windows at the top, a ceramic tile roof in the style of Mexico. They came to a pair of heavy gates that were closed, and Carl beat on them several times before a very old man came to open them. When they pulled in, they saw why everything had looked so foreboding. Everything was built around a central plaza, the house itself, two or three barns, and several smaller buildings. There were at least three wells in the courtyard. Slowly the staff came out to see who had arrived. There were a little over half a dozen cowboys, an older lady who was definitely a cook, she was quite overweight. A couple foolish young girls who were likely the housemaids. They seemed impressed with the three older boys. A middle-aged couple stepped forward and introduced themselves as Hose, the foreman; and Imelda, the housekeeper.

Carl introduced himself as Carl Montrose, the new owner, and said the boys were his sons. Hose had the cowboys unload the wagon, the foodstuff to the kitchens, and the rest to the front hall. Imelda sent the housemaids to light the candles in the halls and the kerosene lamps in the great room, and there were five hand lanterns on a table in the hall for the boys to use as they found their rooms that night. She asked if they required dinner, and Carl said, "Yes, but keep it simple."

Imelda brought out some bread, and cheese, and some roast beef sliced into thick slabs. She served it on the big table at the end of the great room. That was fine for the boys, it eased their hunger. There was cool water, and some wine. When the younger boys made to take the wine, Carl sternly said, "You guys stick to the water. No wine till you are sixteen."

Hose came in and made a fire in the huge fireplace and they all gathered around, pulled some chairs up and huddled a bit.

Carl said, "Well, we are here, we have had dinner, the next thing is to find you all bedrooms. Apparently, there are eleven of them upstairs, but I expect we will want them close to the top of the stairs. What say you guys all visit the privies outside, then we will go up."

When they all returned, Carl said, "Now, how many do we need?"

Ed and Ali said, "We can share a room as long as there are two beds in it, so our feet don't get mixed up when we sleep. "

Mag said, "A room of my own with a big bed," and he muttered to himself, "In case I get lucky."

Des and Chuck looked at each other and Des said, "We don't mind sharing a room, would be nice if it has two beds though." Chuck nodded in agreement.

"And one for me, one bed though, a big one," said Carl. "Okay then, grab your stuff, and a lantern, and let's go find our new homes."

The first room to the right at the top of the stairs was immediately claimed by Mag, "One bed, not too big, see you guys tomorrow," then he entered and closed the door.

The room across the hall opened onto the courtyard, had big windows and some doors that opened onto a little balcony. There were two beds, wide but low, and the room was claimed by Ed and Ali.

The remaining three moved down the hall. They opened the door to the room beside Mag's and found a large room with two big beds and some windows at the end that looked over the stables. Des and Chuck claimed that room. As they looked down, they could see the cowboys putting the horses in the stable for the night.

Carl crossed the hall and entered what would be his room. It was large and had an enormous bed. There was a whole wall of windows and doors and a huge terrace outside.

As they would find out, all the rooms had small rooms with their own tubs to take baths, every room had big fireplaces, and lots of closets. There were tables with pitchers and basins for light washes and there were little stands with chamber pots, which they all vowed not to use.

Mag lay naked in the center of his big bed and wished he had someone there with him, a female someone, but he soon fell asleep. It had been a long difficult day.

After fifteen minutes, each in their own bed, Ed and Ali came to a mutual conclusion. Neither could sleep alone, despite the problem of the kicking feet. They decided they would share a bed, but that each would sleep at the edge so maybe their feet would not encounter each other's. When they awoke in the morning, they found they were sleeping together in the center of the bed.

In Chuck and Des' room, the question became what to wear to bed. Des rummaged in his bag and came up with a couple of night shirts, then offered one to Chuck who said, "What's that? It looks like a dress. I ain't wearing no dress."

"Fine, what did you wear to bed then?"

"In the stable, I had two choices. I could go to bed in the clothes I wore all day, or nuttin."

"You mean you went to bed with nothing, naked?"

"Yup, except in the winter, if it was really cold, Unc would give me a pair of his long underwear. It can get cold in the desert at night. Since it is hot tonight, I guess I am going to bed with nuttin, you can wear your dress if you want though."

Chuck turned down his lantern, kicked off his boots and sox, then dropped his overalls and crawled into bed. Des stood there unsure. He wanted to wear his nightshirt, but it did look like a dress, now that you mentioned it. Finally, he did the same as Chuck. They lay, each in their own beds under the covers and Chuck smiled and said to Des, "See, doesn't it feel good to let them free for a bit?"

Des had to agree, it did. The both soon dozed off.

Carl was the last to turn his light out and go to sleep. He did wear a nightshirt. He had trouble dozing off though. He couldn't stop wondering if he had done the right thing, bringing the boys out here. This was a hard land. Maybe they should have gone to California.

Chapter 3

Big Changes

The next morning the household woke about 7:00. Before he went down, Carl took a tour of the remaining rooms on the second floor. There were five or six other bedrooms, similar to the ones they had chosen, and he found one at the end perfect for his purposes, large enough, wooden floors and some nice high windows. It was also at the right corner of the house for what he wanted.

He went down and found the boys gathered around the big table. The younger ones had large glasses of cool milk and Mag had a cup of coffee. All of them had large plates of flapjacks, eggs, ham, and toast. Carl sat and Imelda came in with a plate for him and a new pot of coffee.

"Imelda, can you send a message to Hose that I would like to see him in a half hour?"

"In the office room?" she asked pointing, Carl nodded, not really sure what the office room was but expected it was the ranch office.

While they ate, he asked the boys if they had slept well and received five vigorous yes nods. "If nothing else is right about this place, the beds are good, and the chow is not so bad either," said Mag.

"But those privies Dad, they are rank," said Des.

"Give me three weeks, and I will have you a lavatory and bathing room equal to those in Chicago. Remember my stops in St. Louis? Those people are right behind us. Now, on my tour today with Hose, I want all of you to come. I want all of us to know everything about the ranch."

After eating, they all wandered into the ranch office and it was indeed a big room. On the walls, there were several maps. There was a big desk, a table to the side with more maps, and about twenty chairs in various groupings around the room. They all found somewhere to sit and when Hose came in, he seemed to be standing in the center of the room holding his hat. Carl said, "Hose, you are going to take us on a tour of this place, we want to see it all, but not the house, that's Imelda's."

When they were outside in the courtyard, Hose said, "The Hacienda is a bunch of houses gathered together inside a big wall. There is the main house, the kitchens in their own building, the stable, and a barn where the cows and pigs are kept, a chicken coop, and several small houses for the workers, for the house and the ranch. It is almost like a small village."

Carl led him over to a small well at the southeast corner of the house, a little off by itself. "I see there are several wells here for the hacienda, I counted seven, including this one, and I assume there is a pump and well for the kitchens. I want you to build a building around this well, about ten by twenty feet, ten high. Beside it I want you to build a windmill tower, about twenty feet high. The wood and a bunch of men will arrive today. The men will be involved in another project, but I will have one assigned to this to work with your men until it is closed in. Then they will take over the inside and your men will just finish the outside to make it look like it belongs."

Hose nodded, and they continued their tour. They entered the stables where they found their eight horses and a dozen, and a half others. The stables were in good shape and run efficiently, the animals well cared for. "Chuck, you come out here later with Hose and he will help you chose a horse for yourself, and set you up with a saddle. This afternoon, I hope we can all take a ride with him and see a bit of the land."

To Hose he said, "Find him a good steady horse, the right size, and when he has chosen, tell the others that is Master Chuck's horse and no one else will ride it."

Then they toured the barns and the other facilities of the Hacienda. Carl said, "Hose, it seems to me the five or six men you have, and the house people are just enough to run the hacienda. This is a sixty-thousand-acre ranch, who sees to that?

"Mr. Jackson had about a thousand head, and he had separate people to do that. They lived in a bunkhouse out back." He led them through a gate and about five hundred feet behind the hacienda there was another barn, several corrals, and a bunkhouse. There was also a cookhouse off to the side and a little cabin.

"When Mr. Jackson left, all the men left too. The cattle are still there, I guess. Once in a while one of the boys from the hacienda goes out and finds one to kill for our purposes. There was a foreman who lived in the little cabin and his men lived in the bunkhouse, about ten of them." They entered the bunkhouse, and Carl was not impressed. It was cheap and shoddy, and filthy. "You get a crew of women out here this morning to clean this up. There is a construction crew arriving today and this is where they will have to live, is there anything else we have to see or is that it?"

"Out on the range there are some small cabins for the men at night, one or two if they are caught, but that is pretty much it, except there is a little silver mine and a little copper mine, a short ride to the east. There are a few buildings at either of them, no one at either now though."

On the way back, Carl reminded Hose to get started on the little building and to get the bunkhouse cleaned, then he said to the boys, "Now, we have a meeting in the office so I can show you what is planned for this place."

A while later, with the boys sitting around him, Carl said as he pointed to a map on the wall, "This is what we have now, sixty thousand acres with the hacienda down in the corner by the road. There is a chance we may get the 60 000 across the top to make a capital tee. Right now, it doesn't make a cent. Loses money. Also, right now, there are thirty thousand longhorn cattle on their way here from Texas, and thirty cowboys. There is also a crew of carpenters on their way here, due today, to build three new bunkhouses for those cowboys. I have two contracts with the army for five thousand head each, deliverable here and those two contracts will cover the cattle costs and the new bunkhouses. The game will be to make the other twenty thousand pay. In addition, we want to make the Copper and Silver mines pay their way too. There is also that crew due here any moment from St Louis to build us that modern lavatory bathing room.

Just before lunch, Carl was in the courtyard with Hose when a rider came in the big gates. As he dismounted, he queried, "Mr. Montrose?"

Carl waved him over. "I am John Jenner, head of the carpenters, there are about fifteen of us and we met a crew of plumbers on the road who were coming here too. We all joined up. Where do you want us, this is a pretty small courtyard."

Carl led him thru the back gate to the bunkhouse. "You guys can camp here. The one existing bunkhouse I want made into a ranch office. Then construct four new bunkhouses, each for about ten people, and a couple of barns, in this shape, to make a compound, and a new mess hall, I think the existing cookhouse can be okay, just tidy it up a bit. The idea is, when you finish the bunkhouses you join them all with walls, like a fort. Injuns." Carl drew on the ground with a stick as he talked. "One more thing, assign one of your men to the plumbers. The locals have started a new building for a pump house boiler room, and we need someone to keep an eye on it as it is built. The locals will finish the exterior to make it blend in with the rest of the hacienda. There may be a few minor things in the house."

"Okay, I will bring the group here to set up, then I will bring the head plumber, of the six or so, you can explain what you need there. I think I know what you want here. We will spend the rest of the day organizing and get a good start tomorrow. We will likely have to send for more wood, but we have enough to start."

"Remember to save all your burnable scraps. They can be used in the boiler house as fuel."

When he talked to the plumbers, Carl showed them the room he wanted them to use, pointing out it was just above the well and boiler house, and that the side of the house it was on was at the top of a steep rise. "Bring the drains down the outside of the house and put dispersion pipes under the slope here. At least there will be one patch of green grass hereabouts. Put tanks up there on the roof and use the windmill to pump it all up there. One side line, hot and cold, to the kitchen sinks. They still are using a hand pump and big pots on the stoves. It must be like hades in there."

When the crews pulled out three weeks later, Carl had his ranch hand accommodations, three bunkhouses, a mess hall, a ranch office, a couple of barns, and some new corrals, along with several new privies and a wash house for good measure.

At the hacienda there was a new boiler house, a new washing room lavatory upstairs and new lines to the kitchen for hot and cold water at the turn of a tap. All the pumping was done by the windmill.

Upstairs in the washing room, there was a long counter with three basins on it, each with their own hot and cold tap and drains you just had to pull the plug out on. There were two separate rooms each with their own tub, taps, and drains. No carrying of water there. There were two lavatories off to one side each in their own little room. They each had tanks over them and chains to pull. No more trips outside to use the out houses.

It all was marvelous technology and a mystery to the staff, but it saved them a lot of work pumping, carrying, and heating water. Carl was lucky that there was one young man, about fifteen, among the locals, who didn't want to be a cowboy. He was a bright boy and the plumbers taught him enough to ensure the boiler never exploded and the pumps kept running, and they showed him how to drain the tanks on the roof periodically. Carl paid him five dollars a week to make sure there was always hot and cold water, and the boy in turn gave a couple of the younger children a quarter a week to make sure the wood boxes were always full. He moved himself into a corner of the boiler house, which was one of the best built worker's houses on the property, counting himself lucky to have been chosen for the job.

The household was waiting for the arrival of the cattle. Carl and the boys had continued with the shooting practice, joined by several of the men in the hacienda. When the men were proficient, Carl gave each of them a rifle and ten thousand rounds of ammunition on the promise that they help defend the hacienda if it were ever attacked. When word came from the cattle drive that they were still a month away, Carl decided he and the boys should take a trip back into town, Tucson. They would leave early one morning, be in town by noon because they had no slow wagon to nurse along. They would leave the next day early enough that they would be home before dark. They did take a buckboard which Carl was sure would be loaded by the time it left town, but it was fast and would not slow them down to any great degree. Chuck volunteered to drive it and was quite good at it.

When they arrived in town, they pulled up to the livery. Carl told the boys to put the horses in the corral and unsaddle them. Deeds saw them and came over with the keys so they could put the buckboard inside. Carl told the boys to see to the horses, and when they were done to come over to the hotel. He and Mr. Deeds would be in the lobby talking. When he went in, Carl told Rafe he would need two rooms that night, two beds each, then he sat down with Lionel.

"Okay Lionel. You seem glad to see us, which likely means you have found some property you want me to look at."

"There are several. Mrs. Dunhill's School for Girls is for sale. She would like to stay there and keep on with her school, but she just wants to be rid of a mortgage. Her mortgage is 56 dollars a month and she is willing to pay fifty rent. The building is in good shape and after taxes you should make several hundred a year. Another is the Blue Belle Saloon. Blake Denver is the owner, but he wants to go back east. One of his barmen wants to rent the saloon, but he can't afford to buy the building.

"Now, this saloon, there are no girls are there? Some of them have the girls upstairs."

"No, this is strictly a drinking establishment. The owner, Denver, has a wife and she would kill him if there were any girls near the place."

"So far, so good, anything else?"

"There is the building where the Peters' Store is. There is the Peters' Store and one other on the main floor. The second store is vacant. Upstairs there are eight apartments, all rented, one to the Peters. Have to be honest on this one. To make the figures work you either have to rent the second store or raise the Peter's rent."

"Okay, let us have lunch, then we will look at the school, the saloon and lastly, the store building. Start say 1:30." He looked up and saw the boys coming across the road. They had their saddle bags and their rifles, but they had apparently left their saddles in the livery stable. Mag handed his dad the key. "Didn't see any reason to drag the saddles around. We put them in the buckboard and locked it all up."

Rafe handed a couple of keys to Carl, "Adjoining rooms, just slide the doors back." They all went upstairs, and Mag claimed one of the beds for himself. "If someone has to sleep alone let it be me." Carl pushed Ed and Ali ahead of him into the other room, "You guys and I are here, that way you can go to bed at a reasonable hour." Then he stood in the doorway between the rooms. "We will have lunch, then Deeds has a couple of properties he wants me to look at. Everyone leaves their guns here in the rooms. Don't want you guys in some fight with a drunken cowboy."

There were several groans from some of the boys. "I thought you guys would like that, one is a girl's school, one is a saloon, and one is the building where the Peters store is." That tweaked the interest of some of them, especially Mag. The group had lunch in the hotel dining room, and then left at 1:30. Deeds met them and said, "We can easily walk, everything is within a block."

When they arrived at the school, Carl took a few minutes to look at the building. It was a big three storey former residence, brick, well kept, and with a little fenced yard out front. The students of the school were grouped in the living room and the dining room with teachers. They looked up when the boys came in and giggled. The boys blushed. Mrs. Dunhill lead them through, past a study into the kitchen, showing them a back porch, then up some back stairs to the second floor where there were eight bedrooms, each of which had two girls sharing. Then they went to the third floor where Mrs. Dunhill and a couple of staff stayed. There was a common living room for them.

Mrs. Dunhill said, "The facilities are out back. Sometimes the young ladies use the chamber pots. Now, Mr. Montrose, I am sure Mr. Deeds has told you, I want to continue here, as a tenant. I want to start thinking of my retirement and if I am going to have a mortgage, I want it to be on something back east I can retire to."

They were shown back outside through the front door and gathered for a few minutes on the front sidewalk. "Deeds, good property, well kept, and I look at property for its long-term value. I like this one. Now let's go to the saloon." This was the one the boys had been waiting for.

As the group entered the bar keep looked up and said, "Most of youse are too young to be in here."

Lionel Deeds stepped forward, "These are the Montroses, I mentioned he might want to buy the building."

"Barkeep, give them what they want," the boys rushed the bar, "As long as it is Sarsaparilla, even the big one who thinks he knows everything," said Carl. While the boys had their sodas, Carl, Blake, the owner, and Lionel Deeds toured the building. The saloon was straight forward, the whole first floor, big main room and a storage room at the back. The basement was mainly storage, but it was clean and dry. The second floor had four apartments, one taken by the owner and three rented. They were simple two room apartments. When they went back downstairs Blake introduced them to Frank Demers, who wanted to rent the place and run the saloon after Blake left. Carl made no comment to Deeds as they walked over to the Peters Store building. When they got there, he said to the boys, "You can go in, buy whatever you need and tell the Peters I will be in shortly."

He and Deeds then went into the other storefront and Carl was impressed. It was clean and spacious, and well kept. The building was the last on the block, so the empty store had a nice corner entrance. They took a quick look downstairs and found a clean dry basement, with a big coal furnace and a boiler. The Peters part next door was walled off. They went out and around the corner to find another entrance to the second floor where there were eight apartments. "They are all rented but one is empty because the new renters don't move in until tomorrow. They went in to find a nice two-bedroom apartment with a living room, dining room, and kitchen. There was water in this building and taps in the kitchen. Heat was by steam radiators. The two stood in the empty living room looking down on the street.

"Okay on Dunhill, good property. Okay on this one, but I will find the tenant for the empty store. Now, the saloon, I don't like Demers, but I don't have to like my tenants. The building is okay. Tell Blake I will buy the building, minus the saloon, I want nothing to do with it. He gives us empty possession of the first floor, and you put something else there. Now for all of them, I want you to have completed contracts, signed by the vendors and a price agreed for tomorrow morning. I will stop in to your office before we leave. I will leave it to you to negotiate price, with the understanding that you will come back with a price you yourself would be willing to pay. Usual deal for your management. You did a good job here. We have a long road in front of us. Now, I had better see what my kids have selected. See you in the morning." Deeds watched him go and thought to himself that Carl knew what he was doing, he hadn't thought much of Demers either.

In the store Des had found something he drew to the attention of Chuck, "See these, they are called under-alls. You wear them under your pants. They would be ideal at night, especially tonight. We are sharing with Mag and God only knows what he wears to bed."

Chuck felt the fabric and how light it was, and he said, "Let's get three pair each, one to wear, one for the wash, and one clean for the drawer. Let's try them, and I was worrying about Mag too." When Carl came in, he found the boys had mainly chosen light clothing. Their wardrobes were suited to Chicago, not the deserts of Arizona. Ed and Ali were still young, and they had chosen a few toys, which Carl did not object to. "How much have they spent so far?"

When he was told about fifty, he said, "Not bad, let them go on for a while. I wanted to talk to the two of you anyway. It looks like I am buying this building and I would like the two of you to expand into the space next door, knock a couple of entrances between the two sides. I will give you free rent for three months because it will take that long for you to get stock in and as the owner of the building I will pay for the alterations. Rent for the whole store will be what you pay now plus fifty percent. What do you say?"

"Mr. Montrose, we have always wanted to do that but never thought we could afford it. We would like to widen the range of stock we carry. If you are sure, we would like to do it, but honestly, the rent is too low."

"We'll talk again in a year. You get your business on firm ground first."

Mag came up and said, "Can I get this Dad, maybe someday there will be something I can wear it to." He was wearing dress boots, dress pants, a jacket and fancy shirt and tie. Carl was taken back for a moment by how old he looked, but he said, "Sure son, I think you have done with your shootin' up. We can invest in some decent clothes for you now."

A little later, as he watched the purchases being tallied, the under drawers went by and Carl snatched up a pair. Des stepped forward, "They are under drawers dad, like long underwear only short, bottom half, and light. It is awful hot here dad."

"Well I'll be, what a great idea. Gillian, see these, give us ten pair for each of us, all six, and we all will give them a try."

Loaded with the purchases, the boys started back to the hotel. On the way out Carl snatched a jar of rock candy and said, "Charge it."

No one knew then what caused it, but that day on the way back to the hotel, something was said as Ed and Ali passed a couple of the local kids their age, and soon there were four children rolling around in the street, beating the hell out of each other. Mag made as if to go stop it, but Carl held him back with, "No, not yet, if we stop it before they are winning, they will never get over it and always wonder if they were tough enough. Give it a couple more minutes." Soon, there was a crowd watching and Ed and Ali were the definite winners. Carl nodded to Mag who went forward and rescued the two locals. The tally on the Montrose side was one blackening eye and one bleeding nose. The locals had two bleeding noses and three blackening eyes between them.

Mag placed the two little ones on the sidewalk and Carl gave them a little push forward with, "Enough, you clearly won. Let them explain what happened to their parents. Now pick up your packages and let's go and get you two cleaned up. I'm afraid it means another bath, considering what you have been rolling in." Back at the hotel, the older boys lolled in the beds while Carl took the other two to the bath room. As they sat in the tub facing each other, he wiped the blood from the nose of one while he held a cold compress on an eye of the other. "So, what started all this?"

"One of them said we looked stupid," said Ed.

"Guys, you really have to learn to let things like that go by. It really means nothing. A stranger like that has no way of knowing whether you are smart or not, he was just trying to get a rise out of you, and he succeeded. Never let people get control over you like that. Always act on your terms, not someone else's." When the boys came out of the bath and dried themselves Carl tossed each of them a pair. "Try these, they are called under drawers or something, look like a good idea to me." Clad thus, he escorted them down the hall to the room. As they came is Des saw them and said, "Dad, you are supposed to put pants on top of those you know."

"I know, but they are such a good idea I see the time when people will go through most of the day wearing only these." Then he told his other sons to get themselves together for dinner. The group ate downstairs then returned to their room and Carl introduced the boys to the joys of poker, at least he thought he did. Mag went along with his dad and pretended that was his first exposure to the game. He was thinking though, "Dad? Was it the same with me and Bobby, when we had our big fight? Did you let it go on till I had won so that I would know? Like with the little kids?"

"Frankly, yes, and it took you a little longer to gain the upper hand. Bobby was bigger than you, but at one point in the fight I could see it. You just decided that you were not going to lose to him, and you didn't."

The next morning, over breakfast, Carl said, "After we check out of the hotel, you guys take our stuff and go over and get the horses ready, and hook the team up to the buckboard. I have to see Deeds for a minute."

"Did you buy them Dad, the school, the saloon, and the store building?" asked Mag.

The school and the store yes, but not the saloon, I didn't like the look of the Demers guy. I bought the building though, without the saloon."

"I didn't like him either Dad," said Mag.

"Good for you, it is important you go by your instincts, trust them."

A little later, the boys were working at the horses, and Carl sat across from Deeds. He had already signed the contract for the school. They were now dealing with the store. "Write a new lease for the Peters, the whole store. Rent will be 150% of what they pay now, but the first three months are rent free. I told them you would drop off the keys this morning." Then he signed the document buying the building.

"Why are you doing that? You could get five times the rent for the empty store."

"I know, but when we got here the first day, they were so kind and friendly. I was thinking I had done the wrong thing, bringing the boys here and they were the first to help me understand I was not wrong. You have to remember, at that point I had met you, but we were still working out our relationship. The only person I had contact with was Chuck's uncle, and he was no great deal, was he? Let's give the Peters a little break and I bet they will soar like an eagle."

The last document was the one for the saloon building. "So, did Demers work something out for the contents of the saloon, are we getting an empty building?"

"Empty, but the rents for the apartment will cover costs, more than, until the space is rented. The location is good."

"I know, but that is what I buy, good locations, good buildings, keep looking for more. Do your stuff and I will get the documents next time we are in town. Transfer another fifty over to the land account. Now, what about the ranch land, have you talked to them yet?"

"Yes, I have talked to the Connors, there is only the old man, Mac, and a daughter Melisa, about the same age as Mag. Mac is really ill, heart, and Melisa is afraid to do anything that might make him worse. I think when he goes, she will take the offer. They are only running about five hundred cattle, fifteen or twenty hands. Must be costing them a fortune, which is probably why they are behind with the mortgage. I have a line on the pieces beside you, either side, 60 000 acres. The one to your east you can have for forty thousand, cheaper because there is not much water." The one west of you is a bit better than yours, has water and the owner was convinced there was a gold mine. He died in a cave in. The wife just wants to go home to South Carolina. Wants 75 000."

Carl reached in his chest pocket and brought out a piece of paper which he handed to Lionel, "Another letter of credit for 250 000. Put it in the private account then buy the two pieces, immediately. My cattle should be here in a few weeks."

"Okay, that pretty much gives you 180 000 acres and when we get the top piece that will be almost a quarter million. I'd say that was big enough."

"Never big enough, Lionel, that's something else you have to learn about me. Keep looking at the adjacent lands. I want the lands below too, which the road runs through, especially the part by the river. See ya next time I'm in, maybe you can have some more gems for me."

Then he went out and crossed the street to the livery. The boys were ready, and the family left quickly, soon reaching a point well outside of town. They stopped at the stream to water the horses, and a stagecoach stopped there too, to water its horses. It was the one from the west with its next major stop being Tucson. The passengers got out to stretch their legs and Carl talked for a bit to the driver.

"I hate this stretch. No stops from Richville to Tucson, often we have to drive all night, it's dangerous."

"You know where the road forks, at Ranchero Grande? Would it help if you had a station there?"

"Sure would, just the perfect place for it."

"Give me a second to write a note to your boss, and I'll see if I can make something happen. We live at Ranchero Grande, and I want to do something out on the road." Ten minutes later the stagecoach was on its way, as were the Montroses.

"I was talking to one of the passengers, asking him what was in Richville. He says nothing, a lot of unemployed miners, a closed brick plant, several saloons, one church, two really bad hotels and a couple of restaurants, oh, an assayer who is open an hour a week and a small smelter that only runs a day every third week."

"Interesting," said Carl, and he thought about things for the next several hours. When they got home, he called Hose in. "Tomorrow, I want to go to the Connors, do you know where they live, and can you show me there?"

Hose nodded, "Will take about three hours each way."

"Tell Imelda we will leave after breakfast, have her make us a travelling lunch and get one of your men to drive the buckboard so the boys can all ride. Hopefully we can be back for dinner." That night at dinner, Carl informed the boys, "Tomorrow we are going over to see our neighbors, the Conners, and at the same time we can get to see what we own. Hose will show us the way, and one of his men will drive the buckboard so you all can ride your horses."

Mag was sitting there looking at his father and wondering what he was up to. Carl was not the type to drop in on the neighbors.

The next morning they had an early breakfast and were on their way. Carl said, "When we were in town, I bought the lands to the east and the west of ours. Overtures have been made to the Connors too, but Mr. Connors is quite ill, and it sounds like they didn't want to deal with an offer. Point is though, they are in financial difficulty so I thought maybe I could help the process along. Now Mac Connors has a daughter. That got your interest eh. Well I have no idea how old the daughter is or what she looks like, so you all behave yourselves. There is sickness in the house and she likely will not want to deal with your hi jinks."

While Carl rode with Mag, the younger ones rode around them, taking little side trips to examine things that interested them. Carl was pleased to see them happy and enjoying the company of each other. At about 11:30 they stopped for lunch. Hose told them they just had another half hour or so. They ate, then carried on and Hose was correct. About a half hour later, they could make out a group of buildings, an adobe ranch house, a wooden barn, what looked to be a bunkhouse, and several small outbuildings. When they rode into the farmyard, Carl saw there were about ten men standing around, all armed in case of need. He dismounted and one came forward and introduced himself as Herb Brown, the foreman. Carl introduced himself and his sons, then acknowledged Hose and his man as people Brown likely knew. He told the boys to dismount and asked if they could water the horses. Herb indicated a well and horse trough. Mag took his father's horse and led the boys over. The front door of the house opened and a young lady, about eighteen, stepped out.

Carl said, "We were out checking our new ranch and I thought I should introduce myself. Can I say hello to your father too."

The girl motioned him in and led him to a bedroom where an elderly man slept, breathing with a soft sigh. "I am Melisa Connors, and this is my dad Mac. Dad gets so little sleep now, I hate to wake him up. As you can see, he is quite unwell. Let's have a seat in the parlor. You didn't come all this way without something you want to say."

They sat, and Carl said, "I know Deeds talked to you, and you know I want to buy the ranch. If you sell, you two can continue here as you are because I don't need the house. I have thirty thousand head arriving from Texas shortly and I need the range. I would like to put five thousand over here and I will hire your men to look after them. I will pay off your mortgage, which I understand is about twenty, and I will give you thirty on top of that."

"That is fair enough, but Dad is the second generation. He would hate for the land to be swallowed and there be nothing left of the Connors after all that time."

"I thought it might be something like that. You know on the road, where it branches to the ranchero, there is a fork. I intend to build a town there. What say we call it Connors, as a way of honoring your dad and his family?"

Carl could see she was interested. "And maybe, as part of the purchase price I could have something built there for you. Say, would you like to own a hotel, with about twenty rooms, and a restaurant? I could build you that. I have offered Wells Fargo to build them a stage station for a stop between Tucson and Richville, and a hotel would be perfect. I have a couple mines on my property, and I intend to get some miners and put them and their families up in the town, and maybe a general store. I have a few other ideas, but I don't want to promise you something I can't deliver."

"That is a pretty good offer. Thirty, you pay the mortgage and we can stay as long as Dad needs the ranch, then I could move to a new hotel."

"And I will take on your men. I'll also pay them any back wages so they will be okay, but they will still be here with you and your dad."

"Okay, I have power of attorney for Dad."

Carl brought a document from his vest pocket and lay it on the table. "It's all here, except for the hotel which I will add in now." After they both signed, Carl said, "I'll send this to Deeds and he will see to the deed and transfer the money to your account, I assume you deal at his bank. He will see to the mortgage too."

There was a creak as Mac Connors rolled out in a wheelchair. "I was listening, and it is a good deal. I was so worried about what would happen to Lisa, could get no peace. Let me sign too, a man should sign when his ranch is sold."

As Carl went out on the porch, the men looked up and Carl motioned them all over. "I have just bought the ranch, but I want you all to continue. I have twenty thousand head arriving from Texas in a day or two, and I want to put 5000 over here and have you all look after them. Ranchero

Grande pays its hands three dollars a week and the foreman five, also I will cover the weeks you have not been paid for at the same rate. Herb, gather your men and make me a list, name and what I owe, and I will pay them now, and two weeks in advance."

Carl stood with his sons as the list was being prepared. When the list was handed over, Carl paid the total without even checking the addition. "Okay men, from now on expenses run through Ranchero Grande, bring a list over to us every two weeks and we will include your needs with ours. I will let you know when the cattle arrive. Herb, you are in charge here now and you answer to me. It may take them a little while to get used to that, and in little things go along with them. Anything big though, bring it to me. Got it?"

"Yes sir Mr. Montrose."

On the way back home Mag had been thinking and then he said, "Dad, if the hands get three a week, what do we get? I know you pay for everything, but it would be nice to have a bit of money in our pockets, at least as much as a cowhand."

Carl reached in his pocket and brought out three one-hundred-dollar bills, which he gave to Mag. "Now you have three hundred dollars. Put it away. But, now you have it, what are you gonna spend it on? Look around. You see anyplace to spend it? Sometimes even a million dollars is no good to you, other than maybe to start a fire."

That night, after dinner, Mag sat on his bed looking at the money and he muttered to himself, "You are right dad. I know what I would like to use it for but there aren't even any of those around here." He put the money in a drawer and went to bed in his new under-alls. They had become quite popular in the family.

Chapter 4

Connors

After the trip to Tucson and the Connors, Carl waited for a message from Deeds, so one day was surprised when Lionel was shown in. He looked tired and dusty. "I took the stage to Richville, and had them drop me at the end of your road on the way back. That is a long three miles."

Mag wandered in to see who had come and Carl told him, "Sit. You might as well hear this, it is your future too."

Deeds stood to continue and went to the large map on the wall. "I got you the bottom plot of land, 60 000 acres more for a total of 300 000 acres, and as soon as you sign the forms in my pocket you own it. $20 000 dollars. I ordered a surveyor from Richville to survey the whole property and to lay out a townsite at the junction of your road and the road to Richville. One main street, two cross streets, then some for houses. I have a diagram here. He laid out locations for the hotel, a separate restaurant, the general store, mining company office, assayer, stage depot, and bank. The stage station is out by the road, the idea being the stage would drop any freight or riders off at the depot downtown, then take the stage to the station. There will be about fifty spaces for houses and at least five unallocated commercial spaces downtown. And, there are a couple spaces out by the road where we could put the required saloons. I know, you would rather not have them, but, if we don't, there will just be a boot-legger. There are big lots for a lumberyard, and a livery stable. In the end the town will be slightly off the road, have three commercial blocks, and start with thirty to fifty houses."

"I went to Richville and bought the brickworks. It will move over here by the river this week, with the brickmakers. They have been told one cent a brick and they will start right away, adobes. I found an engineer who will lay out the water and sewer lines for the whole core town, and will also design a water and waste works, then oversee its construction. That will start next week and three weeks from now we can start on the buildings. The miners will do that overseen by the carpenters. I told them in Richville that once the majority of the buildings were up, the single miners could go back if they wished, or they could form groups and rent houses here. The married miners could bring their families for the first houses; by then we should have the store up and running too. All the miners are willing to work under the carpenters I found in Tucson because they want a nice town for their families. They asked if we were going to build a school and a church, and I said we would do both on the main street."

"Now, for the actual mines, the copper and silver mines are close together on the third lot and the mining engineer seems to feel we could get by with a small smelter shared by the two of them. We will need to put a new road in from the main road, about four miles. The gold mine will need a new road too, a little longer. The engineers feel the gold mine will need a smelter of its own. They all figure the copper and silver mines could operate on two shifts of five men each, five days a week and the gold mine the same, but they think crews of ten. Each smelter could operate two and a half days per week, so same people for each, crews of three. Then there would be a night-watchman for each. Total manpower all mines and smelters are about four dozen, which means four dozen families for the town, just the miners. Then you have all the other commercial people. Total families sixty to seventy when all is considered and a population 450 to 500. There is a retired assayer who is willing to move and work two days a week, and I will work here at the bank two days a week also, but for four days there will only be a clerk. We will need an office for the mining company with at least one man there each day, and we can put the gold and silver in the bank vaults, the copper can stay in the mining company until the runs into the city. Wells Fargo will work with us to schedule the runs as we need them, but we will schedule the gold runs at irregular intervals. A pair of mining engineers will come in this week to look at the mines and I said they could stay here, hope that was okay. I will send a paymaster out once a week to handle the pay for all the crews. All of this will be run through new accounts created for the mining company. The town will be owned by the mining company. Projections lead me to believe that you should have your initial capitalization back by the two-year point, and after that it should all be profit. Life of these mines should be at least fifteen years, and we still have to get someone out here to see if there are any more deposits on your land, which there likely will be. One thing, we made sure to leave enough space on your lands for a railway and a station."

Mag said, "A railway? Here?"

"I have a big chunk of something called the Southern Pacific Railway which is to run from Texas to California, but it will likely take twenty years to get here. They will start from the ends. When it does get here, I will have enough clout to get a station, just planning ahead."

"Now, I am doing all this for the sake of my family. You are done school I expect, but the little uns aren't, and for a school you need people. Des is sorta in between but let's see what he thinks of the mining engineers. Now Chuck, I have no idea yet, don't know him well enough. Mag, is there anything in all this that appeals to you. The only thing you can't have is the hotel, that is promised to Melisa Connors. And don't you dare tell me you want to run the saloons."

"Hey, you wanna be a banker? The bank is your Dad's. I am just helping him with it. Might be nice to have a Montrose in the Montrose Bank," said Deeds.

"Sorry Dad, I don't think the bank would be for me, more likely something to do with the ranch. When the cattle get here let me see what that is like."

"Okay, but life on the range is not all that much fun," said Carl dubiously, "But anytime you find something you find interesting, speak up."

Then Deeds said he had finished all the documents pertaining to all the land. He handed Carl the five deeds and Carl put them in the safe in his office with the other three from the town. "Mag, tell the boys we will take a ride into Tucson tomorrow and take Mr. Deeds home. I want to talk to the Peters anyway." Mag went off in search of his brothers, he knew they would be happy, they liked going into Tucson.

Carl said to Lionel, "You have done a good job for me. It had to be someone from out here to approach the miners. They wouldn't have trusted an easterner like me. Now I have the people to build the town and the people to live in it and work the mines. This is a hard land. I have yet to be convinced that even those cattle from Texas can manage here. The mining is the only thing I see that can make any money."

"When should these cattle get here?"

"One more week, and then I have the two deliveries to the army, for the reservations, that will cover the costs of the cattle and getting them here, but I will be left with 15 000 head. I'll put 5 000 over on the Connors

Ranch and let the crew there look after them, and that will leave 10 000 for my new crew here. In the spring, if the cattle survive the winter, I'll send the crew back down to Texas and do another trail drive with more."

"What is the market for all these cattle? You have to have some outlet other than the army?"

"The only answer will be to drive the cattle to the railhead, which next spring should be Laramie, the Central Pacific. I have some money invested in it too. I also have some money invested in the Southern Pacific, but that is at least ten years away. The only good thing there is that when it starts it will start in California and move east. They are having problems with land rights in Texas."

"So that is the long-term plan, to drive them to the rail-heads until we get our own railroad?"

"Yeah, I think ultimately the west coast will be our market, we are closer."

The next morning the group set off for town. Chuck again drove the buckboard with Deeds as his passenger. Deeds was impressed with Chuck, at how bright he was, and how he could do mental math calculations, as well as read and write. When the group stopped for lunch, Deeds said to Carl, "I think I know who is bright enough to be a bank manager, Chuck."

"Chuck?"

"He said that was the only thing his uncle ever did for him; apparently the man wanted to be a teacher and taught Chuck. With a little more training in the banking industry, he could be the one. He's almost thirteen now. Bring him into the bank next year and by sixteen he could be the one."

Carl was impressed but cautious. "That's is what we think, but what about him? What say we both work on him a bit before we let him know?"

The group arrived in Tucson, and proceeded to their base, the area of the livery stable, the hotel, and the bank. Carl and Lionel left the boys to deal with the horses and the wagon, and they went across to the hotel. Lionel said he was dying for a coffee. They stood for a few minutes outside the hotel and Deeds pointed to several buildings across the street, two stores and one lawyer's office. "Those three are for sale, one owner. They are beside the livery and their property goes back as far. That would give you a whole block and they all carry themselves. Total cost of all three would be about seven thousand."

"Okay Deeds, go for them, I don't have to see any more. It is the property we want anyway.

The boys joined them as they entered the hotel. Carl waved to Rafe behind the desk. Mag was the last of the group to enter and when Rafe saw him, he came out from behind the desk yelling, "You bastard, you used her and didn't care, it's not right to go around using people as if they are nothing!"

Carl and Deeds were restraining Rafe, and Carl softly said, "Rafe, let's take this into your office, stuff like this does not belong here, out in public."

Carl sent the younger boys to have lunch and the three joined Rafe in his office. When the three were seated, Rafe glared at Mag and said, "She is five months now and he was the only boy she was with. So, what are we supposed to do? People are making comments, I can hardly come into work, and she stays in the laundry room and cries. This bastard caused that. He should be ashamed rather than going around like he owns the world."

"Yes, he should, but that will be the subject of another conversation between him and I. Now, let's see if we can solve a few problems here. Can you get Louise, and let's see if we can find out what is best for her."

Rafe sent someone to get her, and when she came in, she sat beside her father and just looked at the floor. Carl said gently, "Louise, your father says you are going to have a baby in about four months, that Mag was responsible, and that he was the only one you were with, so he is the father. Is all that true?"

Louise looked Carl straight in the face and said, "Yes, that is all true. It happened in the washing room the first day you arrived."

Carl remembered Mag's expression that day, like a contented cat, and he asked, "Louise, do you want him to marry you? Did he promise you that?"

"No, he never promised that. He was quite clear, he did not love me, it was just sex. He said I would enjoy it and I gave in. He was so beautiful. It was my first time, my only time, and as far as marriage now, never. I will not marry someone who does not love me. Honestly, I don't love him neither. Thing is though, like this, a single mother with a baby, what kind of life can I have, or the baby? What kind of life can a baby have, the bastard child of someone who never cared about it? And my Dad, his life is ruined too."

Carl looked at Mag and said, "Well, let's see if we can help with some of that. Rafe, I will buy the hotel, and you can go somewhere and start another. Name your price and Deeds will work it out in an hour. I assume there is someone here who can run it for me. Now Louise, you can go with your Dad, and make up some sort of story, a dead husband or something; or you can come home with us and have the baby. You can then turn it over to Mag, and I will see you have a new start somewhere. The baby will then have the life he or she deserves, and Mag will live up to his responsibilities to the child, I will see to that." Mag was looking even more uncomfortable.

"You will do that? It is not some sort of trick to get us together?"

"No Louise, I don't want to see either of you in a loveless marriage. Neither of you deserves that because of a few moments of weakness. When the baby is born you can either join your father, or have a start somewhere on your own. I will help you do that. Now Louise, is that what you want, to come with us until the baby is born, or should we try to find some other way?"

"Mr. Montrose, that is a reasonable solution, okay."

"Okay, Mag and I will leave the two of you with Mr. Deeds to work out the details. Deeds, I will be in a room upstairs when you have something for me to sign."

Carl motioned Mag to follow him and went to the desk to get the keys to two adjoining rooms. He then went to the dining room to check on the boys, leaving Des a key and money for the meals. Then he and Mag went upstairs to one of the rooms.

When they were in the room, alone with the door closed, Carl said, "Mag, I have never said this to you before, but, in this, you have disappointed me. You were selfish, thoughtless, and concerned only with what you wanted. You had no concern for that poor girl or her family. You could care less. You are lucky I had the money to clean it up a bit or you would have found yourself in a loveless marriage. Now, you still have the chance to find the right person, but believe me, you will do right by your child, that baby is the innocent one in all this and deserves as good a life as we, as you, can give it. You made a baby and you will be a father to it. We have the means to have people to help you with it, but you are its father and you will act like it."

"Dad, I agree with everything you have said. I was wrong and admit it. Thoughtless. But dad, what makes you believe I don't want to do right by the baby? I saw what you did after Mom died, you did your best by all of us and I know it wasn't easy. I hope I can be half as good a father; but I have to admit it scares me, to be responsible for someone else like that." Mag's voice was a bit shaky.

Carl crossed the room to stand beside his son and said as he hugged him, "Mag, I was fifteen once and I understand what happened here. But, what is, is. You have to deal with it. I know you though, and once you determine you are going to do something, you do it. So, you are going to be a father to this child, and I know a good one."

When the boys came up from lunch, they found Mag and their father just sitting there quietly. Carl said, "Get yourselves together and we are going to the Peters' store. As usual, get whatever you need. Chuck, you too, and get yourselves something fun too, or even a few books or some games that you can play with each other, cards, checkers, God forbid, even chess. We have a long winter coming up so get stuff to keep you busy, and it's time for warmer winter clothes, good coats and gloves, make sure you all have good boots that fit and maybe winter hats with flaps. We might not get in again until spring."

When they got to the store, Carl set the boys free and warned the Peters. "This is their trip to get ready for winter, so be prepared." Then he drew Gillian aside and said, "We are going to have a baby at the hacienda January or February. Can you put together a package of what we will need? Stu will be sending for a shipment of furniture soon, include a crib and a rocker with that too." Then he had Stu show him about the new store and he saw they had a much broader range of goods. They had some furniture now, and Carl had Stu sit at a table with him.

"Stu, I am building a town for some miners by the crossroads into the Ranchero. Here is a copy of the plans for a twenty-room hotel that will be going up there. Melisa Connors will run it. You outfit the guest rooms, the lobby, owner's quarters and the dining room. Everything, furniture, linens, curtains, and dishes. Also, I told Gillian to put a rocker and a crib on the order. Get it all together, rent some warehouse space if you need to. When you have it all together tell Deeds, we are in frequent contact. When you need some money for this, tell Deeds."

"Now, more important, I want to propose a partnership, you and I. In addition to the hotel I will be building a large general store, and I need your help in getting it up and running. I think I have a person to run it at the end of February, start of March. The store is to have everything for a town of six hundred or so. I will have it built with a couple of apartments above it, one for you two. One of you may have to spend a little time up there to get it going and train staff. The person I have in mind can help too for a little while."

"Who is this person?"

"You know Rafe's girl, Louise? She is going to have a baby, Mag's. Afterwards she wants to continue her life. Mag will keep the baby. I thought maybe she could manage the store when it is up, and you guys could return home.

Stu glanced at Mag, "He, they, are so young. I will have to get some warehouse space to do this, gather the stuff, then get some wagons to bring it up."

"Talk to Deeds, I might already have what you need, space wise, or maybe I can buy it. I'll talk to him, he is in on everything. So, you think we can be partners in this? We can call the store Peters' West. We will try to have the store and the hotel ready at about the same time, so you can do it all at once."

They went back to the front of the store, and there was quite a mountain of goods assembled. Carl asked Chuck and Des if they would mind getting the buckboard and the two hurried off as the bill was tallied. Carl said, "I will get Imelda to put a list together for the winter and send a couple of hands down with the wagon to get it, for us and the other ranch. Here's another thousand to put on the account, that should cover it, and the ranch order. Gillian handed him the baby parcel and he in turn gave it to Mag. "You make sure Louise gets this when she has chosen a room. It's all for the baby," he said softly. Mag blushed, but he nodded.

When the buckboard drew up outside, they all helped load the purchases then got a tarp from Stu and covered it all. Carl told Des and Chuck to take the wagon down to the gunsmith and the rest of them would walk. When they went into the gun store, they were recognized immediately.

"You can't be out of ammunition already," the owner said with a laugh.

"No, but how many of those repeating rifles do you have? I have a big construction site full of builders camping in tents, and will have for a few months."

"I have three dozen I just got in for Wells Fargo, but I can re-order theirs and get them in a couple of days. I think they were stocking up for your shipments anyways. You will need them first."

"Okay then, and all the ammunition you have for them. We have the buckboard outside and can load them now. The boys can give you a hand getting them together."

Fully loaded now they returned to the livery and pulled inside the barn. Des and Chuck tended to the horses. Carl glanced across the street at the hotel and commented, "We can keep an eye out tonight from the room, after dark."

The group then went in to dinner and had a raucous meal. There was pie again, and everyone had seconds. Pie was one thing Imelda had not mastered, it having little to do with Mexican cooking. After dinner the boys sat in one room playing with a newly purchased checkers game. Carl and Mag sat by the opened window in the other darkened room and watched. At about 11:45 there was some movement by the door.

"You or me Dad?" said Mag.

"You take the first one, one shot to the left of his left foot." Mag placed his shot perfectly, and the fellow jumped straight up, then dashed away. He asked Carl whether he thought that would be it.

"No, I think they will be back once more, maybe about 12:30, then that should be it."

Carl was right. There was one more attempt to get in the barn and that time Mag and Carl each took one shot to either side of the men. When they fled, Carl said, "I think maybe they have decided now that whatever is in the barn there is not worth getting killed."

The next morning they went down about eight and Carl said to Rafe behind the desk, "We should be ready to go about nine."

Rafe nodded and said, "I'll send the guy who is going to manage this place for you in, to introduce himself. I plan on leaving about noon, Salt Lake City."

Sidney Green came in to meet his new boss. He and Carl talked for several minutes and Carl said, "Anything big, take it to Deeds next door, we talk frequently."

After breakfast Carl sent the boys over to get the buckboard and the horses ready. "Hook it up and bring it all over here." When they were all ready, Louise and her father came out. They had a long hug, then Carl told Chuck to help her up onto the seat. Mag stayed as far away as he could. The trip back was quick, and they made only one stop at their usual place by the stream. As they approached the road to the hacienda, Carl diverted them to the construction camp.

He sought out Trevor Brown, the foreman of the construction crew. "Trev, here are three dozen of the new repeater rifles and 10 000 rounds of ammunition. Issue them and give your people some practice. By now the Apache know you are here and what you are doing. They won't like the idea of a new town. Have your people sleep with these guns and collect them when the single men move on. I will come down to the townsite tomorrow and see how things are going."

At the house, Carl told Chuck to show Louise to the room beside his and to show her where the bathroom was. He told the rest of the boys to get their stuff in to their rooms. "I'll go talk to Imelda and tell her we will have dinner at 6:30."

Then he went to the kitchen. "Imelda, we have a new guest, and she will be here until well into the new year. Her name is Louise, and she will be having a baby. She will move on after that, but the baby will stay here with Mag, who is the father. She is to be treated with the utmost courtesy, and if there is anyone who cannot do that, find them a job elsewhere. If there is a mid-wife here, have her start checking on Louise."

Imelda was a smart woman, and she knew this was not a situation Carl was happy with. She knew he had told her what she had to know, probably more than he really wanted to. She went up to introduce herself to Louise and see if she needed anything. Louise asked if she could have her dinner in her room and it was agreed. That, in fact, became the pattern. In the mornings she didn't come down until everyone had left, and dinners were usually in her room. During the days, when everyone was usually gone, Louise hung out in the kitchen with Imelda and her staff, helping where she could. The two women became good friends.

The day Carl went to the townsite, he was impressed. The brickyard was turning out bricks by the thousands, and Carl decided to have all the first floors of his buildings done in adobe. Most of the commercial buildings had second floors with living quarters and these would be done in wood. When he saw the size of the bank, Carl ordered it tripled in size. Mag was with him and asked why.

"The bank will also be where people go to buy their houses, or rent them. There is no town office, they will need the space."

Mag also noted that the town needed a building for a sheriff or marshal. Carl agreed and ordered it be built beside the bank, with living quarters above it. He also ordered that priority be given to the hotel, the store and the bank. The school and the church could wait a bit. The absolute last thing to be done would be the saloons. He decided that he could tell Stu he could deliver all the furnishings for the hotel in three weeks, and the stock for the store at the same time.

A couple days later Carl and the boys rode over to the Connors ranch. When they rode up, Herb came out to meet them. Carl said, "The cattle are due any day. Bring all but a couple of your men over to the new bunkhouses, they are empty right now. You will be there when the drive arrives, and you can bring your 5000 right over here. I am sure it will take a couple of days for a herd that size to arrive."

He left Herb talking to the boys and went to the house. Mac had died a week or so before and Carl had brought the boys to the funeral. Melisa came to the door as he rode over. "The hotel should be finished and ready for you to move into in three weeks, right down to the furniture which I have ordered and should be delivered in about two weeks. The first of the married miner families should start arriving this week and you should be able to find a couple women from among them to help you at the hotel. The store will be finished at the same time and its stock will arrive at the same time as your furniture, so you should be able to pick up anything we missed."

Mag and the other boys rode over to the porch after their father. Mag sat there on his horse looking down at Louise, and she stood there on the porch looking up at him. Neither said anything, although there seemed to be a mutual exchange of sparks. Louise just thanked Carl for telling her and said she would start packing for the move down in three weeks.

On the way home Mag rode beside his father who said, "I saw that. Your life is too complicated right now for a new girlfriend."

"I know Dad, besides, what would a decent girl like that see in a guy like me, a man with a baby already and not yet seventeen."

That evening after dinner, Louise was in her room when she heard a light knock at her door. She opened it to find Mag standing there holding a big box.

"I have been meaning to give this to you. Dad got it, stuff for the baby. I'll put it over there by the dresser." He walked over and put it down on the floor. On the way back to the door, he stopped and said, "Louise, take one of the dressers and sort the things out permanently. When the time comes, I will just move in here. This is a nicer room for the baby anyway. Louise, I am so sorry this has all happened. I never meant you ill will. Frankly, I never thought about you at all, something I am ashamed of. That says something not so nice about me. I promise you this though, I will do my best for the baby." Then he was gone leaving her a bit in shock. Maybe the two of them were having to grow up a bit due to all of this.

Chapter 5

The Cattle Arrive

One morning a lone rider came to the hacienda. He was a cowboy from the group with the herd and he was very tired looking; with a few slight wounds and scrapes. Carl had gone to the door at the knock; and he escorted the boy in, for he was a boy much more than a man, about fourteen or so. He told him to sit at the table and called for Imelda to get him something to eat. "What's your name son," asked Carl gently between mouthfuls of food that the boy was shovelling in.

"My name is Dizzy, I keep getting thrown from my horse, they say I keep falling."

"Is that what all the scrapes are from, falling from your horse?" asked Des.

"No, they are from the Indians. They have been at us for the last week. We had to close the herd up, that's why we are taking so long. We left with almost 36 cowboys. Lucky if there are 24 left now, and sometimes we hear them at night with a cowboy they have managed to pick off somewhere. The screams of our man go on for hours. That's why they sent me. I am the fastest rider and they need help if you are gonna get any of your cows. They are disappearing one by one too."

Imelda was in the room gathering dishes and Carl told her, "Get Hose in here quickly."

When Hose was there, Carl said, "Send a runner over to the Connor crew in the new bunkhouse and get them all over here. There are ten or so. Make sure they all have new rifles and a thousand rounds. Get any of your men that you can spare, then button this place up. We leave in fifteen minutes. Boys, all of you get your guns and your rifles, even the little uns, and be back here in five. Imelda, get the fires out and get everyone else armed, men and women. This was why we trained all of you and why we got the extra rifles. Send someone down to the construction camp and tell them to be on alert and have their guns handy. Okay, go."

When the boys were back, Carl took inventory. The all had saddle bags full of bullets, and a little food that Imelda and the girls were going around cramming in. They had full canteens, and all had their rifles. The older three also had their double holsters and Colts on. Ed and Ali had their Derringers stuck in the waist of their trousers, and Carl adjusted them slightly so if they went off the most important parts would not be damaged. Then Carl led his boys outside where they met the cowboys who had their horses. Hose's men were bringing the boys' horses out fully saddled.

"Now, some of you are a little young for this, but I want you all near me. I could not bear it if I got back and some of you were gone. You are all deadly shots, and some of you are worth two men. Now, Dizzy and I will lead, little uns behind me, the rest of you around them, and the crew around that. We all are gonna go fast and if there is an attack, we will go right into the middle of it. If we dismount, make sure you bring your saddle bags and rifles, and the extra rifles you all have for the boys on the trail. None of the Indians have repeaters and likely few of our cowboys out there either. We should be enough to turn the balance."

The men formed up and Dizzy and Carl lead them out. Altogether they were just under two dozen men, a doubling of the force with the herd now. They rushed Southwest and in about three hours they could hear gunfire. They came to a top of a raise and Carl stopped the men as he looked down. There were cattle everywhere, but down in the valley the cowboys had formed a circle to defend themselves.

"Okay boys, we are going down and right into the middle, dismount, take the saddle bags and the canteens, don't worry about the horses. They will stay near by." When they swept down and into the circle of cowboys, there were cheers from the encircled cowhands. Carl made sure all his boys were set up properly and with the new men, and the new rifles, the gunfire out of the encircled group was vastly superior to the efforts of the Apache. It took about an hour, but the Indians were convinced they could not succeed, and they faded away.

When things quieted down, the trail boss, Mason Fellows, introduced himself to Carl. "Well Boss, you came just in time. I think they would have worn us down today. I think when we gather them, there will be about 22000 head. Most of those that were lost went to the injuns in the last ten days or so. As for the hands, we are down to a little over twenty, from the more than three dozen we started with."

"I have a crew of ten who are gonna take 5 or 6 thousand off your hands and take them over to another range. And, there is a compound with three large new bunkhouses waiting for you. That is why they were trying so hard today. They know once you reach the hacienda it will be much harder to get at you. Let's get this show on the road."

It took a little while to round up the horses, but soon the herd was moving slowly, and the trail crew gradually got to know the Connor crew. Cowboys all, they soon were friends.

When they got back to the hacienda, they found that it had been attacked too. The Indians were beaten off by the firepower from the new rifles and the skills of those that had been left. There was one casualty, an old woman who had fallen down a flight of stairs in her haste. It was a long day, but they got the cattle in the valley and the cowhands in their new compound. The next day, the Connors crew would take their share of the cattle over to the other ranch. Carl had a discussion with Mason. "The drovers from the army will arrive next week and they will take five thousand more, should give you guys a chance to rest a bit. One thing I noticed though, you guys still have the single shot rifles mainly. I have some extras at the house which I will send over, and I will order some more. I want all my men to be the best armed. How are the bunk houses? Do you have everything you need?"

"Yeah, it's the best we have ever had. We are going to be comfortable here for the winter. You are thinking of another drive in the spring though."

"Depending on the survival rate of these ones over the winter, probably. Use your contacts there over the winter to find another twenty of thirty men, and a trail boss there to start assembling the cattle in the spring. I am buying a ranch there to assemble them on and gather the people. When you are ready, we will send you to oversee that, and however many men we can free from here, after the second 5000 to the army. I am working on a better way of selling the cattle off. There are some areas of these ranches that could support a lot of cattle if we had the Indian problem dealt with. I am working on that too."

Mason said, "I have to apologize to you though. When I saw the group come over the hill, I wondered what we were supposed to do with all the kids, but when they got down there, they were amazing, dead shots all of them, and those little ones, fierce like tigers. I wouldn't want to be on the wrong side of them."

"Your fella Dizzy there, he is a pretty tough character too. I was impressed by him. "

"Yeah, we all like Diz. He is a bit of a mascot for us."

Carl left and went back to the house for lunch. He found all of the boys were there, along with Deeds who said, "I have just been down at the townsite. The livery and the stage coach station are up and running. The stage coach office is operating, though without windows. The store and the hotel are having their stock loaded in. The mining company office is up too. I saw the bank. Why the hell is it so big?"

"The bank is also going to be the real estate company too, where the miners will get their houses, so I had them do the extra space. The second restaurant, the school, church, and the sheriff office are the ones that seem a little slow."

"They will pick up now the others are done. What did you think of the houses?"

"The miners seem happy with them, the ones that moved in anyway. There are a lot of kids there though. I guess that is what happens with unemployed miners. They really want the school done, not all that eager for the church, but definitely the school."

"Okay, I'll have them put a push on that, we are doing three big classrooms, one for the little ones, maybe 6 to 8 or 9, then up to twelve or so, then the older ones, the teens. Then we will need a library, I thought we could design that, so it was open to the public at nights. A gymnasium that could also be a town hall, a few offices, some bathrooms and lounges. Until we have a church, people, if they want, can have Sunday gatherings in the gym."

The two youngest boys were listening closely. Ed said, "Dad, you are talking about a school, aren't you? Not a school you expect us to go to? You can't really expect us to go from riding the range fighting Indians, to sitting in a classroom."

"Yeah, you two and Des and Chuck. Look, someone has to have some schooling to run all this stuff I am building up. I won't be here forever. For sure we need a banker, and a mining engineer, and someone to run the ranch, and eventually there will be railroads and telegraphs. There should be something there for everyone. Don't worry though. You two try your best and I will make sure you stay together. I know the two of you are like twins."

The two youngest went and joined the others. There was a great deal of whispering back and forth and then Des and Chuck came over, along with Dizzy, who had been spending a lot of his free time with Des and Chuck. Des said, a bit loudly, "When you were saying the other two had to go to school you didn't mean us too, did you?"

"I most certainly did, but I will make sure you all are in the classroom with the oldest kids, in fact you may be the oldest kids. From what I have seen the other kids in town are pretty small. Now Des, remember when the mining engineers were here, how you found what they did so interesting? Some day I hope to turn that operation, the mines, over to you, but that might mean having to go back east for a year or two to college. Chuck, to be honest, we hope you find the bank interesting. With another year or so of school we are hoping to get you working in the bank with Mr. Deeds here. And Diz, when you are good at reading and writing we can try to find you a job somewhere in the operation. How does camp clerk sound?"

"Aw, can't we just be cowboys, work with the cattle?"

"Boys, in case you hadn't noticed, those cowboys have really lonely lives, no wives, no children, no homes. I want more for you three than that; so, face it, you all are going to school for a while, you too Diz." The three boys went away whispering and grumbling. Carl looked at Deeds. "When you get back to town find us some teachers, one woman for the primary, and men for the other two rooms then one to be in charge. We will build two teacherages, one for the men and one for the women."

"I can do that. Maybe talk to Mrs. Dunhill. One of her older girls may be ready to teach the younger children. Now, this afternoon, what say we go look at the mines and the smelters."

Carl yelled out, "Boys, all of you, get your guns and your horses. We are gonna go and inspect all the mines and the smelters."

The group started with the silver and copper mines with their own small smelter. They went over their range to get there, and decided they would take the new road to get to the gold mines. The copper mine was an open pit operation, and it was still quite small. Carl could see the potential though. "By next year, we will likely have twenty men working the copper mine alone, and it will need its own full-time smelter."

A couple of the miners came up and said, "This is good ore, best I have seen in years. This is easy mining if it all is like this."

They left the copper mine satisfied, but Deeds noted, "For the copper mine I think you are in good shape, too bad the price of copper is not all that great. They say though, that when the rail lines go in, they are going to run telegraph lines with the rails, have to for safety on some of the single lines, and then they will need miles of the wire. This is something that has real potential."

At the silver mine, they met some miners too, just coming up for lunch. The silver mine was a real mine, with shafts and galleries. When the miners saw Carl they said, "You got good ore, but you need many more posts and cross braces. Right now, the mine is not safe. I know where we can get the wood in Richfield, but it will cost you about five hundred dollars, two wagons, two days, six men, and then for the wood."

"Okay, you organize it all, here's the money. I don't want you guys going in there unless it is safe. All I need is a bunch of widows and orphans to worry about. How long do you think it will be until you are back in production."

"About a week should do it, that is all it really needs, the bracing."

"I'll be back in a week, so I hope then I can see some silver coming out of the ground."

Carl said to Deeds, "That wasn't bad, I expected worse, but I want them safe. I meant what I said, I don't want a bunch of widows and orphans to worry about. What say we stop in at the hotel and the store on our way? I want to see if Melisa and Stu are making out okay."

As they diverted through the town, Carl pointed out the school and received several groans in return. They stopped and tied the horses in front of the hotel; and Carl led the group though the door to see Melisa trying to move a table in the lobby by herself. He motioned the boys over to help and they did. "Anything else while we are here Mel?" said Carl.

"Well, since you ask, there are twenty beds set up on the wrong side of the room, they are under the windows and should be on the other sides of the rooms." Carl told the boys to go upstairs and move the beds. For the five of them it would only take a few minutes. "I should be ready to go tomorrow. I have hired a couple of miner's wives to do the stuff like the floors, and to wait in the dining room, and I found one that was a cook. She will run the kitchens, and I will handle the front desk. Carl, I think I will be happy at this, at least I will be busy. And thank you for having the boys do that. It would have taken me a couple of hours."

Just then the boys came down the stairs and Mag stopped in front of Melisa and said, "All done ma'am. Twenty beds moved and we lifted them, so we didn't scratch the varnish on the floors." Again, the two looked at each other and there were silent sparks but they both backed away. The group went down the street to the store and entered. Stu was there with Louise. He was staying at the house and had brought her down with him that morning so she could get a feel for the store as it was being set up.

"Hey Carl, guys," Stu said as they came in. The two youngest ones ran over to Louis and gave her a hug, which she returned happily. She had formed a bond with Ed and Ali in the last little while. She crossed to a jar on the counter and took out six jawbreakers. She gave one each to Diz, Chuck, and the other three, and tossed one to Mag as she passed him, which he caught with a grin.

"Oh that grin," she thought, "That was what got me in trouble before."

Carl asked Stu how things were going and he replied, "Not bad, all the stuff is in off the wagons, and it is sorted. We priced everything back in Tucson. We will open tomorrow. Louise said she will come down and work a bit in the back and the office, she doesn't want to work out front until after. I hired a couple of the women from the community who had some experience to help out front, and when I am sure they can handle it, I will do three days here and three back in Tucson."

"And for the next few afternoons I will bring the boys down. They can help a bit, carrying packages, moving stock, and the like. They can be paid in jawbreakers. Hear that you five, we can help back here, and Mag can look after the ranch for a few days until this place is sorted out." The group helped Stu for about an hour then carried on with their trek through the mines. With the kids reinforced with a new jaw breaker, they all remounted their horses and rode out to the gold mine. They got there just at three, when the first shift came out and the second went in. The gold mine had a supervisor that worked ten till ten. Carl made a point of talking to the shift that was coming off duty and was glad to hear there were no problems, the mine was safe and working well. The miners were happy. The supervisor had no complaints either. The smelter crew had their first results that day too. They showed Carl a small bar that represented the first week's efforts.

"When we get going here, we should be able to produce four or five of these a week. The boys in the mine will get better as they get to know the rocks. The purer the gold they send out, the easier our job. The ore is crushed, then they separate out the gold and we heat the ore to get rid of the part that isn't gold so we can keep the rest. The volume can only go up. We can develop the mine so there are multiple mining surfaces and you can put more miners per shift."

Carl called the boys over and let them see and feel the gold.

"I didn't know that gold was so heavy," said Chuck.

"How much is this worth?...... How much?" said Des in awe.

On the way back to the main road, Deeds said, "We have an extra big safe going into the bank for the ingots, and the stage office will have one too. When we have a number, you can send them by coach to the bank in Tucson. Once Wells Fargo has them, we are insured. If they lose it, they give us the value."

They had come back to the main road just as a stage pulled into the station. They went over and Carl talked to the driver, who was one he had met before. "So how will this station work out?"

"It is placed just right. Will be good when the hotel is opened, then we can drop the passengers there and come out here and change the team, then go back and pick them up an hour later."

"The hotel will open tomorrow, with it's dining room. Eventually there will be a second restaurant downtown. The rooms in the hotel are ready to go, we helped position the beds today." They said goodbye to the stage driver and continued back to the hacienda. After dinner, when Deeds and Carl were sitting talking, Carl handed Lionel a letter for him to mail when he got back to Tucson.

"It is to President Johnson. We are good friends you know. I am asking him to establish Fort Connor here, a little south of the town, and offered him the land for free. I told him what happened when we brought the herd in. I also told him I have a lot of investment here and I need protection. I hope he agrees."

Deeds said, "The nearest federal garrison is in Phoenix, so I think there is a good chance."

Carl then said, "There is another thing I want you to work on. I want a railroad from Tucson to Laramie Wyoming, with a spur to Phoenix and from here to Tucson. With my connections to the transcontinental railways, especially the Southern Pacific, I will sell it to them when they reach here from the east or the west, whichever is first. I have a seat on the board of the railway if I want it. I want the line now to make it easier to dispose of my cattle, and the products from the mines. Here is a map of the route I propose. If we start by building down from Laramie, there are six or seven cities that will pay for it right from the start and we can drive the cattle to the rail head. From this end we do Tucson, Connor, Globe. Then there will just be the part between Pagosa Springs or Durango, down to Globe. That block in Tucson that we own most of is where I would like to put the Tucson terminus, a new hotel on the livery stable side, and the station where the hotel is now. I need a right of way between here and there, then north to Globe. I will get investors in Phoenix to pay for their spur and maybe take the line west. Now the hard part, between Globe and the end of the line from the north. Get me some big tracts of land there and I can use the profits from land sales there to pay for the missing part of the line. Then it will just be a wait for the Southern Pacific to arrive."

Lionel was looking a bit shocked, "Do you really have the resources to do this?"

"Yes, but I would like to have this start to become self financing now. The gold and silver mines will help, and I wouldn't mind a few more. If we get the fort, it will become easier to sell off land around here, so see what is available and get it before the news gets out. You saw the size of the bank, that was to accommodate a land sales operation, in addition to house sales to the miners. That operation is what I want for Mag to run, if I can convince him of that."

Deeds said, "You have been planning this all along haven't you, right from the beginning?"

"Yeah, but Mag threw me a bit off course and reminded me he had a little growing up to do. Hopefully by next spring he will be ready. If the fort happens, it will be in the spring, so we have a little time to assemble the land."

Chapter 6

Spring Follows Winter

After their conversation, Deeds went back to town. The silver mine had its improvements and opened again, quite successfully. By that point, the bank was finished, and it's safe was installed, as were bars on its windows and the back door. Every week, after the smelter had finished its week's production, the gold was moved to the bank, as were the silver and the copper. The copper was just stored in a cupboard. Deeds came out on the evening stage once a week and ran the bank for two days, spent four nights and then went back on the morning stage. He usually stayed at the hacienda, although there were living quarters above the bank if he wished to use them. It was just easier to have his discussions with Carl when he was at the house overnight. They often talked until almost midnight.

Sometimes, he would have Stu's company, either coming or going as he was a regular commuter too. The store in Connor was quite profitable and many of the migrants west liked shopping there rather than Tucson. It was less hectic and always had all the stock it needed. The staff that he had hired for the store was efficient and Louise came down sometimes when he was there. One morning though, when he entered the store, he caught a bit of the conversation between the two town women and he chose to make an issue of it.

"You know ladies, rather than gossiping about her, it might be nice if you got to know her. Beneficial too, because in the new year, she will be your boss. She will be manager and part owner. Louise is a good person, and you two are good employees, but if at any time she feels either or both should be let go because of personal issues; I will side with her. Just a word to the wise for people who should know where the butter is put on their bread." There was no more gossiping after that, and the two women did make an effort to become friendlier with Louise. She managed to work through the Christmas rush before she decided to stop coming down. Stu was impressed with how efficient she became at running the store during those months.

On one of the early trips, Lionel brought a letter for Carl from the President, who was pleased to inform him that in January a contingent of Federal troops from Phoenix would relocate to Connor where they would be building a fort on the land he had offered. The army would take a fifty-year lease on the property. The rest of the president's letter was taken up with personal chatter about their respective families and mutual friends. Lionel was impressed how a little word in the right ear could be so effective and he began to realize there was a lot about Carl Montrose he did not yet know.

Lionel worked on assembling the land Carl wanted in Tucson. He first assembled the land around what he already had, and soon Carl owned the whole block around the hotel, a block to the south, and three full blocks to the north. After that he worked at procuring a strip from Tucson to Connor about an acre wide. He got hold of another vast parcel just south of Carl's land and including the river side, figuring somewhere on that would be a good place for a fort. Then he worked on the leg from Connor to Globe, buying several adjoining ranches to provide the right of way for the railroad. Most of the times, the ranchers just stayed on, happy to be rid of the burden of a mortgage, and it was not something they told their neighbors, so Lionel was able to continue his stealthy acquisitions. For the section from Globe to Window Rock he managed to acquire three large ranches that gave him what he needed. Again, the owners stayed as tenants. As a matter of process, Lionel had a geologist survey the new lands and there were several new prospects for gold and silver mines. The New Mexico requirement was quickly met, and Lionel knew he was in the most difficult part, Colorado, Durango to Carson City. Carl told him he had an associate in Laramie working on the Laramie to Carson City leg, working with some of the towns there that were desperate for a railroad. The associate was selling the idea of a Laramie south spur, not mentioning the chance of a line coming up from the south.

About three weeks into September, Deeds brought up four teachers for the school along with a wagon train of building supplies for the lumberyard. Carl and Mag met the train with the buckboard and the new teachers were delivered to their quarters, three men to one and the lady to the other. The younger boys had refused to go with Carl and Mag, preferring to keep as much distance as they could between them selves and teachers or school. Lionel went to the bank while Carl and Mag showed the group around the school. The teachers were impressed with what had been built but had several questions about the student body, how many, what ages, and the range of abilities.

"From what I can see, the numbers tilt to the younger. Most of our miners came as families from Richville, and there was a school there, so the older ones likely have had some education. I have two going into the youngest classroom who I have been teaching for the last six or seven months, relocating and all. Then there are four older ones, fifteen or so, who have had varying levels and types of instruction. I think that is what you will find, broad ranges of instruction at each grade level. You are going to find these western kids have had many experiences you have not even thought of. Example, my two youngest helped fight off an Indian attack for about four hours. One of the older ones was on a six-month trail drive. Another of the older ones went to a private school in Chicago for five years. You try to pin all these kids down to a pre-determined course of study and they will chew you up. Take them as they are and work from there. I think all the kids you get from the town will be about the same. This is the west, a different country from what you are used to."

The teacher who was acting as administrator asked, "How do we go about letting the parents know we are here and ready to start school?"

Carl laughed, "This is a small town and they all knew you were here five minutes after you arrived. If you want to start tomorrow, just put a sign on the door that school starts at nine and the kids will be here. The town is small enough that you can expect them all to go home for lunch." Out of the corner of his eye Carl caught it when Mag flashed one of his devastating smiles at the new lady teacher and saw her get quietly flustered.

The two left a few minutes later, Mag driving the buckboard and Carl on his horse. "Mag, that young teacher is another person whose life you can ruin in as much time as it takes to snap your fingers. This is the eighteen hundreds, and she is a young lady. Any hint of a relationship between her and a young man like you will ruin her. Think about that a bit. Now stop at the bank with me for a minute, there is something I want you to see."

In the bank, Deeds had taken about a third of it, and there was a counter and a couple offices down one side. The other side had some large maps on the wall, and several more spread over several tables. Carl brought him over to one of the tables and told Mag to take a good look at the maps.

Mag found one and said, "This one is around here. There is the ranchero, with the Connor ranch above it, and the ones on either side with the mines and the part below it with the road and the town. They are all yellow, I guess 'cause we own them, then there is more land below them, all yellow, with striped areas off to the sides. Dad, the yellow goes all the way to Tucson in a strip. This is a map of Tucson. The yellow takes up a quarter of it. Dad, does that mean we own a quarter of the city?"

Carl nodded, then indicated the rest of the maps. Mag found the map of Arizona indicating Connors north. This map had solid yellow and striped yellow plots indicated on it. The solid yellow formed a path all way to the part where Arizona, Utah, and New Mexico came together. "Dad, why do you have a path all the way to the borders? It's like you want to build something up there. What? And what is the rest of it all."

"To get the strip we had to buy other parts. The striped parts, we will sell. You are right, the solid parts are to build on. A railroad."

"A railroad to where?" Mag laid out the other maps. He saw there was a little yellow in the corner of New Mexico, a wide swath through Colorado, bottom to top, striped and solid, and on the map of Wyoming there was a little strip to Laramie. There also was a line through Laramie, from left to right. There were little letters on it, "Central Pacific Railway."

"Dad, are you doing this to join the Central Pacific? I thought there was going to be a railway here?"

"There will be, I am on the board and I own a large part of it, but it will be ten or fifteen years. That won't help us get our cattle to market. If we get this, we can sell as many cattle as we want into Chicago. And the idea is, when the Southern Pacific gets here I will sell them all our railroad, and they will get most of the territory or state, whichever it is then."

"Okay Dad, I see what you are doing and why, but shouldn't we have waited til spring to make sure they survive here?"

"They will, I talked to the cowboys who brought them up. They manage through much worse winters than they will have here. We have good water through our land. Just bring them down for the winters near the water then out further for the summer. We can raise as many as we want, and can sell, that is why the railroad."

"Dad, given all that is right, why did you want me to see these?"

"The striped parts, the land that is for sale, I want you to take that on. As the rails push north and the land becomes accessible, we want to sell it off, and this part of the bank is devoted to the land sales company. Next spring, I want to take a herd to Laramie, or the railhead, whichever is closer, and I want you to go along, see the land we are selling, and it will make it easier for you to do that. Now on the maps you might see a few of the striped parts turn solid. That will happen when our geologist looks at land and advises us to keep it for gold or silver, even copper. Then we will keep the land for future mines. All the rest, not needed for the railroad, will be sold. Our ranch will be here."

"Maybe some of the other lands will be safer, without Indians." said Mag.

Carl pulled one of the original maps out and pointed.

Mag looked, "What is Fort Connor?"

"Early in the new year, a contingent of federal troops will arrive to build a new fort here in Connor, and that should be the end of our "Indian Problem.""

"But what makes you think I can sell it?"

"Mag, you are a born salesman. You sell yourself everyday. You ooze charm, your smile is good as gold. You put one tenth of that into selling our land and it will be a sure sale."

"But, what do I know about contracts and things. Dad, you are talking of millions in land sales here. Am I ready for that?"

"Why do you think the land office is in the bank? Deeds there is a lawyer too, not just a banker. He is there for when you need him at first. I have faith Mag, you can do this."

The next morning, Carl went into Ed and Ali's room and woke them at seven. "Up boys, school starts today. Make sure you leave your guns at home. You are going to school to learn." He passed much the same message to Des, Chuck and Dizzy. They had put another bed in the room for him when he started staying over. Carl had had a good talk with Mason, about Dizzy's future. There was no other family but Mason and the guys, and it was decided, Dizzy could have a better future with Carl's boys than he could with the cowboys, and hard as it was to let him go, all the boys in the bunkhouse agreed. Dizzy could do better. That morning that meant the three of them were going to school, minus guns, but then Carl had second thoughts. When the boys came into the hall, he said, "Get your guns, we will leave them somewhere in town. No guns at school, but we have a bit till we get there."

At breakfast Carl said, "Mag, you wanna ride down with us? I almost had them go without their guns and thought better of it. This school thing means they will be going a certain place at a certain time, five days a week. Better if they have some protection. Get Hose to get three of the men to go with us, armed."

Then he said to the boys, "You will leave the guns at the bank. Find a place. We will have men ride in with you in the morning, and after school you guys get your guns back, then go to the livery and get your horses ready, but wait until the men get there at the end of the day to ride you home. Anyone who breaks this rule, if you make it home alive, I will whup you within an inch of your life. If there is a problem, stay together. That is your strength, together."

The first day there was no problem. The second day, the ride in was uneventful but on the way back Carl had this feeling there was something wrong. About half way, in the most remote part of the ride, Carl said, "Boys, we are gonna ride hell bent for leather, but I have a feeling we will have to fight them off." They took off together, but the fire from the woods forced them to dismount when they reached a clearing with some downed trees for cover. As they alit, Carl said, "Be sure to take your rifles." As it turned out, there were six men in the woods, but the group managed to pick them off one by one. When they got down to two, the attackers slipped away. About then, reinforcements arrived from the hacienda, drawn by the gunshots. As the men stood over the bodies of the attackers, they saw the group laying in wait was all white.

Mag said, "They probably wanted some of the young'uns to use as hostages for the gold."

"Yeah son, guess it's time we got that gold into Tucson, get rid of the temptation."

Then Carl checked the children and his heart fell. Ed was the worst injured, he had been shot in the leg and there was a significant amount of blood. Carl and Mag quickly put on a tourniquet and then Mag passed Ed to Carl on his horse. Carl galloped for the hacienda. The others followed close behind, leaving two of the people from the ranch to deal with the bodies of the attackers.

Carl slammed into the hallway calling for Imelda. Louise came too, and between the two women and a little needle and thread, the two managed to stop the bleeding and suture the wound. When they were done Carl said, "It's okay Ed, you can let your self cry a bit now." Carl sat beside him and held his almost seven-year old son. "You have been so brave, and you are only six." It took only a few minutes for Ed to gather himself and no one mentioned a few tears. The rest of the children only had minor cuts and bruises which the two women quickly dealt with. At that point, Deeds and Stu came in. "The news got down to town, that you and the kids were attacked. Who is hurt?" said Lionel.

Mag and Carl looked at each other and Carl said, "We were lucky today. Lionel, arrange to ship our gold and silver out of here. Book a special Wells Fargo coach with guards, and we will send some armed men with it too. Make sure everyone knows there is no more gold to go from here. After that, production will be sent out daily by strongboxes. We want no more excuse for more thieves to think they can get away with this type of thing in the future. Lionel, set this up ASAP."

The next morning, Ed was allowed to stay in bed and miss school, but Carl took the rest down, along with a half dozen of his men. After the livery, Carl walked with the boys to school and the men trailed behind. As they neared the school, they saw that Mr. Simons, the principal, was standing outside with a group of women who seemed to be nattering at him. As their group neared, the women quieted and Carl led his boys to the door and let them in with a comment, "Have a good morning, pick me up at the bank and I'll take you for lunch. There will be one or two men across the street all day."

When the kids were in, Carl turned to the group and said. "Okay, I gather the discussion has something to do with me. Let's get it out on the table but perhaps, Mr. Simons, we could go in the gymnasium and have a civilized discussion with chairs." He then motioned one of the cowboy guards over and told him to get Mag and Lionel from the bank.

When the group had reassembled, Carl stood and said, "Okay, Mr. Simons, what is the problem?"

"Miss Plessy here has some concerns."

"Miss Plessy?"

"I am looking after my brother's family since his wife died. Four children in the lower two classrooms."

"Okay then, Miss Plessy, what is causing difficulty today?" As they talked a few more parents, men too, joined the group.

"After the attack on your children yesterday, we are concerned lest another attempt to be made at kidnapping or something, and our kids being caught in the middle. Then there also is the matter of your eldest son and Miss Grayson."

"I have been informed my son has taken the young lady out to dinner once, yesterday. He returned her to her door one hour later and never even entered the house. What is your concern?"

"We don't want no floozy teaching our children."

"Now that is rather unwarranted, I assure you the most care was taken in assembling the staff for the school."

"That's the point, why did you pick? We had no say in this, them, just like we seem to have no say in the safety of the children."

Carl was angry now. He spoke to Lionel for about five minutes, who then scribbled some documents on a legal pad, and Mr. Simons was despatched with some papers. Then Carl stood and said, "I have had enough of this. When the miners were recruited, I promised the miners a school, and this is it. I have done as I promised. For your information, in order to contract the teachers, it was incorporated as the Connor Private School, with me as the owner. Now Miss Plessy, effective 1 PM today, the Connor Private School will no longer exist. Its ownership will be transferred to the School Board of the Town of Conner. My children will be removed at twelve today and will never return. I shall make no further contribution to the operation of the school and will likely never enter it again. My staff, the teachers, will also leave at twelve and they will be out of the teacherage by 1PM. So, Miss Plessy, you can find your own teachers, run this place as you see fit, do whatever the blazes you want. I will not be bullied by a bunch of interfering narrow-minded women with nothing else to do, and you madam, and your friends there, are just that. Good luck in trying to get yourself elected as school board head, because from what I have seen, miners are very practical people who will not thank the likes of you for taking away from their children what would have been a free high school education. Now they are going to have to pay for this place, which isn't cheap."

"We'll just raise taxes on your stuff to pay for the school." said Miss Plessy.

"No, you won't. Any school board only has jurisdiction in the town of Connor. None of my significant operation is within the town. I shall meet with the teachers at morning recess privately and offer them some options. I owe them that, they are my employees after all. Whether there are classes here later today will be up to your new school board. I should remind you though, that it is illegal to place unqualified people in charge of more than three children in the Territory of Arizona."

Then he and the rest of the group left the gymnasium. The parents that were there were not happy with Miss Plessy, and a confused verbal melee continued the rest of the morning until twelve. Carl met with the four teachers at recess. He told all of them to be out of the teacherages by 1:00 and that he would pay for rooms for them at the hotel. He and Mag and the boys would come and help move whatever they had to. He told Miss Grayson that when Mr. Deeds went into town, she could go with him and that he was fairly sure she could find employment at Mrs. Dunhill's Academy. Mr. Travers was offered a job tutoring the boys at the Hacienda, which included room and board. He could go right out there that afternoon. They could even find him a horse if he wanted. Mr. Simons was offered a job at the bank, operating it on the days when Deeds was in Tucson. Mr. Jessops was offered a position with Mag, doing land sales and he jumped at that.

After recess, the four teachers circulated through the school saying good bye to the children and telling them they had no idea whether there would be school that afternoon. The children were advised to take their personal possessions with them. When the boys came out at noon, they were surprised to find Carl waiting for them. He gathered them around. "I'm sorry, you are done with school here. Mr. Travers will be teaching you at home. Now we have to help them all move to the hotel and then we will have lunch."

The children were not upset, for the most part they did not like school. Of the four teachers Mr. Travers was the youngest and the most desirable. The three teachers that were going to the hotel were quickly moved and Simons and Jessops were told to come over to the bank that afternoon, to find out about their new jobs. Mag apologized to Miss Grayson for causing her trouble. She admitted to him that he was charming and it likely was a good thing she was moving to Tucson. Keep them both from getting into trouble.

Brent Travers became a part of the family. He would go in first thing in the morning to wake up Ed and Ali with some oral math tables. He then went into the room with Des, Chuck, and Dizzy where he woke them with oral mental math calculations. Over breakfast, he entertained the family with discussions of different places in the world, geography. He then gave them a couple hours of freedom until lunch, after which he went into the writing and reading. One day. when they were working, Brent was idly tapping messages in Morse code on a book as he watched them, and Diz picked up on it. As Brent explained, all the rest got interested, and in the end, they all learned Morse code. It became their thing, to send each other little messages as they were sitting around. The constant tapping drove Carl to distraction, and Dizzy was by far the best at it.

Living in the household, Brent could not help but learn the story of the lady who seemed to spend most of her time upstairs in her room. One day, they met on the stairs and introduced themselves to each other. Both found the other charming which was a confidence booster for Louise.

Carl and Lionel arranged the gold transfer. One morning an armored coach pulled up in front of the bank. In addition to the driver from Wells Fargo, there were six or so Fargo guards and another ten or so from Carl's cowboys. The gold and silver were taken from the bank and loaded into the coach. Then the coach would go directly to the Hamilton Bank in Tucson. Carl openly announced that from then on, the most there would ever be in Connors was one day's production.

In November, Carl had done his Christmas shopping with Stu in the store using his catalogs. The gifts began to arrive in early December on the stages and Carl paid the ladies in the store to wrap them for him. He had to send all the way to Colorado for a tree, and one day it arrived on the stage from the north causing quite a disruption in town. Christmas trees were not common in Arizona. It had arrived ten days or so before Christmas and Carl had it taken up to the house and set up. When Carl got home, he found the boys gathered in the great room looking at it. He went to a closet and came back with several boxes of decorations. "Okay boys, put the decorations on. This is a Christmas Tree and believe me, it was hard to get." He went and found the wrapped presents then had Imelda and Hose help him take them to the tree. When the tree was done and the gifts under it, Carl said, "Ten days, that's how long you have to wait. Serves you right for all the grief you guys give me."

Over at the school, there was still confusion at the start of December. Plessy was not elected to the new school board, in fact she was barely talked to by her neighbors. The new school board managed to find two teachers to replace the four they had lost. Whenever any one tried to discuss it with Carl he said, "No, I don't want to hear about it. People around here have to realize, you can push me only so far. I kept my word, they broke the trust, so let them deal with it."

Simons and Jessops, at the bank, had much the same attitude. They would not discuss the matter with any one. They felt the women had ruined a good thing for them, and for the town, and they were a bit bitter about it. They also knew how badly Carl had been hurt by the parents' attitude. The two men did like their new jobs though, and felt they were much better off out of it all. Jessops loved the land sales and got to be quite good at it. Simons fit right in at the bank and Lionel was glad to have him. So, there were some good results out of all of the bad feelings.

The gold and silver flowed into the bank in Tucson, and one day Lionel came to Carl. "You are now working on you second million from the gold and silver, and there are at least three new mines we can operate from Connor. You are a profitable operation now, and you still have the second delivery to the army, let alone what you are gonna get up to next year. For a while there Carl, I was a bit worried, all the money going out, but you have turned it around in seven months. Absolutely amazing."

Christmas that year was joyous. Brent Travers had gone home for a visit to his family. He promised though, he would be back the end of the first week in January. The boys were almost exploding with eagerness by the time they finally got to Christmas morning, and they were allowed to open their gifts. All the boys were treated equally, with Diz and Chuck being equally spoiled. One of Diz' favourite gifts was a practice Morse code set. Carl sat with him and said, "At some point soon, we will have our own railway and telegraph operation, and that will be yours, so learn all you can about telegraph's. Just think, with the telegraph, we can know within five minutes when anything happens in the whole country. That is absolutely amazing, and you can be in charge of all that, from Laramie to California to New Mexico."

Ed and Ali both got a gift they were thrilled with, a double holster set of pistols, colts, just like all the others except for the fact they were sized for them. They had been handmade by the gunsmith in Tucson, probably the only such pair in the country. Carl had ordered matching black suits with hats, boots and Arizona ties for the five older boys. "You guys all have to start looking like what you are, part of the most important family in Arizona, magnates of industry." When they tried on the clothes later Carl had to admit, "Boys, you do all have to grow a bit I think to fit those suits. I'll give you one more year to be kids, all except you Mag. That suit fits you."

After Christmas, winter in Arizona set in. It was nowhere as cold as winters had been in Chicago, but you knew it was winter. There were cold winds off the prairie when the winds came from the north. The cattle had been moved down to the fields beside the river where their life would be a bit easier and the lives of the cowboys that much easier too. The army drovers arrived to take charge of another five thousand cattle. Now was the test. How many more of the remaining roughly sixteen thousand would survive the winter?

January was the month when Fort Connor was established. First there was a captain and a construction crew. Carl had been accumulating wood for the fort in the lumberyard in town. He showed the captain a map of the suggested locations and the captain agreed with him the best was the one overlooking the river. That was confirmed when the two actually went out and looked at the sites.   Construction began and by the end of the month enough of the buildings were completed that the rest of the men could come down from Phoenix. That was when Carl met Colonel Franks, the new commandant of Fort Connor. Colonel Franks and Carl made an immediate connection and in the coming years were a support for each other.

February too, was the month when Mag became a father, and a man. Louise went into labor on the 14th of February, late at night, and delivered just after midnight. Surprisingly, she delivered a set of twin boys. When she was done, Louise sat in her bed with the two babies, one on each side, and Mag came in and sat beside her. "They are beautiful Louise, both of them. I have to admit, I am having a bit of trouble getting around the fact there are two of them. But, I will do my best with them."

"Mag, you know I will be working in the Connor store. Can you bring them around once in a while so I can see them? They don't have to know who I am. I can just be their friend, the nice lady in the store who spoils them a bit"

"Louise, that I would like. I don't want to be mean though. It is better for both of us that they not know. Eventually I will marry and there will be someone they see as their mother. That is good. And for you to get on with your life, it is better we not be open about it. A friendly lady in the store we can cover nicely."

"What about the names then?"

"How about Lou and Les?"

"I would like that."

The next morning, Carl and Mag sat over coffee. "So, now you are a father. How do you feel?"

"I dunno Grandpa, suddenly I feel I have a lot of responsibility and something to live up to. Did you feel like that when you and Mom had me?"

"I sure did, when I looked down at you in your bassinette, I felt the weight of the world, all at once. Having the first child forces you to make that transition from a child to a man, all at once. There is no more doubt."

Carl had a meeting with all the boys to discuss the plans for the spring. "The army has taken their second shipment of cattle. Later in spring all the cowboys will drive what is left to railhead south of Laramie, and we all will go. Before that however, there will be a trip to Phoenix, involving all of you except for Ed and Ali, and will include Deeds and Jessops. We will go by a chartered stage coach and it mainly will involve meetings with businessmen. Jessops has to go because I want him to see the land we have for sale along the way. Deeds has to be there because there will likely be some contracts, and the four older ones because I don't think I can trust them here without Mag or I. Travers should be able to control the two of you, if not, there are going to be some tanned bottoms when I get back, and none of them will belong to Travers. I am going to have some more of the cowboys move closer to the house for safety while we are gone. So, all of you, a trail drive in the summer, and no, there will not be a tutor, unless he wants to go as a cowboy." He had a talk with Herb, the Connors foreman, and told him to put his cattle in with the rest, and bring his crew over to the hacienda for the time the rest would be away for the Phoenix trip. He also asked Colonel Franks to increase his patrols in the area.

Mag had made certain Imelda and her girls would be okay with Lou and Les. Louise had already moved down to the store. Imelda was ecstatic to have the two little ones in her total control. She said she would have the babies in the kitchen during the day and that she herself would spend the nights in the room with them. Mag was satisfied.

In the middle of March, the chartered coach appeared at the hacienda. Carl had hired the coach, two drivers, and six guards so felt fairly safe when you added himself and Mag, as well as the four older boys. Deeds and Jessops, though present, were not likely to be of much use if there were a gunfight. When the coach left, the four men sat on one side of the coach, looking over the maps as they went. The three boys sat on the other side with their books, practice telegraph, and some cards. It took about two days to get to Phoenix. The boys weren't terribly impressed with the new city and felt it was very much like a bigger dustier Tucson.

Carl had two sets of meetings set up. The first was with several of the richest people in the city, the movers and shakers as it were. When they were all settled, he got right to the point. Carl tacked a map up and used it to illustrate. "Myself, and a small group of investors from Laramie will complete a railroad this summer from Laramie south to Carson City then west to Durango, south to Globe, Connors, and Tucson, euphemistically called the Colorado and Arizona Railway. COLAR. I would suggest you leaders from Phoenix should plan and build a spur from Globe to Phoenix, and then west to Blythe or Yuma, depending on where the Southern Pacific enters from California. It is our intention to sell our system to the Southern Pacific when they get here. We do not want to compete with them, just to make sure we don't have to wait another ten years to get rail service. The Southern Pacific has been held up ten years by those court cases in Texas and are just about to get started. I know, I am on their board too and own a big chunk of it. After they get here, I imagine they will join the two cites directly, but in the mean time we would have access to a transcontinental route through Laramie." Carl assured them they would just have to worry about the right of way; a lot of which he already owned and would sell to them, and the financing. He would have two crews work from the north to Globe, then they would split, and one group would go south while the other went west. "Now for my purposes, I don't need the western line, but if you want it and are willing to pay for it, then we will do it and the route to Yuma or Blythe. Additionally, the telegraph shall come with the railways and I shall be running a school in Connors for telegraph operators. My son Diz here will be one of the principals in that school."

The group then came up and examined the maps closely. One of them asked Carl why he wanted the railroad now. "I have cattle, gold, and silver which I want to get to market immediately."

There was a similar meeting the next day with local political leaders. Carl said, "I have made a detailed presentation of these matters to local financial leaders and there is no need to do it again. Politically, which is your area, you just have to decide if you want to continue to be almost totally isolated or whether you want to support those financial leaders in their efforts to join a new rail system to tide things over until the Southern Pacific gets here. There are maps here you can examine."

While they were in Phoenix, Carl directed that they stay in the very best hotel in the city and closely examined it to see what services it offered. He and Deeds toured the several restaurants and shops off the lobby. Mag and the other boys followed them around just wishing they would pick someplace to settle and eat.

As they were dining, Carl said, "You may have been bored by that, but this summer we are going to build a new hotel and station in Tucson, and I was just trying to get an idea of what we will need. Chuck, your livery will be replaced by a hotel with a livery service as they do here. You will simply ride up to the front door and they will look after the client's horse or carriage. Nice feature. As is the choice of the types of restaurants you want, like for a full meal or a quick snack."

The next day, they started the trip back, stopping occasionally when they were crossing property they owned so Mag and Jessops could take a good look. Mag admitted. "This has been good dad, now we can talk about land we have seen."

"The trail drive will give you two a chance to see the rest of it. I agree though, you should be selling land you have seen and felt under your feet and in your fingers. Farmers will ask you that, what did the earth feel like."

Two days later the coach arrived home and the group climbed out wearily. When Ed and Ali came out, Des said to them, "You didn't miss much, days in the stage coach and hours of boring meetings. We didn't see anything."

"We had a good time. Brent borrowed a gun and we spent hours practice shooting. He says he might just take Dad up on it and go on the drive as a cowboy."

"Travers? Really?"

The first thing Mag did was go to the kitchen to check on the boys. He held each of them for several minutes, and checked out their toes and fingers, as if to make sure they were all there, then he said to Imelda, who was watching all this with a small smile, "It was only a week, but it felt like a month. All I could think about was them. God, how things have changed."

"Yes, when you are a papa, there is nothing more important than them. You have learned that queeklee."

When the planning started for the big drive, Mag asked Carl, "Dad, do you think maybe you could do the drive without me? It would mean being away from the babies for a month, maybe two. I don't know if I could do that."

"I was wondering if you would bring that up? If you go, Imelda and Hose and a couple girls will bring the babies into town and stay at the hotel. If you stay, I would insist on that. We will have too many of the hands on the drive to ensure safety at the hacienda. If you really want to stay, talk to Melissa, and make sure she can give us five rooms, one for Hose and Imelda, one for a couple other of the girls. Two adjoining ones for you and the babies, and one that can be set up as an office, in case you want to do some work close to them. And make sure she won't mind having Imelda doing what she has to in the kitchen. Another alternative might be to borrow Deeds' living quarters over the bank. He will be with us, anyway, as will Jessops. That way you could keep an eye on the bank."

"Can still do that from the hotel, it's just across the street. I will talk to Melissa, and we will work something out. So, the plan is to just leave a caretaking staff here?"

"Yeah, just the usual locals. There are about twenty of them, but if there were a concerted effort there would be no backup there. That's why you and the babies cannot stay. You do realise, this is the last time it will happen because once the railway is in, we will load the cattle right there at the stockyard we will build. And it will be a slower rate, not the ten or fifteen thousand at once. We just have to get through this one, and I do understand you not wanting to leave the boys. But there is no way, with you here or not, that they are gonna stay up at the hacienda this year."

"Okay Dad, I get the message. I will see Melissa tomorrow."

The next day he did talk to Melissa Connor. "We need five rooms together from say the middle of March for about three months. Dad and all the men will be away on a trail drive and he doesn't feel it would be safe at the hacienda with no men, other that the domestics, who couldn't repel a real attack. So, we need two adjoining rooms for me and the babies, one for Hose and Imelda, one for a couple of the serving girls, and one I could set up as an office, so I could work from here, close to them. We will bring in any needed furniture, cribs, chairs, desks and so on. Hopefully this will be a one-time thing. Once the railroad is in this summer, there will not be any more trail drives from here."

Melisa immediately agreed, "You can take the five at the left, four rooms there form a little hall and you could use the one on the front for an office, you can see the bank from there."

Carl also sent a message in to Deeds to see if there was something like the Pinkertons he could hire a team from while they were away. He got a positive answer and the arrangements were made. The departure date for the trail drive was set for March 18th. Destination uncertain. The rails were at Boulder but it was not sure how much farther they would get. If they were lucky, maybe Carson City. The two foremen were working together. Both Herb and Mason had done trail drives and both enjoyed them. During the first part of March, the cattle were gathered and counted. Carl was pleasantly surprised. They had gone into the winter with a little less than fourteen thousand. He knew there had been casualties over the winter, but the count brought to him was just over fourteen thousand. Mason said, "We had losses, but the cattle thrived, and we had births. These are the cattle for here."

"Okay then, get your people in Texas to put together another trail drive and a crew. When we complete this one, half the men will come back here and the other half you can take to speed the drive up. We'll see how many cattle they can come up with. Another fifteen or twenty would be fine. We can winter that many and sell them off in the spring like this year. More would be even better."

March 15th Mag and the babies, along with Imelda, Hose, and two of the servers, moved into the hotel. That very first evening Mag took a trip down the street with his sons. They found Louise alone in the store and she was very happy to see the children, holding first one then the other throughout the evening. That night she started the tradition of the twin's special friend in the store.

"We are going to be in for at least a month and a half, so I will bring them down here to see you quite often. He and Louise walked back up the street and in the hotel doorway she handed the baby she was carrying back to its father, and held the door open for them. Inside the lobby Imelda and one of the servers were waiting and they took the children upstairs to get them ready for bed.

Melisa was there too, and she said, "I am glad to see you and Louise friendly. Since Christmas I have gotten to know her, and she is a good woman. She is doing the right thing by her children, as are you."

"The children deserve the best, and we both want that, but we both know nothing would be gained by a pair of parents pretending at something for their whole lives. We will each do our best, and hopefully we will both find the right person to complete each of us."

On the 18th, the cattle left, at least the first part of the herd. It took two days before the tail end of the drive was on the move. Brent Travers did go, as a cowhand. Mason accepted him with, "Well if he wants to. Seems eager enough. What he don't know, he will learn. If nothing else, he will end up with a sore butt from sitting in that saddle." Moving a herd this size attracted all the vultures, animal and human, for miles around. Carl advised his men to try to drive them off without killing them. "If you have to kill, do it, but try to scare the hell out of them first."

Ed and Ali were beside themselves with excitement, the idea of going on a trail drive for a couple of months with real cowboys had them over the moon. Two weeks into the drive, when they really knew how much work this was, they were not quite as excited. Brent Travers was in his glory though. He had grown up as an eastern kid, reading novels extolling the glory of cowhands and the west. Now he was doing it, and frankly doing quite well at it. He never complained and was the first to volunteer to do something. Carl noted his enthusiasm and took him out one day for a little shooting practice with a rifle. "Brent, you seem to really be enjoying this."

"Yes sir, this is the best summer I ever had. I read books about this when I was a kid and I am so grateful to have a chance to really do it, not just read about it." They spent the better part of a morning together and as it turned out, Brent was not too bad with a rifle either.

As they got further north into Arizona, they got deeper into Indian Territory. More and more cattle seemed to just disappear during the nights. Fred and Mason were beside themselves, but Carl was less irritated. "Look, if they are taking the cattle it is for food. The Apache do not ranch. Maybe they can get fat and lazy and just leave us alone. I have seen what they can do, and I would rather not have to fight them off. The longer they are content with a couple cows at night, the better off we are."

Inevitably though, there came the day when the Indians made a concerted attack. The herd was just too big a target. They chose to come at night and used the dark to sneak close to the encampment. They had signals worked out and the outriders on the herd were attacked at the same time as those in camp.

Carl had been worried about just such an event and he had had the boys sleeping with their rifles and guns. He had also had them sleeping close by him so at the first war cries, his boys had formed a circle around him and were fighting off the attackers. Brent, who was at the edge of that circle, had another dose of the romance of the west. He had to admit, he didn't like this part of it quite as much as the rest of it. The attack lasted about an hour. Many Indians were killed but for the most part, managed to take the bodies of their casualties with them. They also managed to take a few live cowhands too. All during the night the cries of these poor souls tore the hearts of their comrades apart as they were tortured. There was no point trying to find them as it was impossible to discern a direction in the dark, but in the morning, the circling vultures told them where to look. The bodies were found in much the same condition as the bodies had been that day with Mag. Carl let the boys see what had happened to the cowhands, mainly so they could have a full understanding of what they faced. The trail hands were recovered and buried. That night, when they camped, extra hands were stationed around the encampment and people only slept in snatches. Carl found Ed and Ali chose to curl in right beside him and he put a protective arm over them. The others were not far away. They all had seen far more than children their age should have but they now understood what life in the west was like, and it wasn't like what was portrayed in the books. Brent Travers had learned the same lesson that day too.

The trail drive continued north and east for day after day. People soon lost track of how many days they had been doing this, and just settled into a routine, day after numbing day. One day, a small town appeared on the horizon, and one of the cowboys rode ahead to find out where they were. The town turned out to be Window Rock, right on the border where

Arizona became New Mexico and more than half way to their goal. The men gathered excitedly around one of Carl's maps as he showed this to them, where they had been and where they were going. They were only in New Mexico for a few days before they crossed into Colorado just south of Durango. They closed on Pagosa Springs, Fred and Carl rode into town. Carl was interested in finding out how far south the railhead had gotten. The telegraph had made it to the Springs and Carl was able to send a message to the builders of the railway. The line was nearing Carson City where they expected to stop. Carl asked if he could have a meeting in Carson City in two weeks, and the rest of the principles agreed as he was one of their major investors. Carl also wired them to have stock cars accumulated in Carson City, as well as pens and loading ramps for the cattle, and that he had about fourteen thousand head if there were any cattle buyers interested.

A little over a week later, one of the outriders brought in a pair of city dudes. They had ridden south from Carson City in search of the herd and had found it due to the large dust cloud it raised. They were cattle buyers and they wanted to be the first to make Carl an offer for the herd. They identified themselves as buyers for Armour, in Chicago. "We can offer you nine dollars a head at the railhead in Carson City. We already have loading pens there, but it will take us several days to load a herd like this one. About how many head are there?"

Carl said, "About fourteen thousand, give or take a few hundred."

"Well, in that case maybe we should say six a head."

Carl said, "No, its nine, as you offered, but you can sell some off to the other buyers, I don't care. My deal is with you, nine a head, about fourteen thousand. I make that about a hundred twenty-six thousand. Twenty-six cash, and a draft on the Central Commerce Bank in Chicago, where I have some accounts. You have a couple days to arrange that before we get there."

As he watched them ride off towards Carson City, Carl thought, "Not bad, I paid twenty-six cents a head in Texas, and even with the cost of the drives and the cowboys all winter, I will still make over six bucks a head."

Three days later, as the herd approached Carson City, Carl instructed Fred and Mason, "There are new stock pens and loading chutes. I imagine once they start loading, they will handle two or three thousand head a day. As the men become surplus, you can let them go into town for a night, but they are your responsibility. Here's five thousand dollars, you can pay them up to date, just have them sign for it. I have some business with the railroad people, but I should be ready to head home with the first half of the men. One of you come with us. The other will stay till they are done and ride home with the second half."

Carl told the boys, and Deeds and Jessops, to get packed. They were going into town. He asked Brent if he wanted to go with them, had the romance of the west worn off yet? Brent replied, "Be glad to come with you. The romance of the west wore out a while back, when we saw what the Apache did to those poor cowhands." Shortly after, the group left. Deeds and Carl rode together, the kids slightly behind, and the rear was brought up by Jessops and Travers.

The group rode into town and found what looked to be the best hotel. At the desk Carl said, three rooms, each with two beds, two of the rooms adjoining. When he got the keys, he passed one over to Deeds, Jessops and Travers. "Here you go, you three figure it out. Travers, you mind taking on the two little uns tomorrow? Deeds, Jessops and I have a meeting with the railroad at nine. I'll take the three older with me. They might as well see it, they may have to do it some day. But Ed and Ali will be just bored out of their minds, and they can get into a lot of trouble when they are bored like that." Brent readily agreed, he was ready for a return to his role as a teacher. When Carl entered the room with the five boys he said, "You three, take that room, and the two little uns will take this bed in here with me. Now you guys have an hour and a half. I want all of you to have a bath and get changed for diner. You all smell like cows, understandable given what you have been doing for the last few weeks, but still." The boys cycled through the bath while Carl read a paper. At five o'clock they all went down and met the other three in the dining room. Deeds had kept them a table that sat them all. Carl said, "Well guys, that was your first, and I suspect last, cattle drive. That is something that is going to disappear in the west as soon as the trains arrive."

"No loss," said Brent, "A lot of hard work, little return, and really not all that romantic. Not at all like the books. I will be glad to get back to my old job."

On that note, the meal progressed. They all were relaxed and had a feeling of accomplishment, a job completed. Carl and Deeds actually were looking forward to the meeting the next day. The three boys were not, but they all felt at least it was better than facing marauding Apache.

Chapter 7

Building a Railway

The next morning, Carl gathered Deeds and Jessops, and the three boys. After breakfast, he turned the other two over to Travers for safe keeping and amusement. Carl and his group made the short walk to where a private rail car sat on a siding for their meeting with the four railway owners who waited inside for them.

Carl led his group up and entered the car. On one side of a long table sat the four owners of the railway. Carl sat opposite them, with Deeds and Jessops on either side. The boys filled in three chairs behind them, against the windows.

Carl began, "To my right is Lionel Deeds, my banker and lawyer, to my left is Mr. Jessops, he works in my real estate department and has prepared most of the maps we may be examining. Gentlemen, my congratulations. You have built what looks to be a good railroad and you have reached Carson City by the time you promised. I am quite pleased with my fifty-two percent ownership of the line. Now I wish to continue south, to Tucson. You have two crews to lay rail, I understand. I want both crews used, dawn to dusk, seven days a week, Carson City to Globe. At Globe, one crew will head west to Phoenix. The costs of that part will be borne by a consortium of Phoenix business men. The other crew will head south to Connor, then Tucson. There is already a station, a stockyard, and loading facility built in Connor. We just need the rail line and the siding. This summer a new station and a railway hotel will be constructed in Tucson. After the rails are done to and in Phoenix, the rail crew will continue west to Yuma where the Southern Pacific has assured us they will enter from the west. From the east, the Southern Pacific will build a short line from New Mexico to Tucson and perhaps a direct route, Tucson to Phoenix. Otherwise they will have all of Arizona covered. It is my intention when the Southern Pacific enters, to sell them the part of the railroad I have constructed, as is the intention of the Phoenix group. I hope you all will come to the same conclusion about this part, but although I could force the issue, I won't. The new railroad would be the only north south connection between the Southern Pacific and the Central Pacific this side of the Rockies. All railroads shall have accompanying telegraphs. If you agree, we should be able to get two of you on the Southern's board, and the other two on Central's. I am on both. The entry of the Southern Pacific is at least eight, maybe ten years away, so for that period we have a railroad to run."

"Now perhaps you could call your engineer in. There are a few things I wish to tell you that he should know too, saves time." When he was added to the group, Carl went on. "Here is a map of the route south to Globe. The Rights of Way have already been purchased by me, along with a lot of other land which Jessops here will be involved in selling. On the map, you will see there are several sidings marked. They are to be built as we go but there is to be at least 300 feet between the main rails and the sidings, to allow for the construction of a small station at each one. They all represent areas where I have procured property for gold or silver mines. Each one will have their own small station and telegrapher. The mines will mine their ore, and when they have enough for a fifty-car train they will telegraph for a train of hopper cars to be spotted in, and a couple days later for it to be picked up. The train will then proceed to a large smelter in Boulder, which I will also build, but will be available for whoever needs it. The two mines I have in Connor will continue with their own small smelters and produce refined gold or silver, but all the rest of the production will have centralized smelting services. The cattle I produce on the ranch in Connor shall be brought north by rail then east to Chicago, probably daily shipments. Connor will also be the place where I run a telegrapher's school to meet our needs. Connor also already has a station, and a stock loading facility."

"These operations will require some specific rolling stock. I would think three trains of fifty hopper cars, an engine and a caboose for each and perhaps one coach for each train. We will also need armored baggage cars for the transportation east of the gold and silver. Maybe six. I also would like a private car like this one for the family. That car will be stationed in Connor. Then, there will be the added needs for passenger and freight service to the entire area with two trains daily in each direction. The stock for my operations will be paid for by me. Just guessing from looking at the maps, the other stock should be charged out at 15 % to the Phoenix group,

20% to this group and the rest to me. The Southern Pacific has agreed to buy all of our general rolling stock when they buy us."

"We anticipate the need for two trestles in my areas and the Phoenix section one. Naturally each of us will pay for our trestles but I assume you have the people to build them. I think they should be sent ahead of the rail laying teams. One of them will be near Fort Connor and I will see that the army provides protection. The land sales throughout Arizona will be based in Connor, but we might use some of these new small stations as sales offices for a time. The construction of the new stations has been arranged. There are also two sidings for me that have to go in for new mines in the parts of the railway where you have finished, but they can wait til after all the rest is done, as those mines will not be opened until next year."

When he was done, he asked if there were any questions. The four business men from Laramie had none, they just sat there looking shocked. They had gone from a small local line to one involved in five states. The boys were sitting there shocked too. This was the first time they had seen their father in action this way and they were impressed. When they returned to the hotel the little ones ran to meet their father. He asked what they had done that morning and Ed said, "Travers, Mr. Travers, took us to this place where there were some women."

"What..?" said Carl with a sharp look at Brent.

"A school sir, it was a girl's school."

"Yeah, it was a school, and the girls asked us questions about the cattle drive. We told them about the cattle, and what we had to do to look after them."

"And we told them about the Indian attacks, and poor Ned, who the Indians took and killed," said Ali.

"One of the teachers at the girls' school was an old classmate from Virginia. When I saw the name of the school, I dropped in on impulse, and it was good for the girls. They had no idea what a trail drive was like, just as I didn't before I went on one. Besides, the boys enjoyed it."

"Yeah, those girls said we were cute."

"One of them even gave us a kiss goodbye," said Ed.

Carl was smiling as he said, "Looks like you two made some important discoveries today. It is good that you had some fun and I will trust Mr. Travers not to take you too far into these other areas before you are ready."

The whole group took a walk to the rail head and watched as some rails were laid. The line was already leaving the town limits heading south. Deeds and Jessops were talking. "It should go quickly now, with the land changing from mountains into prairie, and until the line reaches Globe, there will be two teams, dawn to dusk. That's at least fifteen hours a day."

"At that rate, they will be in Globe in a month. It'll take us half that to ride home."

At home in Connor that day, Mag was the first up and he went into the front room he used an as office. He was sitting at the desk when he glanced out the window and noticed some smoke at the edge of town, about where the Wells Fargo station was, and realized the station itself must be under attack. When he leaned out the open window, he could hear the shots. He went in the hall and there was a fire alarm bell, he rang it. Mag immediately found himself surrounded by several people. Hose and Imelda were there as well as the two girls from the hacienda. Melisa Connor was there and about eight men who seemed to be together and staying in the hotel.

Mag said, "There is an attack going on right now at the stage station. Must be Indians, they will be here soon enough. Now, you two girls run downstairs and close and lock all the window shutters, and make sure all the doors are locked, then come back up and find Hose and Imelda. Hose, take one of these interior rooms, away from gunshots, tip the beds and get extra mattresses to make a hideaway for you and Imelda and the babies, get in there with the girls, take your rifle and a couple extras from my closet. We all will fall back on you. One last thing Hose, make sure those babies are not taken. You know what you may have to do." Then he turned to the others, Melisa and the men. One of the men said, "Mr. Montrose, there are ten of us and we are your Pinkertons defence shield. We were told to be there, but unknown, till or if needed."

"You are needed now. There are extra rifles and shells in the closet in my room. Get arms, then we will go down and barricade all the doors. A couple of you men make a barricade up here at the top of the stairs. If we fall back, we do so on the room where Hose and the babies are. Everybody, have a pistol too. Remember, you do not want to be taken alive by them. With the first floor being adobe brick, the walls were safe enough. They checked the shutters all around the hotel. Mag and the Pinkerton head stationed four men downstairs on the first floor, and the rest went upstairs. Mag showed the remaining men the corner rooms with their good range of fire. Everyone had at least two rifles and a pistol, including Melisa. Melisa and Mag stationed themselves in the corner room he was using as an office where they had a clear view of the two main streets, the bank, the Wells Fargo office, and the almost finished new restaurant. Gradually, the shooting, yelling, and screaming got closer as the Indians crept down the street. Once in a while a squad of mounted Indians would ride the street, from one end to the other, in order to draw fire so the ones on foot could then try to take the source of that fire out. It was a pretty good tactic so Mag yelled to the men, "Don't shoot at the mounted ones, they can't hurt us, it's the ones on foot that follow them that we have to worry about. Mag and his men saw the tactic work on the stage depot. The defenders revealed themselves when one of the Indian groups rode by, and they were quickly overwhelmed by the ones sneaking along behind them who burst from the shadows in large numbers. Mag whispered across to those in the other corner room. "Let them get between us, then we will open fire on them from both sides and catch them."

Soon, that is what happened. The natives were creeping up on the corner entry door for the hotel, hoping to force their way in, and when they were between the two corners of the building the men opened up from four directions, catching fifteen or so and killing them. That caused the Indians to have to regroup. They decided the hotel was the strongest source of resistance and would have to be taken. They furtively tried all the doors and found they all were too strong. A group tried the back stairs to the second story. They were half way up the stairs, when one of the shutters on the first popped open and three men leaned out and fired up the stairs, then sealed themselves back in. The seven Indians on the stairs were wiped out. The chief was furious. He had lost about two dozen men and hadn't even gained entry to the building. He chose one of the downstairs windows and concentrated his men on it. They managed to break the shutters open a crack so that it was only a matter of time. Mag positioned about four men at the end of the hall outside that room just by the stairs to the second floor. "They will get through the window and build up in the room. One or two will try to get out, and only one of you shoot but get each of them. They will think there is only one shooter so will come out in a mass in order to overwhelm the one, and that is when we all open up and wipe out the group, then we hike it up the stairs before they can recover. The stairs and the landing are the choke-point, we can hold them off for quite a while there. Surely by now the soldiers must know something is going on over here."

At the fort they did know, but it takes a little time to get a couple of hundred men moving. They were bursting out their gates at about the time the hotel was repelling the Indians on the back stairs. The army swung in by the coach station and quickly found all the men there had been massacred so they swung towards town where there was still the sound of shots. The Colonel split his men into two squads and had them enter each on one of the two main streets.

In the hotel, it went as Mag thought it would. The initial two or three were quickly dispatched by a lone shooter. When a massed group of fifteen or so forced their way from the room into the hall, they were mowed down by the five or six repeating rifles, and then the defenders hot-footed it up the stairs before the Indians could again recover. When the Indians regrouped and then rushed the stairs, they were mowed down by blistering fire from above. That was the point the army charged down the streets and the chief decided it was time to flee, having lost the better part of four dozen men at the hotel and having nothing to show for that.

Several more of the Indians were killed by fire from the angry soldiers as they tried to flee from the several building they had managed to enter in the community. Total civilian casualties were just over thirty, with some women and older girls being assaulted. They were lucky though, assaults by Apache warriors usually end in the death of the victim. As the sounds of fighting died down, and the sounds of the Cavalry became more pronounced, Mag brought his group down. The babies, with Imelda and Hose carrying them, were surrounded by a circle of Pinkertons with Mag and Melisa. Soldiers were entering the hotel, removing, the bodies of the dead Indians, and laying them on the street in front of the hotel. Mag and his men had alone accounted for almost three dozen of the savages. When he was sure it all was over, and they would be safe, Mag sent the babies back up with the three women from the hacienda to feed and then put them to sleep in their room, but he said not to leave them alone. He would be up soon. He, Colonel Franks, and Melisa Connor then talked for a few minutes. The Colonel said, "We lost six at the stage station, another four or five at the stage depot, a couple of men around town, and another five or six women raped but not yet killed. No abductions that we are aware of yet. We are hurt but it could have been much worse if they hadn't got delayed here at the hotel. I bet they were heading for the school to try to take as many kids as they could."

Mag said, "Can you send some men to the store to see how they made out. Likely three women there but I am not sure if Stu was this morning." The word soon came back, the three women were safe. They had barricaded themselves in a room in the basement with two guns. They were okay, almost shot the head off a trooper who went looking for them though, was the report. Mag asked if it would be possible for the Colonel to have men patrol the town for the next few days until the townspeople had settled a bit and he agreed. One of the men from the hacienda came to report to Mag. "There has been an attack there too, likely after the town. It was like the Indians were just mad, not determined. They set fire to a barn and took all the horses, and later there were two fires at the Connor ranch, likely the house and the barn or bunkhouse."

"Well, Colonel, we were lucky today. There could easily be a couple hundred more dead, and tens of children taken. I trust the army will do something about this."

A day or so later, Carl and the boys returned; and they walked into the lobby to find Mag and Melisa sitting there, each with a baby and a bottle, for one of the morning feedings. Carl was glad to see the four but commented, "Looks like there have been a few problems around here."

"No problems Dad, just a hundred or so bloodthirsty savages, and there was a raid at the ranch too, so I am not sure whether you can go right home at once." Carl looked at Melisa and said, "You have four or five extra rooms?" and received a positive nod. Carl turned to Travers. "Take them over and check them in. You and the three, me and the young uns, then two rooms between eight of the boys, so we have some power if we need it. Deeds and Jessops have their accommodations here in town. The rest can go up to the hacienda and clean up what they have to. Let us know in a couple of days when things are ready for us to come home." Then he sat with the two and the two babies.

"Good call, having us move down here and the Pinkertons here too. Without them, we might have been in trouble."

"Next time, we all go together. By the end of the summer we should be able to do that in our own rail car. I see you are done now son, how about giving me Lou to hold?"

"How do you do that Dad, I can't tell them apart, how do you know?"

"There is a slight difference in the shape of their noses. Lou has more of your mother's nose, and Les has mine."

"So Dad, how did the meeting go?"

"We are getting our railroad, likely by the end of the summer, and I talked to Deeds on the way back, he is going to tear down the livery, the whole block, build a new hotel there with a suite reserved for the family, a new hotel livery just behind it. His bank will move into the lobby of the new hotel. Then that side of the street will be razed and a new station built, with the needed platforms and yards. It will be sized to accept Southern Pacific trains too. The Peters store there will be all that is left of the block as we know it. We are going to start advertising the land sales in the northern Midwest, and feed the clients down thru Laramie to Carson City. Jessops will go and run an office there for a few months. He got a real feel for the land on the trip. Once we have the rail line in, we will start advertising in the South East feeding the clients through here and you, and eventually we will have only one office, here. They have the maps with all the sidings we discussed for the mines and we can use those sidings to settle the new farmers. Take two or three farmers in the one area, put together a small train and spot them into a siding near their new home, giving them a couple of days to get their stuff off the train before we go back and get it. Reminds me, we want to get our lumberyard to start building up it's stock. Those farmers are not gonna want to be building with adobe, and son you sure can go for miles and miles on that prairie without a tree."

"What are we gonna do about the Indians? After what happened here how can we send farm families out there to live? We were lucky we didn't have a massacre here." Mag went on to detail the events in Connor the day of the raid.

Carl listened carefully then commented, "I think it is time for another letter to my friend, the president. If they want the west settled and the territories to become states, then they have to make it safe, which means getting the Apache caged up, and they need to do it now. I will make that clear to him, we are right on the edge, within months, of putting a lot of people out there, and it won't look good in the eastern papers if whole families are being massacred. I'll have a talk with our friend, Major Franks, so the same message is getting sent up through the ranks in the army."

During the next few months the Apache realized what the coming of the rails would mean and they attacked the rail crews mercilessly. Carl and his partners complained loudly to the political powers and to the press. There was a clamor in the press to protect the brave Americans trying to settle the west. There were daily graphic stories in the papers. It wasn't long before there were more soldiers sent to Fort Connor, and patrols sent out with all the railroad crews. In the end, massive campaigns were mounted by the army to press the Apache back, with many native casualties.

The railroad reached Globe and split into two. The workers who prepared the area in Tucson for the rails gradually moved northward toward the line moving south. Bridges were completed well before they were needed. The hotel and the station were finished. When the rail laying crews reached the prepared road way, they moved astonishingly fast. One day Carl was there with Mag when their private car was spotted onto a siding.

They inspected the car together. They found there were berths for about twelve with a room with two tiny berths for the babies and one adult bed. There was a complete galley and a large lounge where some of the seating converted into berths too. Mag commented, "Dad, this is beautiful, no more hours in the saddle to get to Tucson."

"Not just Tucson, try Phoenix, Chicago, even New York or California. The access to the Central Pacific opens them all up." The family decided they would start with the grand opening of the station and the hotel in Tucson when the rails got there.

So, one day late in August, the family, with Imelda to look after the babies, all boarded the car. There was a second coach attached full of cowboys whose sole purpose was to be a private army if required. They were shunted into a private siding. When they all alit, the group went out the front door of the station and saw the new hotel. The boys were shocked and Diz said, "That is what? Seven or eight storeys high. How do people climb those stairs?"

"They have little rooms that move up and down, to take the people to the top floor. That is where we will be, the top floor. That floor is set aside for us." The group crossed the street to the hotel and a manager was waiting to escort them up. It took two cars to accommodate them all but soon they were upstairs and shown into their suite, which would be kept only for them. There were nine or ten bedrooms, so everyone who wanted one of their own could have one. Imelda and the babies settled into one that had a bed and two cribs. Ed and Ali claimed one together, and the three other boys chose to share. Brent Travers took one of his own. Carl had one and Mag one across the hall from Les and Lou. The suite was luxurious, as befitted the owner of the building. The views were spectacular. The room even had its own telegraph station, which Diz was immediately enraptured by. There were a couple maids attached to the rooms by the hotel, just on the days it was occupied.

Deeds arrived to accompany Carl to the ribbon cutting ceremony. "There are representatives of the other major railways, the Governor, and lots of politicians, local and territorial. Whether you want to be or not, you are now a big deal in territorial politics, and when we become a state, that too. So, smile, and be nice."

Chapter 8

Developing the Seasons

It was New Year's Day, 1869 and Carl was having a family meeting. They were in the Great Room at the hacienda. "Just wanted to bring you all up to date on family business and talk a bit about next year. About time some of you started to take an interest in all this. At the moment, the three mines on the ranch are doing quite well. The copper is even starting to be worth the trouble it takes to get it. The cattle from the ranch are being sent to Chicago at the rate of about 200 a day, seven days a week through our facility in Connor. The railway is running full steam, and it looks like the Southern Pacific is still 8 to 10 years away. Along the line we have opened eleven new mines, 5 gold, 4 silver, and 2 copper. We have sold land to about 1400 farmers. There are three new towns. We own the whole telegraph system from Laramie along the line and in almost all parts of Arizona, and we have stations almost everywhere, including our living room, thanks to Diz. I think we have about tapped out the potential of Arizona, so for this year we are going to start looking further afield."

"Oh uh," thought Mag. "This doesn't look good." He looked down at the twins sitting there on the sofa beside him, three years old, ready for anything, and wondered what this new outlook would have in store for them. Des glanced over at the other two fifteen, and sixteen, year olds sitting on the floor beside him, backs against a sofa and he too wondered what this meant for them, nothing good, he thought.

Ed and Ali looked at one another too. Ed thought, "Now this might be promising, something new." Eleven and ten-year old boys were always ready for something new.

"Boys, we are going to spend most of next year on tour. I have purchased a string of hotels in the east and south and they have to be inspected. Additionally, it is time you three middle ones are finished properly and learn what real society is like. I hope you do better at it than Mag did. We just got him out of town before I had to deal with a herd of angry fathers.

End of the month, we go to Chicago to get you guys outfitted properly. Spring in New York, summer in Southampton, the fall in Virginia. Did I tell you all that I bought Oakside back and had the mansion rebuilt? We have to check on that. Then, we will winter in Florida and along the gulf, most of the new hotels are there, aside from Chicago, New York and Washington. We shall take the rail car and Mr. Travers will be going with us to look after the schooling. In Chicago, we are going to pick up a new tutor for you three middle ones, to teach you some manners and how to dress and act in polite society. Now Mag, if you want Imelda to go with us for these two, she is willing, in fact looking forward to a change from here after the accident that took Hose. For security, I have engaged a double team of Pinkertons, twelve men, and a second railcar will be spotted in with them before we leave. Deeds is going with us, at least part way, and he will sleep in the other car. So, what do you all think?"

"Dad, sounds interesting but I am just starting to get friendly with Melisa, and going away for a year isn't going to help that much," said Mag.

"I thought of that. That's why I want to ask her to come with us. After all, it is a tour of hotels and she owns one, doesn't she? She must be getting bored stuck here all the time."

"Dad, that is such a reasonable suggestion I can't help but wonder what you are up to," said Mag.

The next day, when Carl asked Melisa if she would like to go, she was a bit taken aback, "I think I would like the trip, but how would we explain me and Mag, how would you introduce me?"

"Mel, what should I say, this is the girl who has waited almost two years for my cowardly son to get up enough gumption to approach her, or maybe by the end of the trip I can introduce you as my son's fiancé. If nothing works out, you can just come home, or maybe find a rich husband in the Hamptons. If you come, at least you two will have lots of time together. There is lots of room, the car has ten staterooms, and we only need five, and if we add the two tutors there are still at least three left for you to choose from.

On January 29th, the family and Melisa entered the private car at the station in Connors. The two cars had been spotted onto a siding. Carl stood on the platform as the boys boarded. As usual, the three had a couple rifles and both holstered pistols. Carl stopped them and said, "Now, normally I wouldn't allow all the artillery, but we are going through Indian country.

However, before we get to Chicago it all goes in one of my trunks. The dangers you all have to learn to face this trip cannot be handled with guns. The three found a cabin with four berths and threw all the baggage on the spare upper. Edwin and Ali took their usual with two berths. Imelda and the twins found theirs with one big berth and two smaller ones. Mag, Melisa, and Carl all found staterooms with large singles. Travis had one of his own and there were still two for the new tutor to choose from after Chicago. Carl went and checked on the Pinkerton men. He found Deeds unpacking in a stateroom and said, "Come back to the lounge when you are ready. We are not gonna leave you to your peace and quiet, so you better get used to it right from the start."

The family gathered in the lounge as the train pulled out of the station. The Montrose car was the last on the train, with the other private car right in front of it, the arrangement that would be maintained all the way to Chicago. When they slowed to go through towns a couple of the detectives would come though to stand on the rear platform. The two littlest ones, Lou and Les, were really only concerned with what went on in front of them, their toys and their people. The other five though had their eyes opened on the trip to Chicago. They had been in Arizona long enough to be used to flat desert lands and cacti. On the route to Chicago they saw mountains and forests in Colorado, the prairies of Kansas, Nebraska, and Iowa. There were streams and lakes, and in Illinois a great deal of settlement as they neared the city. When they had moved west, they were still too young to remember much about Chicago. The three boys spent many hours hanging over the back of one of the sofas looking out the windows. Mag and Melisa spent many hours playing with the boys or holding them up at a window to see something interesting as it went by. Carl and Deeds spent most of their time huddled together planning their next financial conquest.

Finally, the group arrived at the station in Chicago and their two cars were shunted into a private siding where four cabs and a couple wagons waited for them, along with a representative of Carl's bank, First National Indemnity, whose only job as long as Carl was in the city was to help things along. Melisa, Mag, Imelda and the twins took one of the cabs. Deeds, Carl, Ed, Ali and the man from the bank a second, Travers and the three the third, and four Pinkerton men in the fourth. The luggage and the wagons followed behind. When they arrived at the Chicago LePrad, the LePrad hotels being the chain purchased by Carl, they were met with appropriate ceremony and escorted to the owner's suite. The hotel had manual elevators, and they were used several times to get all the people and luggage up to the tenth floor. Once they were shown to the suite, two of the Pinkerton men stationed themselves outside the door and the other two went to see to rooms for the team and to oversee the movement of the luggage.

In the suite, Carl was saying to Copps, the man from the bank, "Tomorrow morning, 9:30, I want you to have a tailor and a valet up here. All the boys, and us too I guess, need to be outfitted properly, and tell that new tutor to be here for nine. That's all we need tonight. We will likely stay in and just use room service today. Tomorrow, when the tailors are here, I would like you to escort Miss Connors to an appropriate ladies' dress shop to be attired for all the events we are likely to encounter, with the bill going to my bank."

After Copps left, Melisa started to protest. "I am not sure I want to go to the events if I don't have the proper clothing now, and in any case, you shouldn't be paying for them."

"Melisa, just think of this as a thankyou for harboring my son and my grandsons during the Indian Raid. I don't know where I would be if I were to lose any of them. Besides Mel, for a guy with a dozen functioning gold mines this really is nothing. It makes me feel good to see you enjoy yourself, but you did notice my dear, Copps, not me or Mag, will be accompanying you to the store. Be merciless." Mag. Mel and Carl all laughed together.

The next morning they all had breakfast together in the suite. At nine o'clock there was a soft knock at the door. Carl answered and showed in a very pretty young lady, blond, slim, and impeccably dressed. As he brought her into the dining room; Deeds, Travis, and Mag stood but the others didn't. Carl said, "Boys, this is Miss Stevens. She is the new tutor for the older ones, academic and social. Now, my manners are a bit rusty but if I remember correctly all gentlemen rise when a lady enters a room, and one of them, you Des, should help her have a seat at the table. And I will ring for some coffee. My dear, would you like anything else."

The boys were sitting there open mouthed, frozen, and Mag kicked the foot of Des' chair to get him moving. Des rose and went over to an empty chair on the other side of the table, opposite her three "students", and said, "Ma'am, may I help you?" He pulled a chair a little to the side to allow her to enter and slid the chair slowly in as she sat.

Miss Stevens said, "That was pretty good. Someone taught you a little of this before.?"

"Yes ma'am. We lived in Chicago until three or four years ago, so I guess a little rubbed off. Don't remember a lot since that sort of thing is not used all that much out west."

"Now who are the other two, Chuck and Diz? That's a new name for me Diz, never heard that before."

"Diz is short for Dizzy. When the cowboys first got me, I was kinda little and kept falling off the horse. Sometimes I was kinda dizzy, so they just shortened it to Diz, but I think you are gonna have a harder job wi me and Chuck, nobody done teached us no manners."

Miss Stevens shot a quick glance at Carl, but said, "No problem, we have a month before you have to face the dragons in New York, more than enough time to brush up your manners, your grammar, and how to dress; and to teach you how to act in polite society, and also to dance. I was once part of that New York scene, and you better be ready before you go into those waters. Lots of sharks."

"A tailor and a valet will be here for 9:30 and the three there, and I guess all of us too, will have to be outfitted. Your help with these three would be appreciated. I think Mag and I can manage, and I guess knickers and high socks are still the uniform for Ed and Ali?"

"For the younger crowd caps are in too." She looked around the room at all the scattered cowboy hats on the sofas and said, "Cowboys hats are definitely not acceptable, nor are those cowboy boots that you all are wearing. Leather boots yes, not with large heels, and if a dance, thin leather shoes."

A message came up from the lobby. Copps was there to escort Miss Connor. Shortly after, the tailor arrived with a valet and a couple underlings with a large clothes rack on wheels. They all took over the dining room. Deeds had wisely absented himself, but Carl said, "The rest of the men in the room are your victims, including Travis there. You and Miss Stevens will have to accompany us, to keep an eye on those three. There will be some places Miss Stevens cannot go. We will need day wear and formal evening wear, like for dinners, and I expect for dancing too."

The tailor said, "We'll do two frock coats for everybody, a cutaway for riding, and a coat with tails for formal dining. A cape, and an overcoat. Two dozen shirts for each, assorted styles. Pants, a dozen assorted. Then the usual suspenders, underwear, and studs. Hats, six for each, cumber's for dinners. White gloves, three dozen each. Collars, four dozen. Ties, cravats, and bow ties, six assorted of each. Boots, black, brown, and grey, and shoes, thin for dancing, black and brown. Cane, umbrella. All that will get you to New York. I understand you will be summering in the Hamptons. For that you all will need swimsuits, say four each, Sack suits, six assorted, with short sleeve shirts, a couple straw hats each, you can use the same collars and ties. A couple more low and light shoes. That should do it. I would suggest with all those clothes and all of you, the family should engage a valet. Now for the two less than ten, hats, shirts, knickers, hose, shoes say six or seven of each, assorted underclothing. They will need swim suits too, and a coat. Now, we need sizes. The tailor nodded to one of his helpers. Carl had been sitting there with Ed on one side and Ali on the other. Carl pushed Ed out into the middle of the floor and the tailor advanced with his tape, started measuring and calling out numbers.

"Name?"

"Ed."

"Hat 7, neck 9, chest 15, waist 13, hips 15, inseam 14, shoes 9." Then a flustered Ed was pushed back. Ed was saying, "Did you see where he stuck that tape?"

Ali was dragged forward and a whole string of numbers again recited. Then the tailor turned to the other three and pointed at Des. "Okay, you first. We have to have real measurements to get a good fit. Strip all those clothes off so we can see what we have to work with. Then the tailor and a helper started undoing buttons far faster that Des could resist until he stood there naked except for his under drawers. When one of the helpers reached for those Des grabbed his hand and spoke softly, but icily cold, "You touch those and I will break your arm, and when you need an inseam, I will hold the top end of it."

Carl and Mag grinned to each other. Mag said to his Dad, "Some one did some growing up when we weren't looking."

Carl grinned but said, "Way to go Des. Don't let no one touch those drawers, that will keep you out of a lot of trouble. Now, you guys, I think you can get enough measurements like this, and you ain't getting Mag and I in our drawers. Let's get this over with."

The tailor and his assistants did return in about two hours. The hotel also added the services of a valet, especially useful to the three boys, as they tried their outfits on, and to make sure the clothes were hung up properly. He struggled mightily to get the three into the formal dinner outfits and he proudly brought them out to see Carl and Mag in the lounge, both of who were totally shocked. The boys looked two or three years older, and oh so handsome. There was going to be many a broken heart left in the wakes of these three. Carl said, "Boys, amazing. You look like a million dollars and when we get those manners spruced up a bit you will be worth that."

Mag said, "You do know Dad, when the girls here, and the ones in New York; get an eyeful of them, any of them, there is gonna be four or five after each of 'em."

"I know son, and I know too the boys would have better odds if we replaced the girls with twice the Indians. But this is something we have to teach them, as you will with your two. With the family wealth, the boys will always be targets. They have to learn to deal with the gold diggers as much as they had to learn to deal with the savages. I just hope they can come through this without gold digger wives."

"Not virgins too dad?"

"Mag, I can hope, but look at them, and there are three. What are my odds of getting that too?"

"One in a hundred if you are very very lucky," Mag laughed. "I think you are more likely to end up with gold digger wives for each of them."

Carl heard some commotion from Ed and Ali's room, and he went to investigate. They had on only shirts, which were long enough to cover them, barely. Travers was standing there holding out long stockings to them. Ed was saying, "No way."

When Carl entered Ali came over, "Dad, these knickers are short pants and you wear them with long stockings. We fought Indians. We went on trail drives. Ed got shot. There ain't no way we are going back into short pants."

A second later, Miss Stevens strode in and the boys scrambled to pull their shirts down and hide their nakedness. She said, "I heard the last part of that, and they are right. They have earned the right to wear long trousers and I will get that tailor back up here immediately; but boys, one thing you two have to learn. If you want to win an argument, especially with a lady, you should never let yourself be caught without your drawers, no matter how absolutely adorable you are."

The boys blushed deep red and Travers and Carl burst into laughter. Miss Stevens set off in search of the tailor. Carl said, "Boys, find some trousers out of your old clothes and some of those under all things for now. You guys are too old to be going around half naked. Lou and Les can get away with it, you two can't."

The tailor bustled in shortly and started to protest when Carl directed him to equip Ed and Ali with long pants. "Look, I don't care whether you think it is proper. The boys are right. They have been on trail drives for two months straight and they have fought off savage Indians. They have earned long pants. Now, do it." The tailor complied and when the trousers came up, there were a couple of small frock coats for each, and some pre-tied bow ties and caps the boys thought were neat.

Melisa came in with a parade of bellhops and boxes. Copps was trailing and looking a little stressed. Carl announced to all present, "We are going to eat in tonight, but in full dress, and we shall have full table service with dinner to practice." Dinner was ordered for seven o'clock. Miss Stevens arrived back at five, dressed in a fabulous evening gown and followed by two bellmen, carrying a Victrola and a stack of records. She had the three middle boys stand and did an inspection. She pulled and prodded here and there, then pronounced them, "Suitably attired and handsome as hell." She had Ed and Ali stand also, and after inspection, said, "You two aren't so bad either. You will beat out any other ten and eleven year olds, and could probably mop up any twelve years olds who dare to confront you. Oh Mr. Montrose, there are going to be so many broken-hearted girls in the wake of these five, I hope you are ready for what is to come."

She called Brent up. "Come on Brent. We went to the same parties back in New York. Help me show these boys what it means to dance." Brent came up a bit self-consciously. "Note where his hands are, and the fact there is space between us for a whole other person. This is dancing, and no matter how much you guys want to rub up against the girl you are dancing with, you can't." At this she glared at Des, Diz, and Chuck. They blushed, all three. "Now Brent, put something on the Victrola, and Des, you come up here, we'll start with you."

Carl and Mag took turns dancing with Melisa. And Des was forced to dance with Miss Stevens, taking turns with Diz and Chuck. Several times she made the three watch while she demonstrated a step with Travers that they then had to practice. Although they would never admit it, the three enjoyed the sessions and were secretly excited by the idea that they would soon be using these skills with girls their own age. They had never had much contact with girls at home, of any age.

Seating the lady was again discussed. "You have to realize, the ladies at these dinners are dragging around ten yards of cloth with them just in their dresses. They have to manage all that as they are seated. That is why they need your help." When dinner was served, the lessons switched over to table manners and cutlery. "With the cutlery, work from the outsides in. The table will be set to deal with what is being served. If you have four forks left, don't be tempted to use the fork nearest the plate just because it looks right. If you are really at sea, stall, talk to one of the people beside you until it is clear what all the others are using. So, part of dealing with dinner is learning to talk to the people at the table with you. A good hostess will ensure you are seated beside people that at least speak the same language as you do and hopefully have some interests in common, something to talk about."

They worked their way through dinner with Miss Stevens making sure they had the correct fork or spoon for what was offered and how to hold and use it correctly. "Remember, unlike the meals in the west, the purpose of dinner is to socialize. You do not just chow down. My Dad used to eat dinner before he went to dinner, because he said the courses were so slow that by the time they brought him something he was interested in eating, he would have starved to death. It is important too that you only take small bites. One of the people beside you may ask you something. You have to be able to quickly swallow what you have in your mouth and answer."

Diz said, "Gosh, this sounds terrible. Why do people go to large dinner parties?"

"People get dressed and go in order to be seen, and to see. They go to talk business. They go to meet people and they put themselves forward to find the right match. There are lots of reasons, but none of them are because they are hungry. Just think about it. Your Dad has not brought you all east because you are hungry. Why will all of you be going to these dinners? Ask him."

Carl was thinking to himself, "I told them I wanted a strong woman tutor who spoke her mind, I guess I got what I ordered." He said, "Miss Stevens is right. I brought mainly you three east, so you could see the real world, where the real power is. This family is wealthy and getting more so.

If we are going to exercise the power we should, we have to understand the world that power is wielded in. And she is right, a lot of it is wielded socially at these god-awful dinners. All of you have to understand how to navigate in that world. There are more dangers there than there are out west with its savages and rattlers. At least they are visible. The dangers here in the east will look you in the eyes and smile at you while they knife you in the back without a thought. Their daughters will tempt you, and let you believe they love you while all they really love is your money and power. You three are ready to learn that lesson, and most of all, you have to learn to keep your wits about you, always to be vigilant. The pretty girl sitting beside you at dinner may be preparing to slit your throat."

Mag laughed, "Nice Dad, good dinner conversation."

Miss Stevens then spoke up, "Your Dad is exactly right. The people you dine with will be oh so polite, so friendly, so kind, you will never know what they are thinking or doing. You have to learn to not be drawn in. If one of your Apache was smiling at you and offering you a piece of roasted meat but had one hand behind his back, what would you do?"

"Shoot him," said Diz, "He likely has a knife behind his back."

"Then, how do we deal with these dinners?"

"You are friendly and polite, you never say anything important because they are always pumping for information they can use. And, most importantly, you never let anyone get you in a compromising situation that can be used against you," said Miss Stevens. "I learned those lessons, but I just got tired of playing the game and I came out here to Chicago; and I daresay that is why you have Mr. Travers with you in Arizona."

"She is right, as is your Dad. The people in the finest dining rooms of New York can be every bit as evil as those Apache out west. The beautiful young girl who takes you for a walk in the garden is always seeking some information she, or her father, can use against you and your family. But, as she says, if you are always aware of that you can use it too. Just as she is looking for information on your family, you can get information on hers. If you know she is trying to get you into a compromising position that she and her family can use against you and yours, you have to protect yourself and make sure it doesn't happen. You wouldn't take a walk outside at night at home without your gun, back east you have to be as watchful. Just different kind of savages and no guns."

Melissa was looking at all of them shocked. "I thought this was going to be a vacation, not a war."

Mag said, "I knew this to a degree, when we were back here in Chicago. I wasn't very smart then though. I let the girls charm me and draw me in. That's the point though, isn't it? I was stupid, and if we hadn't moved out west there would have been problems. Everyone is telling you this so you can protect yourselves, know what you are facing so maybe you can do better than I did. And you guys learn how to do that, to use the people trying to involve you, for your own purposes. It's just like fighting the Apache, be smart, be vigilant, always keep your guard up."

After dinner, they got the Victrola going again and practiced dancing some more. About ten, just before the boys retired, Carl said, "Tomorrow, for lunch, we are all going out to the biggest and fanciest restaurant we can find and give those manners a test run.

Chapter 9

And It Begins

After breakfast, Carl announced the family was having lunch at Fredricos, the biggest and fanciest of the Chicago restaurants. The party would include the five boys, Miss Stevens, Mr. Travis, Melisa, Mag, Carl and Deeds. Imelda would stay with Lou and Les. The boys were told to be dressed for eleven thirty. The reservation was for 1230 and this was a bit of a test to see what they came up with.

Ed and Ali were out first. They had on dress shirts with the pre-tied bow ties, long black trousers and black leather eastern style boots, and their tailor-made frock coats. On their heads were black leather caps. Even their long blonde hair was combed. They stood before Carl for inspection and he glanced at Miss Stevens who nodded. "Okay guys, you pass."

After they wandered away, Carl looked at Mag. "Okay, they are ten and eleven. Why do they look like thirteen all of a sudden?"

"And cute as hell," added Melisa.

"Got to be the frock coats and long pants," said Mag in amazement.

Then Diz, Chuck and Des came in. They had chosen light frock coats over dark pants, dark cravats and snowy white dress shirts. They each carried a bowler hat and gloves. "Aha, three fine young gentlemen who look like they are twenty but really are fifteen. Remember that when the girls swarm you three."

When the ladies arrived, they set out. The restaurant was only half a block away. The group looked as good as any other prosperous group in the city, and as they walked down the street the crowds seemed to just dissolve before them. When they arrived at Fredricos, the maitre'd took one glance, then sent them to one of the more visible tables for twelve by the windows. They were seated and menus were produced. Ed was looking at his for a bit then said, "Dad, can we order what we want, from whichever part of the menu we want."

Carl smiled, "You think I haven't been in this position before? With ten-year olds? You can order three desserts, but you have to order at least one thing that is real food."

"Aw gee Dad, this dessert page looks really good all by itself."

Mag whispered to Mel, "I used to try that too when I was little. Got away with it a couple of times too."

"Oh, I'm sure if you got away with it, your Dad knew and just went along with it."

"Looking back on it, I think you are right. Really, not much gets past Dad that he doesn't want to."

Dinner went well, no major faux pas, everyone was pleased. As the waiter brought coffee, he said, "If your young gentlemen want, there is a sort of conservatory play area. There are swings and slides for the younger kids, but there is also a Koi pond, and some caged tropical birds and the such. Just through those doors on the other side of the room." Carl looked over at Ed and Ali, they had that pleading let me outta here look. "Okay, ten or fifteen minutes, then back and we will be ready to go. We are just having our coffee now."

Ed and Ali were gone in a flash. When they entered the conservatory, they found it hot, but unlike Arizona, very humid. They wandered around and saw many plants they had never seen before, and the Koi pond, they assumed the Koi were those large orange fish. There was a sign by the pond that said some of the Koi were over twenty years old. They stopped for a few minutes at the swings but that didn't seem as much fun as it used to. The place was almost empty, so they were surprised when they got to the end that there was a commotion coming from the far corner behind some trees. They peaked around a corner and saw a tall gaunt man had two girls forced into the corner. He was saying, "Give me your money. You rich kids always have money and I want it." With that he gave one of them a push back against a tree. Ali and Ed looked at each other and nodded. They both took off together with Ali kneeling behind the man and Ed pushing him, so he tripped over the kneeling boy and fell backwards to the ground. Then Ed jumped on the man and pummeled his face while Ali struggled to hold the man's arms down. The girls ran screaming back to the dining room and soon were back with several waiters, their parents, and the Society Editor of the Globe with his photographer. He managed to get a couple pictures of Ed and Ali before the attacker was freed from them. The Society Editor knew a story when he saw one, and the two girls were Von Steddings, one of THE prime families in town.

Lisa and Lana both thanked the two boys, and there was a picture of each of them getting a kiss on the cheek. They told their mother and father they were afraid the man was going to hit them to get their purses and their money. Mr. Von Stedding thanked the two boys and asked them how they knew what to do. Ali said, "We are from Arizona, we fight Indians and robbers all the time. My brother Ed was even wounded once."

"So you don't live in Chicago then?" asked Mr. Von Stedding.

"No, our Dad just bought the hotel down the street and we are going to spend some time visiting the rest of them, you know, checking them over."

The reporter cut in, "Just for our story, what are your names and how old are you?"

"My name is Ali and this is my brother Ed. We are eleven and ten. We are Montroses, from Arizona."

Carl and Mag had been drawn by all the excitement but had not interfered. The boys had been doing okay without their help. When they heard Ed say it was about time they headed back, Mr. Von Stedding said, "Wait a minute while the girls gather their stuff, and I will walk you two back." Mag and Carl rushed back, and they were seated only a couple minutes before the Von Steddings appeared with their daughters. The parents of the girls introduced themselves and briefly described the incident, saying how thankful they were the boys had been there, thanking the boys again. Carl graciously accepted the praise of his children and noted, "It usually doesn't take them long to nose out some sort of trouble."

Carl told his family it was time to go. As they left the restaurant Carl noted Mr. Von Stedding berating the restaurant owner with, "..and this is supposed to be the best restaurant in the city. If you expect to have our friends and us dine here again, you had better make sure nothing like this can ever happen."

After dropping his family at the suite, Carl went on a tour of the hotel with the hotel manager. He was reasonably impressed, the hotel was in good shape and efficiently run. The staff seemed happy and the guests well cared for. On his way back after the tour, Carl stopped in the tobacco shop and got a couple of cigars and an assortment of newspapers. When he got back to the suite, he handed Deeds a cigar and half the newspapers, then they sat together companionably. Carl was about to throw aside the society section of the Globe when his eye was caught by a couple photos of the boys, including one where the two were pummeling the attacker, accompanied by a lengthy article detailing the events of the afternoon and quoting Mr. Lucas Von Stedding, and his wife Marta, as saying they were forever grateful for the bravery of the two boys for having saved their daughters from heaven only knew what might have happened had they not come to their aid. "The boys are the youngest sons of financier, industrialist, and mining mogul, Carl Montrose, currently visiting Chicago on his way to the east coast." The article went on to say the family normally resided on their ranch in Arizona. The owner of the restaurant was quoted as saying no comment but security around the establishment was noticeably stronger after the incident. Carl handed the section to Deeds with the comment, "You'd better read this."

There was a knock at the door and the afternoon maid came in with the head of the Pinkerton's security team. He opened with, "We did as you said sir, we only did night security here in the hotel. But now, you all are famous and targets, people will be only too eager to prove you are not that tough. And the kids, definitely, there will be people who resent their fame. From now on, you have to take us when you go out, not to say that if we had been with you this afternoon, there would have been none of this."

Carl had to reluctantly agree, to the fact it would not have happened if the detectives were there, and the need for security from that point on. Then, there was another knock at the door. The maid came back with an envelope addressed to Carl Montrose. He read it then called Ed and Ali. When they got there, he handed the card over for them to read. Ali said, "What is an Ice Cream Social?"

"It's like a small dinner party for kids. The only food is ice cream and cake. There might be some dancing, but likely not. You all are still young. The party is tomorrow. You have to decide now, the fellow that brought the invitation from the Von Steddings is waiting in the hall for an answer either way."

"Why not go? It's only from 1 to 4?" said Ed. "Besides I thought both those girls were kinda cute."

Carl smiled and thought to himself, "Already, and you are only twelve," and he said, "Okay then, a couple of the detectives will take the two of you and wait with you to bring you back. Now, I will have to write them a note to that effect."

After the note was sent, Deeds and Carl talked. Deeds said, "You know what this is eh? They are using this little opening with the kids to try to open you up. Next, there will be an invitation to dinner or perhaps shooting or some such. Do you really want to get back in this again?"

"Me? No. But the boys have to if they are to prosper. When we came out west, I had already done several years of this, and I was tired of the games, still am. Mag and the other three have to learn how to manage this if they are going to take the money they will inherit and make it into really great fortunes for each of them."

"What if they decide they want something else?"

"That's okay, if they are happy, but they should have the choice."

The next afternoon, at 12:30, two of the Pinkerton detectives left with the boys for the address listed in the invitation. One of the detectives positioned himself across the street where he could watch the front and the exposed side of the house. The other went with the boys to the door whose ring was answered by Lana and Lisa. The three were admitted and a maid took the detective to wait in a room populated with governesses and tutors. The girls took Ed and Ali into the room where the party was.

All the children at the party were 11 or 12, an equal number of boys and girls. Ed and Ali, when they looked at the other boys at the party, both came to the same immediate conclusion, "A bunch of wusses." The sight of even one Apache would have sent them all running for their fathers. Both boys then concentrated on the girls who had invited them, Lana and Lisa. The group was playing some games, at that moment it was Pin the Tail on the Donkey. Soon it was Ali's turn, and he found himself blindfolded and spun around. He groped forward looking for the donkey then he heard a door close and a tiny giggle. He tore off the bandana and found he was alone with Lisa who said, "Finally got rid of all those babies. Come and sit here on the settee with me."

The two sat together on the couch, Lisa advancing from the right with Ali retreating to the left until finally he was wedged in a corner with Lisa almost sitting in his lap.

"I knew you weren't like the rest of them, you are so much older than they are." She leaned forward and kissed him tenderly on his lips. Ali was surprised, finding he enjoyed it, but he had never done anything like this before and both his arms were still on the arm and the back of the sofa. "You can hug me you know." Just as Ali embraced Lisa, the door burst open and Ed said, "Stop foolin' around Ali, they are going to serve the ice cream and cake now. Come on you two, this is the best part of the party."

Lisa wasn't too pleased when he struggled to his feet, but he said, "Come on Lisa," and he held his hand out to her to help her up then they went into the other room, hand in hand, to the table. The boys enjoyed the ice cream, they had only tasted it a couple times before in their life. Ice was necessary to the production of ice cream, and ice was a very rare commodity in the deserts of Arizona. After the ice cream was finished, Lisa asked the party goers what they wanted to play now. The boys were silent but several of the girls called out, "Spin the Bottle." Lana formed the group into a circle to sit on the floor and Lisa went to find a bottle, a crystal one at that. Lana said, "The rules are you spin the bottle and have to kiss the person it points to, but only if it's an opposite. Boys don't have to kiss boys or girls, girls. If that happens you get to spin again."

Lana was the first to spin, and she got a boy called Ralph. He closed his eyes and leaned forward. Lana didn't like him, so she kissed him on the cheek. They took turns and when it came to Lisa, she gave it a good spin hoping for Ali, but she got Ed who closed his eyes and leaned forward. Lisa put a hand on each of his shoulders and leaned in, giving him a big kiss right on his mouth. It was a long tender kiss and when Ed leaned back afterwards, he felt good.

The next to spin was Ali. He was a little miffed that Lisa had bestowed such a kiss on someone other than him so when his spin turned up a girl called Samantha, he figured, "What the hell, two could play that game." Samantha was leaning forward, eyes closed, and Ali leaned forward, put both arms around her and gave her a long deep kiss. When he broke off, he found he was looking into a pair of amazingly beautiful blue eyes. They both giggled. It was Lisa's turn to be miffed.

Shortly after, Mrs. Von Stedding called an end to the party. A dozen cabs had been ordered for four and all the guests were reunited with their adults to be returned home. She did notice the good byes bestowed on the Montrose boys by her daughters and was pleased. They were nice boys and a step above the norm.

When the boys got back to the hotel, Carl asked how they had enjoyed the party. Ali said, "The kids were nice, but I met a real special girl called Samantha, don't know her last name."

Ed said, "Yeah, they had a real long kiss in Spin the Bottle. I had a nice long kiss with Lisa. First kiss I really had from a girl."

Curious, Carl asked, "Was Mrs. Von Stedding there when all of this was going on?"

Ali said, "No Dad, she left after the ice cream. You don't think we would do stuff like that in front of parents do you?"

"I would hope not, but I never thought I would be discussing long tender kisses with my twelve-year old sons."

"I know Dad, it should have been years ago but there are not that many girls out there in Arizona," said Ed. Ali nodded in agreement.

The group dressed for dinner that night and ate in the hotel dining room. The manager made sure they had extra special service. The group finished and came up to find a messenger waiting at their door. There was an envelope from Lucas Von Stedding, inviting Carl, Deeds, Mag, and the three older boys out to his place on the shores for an afternoon of shooting with himself and a few friends. There was a map enclosed. Carl assembled the prospective guests and explained the invitation.

Diz said, "What do we shoot?"

"Around here they shoot at little clay discs, called pigeons, and they use shotguns. I think we will surprise them a bit and take our rifles." Carl composed a response.

"I appreciate the invitation, as do my sons. You can count on six guests at about 12:30 but we will have to leave about 4:00 because of a previous dinner commitment. We will bring our own shooting instruments." He went out in the hall and showed his response to the detective stationed there before he gave it to the waiting messenger. After the boy had left, he said, "Tell your boss and have him arrange the coaches. We six can share one, but he can decide on how many of you go and how many coaches you need."

Then he went inside and hunted up Brent Travis. He told him what they had planned for the next afternoon. "Here's a couple of hundred dollars. Ed and Ali are going to be disappointed, they can shoot the best of all of us, but maybe you can plan something special with them, and Miss

Connors and Miss Stevens. We will be back for dinner. Have Miss Stevens choose a restaurant and make a reservation for all of us."

During the morning, preparations were made. There was some discussion about appropriate wear for an afternoon shooting. They came to the conclusion boots, dress pants, sweaters and coats were in order, and they all chose to wear their western cowboy hats. That was Carl's idea, "Let's let them think we are a bunch of country hicks and we will mop them up in the competition."

Mr. Travers, Miss Stevens and Miss Connors put their heads together to decide what they would do for the afternoon and from one of the morning newspapers got an idea. There was a carnival in one of the parks by the lake. Some rides, sideshows and the sort. "That sounds like fun," said Melisa. So, it was decided. When Ed and Ali heard, they were in favor too. When they mentioned it to Carl, he agreed, only cautioning Brent to let the Pinkertons know because some of them would trail along.

A little before twelve, the shooting party left. The family took one carriage and the Pinkertons another. As they got there, Mr. Von Stedding came out the front door. He greeted the three older men and shook hands, then nodded at the detectives, who had spread out over the drive. "My security team, Pinkertons, just ignore them and they will do their thing. It's almost gotten so I can forget about   them. I'll tell you one thing though, if you ever need security, they are the ones to get. Not long ago a team of them saved Mag there and his two infant sons when savages over-ran the town. If needed, they do their job."

Des reached back in the carriage and pulled out the six rifles. Von Stedding said, "We were planning on shooting skeet. You people will be at a real disadvantage with rifles, not shotguns"

"Don't worry Lucas, we usually hit what we shoot at."

Just then another five people came out of the house. They all had shotguns and one had two. Von Stedding introduced them. "This is my son Fritz, he is a sophomore at a local military school. These are Mr. Leo Graystone and his sons Jake and Clem. And the gentleman in the back is another of my business associates Ronald Scott."

Carl returned the honor, introducing, "My oldest son Mag, my three middle sons, Des, Diz, and Chuck; all sixteen. And this is Lionel Deeds, one of my solicitors and a good friend. Now, shall we go shooting?"

The group went around the building and down towards the lake. The older men walked a bit ahead and the younger ones formed a small group of their own, sizing each other up. Fritz said, "Come on, you guys can't really expect to do well with a rifle, do you? These pigeons are only the size of a hand. Most people need the spread from a shotgun to even get a corner of them."

"Oh, we'll do okay. The only problem is, we are used to aiming at living things, not little clay things. Sorta takes the need out of the process," said Chuck.

Jake said, "What do you mean living things? You mean deer and such?"

"Deer, cattle, groundhogs and other varmints, and of course the Apache. The need to hit them with one shot is really urgent when they are coming at you looking to take your scalp. Sometimes you only get one shot," said Diz.

"Come on, you can't really mean you have had to fight off Indians," from Clem.

"We were on a trail drive that lasted two months, and they attacked at least every other day. They occasionally got one of us alive when they attacked. I remember one night they got Ned. Their practice was to scalp their victim alive and then torture them slowly til they died. We heard Ned for hours and hours. That's what I mean, it was kinda urgent you got the target with your first shot, you might only get one," said Des.

"On that trail drive we lost nine men, a quarter of the total force with us," said Diz.

The group in the front was also having a conversation. "I had my people do a quick check, after the event at Fredricos, and you seem to have a wide range of investments, the three nationals, the Arizona railway, mines, and land out west, a huge ranch and cattle herds sold to Chicago, land in Virginia, now the hotels all over the east and the south, as well as investments in industries all over the east, and there are even rumors of oil in Texas and Oklahoma, as well as Pennsylvania. My people felt they had uncovered less than a quarter of your investments."

"They are about right in their guess. I must admit, I have been lucky with my investments."

"People aren't that lucky, you must have a talent for this?" said Leo.

"Well I did make some purchases early, before they got really expensive. Is that what you are looking for? Investment tips?" said Carl bluntly.

"No, not tips. Just general knowledge. Us investors in the east are just starting to turn our eyes west. You have actually moved out there and live there. By the time all the railways get finished it will be too late. What are the areas of growth out there? Where should we be looking, and for what? Just general trends."

"Well, the way I see it, in what will be the states of the west and the mountain west, there will be states with a lot of area and very few people, the Dakotas, Wyoming, Utah, Oregon. Unless you want to get involved in mining things, not much there of interest. For myself, I have some copper mines, but I have mainly concentrated in gold and silver. When you get to the coast there are areas of growth, like it will be in California. Beautiful land and a wonderful climate. At some point, I can see the day it is the state with the most people in the country. With a little irrigation, some of the land could be quite productive. The area that interests me is the Southwest, Arizona, New Mexico, Texas, even Louisiana. Right now, Louisiana is known for cotton, and Texas for ranching. I think the future of both will be oil. Arizona and New Mexico are still territories. Land is plentiful and cheap. There are very few people. You can get in there with new ideas and modern methods and do well because the land is so reasonable. The long-term investments are California and Texas. The territories are still adventures, but they can be profitable. The key to the western states, including California, is water rights. Get in early, and get the water rights, and eventually the land will be golden."

Leo Graystone said, "I don't think I understand this thing about water right."

"My main ranch, Ranchero Grande, is surrounded by five or six other tracts of land. During the rainy season, we graze all of it. Towards the dry season we sell the cattle off and bring the core of the herd into the main section where the river and the water are, and then we expand again for the next year. The great ranches of the west will all do the same, and even in California, the farms. A core operation is where there is water. It will expand out for part of the year but always return to the core where they have the rights to water. The cities will be along those rivers, the land the most valuable."

"But don't bother looking in Arizona, he already has all the key rivers buttoned up," said Deeds.

"See, I told you, a man like that wouldn't be out in Arizona raising cattle. He is there to obtain a state for the future of himself and his family for generations to come," said Lucas Von Stedding.

By this point the group had arrived at the shooting area. Lucas had arranged for one of his grooms to run the Skeet machine. The shooting began. They ran through each team, three clay pigeons each, and totalling the score. Out of the possible eighteen in the first round, the men from Chicago got fourteen. They looked a bit smug. Then the western group had their chance, and out of their eighteen they got the full amount, eighteen. There were several rounds like this when Von Stedding's crew got almost eighteen and Carl's side did. The men from Chicago were good. The Arizonans were better. The Chicagoans got ninety-five percent of their shots. The Montroses got one hundred percent of theirs, and with a rifle; even Deeds. They took their feat in stride, but their opponents were impressed. Lucas said, "You guys are deadly at this, and with rifles too."

Des said, "But this is boring. Can't you speed them up or double them or something?"

Fritz Von Stedding yelled to the boy handling the machine, "Double the pigeons up, and double the speed." Des and Diz took them on, as a duo, given the fact that between the shots they had to manually eject the cartridge, but they kept up, never missing a one.

Von Stedding said, "The only limit you guys have is the rifle. Apparently, Remington is working on an auto eject rifle, might solve part of the problem. In any case, what your boys can do with what we have is amazing."

"Amazing how motivating a band of attacking savages can be, isn't it?" said Carl. About three, the group headed back to the lodge for some hot coffee before the Montrose group headed back to the city. The six younger boys gathered with their coffee around the billiards table. Fritz explained the game and the three from the west said they would like to try, but that they had never done it before. Jake, Clem, and Fritz, were ecstatic; they had found something they were better at.

The men had gathered in another room over their coffee. Lucas said, "I understand you are doing the New York season, then the Hamptons. The

Von Steddings are doing the same this year so we will likely be running into each other a bit, I would daresay. Your two little guys have made quite an impression on my little girls. It would be nice if they became good friends, wouldn't it?"

"You might not think that if they really did become friends. Ed and Ali are true creatures of the west, free and wild and always in motion. You never know what they will come up with or say. They will have the hardest time fitting in to this eastern society, to the politeness of it all."

At 4:15 the group headed back to the city. In the carriage on the way back, there was a long discussion. Carl asked the boys what they thought of the youngsters they had just met. "Jake and Clem seemed like normal kids, just rich ones. I don't think they would last long out home. Too soft," said Diz.

"That other one, Fritz Von Stedding. He is always watching, scheming I bet, he's one you have to watch. He is always looking for an advantage over you, and there is something really strange about him, but I cannot put me finger on it. One thing I am sure of, you could never trust him with your back. He is out for himself, of that I am sure," said Des.

Chuck added one more comment, "I didn't like any of them. I like people to be and act the same way. Is no one real out here?"

Carl commented, "Now boys, you are getting an idea of why we are doing all this. In the business world, where most of our money has to work, you have to deal with people like these. I am not saying they are bad people, it's just the world they live in. They are more to do with appearance and reputation, and less on the actual doing. That is why they are always looking for something to give them an edge, something they could use if they ever got desperate, and that is why you always have to keep your wits about you."

Deeds said, "Are you sure you didn't give them that edge with all your talks about water rights in the west? They had no idea."

"I did that on purpose. A year ago, I wouldn't have, but now I have secured all I have to, across the Southwest, Arizona, New Mexico, Texas and California, even what I need in Louisiana and Mississippi. Now if they want to spend money out there, that's okay. They will never be anything more than junior partners and allies. It makes anything I want to do easier if they consolidate the other ownership a bit. So, it suits me if they spend cash out west consolidating water rights. Nothing they do now can curtail any of my plans."

Des said, "Then Dad, you were playing them while they thought they were playing you?"

"Best way to conduct business boys, a lesson to learn early."

During the same afternoon, the boys, Brent, Melisa, and Miss Stevens attended a carnival not far from the hotel, accompanied by a half dozen or so trailing detectives. The carnival, when they arrived, had a whole lot of sideshows, some games, some rides, and lots of barkers, people selling things. The sideshows, and some of the world's greatest whatevers, were absolutely revolting to the women and they often found themselves standing chatting as Brent took the younger two in. Melisa said, "This is nice, more like the real world, not like all that nonsense with the dinner parties, and the clothes, and the phoney manners, and all the pretending."

"Glad you have seen through all the phoniness, that's the biggest part of learning to live in a place like this. New York is even worse. Hate to tell you that as that is where you are going. The Hamptons are a little less formal."

"Sometimes, I wonder why I even did this trip. I doubt if I will stay to the end," said Melisa.

"Honey, I know why you made the trip. That is clear anytime you and Mag are together, each of you adores the other. Both ways, I can see it."

"Frankly, I do adore him, and Lou and Les; but why can't he bring himself to say something if he feels the same way?"

"Mel, you have to understand something. Mag is what? Twenty, and he already has two children he is responsible for, three years old. Men like to grow into responsibility slowly. He is afraid to ask you, to at his age have a wife and two children, and then what? He is still trying to sort out where his place is in the Montrose empire. I think once he has a direction, then he will ask you. It is clear he adores you."

"You think that's it, he just needs to find his direction? I have a hard time seeing him as afraid of anything. You forget, I saw him fight off fifty or sixty Apache to save me and his children."

"A man would rather face a hundred screaming savages than to face a wife he has disappointed."

Brent and the boys returned laughing. "That was all so phoney, who would believe any of it, but it was funny?" said Ali. They went a bit further down the aisle and found a shooting booth. Ed and Ali glanced at each other and came to the same conclusion, they should be able to clean up in a place like that. Brent gave each of them two dollars and then he and the ladies stood back to watch the fireworks. The three had come to the same conclusion, the boys should be able to clean up in a place like that given their background. About ten minutes later Ed and Ali came back disappointed. Ed said, "We didn't win nothing, didn't hit any of the targets. I don't know how we could have missed."

"Yeah, and both of us, both of us missed everything. Don't see how that could be," said Ali, quite dispirited.

Brent said, "It likely wasn't you guys at all. These people in the booths earn their livings with them. Quite likely they have shaved their sites ever so slightly to make sure the good shooters like you two can't hit anything. For most of the clients it makes no difference, they couldn't hit any of the targets anytime. Not fair to real shooters like you two though."

The boys listened to this explanation getting increasingly indignant. No one understands and is as committed to the idea of fairness as two twelve-year-old boys. When they saw a policeman standing nearby, they let go of Brent's hands and scurried over to the cop, one tugging on each of his arms.

"Hey, sir, you in charge of these people in the booths too? There is one back there, where you rent a rifle to shoot at targets and they rip you off. They must have done something to their rifles, and it is not fair."

"You really should do something about them. They shouldn't be allowed to rip off kids like us," said Ed innocently.

The officer leaned over and said, "Boys, you are right. Let's go have a look, why don't we." The officer and the boys led Brent and the two ladies back to the shooting gallery where Officer O'Brien demanded to see one of the galleries guns. The owner reached under the counter for number 37, the only gun in the place that had not been altered, and handed it to O'Brien, who took a couple of shots, hitting the targets. The policeman spoke to the owner of the gallery, "Now, these boys are disappointed and were saying there was something wrong with the rifle they had. Now, you have two choices, you can either let them have their shots again with a gun that works, or you can close for three or four days while we confiscate all the guns to check them down at the station."

The owner was quick to get the point and said, "Here boys, take your ten shots over, this gun is fully loaded." Ed took two shots, and got a pair of binoculars, three more shots and he got a big pocket knife, then he handed the gun to his brother. Ali had set his eyes on a telescope, for which he had to ring the alarm three times, and a little wind up lantern. When they were done, Ali turned to Brent and said, "Hey, why don't you win a couple of bears for the ladies." Brent good-naturedly handed over a dollar. The bears needed three rings each, and he won a blue bear for Mel in four shots, and with three more he won a black bear for Miss Stevens. He then handed the gun back to the owner and the group wandered off, after the two boys thanked Officer O'Brien.

After they had gone, O'Brien said, "Jasper, I told you, I don't care about all the drunks you cheat at this place, but when a nice young family like that comes in, you at least give them a good gun, most of the time they won't hit anything, but at least they have a chance. Now either you get the point, or we will take all these guns in for inspection and you had better hope we don't find any of them altered. Today it cost you two bears and a couple of trinkets, next time it may be a few years in jail."

The rest of the group continued through the carnival. There was a Roller Coaster which they all rode together, Ed and Ali in the first seat of a car, and the three adults crammed into the seat behind them. The boys held their arms up on the dips. The ladies held onto their hats, and Brent had an arm over the shoulders of the two. There was a maze the boys went in while the adults waited at the other end. Half way through Ed and Ali met an older kid who offered the two a cigarette, and Ed and Ali accepted. The three stood around smoking and talking until the cigarettes were done, then the boys quickly found their way to the end."

The boys each had a ride in the back lot on a camel. That, they found interesting. "Not a bit like a horse," said Ed.

They each had some cotton candy and a waffle cone, chocolate, and then it was time to get back to the hotel. On their way out, the group again stopped at the shooting range. The owner came over and said, "How about before you start, I give each of you two, five shiny dollars to just call it a day." Ed and Ali agreed.

Back at the hotel, the skeet shooters had returned. The little kids showed the older ones what they had gotten from the Carnival.

Ali was showing Des the little lantern. "I don't know how it works but it looked neat."

Des said, "You take this little crank on the side and you turn it. There is a little dynamo inside it that makes something called electricity, and see, when you turn it hard enough the little lantern lights up." Carl had been listening to this conversation and then he went and sat beside Deeds.

"You know that offer from those people in New York, the dynamo thing and electrifying the city, get it out again willya. I think we have someone who can explain it to us." When Deeds got the material, Des was called over and the three of them spent half an hour discussing the offer from the inventors. Des said, "These guys have developed a dynamo, a type of machine that turns to make energy, electricity. It can be used to run machines, electric machines, say fans, and most important, lights, electric lights instead of kerosene or gas lights like in a city. They need to test their dynamo though, they need investors and a place. But Dad, do you see the potential, one dynamo could provide enough electricity to light up the whole town of Connor."

Carl thought for a few minutes then said, "Lionel, after we get back from dinner write them. Tell them we will invest the ten thousand, but they have to prove their concept by electrifying my plantation. Tell them there is a river there. They are to electrify Oakside Plantation, near Oakville, Virginia; with all their equipment and if they can electrify the plantation; we might have a deal. And Des, this will be your project, you keep an eye on them for me. You learn everything you can about this electricity thing. I have a feeling there may be a future there."

Carl then took the family out for dinner. Miss Stevens had chosen a restaurant in Little Italy for Italian food. They came in and immediately saw they were the best dressed of all the diners, but the owner immediately seated them and made them feel comfortable, one of his family. Soon the family was into an enjoyable meal. Carl had a moment to ask Miss Stevens, "Why didn't you tell us to tone down a little, the dress, so we didn't stand out so much?"

"I did that on purpose, so that you all had to cope with something that was uncomfortable, outside of that little cocoon you can be living in."

"Well, you did that, but I have to admit I like this place, and by all the smiling faces, I would say they do to."

They both looked out on all the smiling faces of the boys and Melisa, and it was clear this was a place they all would like to visit again; unlike many of the other places they had dined in recently. By the end of the evening the whole family was on a first name basis with Luigi, the owner. When he was presented the bill at the end of the meal, Carl added an extra two hundred and said to Luigi, who started to protest, "Luigi, look at them. For the first time since we left home, they have been totally comfortable and happy. This is now our favorite restaurant and you can be sure we will be back several times before we leave for New York. Thankyou my friend."

They had taken two cabs to get there, and did so on the way back to the hotel. On the way back Carl said to Lionel, "Find out about Luigi's building. If he doesn't own it, buy it. I can invest a bit in Little Italy in order to ensure that a place like that can always be there."

When they got back to the hotel, there was a messenger waiting for them again with a note addressed to Mr. Montrose. Again, Carl had to call Ed and Ali, and Miss Stevens. "I have here an invitation for Ed and Ali, twelve thirty to three thirty, for a riding party tomorrow afternoon at the stables in Lakefront Park. You are both being invited by one Miss Samantha Green. Now, Miss Stevens, what is a riding party?"

"You have to remember, most of the children here that same age as Ed and Ali, do not know how to ride. Likely, for most of the time, the horses will be on tethers in a fenced paddock. There are riding costumes available for children. We can get a couple sets in the morning if we wish."

Carl looked at the boys, "Look, it's up to you, but I have a feeling the two of you are going to be bored out of your mind. This doesn't sound much better than the pony ride at a carnival."

The boys talked between the two of them. They gave each other one last look and then Ali said, "Okay, we want to go."

"Now look here, I know the two of you and I know that look. You think you are going to go to this party and once you are on a horse you will get loose and ride. Before I write that note, you two will have to make me a promise. Now, come over here and stand by me where I can see you. No crossed legs, no crossed fingers, no crossed eyes. You two have to promise me that you will behave yourself and do what the other kids do."

The two boys solemnly promised. When they had returned to their room, Carl looked at Miss Stevens. "They meant that you know, but twenty minutes riding around in a circle will drive them crazy, they will break away from the others, and there will be nothing you can do about it. But, when they stop, and get off the horses; you bundle them home where they will have to face me and bear the consequences."

"If you know what is going to happen, why are you letting them go?"

"They have to learn that when they give their word on something, especially to me, they better keep it or there will be dire consequences."

"What kind of consequences?"

"Miss Stevens, they will get a whuppin."

"But, ..."

"Miss Stevens, I value your opinion, but this is between me and them. They looked straight in my eyes and gave me their word. The word of a man has to mean something, and they have to know that."

Miss Stevens nodded as Carl wrote the acceptance note. He showed it to the detective on duty then sent it with the messenger. Miss Stevens went in to see Brent and told him what had just transpired. "Brent, I understand men have to understand what it means to give their word, but they are twelve years old, they are not men, they are little boys."

"Those little boys have bore the burdens of men. When they were fighting off the savages, if they had been captured, they would have died in exactly the same way as any of the other men. They knew that, and they fought as men. They shot, and they killed. Do not deceive yourself. When they made that promise today, they knew what it meant, and they fully understood the consequences of what it would mean if they broke their word. Whatever happens now will be because they choose for it to happen."

The next morning, Miss Stevens arrived with two sets of riding gear for the boys, complete hats to boots. She was early, in fact the boys were still in bed when she strode into their room. "Here is the accepted riding gear for people your age."

The boys looked at what she held up. Ed reached out and felt the leather of one of the boots, then said, "The boots feel real nice, soft. And I see how the britches are made to fit inside the boots, and the black jacket, sorta goes with the boots. But what's with the frilly thing at the neck, and the hat?"

That frilly thing at the neck is an ascot, and it is to hide the fact you don't have much of a shirt under the jacket, and I know the hat is silly."

Ali said, "Okay, boots, pants, jacket, even that ascot thing, but no way to the hats. We will wear our cowboy hats, and that's that."

"Okay then, get dressed and we will let your dad see you before we go." Then she left, thinking to herself that she had done well to get what she had gotten.

When the boys came out, Carl was still at the table with his breakfast. He looked at them and gulped. "That is what they wear here now for horse riding? Somehow, I don't think they wear cowboy hats, what does the real hat that goes with that get up look like?"

Ed held up a hand with the little billed hat on it and Carl looked at it. "Well. I can see why you want the cowboy hats. Okay, but we are paying a real price to try to fit in. To let the two of you go out in that gear is almost embarrassing."

"Dad, one nice thing is the boots. They are light and soft, almost as if you have nothing on. I like them," said Ed.

"We'll see if you feel the same way after a half ton horse steps on your foot," said Carl. Miss Stevens got a cab for the three, and a second cab followed with three of the Pinkertons. When they arrived at the stable, they found Samantha there already, with her governess. She greeted both boys warmly, especially Ali. Miss Stevens noticed but made no comment. The next to arrive was a young boy. When he saw the two boys in their cowboy hats, he let out a cheer and reached into the bag he was carrying. "Mom told me I couldn't wear it unless some one else had one. Thank god, I hated that other hat. Looks like a duck."

Ed said, "I gather you are not from here then?"

"Until two months ago we lived in Laramie, Wyoming. When my uncle died, my grampa made my father come back to help with the bank. My name is Roger Birch. You guys aren't from here either."

"Our ranch is in Arizona. We are taking a tour of my dad's new hotels."

Just then Lana and Lisa arrived. Lisa was especially friendly with Ed. Lana gave Roger a hug. The six stood around talking. Ed said, "Sam, is it true they will have us ride around in circles on tethers?"

"That's what we normally do."

"Look, there are three of us here who know how to ride, and three who need some help. Why don't we pair off and help each other? We can stay in the field, just not ride in circles at the end of a tether. Tell them you want six horses in western saddles, and we will take care of the rest." Sam turned to her governess and said, "Get us six horses, western saddles, and we won't need the grooms."

The governess started to protest but Sam stamped her foot and said, "Now, Agnes." The horses were produced as directed. Ed paired off with Sam, "You put your left foot in here, grab the pommel and pull yourself up, then I will adjust the stirrups. None of that stupid side saddle stuff. In this saddle you will be safe, and I think you will enjoy it more." The other boys helped the rest of the girls. Once everyone was on their horse, they gathered in a circle and Ed said, "Now girls, doesn't that feel better, and you can feel the horse with both knees. Now we will break into pairs and just let the horses walk until you feel secure, then we will speed it up a bit." It took about an hour, but the girls were soon trotting about the pasture.

At the side the governesses and tutors were watching. Sam's governess had stopped worrying and saw that Sam was in good hands. Miss Stevens was also impressed. Ed had taken charge and now all the children were trotting happily around the field. About half way through the afternoon they all moved out to the track and the couples loped easily around it. Just before they quit for the afternoon, Ed said to Sam, "You girls mind if the three of us race around the track one lap?"

The girls cheered the boys on as they tore around the track. And they all were pretty close to each other. Ali won by a nose, but they all were elated, and a little of the excess energy was worn off. As they came into the suite the boys were laughing and joking, and Carl was surprised to see there were three, and all wearing cowboy hats. Ali introduced Roger, "This is Roger Birch, until a few months ago his family lived in Laramie, so I guess we were almost neighbors. His Dad works at the bank across the street and will pick Roger up when he is done at five. We just wanted a few more minutes to hang out together. Is that okay?"

"Sure boys, I'll let Roger know when his Dad gets here." The boys went down to their room and Carl turned to Miss Stevens. "So, did they ride around in circles?"

"No, but no one did. Ed took charge, got them paired off and outfitted in Western saddles and each of the boys taught one of the girls how to ride cowboy style. They all had fun. At the end, the boys had a race around the track, one lap, Ali won."

"Ed took charge and made all that happen? Amazing."

Then Carl sat with Lionel, "Birch? Why is that name familiar?"

"Randolph Birch, died in a shooting accident four or five months ago. He was running Fidelity Trust, his father's bank. The old man was almost retired. I guess that's what Roger meant when he said his grandpa made them come back. The old man must have made his second son come back to run the bank. Fidelity Trust has a pretty good rep, sound."

Later, there was a light knock on the door and Carl went to answer it. He opened it to find a youngish man, conservatively dressed but with an engaging manner. "Hi, I'm Charles Birch, I believe my son is here."

"Hello Charles. I am Carl Montrose. Come on in. I was hoping to have a short chat before you left. Perhaps you'd like a brandy or something. This is one of my lawyers and bankers, Lionel Deeds."

"Actually I have heard of both of you. Mr. Deeds, you have a small bank in Arizona, but a bit of a powerhouse. And you, Mr. Montrose, you developed the railway from Laramie to Tucson. And you brought a massive trail herd to Laramie a while back. What did you want to discuss?"

"What I wanted to discuss is the formation of a new bank, to help in the development of the west and centered in the west. I own a bank in Connor Arizona, and Deeds here owns one in Tucson. I also own a bank centered here, First National Indemnity. I would like to put all of those together with your bank, Fidelity Trust, which I am prepared to buy outright from your family. Any western bank would need eastern connections if it were to succeed. The new bank, for now let's call it First Western Fidelity, would have its head office in the west, let's say in Laramie, with branches in Chicago, and all of the other places noted, as well as some new places. I especially want a presence in California. You may know, I have a significant investment in gold mining and silver mining in the southwest. I also have gold interests in California. It is a different kind of mining. The new bank will also move into Texas, Oklahoma, and Louisiana, where I have oil and ranching interests. I am not a banker, I like to find and make investments. I would like you to lead the bank, and I think you might like that too, if it takes you and your family back to Laramie. I assume you still have your property there."

Charles was looking at Carl, a little surprised. "My wife and I, and Roger, would love to go back west. That is why I kept the ranch. It is an interesting proposition. I might be able to get my Dad to agree. He is quite old now, doesn't have that much time left. There is no other family left here so a move west would be easy once he is gone. I think Roger would like to go back."

Just then the three boys came out and Roger ran up to his Dad. "Dad, this is Ed and Ali. The are from Arizona. Finally, someone I can understand. And see, we all have cowboy hats, and we actually rode horses today, and not just around in circles. And Dad, there was this girl today, Lana, I think we need to have a talk."

Charles looked over at Carl and said, "It may be too late."

That spring "Western Style" riding parties became all the rage with the younger set in Chicago. Roger, Ed and Ali became the most popular guests in the 12 year age group. The merger of the banks and the creation of First Western Fidelity was accomplished and the plans for the relocation of the Birches back to Laramie were set also. Roger and the two Montrose boys were a little sad that what had become a strong friendship might be broken but Carl assured them all that the needs for Carl and Charles to meet would be frequent, and they all had agreed there would be chances for the boys to renew their friendship.

Mag had finally worked up enough nerve to ask Melisa to marry him and she quickly agreed. When they told Carl, he was receptive. "Frankly Mag, I was wondering what was taking you so long." It was agreed that there would be a small family wedding just after they got to New York. It was planned for the family to leave for New York on April 25th, with a one-night stop in Boston to check out the Boston LePrad, and then the move to New York the next day. Therefore, the date set for the wedding in New York was April 30th. The New York LePrad was notified of their arrival, their requirement of the Owners Suite from their arrival to the end of June. Carl also reserved the Honeymoon Suite for Mag for a week from April 30th.

On April 25th Charles brought Roger to the station to say goodbye to Ed and Ali. He and Carl had a few words and the two decided the new headquarters in Laramie would be in a new building of its own within a year. "We want to project an image of modernity, but also stability, and the building has to be impressive, so the investors understand there is wealth behind the bank. Make sure you get a telegraph line, even now in the temporary quarters, and I will get one put in the New York suite and at the shores too. Contact me anytime, we have our resident telegraph operator in Diz. Actually, with the wire, we will have better contact than we would if we were in the same town. Deeds will stay with me at least till we get to Virginia in the fall. I think we will be at Oakside from September until Christmas, and that we will move South in the new year. There are gulf hotels to check and I just completed the purchase of a new ranch in Texas I want to see. In the new year there will be a couple new gold mines to open along the railway and the banking will go through you, but we hope to be in production within three months. Make sure the new bank has a good private vault for me to have the newly smelted gold bars stored in. Just so you know, when we are at Oakside my intention is to set the direction for the plantation, and it will not be cotton. We are going to electrify the place and I want the economy of the plantation to be based on something from the future, not the past. So, there may be some capital needs for Oakside in the fall. Once you have the new bank up and running, review all the banking arrangements for the LePrad hotels with an aim to simplifying what we can. These old organizations are often knee deep in old employees and tradition. The hotels are good, and I want the financial framework to be as good too. Charles, I'm sorry, if I own a bank, I aim to make optimal use of it. All the old mining stuff is running through Connors bank and eventually we will fold that into your operation in Laramie too, but do the other stuff first. At that point, Carl called the three younger boys in. "Roger, I have a gift for you. We found a gunsmith in Tucson who made Ed and Ali pistols that were the right size for them, and we had a set made for you. Now, you practice with them when you get back to your ranch, and when we get to Texas, we will send our train car to Laramie for you and your family to come visit for a week or two. You boys can visit, and your Dad and I can catch up on the bank." He handed Roger a box and when he opened it, he found a set of matched pistols just like the ones Ed and Ali had. Carl quickly checked to make sure the guns had no ammunition in them and then let Roger try them on. They fit perfectly. Ali said, "They won't look so bright and shiny for long, but that is the way it should be."

Carl handed Charles a box too. "This is the ammunition for those guns. The gunsmith's name is on the top and I am giving you the first ten thousand rounds. Seems like a lot, but it's not, so once you get out west you will have to place an order."

At that point, they felt the engine taking hold of the two cars, theirs and the Pinkertons. A conductor came aboard to say they would be ready in ten minutes so there was a hurried round of good byes, and the people on the train waved back to those on the platform, Roger, Charles, and Copps from the bank, who was glad to see them leave so he could go back to a slightly slower pace. Charles, feeling a bit like he had taken hold of a tornado, strode up to Copps, "Mr. Montrose spoke so highly of you, I had you transferred over to me. You be at my bank for nine. Now that you are finished with the Montroses, I will give you a new assignment. Pack some bags, you are going out west. Hey Copps, you are single, aren't you? Good, you may have several assignments out there for me. I think you will be my go-to, for all those little unusual assignments that come up from time to time. Your first assignment will be to go to Laramie and find the land for the new headquarters, secure it, have it cleared. By that time, I will have the plans for you, and you can supervise the new construction. By the time we get out there, I want the new building, if not finished, at least habitable. Get a telegraph station put in to your new quarters and get someone to teach you how to use it in your spare time."

The train steamed east, ultimately for New York but with a brief sojourn for one night in Boston. Travis and Miss Stevens had both agreed to continue with the family and they were trying to organize an educational day for all the boys in Boston. Deeds and Carl would have the whirlwind inspection of the hotel, and Mag and Melissa looked forward to some quiet time with the babies.

As the train steamed towards New England, Carl met with his sons to see if the trip was teaching them anything. "So, we are off to New York, with a brief stop in Boston. What have you all learned about the people back here.

Mag said, "They are liars and cheats and you can't trust any of them. I hope Mel and I can find a place where we can be more relaxed and just raise our family. I felt I had to be looking over my shoulder with them back there in Chicago; and I bet New York will be even worse. Glad to be rid of em."

Ed said, "I found most of the guys sappy, very few I could trust with my back, except for Roger that is. I think we will be friends forever."

Carl agreed, "Yes, I think the Birches will be good friends to the Montroses over time. They were a good find, and we can thank you two for that."

Ali said, "We made some good friends among the girls, Lana, Lisa, and Sam. I think the six of us are going to be a group, for a long time."

"A group of six, or three pairs?" asked Des shrewdly.

"I guess pairs, me and Sam, Ed and Lana, and Roger and Lisa," said Ali.

"Now guys, you are just twelve, let's not get carried away too early in our lives."

"Dad, when a person meets their friends they know it, and remember, we are all gonna be at the shores this summer and you promised to try to get Roger there too, with us," said Ed. More and more Carl had been noting that Ed spoke for his brother and for their little group. He seemed to be the leader, even though he was among the youngest. Carl had been unsure about letting the boys get paired off at such an early age but more recently he had become a little more accepting. If the three boys had found their true intended that early in their lives, they would be saving a whole lot of angst and drama later. He had decided to just sit back and see what happened.

Des spoke for the last three. "With all the social stuff in Chicago, we met a lot of people, girls and guys. We didn't like any of them because none of them seemed real, everyone just playing a part. A role. Sometimes, like with Clem and Jake Graystone, it's not their fault. They are trying to be what their father wants them to be, not what they want for themselves. Fritz though, he has an idea what he wants and will use anyone or anything to get it. Somehow, I don't feel his goals are all that honorable. The girls were all like silly geese, rushing around after one another making all sort of noise."

"Here the people try to appear so kind, smiling all the time, fake."

Dizzy added, "I would rather face fifty Apache than to face a bunch of these people. At least you know what the Indians want, to kill you. Here, the people are usually phony, you can't tell what they are thinking, really wanting. Everyone is so selfish, but you can be sure of one thing, what you want or need means nothing to them."

"It sounds like you older ones are learning the lessons I brought you east for."

Chapter 10

Boston and New York

As the train neared Boston, the younger boys were looking out the windows. Boston was such an old city, even compared to Chicago, and especially when compared to the cities in Arizona. Once in a while, they got a glimpse of the bay, which was really the Atlantic Ocean. None of the boys had seen the ocean.

The plan for the next day was for the two tutors to take the five boys, see the city and all the historic sights, and even a bit of the fishermen and the harbor if they had time. Carl and Deeds would spend most of the day going over the Boston LePrad.

Their cars were again shunted onto a private siding and the party was met by an assistant manager from the hotel who had been warned by Chicago. He had a wagon for luggage and four cabs for the family and the security people. Pulling up to the hotel, Carl was pleasantly surprised. At an estimate, it would seem to have well over 100 guest rooms and was an old brick building. On his way in Carl saw a cornerstone dated 1793. For a building that old it had gas lighting and even one of the new-fangled elevators. There was an air of history about the place and it was quiet and subdued. The lobby was quite luxurious. The manager met them and ushered them to the owners' quarters on the top floor, the fifth. Legions of bellhops were dispatched to struggle up the stairs with the luggage. There was a lot of luggage even though a lot had been left on the car under the care of a couple Pinkertons as they would be leaving the next morning.

The tutors started to gather their charges immediately. Mag and Mel made sure Imelda was settled with the babies and had everything she needed, then joined the group. Carl cornered Travis and said, "Here's five hundred dollars for lunch and dinner for the group. Pick something historic for each meal, something with atmosphere. None of them will likely ever see Boston again so try to make it memorable."

Then the group was ready to depart. When they left the hotel, Brent saw a small horse drawn bus standing there and he asked the driver how much to rent the bus for their party for the day, five kids and four adults; they wanted to see the sites of the city. The driver said he would take the whole lot wherever they wanted to go for the day and back to the hotel at about nine for thirty dollars. Brent paid the man and loaded the group. They had plenty of room. The driver suggested the Bunker Hill monument for the first stop. When they arrived, the two teachers went into the appropriate history lessons. They all climbed the 294 steps to the top of the monument for a breathtaking view of the city. When they came down, they toured a little house that displayed some of the old uniforms and muskets from the Revolutionary War. There was a small cemetery near by called "The Granary Burial Ground". They stopped there and looked at the tombstones. Some of the names the boys recognized, Paul Revere, John Hancock and Sam Adams. There were lots of names they did not recognize, and Miss Stevens explained they were citizens who had been killed by the British during the Boston Massacre. Then, they visited The Old North Church. Des knew what it was famous for, the lantern that Paul Revere put up to warn the people the British were coming, and where he commenced his famous ride. They also saw the house Paul Revere lived in the night he rode. By that time, the group was eager for lunch and the driver found them an old traditional inn that served meals at noon.

As they all sat around a big oak table and ate, Brent said, "When you see a city like Boston with it's history, it really shows you how young where you live out west is. When you get to New York, you will see parts of the city are the same age but somehow it doesn't feel as old. The main thing you feel in New York is the constant activity."

The afternoon was spent in the harbor area. They saw where the Tea Party took place and they watched the fishermen coming in with their daily catches. They went to a fish market and all were astounded at the variety of the fish available. Nearby, there was also a farmers' market where the farmers that lived just outside the city displayed and sold their produce, again a surprising sight to the boys. They had never really given much thought to where all the food came from, other than beef of course. For dinner, they found a small waterfront café that specialized in a fresh fish fry, and they ate at a big table overlooking the harbor. There was a big roaring fire in a pit between their table and the next, to keep them warm.

After the rituals and restrictions of the society in Chicago they all enjoyed the day and the freedom to be who they wanted. Mel and Mag had found several times during the day when they could walk discretely hand in hand and not feel self conscious. The boys loved the freedom to be as loud and boisterous as they wished. Even Miss Stevens and Mr. Travis seemed to be more relaxed.

When they boarded the bus for the trip back to the hotel, they all were a little subdued at the thought of having to return to the strictures that were ever-present at their social level. They got back to the hotel just before nine, and they all made a point of thanking their driver for the day. He was surprised. Most people of their class hardly even admitted he existed. Nice family, he thought.

Carl and Deeds had had an interesting day too, poking around the hotel. They saw everything from the furnace room to the laundry. Just like all great hotels, there was the glamorous front side, and behind that there was a simpler, dirtier, and noisier side that made the place work. Both sides of this hotel were well managed and efficient. Carl found nothing to complain about and could leave the next day secure in the knowledge that this hotel was doing fine. The two men had just had their meals in the small restaurant in the lobby. They were sitting in the lounge in the suite when the family returned, and they could tell they had had a good day. Ed and Ali came over to tell them about what they had seen and done. "Dad, this place was so much better than Chicago, there was no one hushing us or frowning if we didn't behave like they expected us to," said Ed.

"I know you all, we leave for New York tomorrow and there will be another set of rules and a whole new set of rule keepers, that was why I wanted you all to have today. But, we will be there less that two months and then we move to the Hamptons, and that will be a lot less formal, I hear. I think you will enjoy that; and then the fall in Virginia. That will be just like home, without the desert, but with the horses, and on our estate, you can ride them dressed anyway you want. Before the war, society used to be a lot stricter, now you kids will be able to get away with a lot more. So, two more months, then the pressure should be off, but remember why we are doing this, so that if you find yourselves in these situations you will know how best to behave." The next morning, about eight, the Montrose party checked out of the hotel and proceeded back to the station where they re-boarded their car. It was picked up a little after nine and put on the end of a fast freight to New York City.

As they neared the city the buildings got closer and closer, and bigger and bigger. The city seemed to go on for miles and miles. Ed said, "Dad, this place is much bigger than Chicago, isn't it?"

The train went over a couple of bridges, even through a tunnel, and got to Manhattan Island. At the station, they were shunted off onto another private siding and were met by hotel staff. Because they would be staying for two months, they had to take all their belongings. The rail car would be put in a storage facility. The stewards would stay on the car and prepare it for storage. With two wagons of luggage, and four cabs again, the group set off for the New York LePrad. This was one of the flagship hotels of the chain. Rather than tying up the whole front entrance, they were taken to a private entrance at the back. Even that entrance was perfect. Carl could hardly wait to see what the front entrance was like. The building was about fifteen storeys tall and there were several elevating rooms. When you wanted room service you rang a butler on your floor. He sent your order on a series of dumbwaiters to the kitchens and the food came back the same way. Their suite had ten bedrooms, a separate dining room and three lounges, even a small kitchen. There were several washrooms and bathing rooms; and hot and cold water in all of them. This truly was the epitome of hotel accommodations in the country at that time.

One of the managers met them to make sure they had all they needed. "We think you have everything you need. We even got your telegraph unit installed in one of the living rooms today." After the manager left, Carl called Dizzy. "Check with our station in Connors to see if our set is working okay, then if you want to listen for a while it's okay. If the clicking bothers us, we can go into one of the other lounges." Diz loved to just listen to the set, to other people's traffic.

There were some notes waiting for Carl. The Von Steddings were in town for the season, as were the Graystones, and several other Chicago families. There were dinner invitations from the Astors, Sinclairs, and the Whitneys, as well as the New York Roosevelts. Carl didn't know any of them, but his banks did. These invitations were entry through the doors of power. Mag wandered in and Carl took the opportunity to talk to him.

"So, are you ready? Tomorrow is the big day. You know you are making me happy with this. I think she is the right one for you and for the boys. I thought so for a long time."

"Dad, I love Mel, I have from the first time I saw her. The only thing is, I still don't have a direction. I have a family, and soon a wife, and I still don't know what I want to do. Dad, the land sales in Arizona, that never really clicked with me. Jessops loves it, and he can probably handle it all on his own. Frankly, I hate Arizona. There has to be someplace better. I am sorry Dad, I know you own half the territory, but between the Indians, the dust, and the heat, it really isn't that nice a place. And ranching, do you like that, the drives and the dragging the cattle out of the mud, day after day? I'm not that fond of that either. I think I would like having a place to build, more like a farm, where you can grow something. Something Mel and I could grow together."

"You know Mag, I am not blind. Two years ago; I knew you didn't like the west, but you tried. One of the reasons for this trip is to see if we own something that interests you. For example, any of the hotels. Mel runs a hotel. Perhaps the two of you would like to run one of the hotels, not in New York or Chicago, but there will be others. Then there is Oakside, in Virginia. You seemed to like it there before we left to avoid the war. We don't have a direction for it yet, but maybe you two could help with that, figuring out what we are going to do with it. And, you know, I am not that fond of the desert either. That's why part of this trip is to look at a new ranch I bought in Texas. I think Texas is going to be big in oil, and I have been buying a lot of prospective oil land, and in doing so we came across this real nice ranch too. Maybe you will like that. Just because it is a ranch, we don't have to fill it with cattle if it is pumping oil by the hundreds of barrels a day. So, in short settle down, enjoy the family, and let things unfold. You will find your place. Oh, by the way, here is a key. I reserved the honeymoon suite for the two of you for a week. A newly married couple needs some time alone to start and we have Imelda for the babies. No dinners, nothing, just the two of you. And here is your wedding gift."

Mag looked in the proffered envelope. It was full of hundred-dollar bills. "Dad, what is here, a hundred thousand? What am I supposed to do with that?"

"Mag, check the last piece of paper. There is a credit line there for a million. You spend a couple thousand on your honeymoon, and if you invest the rest, even with our bank, there will be a comfortable living there. But, on the trip, if you see something that really appeals to the two of you, you have the money to invest. You and Mel have a good talk in that week the two of you have alone. All of your brothers will get the same treatment when they start their married lives. I don't much believe in hanging on to all the money and leaving it for you when I die. You all should have your share to make your lives with. You are of age now."

"Gee thanks pop, now you've given me another million things to worry about."

"You know son, there are many who wouldn't see a million dollars as a burden, but rather an opportunity."

"Dad, the burden is not the money, but rather the need to live up to your expectations. You know Dad, you have always expected a lot of all of us."

"That I have son, and for the most part, that is what I have got from all of you. Mag, look at your brothers, all of them. They are well on the way to being good men, all of them. That is because they have not been babied. A boy becomes a man when you treat him as such."

Mag had no response because he knew his father was right. Anyone who looked at Ed or Ali could see they were wise beyond their years. A lot had been asked of them and they had delivered. "Well Dad, as usual you are right."

The two sat there companionably for the rest of the evening. Carl felt no need to counsel Mag on his husbandly duties, there was clear evidence he knew what he had to, as proven by Lou and Les.

The next morning, the minister had been ordered for 11:00. Miss Stevens helped Melisa get ready. Des served as his brother's best man, and all he had to do was straighten Mag's tie for him. The group gathered by the fireplace in one of the lounges. Imelda brought the babies and shed the required tears. The ceremony was quick and soon the two were Mr. and Mrs. M. Montrose. Both got congratulatory hugs from all of the new brothers-in-law and the new father-in-law. Miss Stevens and Mr. Travis also attended and congratulated the new couple. The minister had stayed for coffee, and Carl pointed to him as he said to Brent Travis, "We have the parson here. Are you ready to stop mooning over this lady and ask her, or do we have to wait six more months?"

Travis and Stevens were both shocked but gradually a smile crossed Brent's face. He turned to Miss Stevens and said, "He is right you know. We should have done this years ago when we first met, and now we have a second chance. Not many people get a second chance. Sally, will you marry me? I don't have much to offer. I think I am still disinherited, and you will be by your family if you agree to marry me, but I do love you, and I think you do feel the same, for me."

Sally Stevens gave her consent to a match she had feared never would occur. She had no idea what would happen, but she looked forward to whatever the fates may bring them. There was a little bit of a scramble to find another ring, but one was found in and removed from the nose of one of the babies' toys. An amused Parson performed another ceremony. There was a heavy round of congratulations again. Carl rang down for a manager and when he arrived said, "We have had another surprise wedding, so we require another Honeymoon Suite for a week. Everything is to be billed to the room and paid by me." The manager left to see to arrangements and said he would return shortly with the key. Carl turned to Brent and Sally and said, "You two have a week off with pay. And bill everything to the room. A newly married couple should start off with some time together." He motioned Deeds over.

"And here is your wedding gift. We were prepared in case you said yes." He handed them an envelope that had a hundred thousand dollars in it, and a bank draft. "Now, I hope you still stay with us, at least for a while, but this may help you to take advantage of opportunity if it knocks."

Shortly, the manager returned with a second room key and gave it to Brent. The two couples chose to leave at the same time and shared an elevator down to their floor. When they got off the elevator, they turned in different directions. The suites were at opposite ends of the hotel.

Up in his suite, Carl sat in a chair beside Deeds, looked across at the five boys arrayed on the opposite couches and said, "Well boys, we got a bit of a problem. What are we all going to do for a week?"

Des said, "Yeah Dad, at home you could always send us out to herd cattle or kill some savages, but here we don't have any of that. You better think quick because you know how much trouble we can get into if we are bored." The other boys all giggled.

Carl said, "Well Des, you are wrong one way. There are lots of savages here, but you can't shoot them."

"More the pity," said Deeds, but he held out a newspaper to Carl.

"Boys, we are saved, at least for today. Do you see what Deeds here has found for us? A rodeo, right here. This afternoon." Carl said, "Boys, get dressed, and you can wear what you want, and your hats. There is no uniform for the rodeo. You can even get your guns out of the trunk, just don't load them." When the boys came out, they looked like they were dressed for a trail drive. Deeds and Carl ushered the boys down to the lobby and had a cab hailed. The group drew more than a few glances as they waited. New Yorkers did not often see five armed children. The rodeo was being held at the fairgrounds in the Bronx and it took about half an hour to get there. When they arrived, they found there was a crowd by the ticket booth, but no admissions were being sold. One of the men in the booth was saying, "Sorry folks, we don't have enough men to put the show on. Nine of them got arrested last night for being drunk in public. We just don't have enough people who can ride to do the show."

Ed pushed his way forward and said, "If all you need are people who can ride, we can help. We just came here from Arizona, and we can shoot too. There are seven of us." The owner of the show looked down. The kids did look like they were the real thing, but the two men looked like bankers. Several of the prospective attendees yelled out, "Give the kids a chance. We want to see a rodeo."

"Boys, come around the fence. Folks, give us ten minutes to see if we can make this work, if it does, we will try to start selling tickets then." When the group gathered behind the fence Carl took charge. "First let's settle the doubts about Deeds and I. Some one, give us a gun with real bullets."

Des handed over one of his and a charged cylinder. Carl snapped it in and pointed to a line of little wooden corbeilles along the top of one of the rodeo wagons. He fired off six shots and six of the little trim pieces lost their heads, then Deeds did the same. Then he looked at the owner, "That settled, now you get an armorer over here. All the boys' guns take real ammunition. You want that to make sure it all has been collected and replaced with yours or you are going to have a lot of real dead Indians."

At that, there was some mumbling among the shows Indians, who were watching real closely as the armorer did his job. Carl went on, "As far as the riding, the littlest two are absolutely fearless, as long as you can find them a horse that is small enough, the older three the same, only bigger horses. We all just spent two months on a trail drive."

The owner took a chance. "Start selling the tickets, get the two older guys to wardrobe and add a bit to the five kids. Calvin, make sure we don't have any dead bodies when we are done. Get the first number together and fill the kids in. Alert the band." In only a few minutes the boys and the regular cast were mounted on appropriately sized horses and were gathering at the entry point for the ring. Then the alarm went up. "Who is going to sing? Usually it's Eddie but he's in jail. No one else knows the words, do they?"

Ali edged his horse forward. "Give me the flag, Mr. Travis taught us the words. It won't be an opera, but I can get the job done."

"Okay guys, you all circle the ring three times then stop in the center, this kid forward, the band will do an intro frill, and the ringmaster will ask that crowd to stand, then the bandmaster will give one more frill and follow you. Okay?"

The whole group entered the ring together and circled at high speed, yelling and shooting blanks. At the third circuit, they slowed, and Ali found himself to the front facing about a thousand people. He held the flag firmly and edged his horse forward a couple steps. He looked at the bandmaster and nodded. The band gave a little frill and ended and held one note for him. Then Ali belted out the anthem, loudly and clearly, so that everyone in the stands could hear. He thought some would join in, but no one did. They just listened, entranced by what they heard. Everyone, his family included, were astonished at how well Ali was doing. When he got to the end there were loud cheers and clapping. The group left the ring and when they got backstage, Ali's brothers gathered around him and clapped him on the back in congratulations. Carl came up and hugged his son, "You know you guys, there are times when one of you does something so unexpected and so wonderful that it leaves me speechless in pride. Ali, this was one of them. Thank you." The afternoon continued. All of the real performers had managed not to be arrested. The men who competed in the riding and roping events all were still there. The Montroses were mainly used in the mass events, like the beginning and ending ceremonies and the staged events, like the Indian attack where they helped fight off the savage swarm. Deeds had been made an Indian for that event and the boys took great glee in "shooting" him. The three older boys saw the rodeo owner had a skeet machine and convinced him to let them shoot skeet for the audience with their pistols. It was quite a sight when the three of them took center stage together, both pistols drawn, and blazed away at the skeet over their head being launched as fast as they could be. The audience loved it. The two little ones staged a center ring shootout for the audience, and both managed to get themselves killed, much to the delight of the rodeo goers. The closing ceremony saw the whole family and Deeds take part. Ali was given the honor of flying one of the national flags as they all circled the ring. The whole show got a thunderous applause. The owner of the rodeo hunted them up afterwards and said, "You guys saved my bacon this afternoon, would you like to come back for tonight's performance at seven. All of you are the real thing and the audience loves you, and Ali, I really would like to hear the anthem again."

The boys all looked at Carl who said, "Sure we will come back tonight. This was the most fun the boys have had in months. Right boys?" Carl took the boys for dinner to a little café just down the street from the fairgrounds, a place that was totally informal and where the food was wonderful. After dinner, Carl talked to the boys. "You know, today has proved something to me. While I still feel you have to learn the skills you will use here in New York, I am convinced none of you will want to live here full time. These skills will be like tools, to be brought out as needed and then put away, and that is okay as long as you know how to use them. We are all meant for something a little less, a lot less, formal than this place." All the boys nodded in agreement, relieved that Carl had seen what they already knew.

The whole group returned to the fairgrounds for the evening performance, in fact they did all seven days of the rodeo. The owner even wanted them to go on the road, but Carl said he was sorry, but they all had other commitments. Ali did the anthem every day. The two younger ones also worked up a bit with the rodeo clowns that was a real crowd pleaser. The three older ones modified their skeet bit with the pistols to also include a rifle which the three tossed back and forth without a pause in the routine. Carl watched the boys, amazed at their skills and delighting in their joy. On the way back to the hotel, after their final performance, Carl said, "Well, that solved, the problem of the week, how to keep you all occupied.

Tomorrow, the tutors and Mel and Mag will all be back, and it will be back to the old routine, but I want all of you to know, I really enjoyed this week with you."

The next morning, all the newlyweds returned. Mag looked at ease with his situation now, at peace with the fact he was married and had two children. The two of them were overjoyed to see Lou and Les again. Mag slipped Imelda an extra two hundred dollars for having been on duty full time for the last week. Then he and Mel each took a child and sat with them in the lounge for a couple of hours.

Sally and Brent both looked content, also. They both were satisfied with their new situation. Both had written their parents to bring them up to date and neither cared a whit how they reacted. Both sets of parents were in the city but neither had made any effort to get together with their children. The new Mr. and Mrs. Travis were reconciled to the fact and were looking forward to their future together. They both had missed their charges for the week they were gone, and both were quick to ask what the boys had been up to during the week. The boys all relished telling their tutors about the week at the rodeo. Ed made a point of mentioning Ali's new-found talent at singing. Mel and Brent both had the same thought at the same time. "Maybe we should add something to our approved activities, the opera, and the shows on Broadway." Brent mentioned it to Carl and received immediate approval for the set up of a couple evening for the whole group. The boys were not as eager for a night at the opera.

Their first visit to the opera was Carmen. Everybody was all dressed in new tuxedos and the ladies in their finest gowns. That afternoon Carl made a quick trip out. At dinner, he gave a box each to Brent and Mag, "On Loan" as he put it. "Mag, these were your mother's and they have been in a vault all these years but maybe they deserve a night out too."

Mag's box had a diamond necklace and the one for Sally was diamonds and sapphires. Both women were intrigued with their loans and went to the mirror to have a look after their husbands had attached the clasps. They both agreed the necklaces were gorgeous and it was a privilege to wear them. The two women were beautiful in their own right, but the jewelry made them more so.

They took two cabs to the opera. Deeds rode with Mel, Mag, Sally and Brent. Carl rode with the boys who were all subdued. "Come on guys. This is your first opera, cheer up, you might enjoy it. It will be all in Italian, you won't understand the words, but just watch it and the action, and listen to the music. Just go for the mood and the atmosphere." The boys were looking at him doubtfully. "Look guys, you probably will only go to an opera a couple times in your life, we just want you to experience it, while we are here in New York." Again, he was met by five resistant looks, slightly hostile from the older three, and definitely hostile from the younger two. "Now look guys, I spent a whole week, two shows a day, with you all at the rodeo. All you have to do here is behave yourselves for a couple of hours."

The gong went to have the audience get seated and they went up. The family had a box of their own. Carl sat the boys in the front row and the adults took the second. The boys were fidgety until the curtain went up then their attention was riveted on the stage and the music. It didn't matter that the lyrics were in Italian, you could still follow the story. Halfway through there was an intermission. As the curtain went down and the lights came up, the boys turned to their father.

"So, you have seen half an opera, was it that bad?"

Ed said, "A little too much kissing, but the story is pretty good."

Ali said, "I liked the singers. They likely trained for that all their lives. I wonder if ten would be too old to start."

Carl glanced at Brent and said, "I think one of the things Mr. Travis can do with you while we are in New York is the take you around and show you some of the music schools in the city." He then told Mr. Travis about the amazing events at the rodeo all week. "I think that is a side he has just discovered. Take him to see what might be available there, but make sure he sees it all and knows the price."

By this point, they had made it back to the lobby for the intermission refreshments. Carl stayed with the ladies and the boys while Brent, Mag, and Deeds went up and got the drinks. Across the room his glance met Lucas Von Stedding who escorted his wife, Marte, and son, Fritz, over. Carl's boys gathered around Fritz, glad to see someone they knew. That evening Fritz was wearing his dress uniform from his military school. This impressed Ed and Ali. They thought he looked handsome, and like an officer.

Carl mentioned it, "My little ones are impressed with Fritz' uniform."

"The only positive thing I can say about that school is that they have nice uniforms. Academically, he doesn't do so well, and he is having a problem with making friends in school, not sure what the problem is, we have been thinking about finding another school for the fall."

"Really? I went to VMI as a child, from a little older than Ed and Ali are now. I grew up in Virginia, so I got to come home on weekends. Our plantation, Oakside, is not far from the VMI campus." The three returned with the refreshments and passed them out.

"I didn't know you were a southerner originally. You were part of the industrialist cartels financing the war, as far as I knew."

"When my youngest, Ed, was born; my dying wife made me promise to get all the boys out of the south before the war. I sold Oakside and moved to Chicago. The plantation was destroyed during the war. I just recently bought all the land back and there is a new house being constructed as we speak. That's one of our destinations for this trip, to check on it and get it going with a firm foundation."

"You are an amazing man. I bet you got top dollar when you sold it and paid peanuts buying it back. "

That's all true, but I have to replace the house, and cotton is no longer the crop for these big plantations, labor costs now you know. So, I have to figure out something else to do with it. One thing we have decided is to electrify it, which is convenient now as all the wires can be run properly during construction. Be the first one in the south. Maybe that will show us where to go with it, something modern."

The boys were talking to Fritz. Ed was really impressed with the uniform. "Is that what you wear all the time at Military School?"

"Nah, this is the dress uniform for special occasions. There are regular day uniforms that you wear for classes. There is a lot of marching around with weapons, and there is wrestling and boxing, and a lot of running to keep you fit."

"What about the school part? Is it hard? Do they make you work?" asked Chuck.

"That they do, and there is no fooling around. They are very strict about discipline. Parents send their kids there to make sure they are educated and to get them ready to go to a college. That's why my dad did. And then there is this thing about honor and self motivation."

"How did you get away from there to be here?"

"They are pretty lax for the season, in New York. There are a lot of kids there from the "best" families, so they know they have to let some of them loose occasionally, especially as the boys get older."

Marte was talking to Mel, Mag, Brent and Sally. "So, Mag and Mel, the word is out that the two of you are married, congratulations. We hope you will be happy. And that looks like a family heirloom around your neck dear."

"Dad says they were my mothers'. First time I saw them," said Mag.

"Dear, your mother was an Atlanta Turner. They made their money in shipping. I would bet those are diamonds from South Africa. There are probably a few more in the vault. Your mom was the only daughter in three generations."

Then she turned to Sally and Brent. "Word also is out that you two are married too. You make such a fine-looking couple and both so intelligent. I am sure you will do well. Is it true that the two of you were almost inseparable a few years back but that your families were feuding? That is so romantic, that you got together in the end, a Romeo and Juliette thing, without the sad ending of course. Did your families make up for the wedding?"

Brent said, "We didn't tell them until after, and even then, by letter. We did this for us, as we should have done several years ago. What our families think about it will be up to them."

"Hurrah for you two, a quite sensible reaction, although don't tell Lucas I said that. He is all into that family status and honor thing. Drives me crazy. People should just live for themselves. And these New York families are even worse than the ones back home. Ridiculous."

The gong went for the second half and the two families separated. As they went back to their seats, Lucas and Marte talked. "Both pairs confirmed it, they are married. Carl looked happy tonight, so I guess he is okay with it. But, with Travis and Sally Stevens, I doubt if there is much joy in those two homes. Both of the fathers thought they had put an end to that years ago, and now it is done. They have to make a choice now, accept it or lose their children completely. When they broke the two of them up the first time, the fathers were so gleeful, thought they had won, but both of the children just left and went out on their own, both as tutors. That took some wind out of the sails of both families, with their status and having children who worked for others," said Marte.

Lucas replied, "Served the two old fools right, letting something get to that point. If the family reputation is so important you have to make sure nothing comes up to sully it. You must act early. That my dear is why

I insisted Lana and Lisa not make this trip. They were getting far too close to Carl's youngsters. It is better that be tamped down a bit."

"For heaven sakes, they all are barely eleven, and Carl seems to have half the money in the world."

"Grant you, he has the money, but I am not sure of the pedigree. My people can't find much out."

"Well that necklace around Melisa's neck was Mag's mothers. She was an Atlanta Turner; and there is no way they would have let her marry Carl if he did not have the right background."

"I forgot that, Carl's wife. Before the war the Atlanta Turners were the royalty of the south. And Carl admitted tonight, he went to VMI for most of his school career. Before the war, only the worthiest got into VMI, even so now," said Lucas.

Marte replied, "The Turners lost a lot during the war, but they kept the most important things, their land and houses, and none of them were sacked by Sherman. The rumor is there are a few Turners in the Sherman family tree. They will be back on the top of the heap soon enough, and I bet they kept a few of those necklaces somewhere safe too, maybe Europe, maybe even New York."

"Wouldn't surprise me, old money is smart money," said Lucas.

Both families settled for the rest of the opera. Fritz had located the Montrose box and sat there quietly thinking and watching unseen. At the end of the opera, the two families just waved in passing as they located their cabs. One of the Pinkertons had gone out early and secured the three cabs they would require.

On the way back to the hotel Carl asked, "So? Would you guys like to see another opera."

Ali was an immediate and enthusiastic yes. Ed reluctantly said, "I didn't think I would like it, but I did. I forgot it was in Italian. You could tell what was going on."

Des said, "I would go to another opera, but I think I would rather go to a show in English. Are there any of those? Maybe something with music?" The other two older boys nodded their agreement."

Carl nodded to Deeds and said, "I am sure there must be, so we'll check into that. There is a part of town just coming into its own called Broadway. Apparently, there are shows there, dramas and musicals. We will see what we can arrange."

In the other cab the Montroses and the Travis' were discussing the evening. "Marte Von Stedding was her usual self, nosing around. From what she said you could tell all four of us had already been well discussed by her and her friends." said Melisa.

Sally said, "Don't let it bother you. She and her friends have nothing to do but gossip, just like all the society women here. None of them has a real life. You should pity them. At least at the end of your life you will have done something with it, and you will have kids that know you because you raised them, not like Marte who has had someone else tend her kids. They are lucky she even knows their names."

"That's true, I want to know the children and be involved in their lives, no matter where we end up and what we do. One thing I know already, it won't be here, or Chicago. There is nothing I like about either of the places," said Mel.

Mag said, "We still have a lot to see on this trip, maybe we will find a place that appeals to us."

The rest of the New York Spring was a round of dinner parties and evening dances. Carl's wealth got them all the invitations the family could want, and Carl chose the invitations carefully so as to expose the boys to the broadest range of experiences and people. For some of the dinners, he included Ed and Ali so they could learn how to behave in society. They were their usual bubbly selves and usually were a big hit at the children's table. In fact, as in Chicago, they got a whole round of invitations of their own and were soon immensely popular in the younger set. There were many of the younger girls who were as bewitched by the two as Lana, Lisa, and Samantha were in Chicago. Carl saw this and demanded reports from the Pinkertons after each excursion to make sure nothing improper had happened. Usually Brent or Sally went with them and he directed that they too keep a sharp eye out on the boys. The worst that ever happened though were a few furtive kisses. Carl was never sure though whether that was because he had raised gentlemen, or because all the children were so strictly supervised at these events. He was not the only parent who did not want even a hint of a scandal with the youngest of their children. One night, after everyone had gone to bed, Carl was looking for something in the darkened study when he saw Ed and Ali slip by and heard the front door click shut after them. Carl went to see where they were going and went out the door. There was only one Pinkerton man there and he was looking a little embarrassed.

"Where is your other man?"

"He went downstairs with the boys."

"Where to?"

"Umm, ahh, well I guess to the back entrance. That's where they usually go."

"And why are my ten-year old sons going down to the back entrance almost in the middle of the night? And why haven't I been told about this before?"

"Sir, you have to understand, in the security business our job is to keep the client safe. It is better one of us goes with them than to have them sneak away without us. That's why we can't tell on them. As long as what they are doing doesn't put them at risk. We are not their parents."

"What are they doing?"

"Sir, they like a cigarette before they go to bed."

"A cigarette? What the hell is a cigarette? And where did they learn about cigarettes?"

"I think they must have first encountered them in Chicago. I never saw any when we were out west. Cigarettes are like tiny cigars. Men and women smoke them. Women can't really smoke cigars. They are about three inches long, and about the thickness of a pencil. They buy them in the smoke shops, two cents each, no restrictions. They probably wouldn't be sold cigars, but these things are harmless."

"Thankyou, I am glad one of you goes with them and that they are not sneaking away. I also understand the difference between guarding two young boys and parenting them. But, it does raise a question. What if one of the older boys were sneaking out to visit a whore house. Would someone tell me or would one of you just go along?"

"Sir, frankly, for me it would depend on the whore house. Some of them can be very dangerous, but some are harmless. With the age of your older three, this may become a real issue soon. They are old enough to want this. So far, I have not seen anything happening at any of the events we escort you to, but there may be the same issue there too. What are we supposed to do if we see them get involved with any of the young ladies at some dance evening? Do you really expect us to rush in and stop them?

What would happen next time it happened, then they would sneak around, and the risk would be even greater for the client? You have to remember, our job is to save the client from being attacked or murdered, not to keep him from moral compromise or getting some girl pregnant. Now, if you had girls, it might be a bit different. Funny, the double standard, isn't it?"

"Well, Frank isn't it? Frank, you have given me a lot to think about, and then I think I will have to talk with your boss, and the boys." Just then the door from the stairwell opened and the three came out laughing. They all skidded to a stop when they saw Carl and the laughter died. Carl pushed open the door and pointed in. "We are going to talk, since you are awake anyway." The two security men glanced at each other, trying not to grin. They both knew this would happen at some point.

The two boys went in, somewhat embarrassed. Carl ushered them into the study and chairs opposite him. "Now boys. Show me one of these cigarettes." The boys, who thought they were going to be yelled at, quickly complied with his request. Carl reached in his vest and pulled out a match, then lit it. Without a word, he smoked the entire cigarette. Then he said, "Ed, Ali, you are eleven, twelve, years old. However, you have had the responsibility and duties of men at times. I have depended on you to the same degree as I did your older brothers. The fact you have come upon these things, tried them and liked them, is not surprising. You have been many places ten-year olds normally never go, and that is my fault. However, I really am not sure what the health risks of these things are. If you were smoking a cigar or two a day, I would be tanning your hides right now. These things seem pretty mild. The sneaking down at night with one of the Pinkertons puts them in a terrible position. They feel they have to protect you, and they can't tell me because that would just mean you would sneak away from them and they couldn't do their job. There is a lesson in this that you have to learn, you should never put the people you have control over in positions like that, where to do their job they have to be disloyal to someone else. So, that must stop. However, I gather you have been doing this a while and that you are used to them. I know I would be upset if you took away my one a day cigar. Therefore, I will agree to three cigarettes a day, but you will have them up here on the terrace or in the smoking room in the suite with Deeds and I. You will not take your smoking habit to the ice cream socials or whatever, where there are innocent children. And you will not embarrass me by smoking or talking about smoking with any of the other parents. Now, do you understand and agree to all of this?"

The boys looked at each other, smiled and nodded. "Yes sir," they said together. Carl ushered them out of the room expecting them to head back to their room, but they headed for the terrace. "Now, where are you going?"

"You said three, we were limiting ourselves to two, so we thought we would go have the third before bed," said Ed. They continued out to the terrace. Carl stood there a second then said, "What the hell." He went outside and joined them, "Give me one too, I'll pay you back tomorrow." They sat there and talked well past the time it took to smoke their cigarettes.

The next morning Carl went down to the smoke shop in the lobby and bought four packs of the cigarettes. When he went upstairs, he tossed a pack to each of the boys. "Paid back. Now remember our deal, no more than three a day, and only on the terrace or in the smoking room."

"Yeah Dad, we get it, and we know you don't want the news to get out of the household," said Ali. Carl didn't mention it to anyone so the first time they came in the smoking room, Mag and Deeds were there with Carl. Ed and Ali sat on one of the couches and helped each other light their cigarettes. They sat back and exhaled a cloud of smoke as Ali said, "Wonderful day isn't it," to two of the shocked adults sitting there. Deeds and Mag both looked at Carl. Mag said, "Jesus Christ Dad, what are you letting them do now?"

"Look guys, have you ever heard of the lesser of two evils? They were doing it anyway, and they were sneaking around and involving the Pinkertons. Now they are limited to three a day, and only in the smoking room or on the terrace." He pulled out a pack of cigarettes and offered one to Mag and Deeds. "Try one, they are amazing, and I think the boys have found for us the crop that will replace cotton on Oakside. It can be harvested mechanically. There is a drying process that we can speed up with electric fans, since the plantation will be electrified. And, I am researching the process of making these. If we can develop a machine, maybe we can have our own factory on the plantation, do the whole process in house, even the shipping. By the way, I have ordered a spur be put in to Oakside, wouldn't have done it except for the fact we can use the spur to ship the cigarettes and the tobacco. Freshest tobacco will get the best prices. And as a by product, it will make it easier to deal with the rail car.""

The first time the three older boys walked into the smoking room and found Ed and Ali sitting there smoking a cigarette with Deeds and Carl, they were shocked and rather upset. "Hey, what's this? Is smoking allowed now for us kids?"

"I would be a hypocrite if I said no. Same rules though. No more than three a day, only on the terrace or in here. Never out of the house and never with the other kids or in front of other adults. Here, you want a cigarette."

The three boys each said no. Carl went on, "This whole thing with them and the Pinkertons, who they were putting in an impossible position brought up a whole other situation which mainly pertains to you three at this point. The Pinkerton man said to me, their main job is to protect you, not be your father." The three were looking confused. "He asked me what I thought they should do if one of you snuck out to a whore house. Would it be their duty to protect you, or tell me, or both? That got me thinking. Their first duty is to protect the client, but if the client knew that protection would cause them trouble, then they would try to do it on the sly and thus increase their risk. It puts the Pinkertons in an impossible position. The main reason I agreed to this agreement with Ed and Ali was that they were putting the Pinkertons in an impossible position sneaking out at night for a smoke and we had to stop that. I told these two that they must not put people who work for us in such a situation. I am telling you the same. It is not right. They have a job to do and you must not make that job more difficult. You are all sixteen, so I do not think it unreasonable to expect you not to get into situations with girls that compromise them and you."

"At sixteen, Mag let himself get caught in a compromising position and we saw what happened to him. If Louise had wanted to get married, I would have agreed. You should remember that, lest you find yourselves with a wife and child. Very soon, if it has not happened already, girls will be throwing themselves at you, for you, since you are all handsome young fellas, but also for the sake of the family money. Let me be crystal clear. If you let yourself be caught by a fortune hunting wife, she will not get at it. One way or another, your share of the family fortune will be denied her and pass to any children the two of you may have. Sure, you will have a place to live and food on the table, even something to do with one of the family businesses. The real wealth however will be denied you and her. You will be limited to what you can earn and that will not be enough for a woman like that. You will have no end of grief. Solution, avoid getting caught and instead look for your real match, a relationship based on true love and a desire to work together for something, like with Mag and Mel, or Sally and Brent."

"So, in short Dad, what you are saying is, get to know some of the girls, to a degree, but above all keep it zipped up or be ready to live with the consequences," said Des.

"Jesus Dad, don't you think we already know that?" asked Chuck.

Diz added, "Yeah Dad, we want the same thing you do, the right person to spend the rest of out lives with; and we do recognize the risks. We may be sixteen but all of us have had lives that demanded more of us than the usual sixteen-year old. I think we have all learned a little. Our bodies may be young, but our spirits are older, much older."

"I know all that, it's those sixteen year old bodies I am worried about and what they can get up to. One last thing. If it ever develops that you are serious about a woman to the point where you are considering having intercourse, then I want you to come to me and we will talk. I will not lecture or harangue. There are items available now to stop the conception of a baby that the man can use. They are not talked about in polite society and you three have likely never heard of them. But, if such interaction is about to happen I will explain them to you rather than see you in the situation Mag was. They also are good at stopping certain diseases I really don't want to talk about. But, enough for now."

Carl's concerns were timely. In New York that summer the girls did discover the three Montrose boys and they all were very popular. Not a day passed without an invitation for one or all of them. Carl was concerned. He remembered what it was like to be sixteen, even in the conservative South, and he knew what temptations the boys were facing. Girls were much more forward in current times. All he could hope was that the way the boys had been brought up would protect them, but he really did not have much trust in that.

Surprisingly enough, the first to visit him was Dizzy. He came into the study, red faced, and closed the door behind him. He sat across from Carl then said, "Dad, remember a while back you said if we were ever in a position where we were close to doing it with a girl, we should talk. Dad, I am there. There is a girl I have been seeing, and it is really serious but, so far, we have been able to hold back, but Dad, that has been so hard. We just start with a kiss, that's all, and then the kisses are longer and there is a little bit of touching, then more. Last night it almost happened. At the last moment, I held back. Some day though, I know I won't be able to. Dad, we like each other, but I really don't think either of us wants to get married, at least not yet. What is it about this age, the girls are like magnets and you just can't help wanting to be with them, and when you are, things happen? It's embarrassing Dad, what happens. But I really don't want to be a father at sixteen."

"First of all, if it were to happen it takes nine months between when you do it and you have a baby, so you would be seventeen. However, I do not think you want to be a father at seventeen either. Now I do understand what you are going through, I am not that old, and I have to admit when I grew up girls were much more modest than they are now. Thing is even then, there was enough temptation, and in all truth I did succumb. Lucky though, we were not caught, but we could have been, and when I was your age there was no choice, I would have been married, and that is pretty much true today in our social circle, so I am glad you have come to talk to me. Today there are things you can use to avert disaster. Don't get me wrong, I am not saying go out there and use them…, I would prefer you didn't. But, accepting the fact it might be going to happen, then you should use these, for your sake and that of the girl." Carl reached in his desk drawer, brought a condom out in its little package, and handed it to Diz. "Open it, carefully. You have to make sure you don't tear it. Once it becomes clear it is going to happen, then you should put this on. If you wait too long things may get beyond control, and you might get carried away."

"How do I use this?" said Diz with one unwrapped condom in his hand.

"When you get involved, you start to get hard and bigger. It is meant to go on when your penis is larger than normal. Once it is on, you will still get larger and it will get tighter, so it doesn't fall off during intercourse. Now if you look at it closely you will see it is rolled. You put it on top and roll it down as far as you can. They are fairly light and will not really affect what you feel, or the lady. It will still be as pleasurable. When you are done and get soft, you can pull it off. If you decide to do it again, get a new one."

"What? Again?"

"Oh Dizzy, you never thought of that did you? Sometimes, soon after you do it, it does happen, you do it again. So, make sure you always have two or three of these with you if you are seeing the lady in question. But again son, these are not permission slips, just an acceptance of fact. Now I would suggest you take that one you have opened and go to the washroom. Try it, see how it works, then flush it. You cannot use it again."

"Where do I get these?"

"You can buy them at the druggists, but I know what will happen, you will get inside the door and chicken out. It should be true that if you are old enough to use them you should be old enough to buy them, but as I said, we are dealing in truths here. So, there are a couple boxes here in the desk, take them as you need them for now. At some point I will just tell you guys enough, and you will have to buy them. For now, we will do this. And Diz, it is not your role to tell your brothers about this. Part of this is facing the truth, and part of that is for them to come and see me."

"Thanks dad, I really appreciate this, and as for the brothers, if I had to bite the bullet and do this then why should I make it easier for them?" A few minutes after Dizzy left, Mag came in and sat opposite his father. "Now Dad, why didn't I get the talk like that?"

"Mag, when you were young, I was deluding myself. I never thought my fourteen-year old son would be sexually active. I thought I still had years, but you proved me wrong. Before Louise, there were many times I suspect when you could have been caught up. You were just lucky. I realize now we can't count on that."

"I could have used the talk Dad, I have never used one of those. At some point I will have to if we don't want fifty kids I guess."

Carl laughed and said, "But you are an old married man and can get your own at the drugstore. Honestly though, when you are a kid like them, do you have time to use one or are you just carried away by the moment? Am I deluding myself?"

"Honestly, I hope they do, but looking at my experience, it all just happened, never intended it to, things just happen. I imagine it is the same for them."

A few weeks later the next to visit Carl was Chuck. "Dad, can we talk? I have met someone, Abbie Somers, she is the youngest of the Somers girls. We have managed to keep things under control so far, but it is getting increasingly harder every day. I don't know what to do about this."

"If this is truly the girl for you, the one you love, then you have to protect her. I am not sure if at sixteen you know what true love is, but if I grant you that you do, or think you do, then are you sure she feels the same way? This is a huge commitment, for the rest of your lives. You owe it to each other to be absolutely sure. Let me make a suggestion. Is this girl going to be in the Hamptons?"

Chuck shook his head no.

"Then, here is what I would suggest. We are going to leave New York shortly. Go the summer, who knows, you might meet someone else, but at the end of the summer if you still feel the same way, and she does too, after a summer of writing to each other, then I will bring you up to New York and arrange a meeting with the girl and her parents and I. The two of you can try to convince us that you two belong together. If I am convinced, I will support you and the two of you can get married. She can come with us to Virginia, Oakside. I have an idea for Oakside that may interest you, and her. But, the two of you have to control yourselves and take the summer to really think this through. And, until the fall when you are married, if that happens, the two of you have to not let things go any further than they have. You do not need the added complication of a baby on the way to complicate things if in the end you decide the two of you are really not meant for each other."

"You mean you would agree to us being married?"

"At fifteen, you two can get married in New York with parental permission, but you both need that permission. If it is right and what everyone wants, I would agree."

A few days later, he had his visit from Des. "Dad, we have to talk," he said as he came in, closed the door, and sat. "There is this girl I have been seeing most of the summer. Her name is Shaney Lacey. We have been, uh, intimate, several times."

"You mean you have had sex several times. And, you have not come to see me, so I assume that means you did it without protection. Why were you so reckless?"

"Shaney is a bit older than me, she's seventeen. She said she had it covered, she had a diaphragm, so she said it was safe to do it."

"You twit, you believed that. A man never believes a girl when she says that and he never turns control of his destiny over to anyone else, ever. Had? Was? What has changed?"

"Shaney says something must have happened and she is pregnant."

"Now that is interesting, we have only been here a little less than seven weeks. How long ago did you first have sex with each other?"

"First time? About a month ago."

"Most important question, do you love her, and she you?"

"Love? Like forever? No, I have never felt like that and she has never said anything like that to me."

"Then Des, what the hell has been going on for the last month?"

"Dad, we were just having fun. She was there and available, as were a lot of girls. She said it was safe, and we both enjoyed it. I had the feeling she had done it before because she sort of taught me. Anyway, we did it and she is going to have a baby. I guess I am going to be a father."

"And what do the two of you want to do about this?"

"She expects to get married, quickly, so we can hide the fact she is going to have a baby."

"And you?"

"I don't really want to get married, I don't want to be a father yet, I was just having… uh fun. But, I have to admit I must be the father so I guess I should get married," said Des sadly.

"The only thing I admire in all this is the fact you are willing to accept responsibility. The rest of it all is disgusting. Sex should not be just for fun, and the fact that you turned responsibility for your future over to someone else, because she said it was covered, is absolutely unforgiveable. You should have known better. Now I will send a message, to arrange a meeting here tonight, you, me, her, and her parents. And I tell you right now, you will keep your mouth shut. Now go back to your room and do not mention anything to anyone, even your brothers."

Deeds came in a few minutes later just as Carl was finishing his note to the Laceys. Carl gave it to him to read, then said, "Des has been having a relationship with their daughter, Shaney. She is seventeen. He did not use any protection because she said they were safe, she had a diaphragm. Now, after a month, she says she is pregnant and wants to get married, quickly."

"I think we need to set our Pinkertons loose, at once. And I think we need a doctor here tonight for the meeting."

"I agree, the little fool has stepped in it I think."

That evening the Laceys, and their daughter Shaney, arrived at 7:30. They were shown into the lounge where Carl and Des sat, along with Deeds and a gentleman introduced as Doctor Smythe. Carl began the conversation, after the usual pleasantries. He addressed the parents. "Your daughter feels she is pregnant by my son Des. That is the first thing that must be determined, which is why I have asked Dr Smythe to be present.

He is the best Obstetrician in the city. Ma'am, if you and your daughter would accompany the doctor into my study, he will quickly determine that fact and we can complete the arrangements."

The three left shortly and came back quickly. The two women seemed rather smug. Doctor Smythe handed a note to Carl and then excused himself. Carl continued. "The only admirable thing in this whole sorry event is the fact that Des is willing to accept responsibility for any child he has fathered. And I am willing to provide for any grandchildren I might have through my sons. There even is a ranch at home, the Connor Ranch, that could be turned over to the two, and their new family, in Arizona."

Lacey leaned forward, "I don't want to go to Arizona, it's all desert. A place like this here would be fine." Her mother nodded in agreement.

"Then it is fortunate that Dr Smythe feels you are two months pregnant and will deliver in a further seven. Two month's ago we were in Chicago. Des therefore could not be the father. Perhaps, Mr. and Mrs. Lacey, you should turn your attentions to one Timothy Saxon, a resident of the hotel across the street. I have a report from my detectives that he and Lacey were seeing each other daily at his residences for several hours at a time, and that those rendezvous have continued until this very day. That may be why Shaney would like to live here, in the LePrad, since it would make it easier to slip away from her husband and child to meet the father of that child." Carl glanced over at Des, who was looking rather grim and a bit nauseous.

"Now Mr. Saxon is not as well off as Des here, which is likely why Des was selected to play the role of father, so I would suggest you turn your attentions to Timothy and our business is settled; unless perhaps you would like me to have my detectives continue their investigations and perhaps uncover some other areas of , perhaps collusion, between Shaney and Timothy, and perhaps even her parents too, or even fraud. Mr. Deeds here will show you out." The three left quietly, aware the jig was up.

Carl looked across at Des, who looked both shocked and relieved.

"Remember, a long time ago I told you three our wealth would be a magnet for that sort? Now you have the proof. There is a lesson there you better have learned. And you, young man, will come with me into the study where we are going to have a discussion about how a man, not a reckless boy, should act so that he can retain control over his own fate. You squeaked by this one, but you will never put yourself, or me, in this position again."

The Montroses left New York in the private car three days later. They were bound for the Hamptons, and a "cottage" that Carl had purchased there, hoping the family would be able to use it for several summers. On the way out of town there were a few moments he could talk to his sons. "Now, you youngest two. You have grown about six inches, at least that was what the tailor said when we had him up before we left. You discovered girls, only a bit I really do hope. Ed has shown his leadership skills, surprisingly enough. Ali has discovered a wonderful talent he has. Ali, I trust Mr. Travers has shown you around to see some options that you are thinking about and that we will talk about soon. You older three have learned some lessons, and I expect will learn more this summer. Self-control, self-discipline, and the absolute need to maintain control of your own destinies, and to never cede that control to someone else. You have to realize that above all you have to be true to yourself and your core beliefs. You all are now coming out of New York having survived the social dragons, with the manners that are demanded of you in polite society. You all have accomplished quite a bit this year, but there have been a few hiccups. Now, the Hamptons will not be as formal. There will be new accepted behaviours, new norms, but they can be as dangerous. You have to keep a hold on those core values if you are going to make it through these waters. There are sharks here too and they are not all in the water."

Chapter 11

The Hamptons

The train pulled into the station and was shunted as usual onto a private siding. This time however, the car was parked on a siding full of other private cars. Well over a dozen of them. "Looks like we will have company here this summer," said Carl dryly.

Arrangements had been made to have the train met with several carriages and wagons. The detectives supervised the moving of the luggage from the train cars. As with any of the other arrivals that summer, they made quite a procession to the "Cottage".

As they drove up the drive, a long circular one with an enormous front lawn, Des said to his Dad. "Dad, you said you had bought a cottage. This place is three times as big as our new hotel in Tucson."

Carl said, "I have to admit, their definition of a cottage here is a bit strange. I bought this one from one of the Astors. But, you have to remember, this has to accommodate all the house staff and the Pinkertons. And also, there is a ballroom here, so we cam repay a lot of those invitations we received in New York, and maybe Chicago. The Von Steddings are here too, for the summer. In fact, I had a note, Fritz is going to stop by this afternoon, about getting you three older ones into sailing down at the yacht club. He has a boat."

"God, I wish Fritz would stay away from us, he gives me the creeps," said Des.

To that, Carl said, "You know boys, when you get a feeling like that, when the hairs on the back of your neck stand up, that is something to pay attention to. If you really feel danger, don't let the social implications cause you to do something that you would rather not do."

When they went in the door, they were met by Mrs. Langley. "Welcome to SeaView, Mr. Montrose. The room at the stop of the stairs is the master's, I will have the girls take your luggage up. The rest can choose their own rooms I suspect. There are twenty-one rooms on the second floor for the family. The household staff is on the fourth floor and your staff can choose rooms on the third. Is that acceptable?" Carl nodded at the head of the security patrol and he took most of his men up to the third floor. Two remained at the front door and would be spelled shortly to stow their gear. Carl said to the boys. "There are lots of rooms to choose from and you can set yourselves up any way you want, shares or singles, up to you. We will have lunch at one out on the back terrace and discuss what we are going to do for the summer. Is that okay, Mrs. Langley?"

Ed and Ali chose to share a room and found a nice one with a view of the ocean, as did Mag and Mel, and Brent and Sally. Deeds took one that overlooked the front drive. He liked to see who was coming and going. Des, Diz, and Chuck, for the first times ever, chose to take separate rooms. Somehow, they felt they had grown up a little in the past while."

When everyone showed up for lunch, they were all entranced by the view of the Atlantic Ocean. There was a wide back lawn, then an area of tall beach grasses and then a wide sandy beach with waves rolling in. Carl made comment, "Perfect place to shoot skeet. I think I will get a skeet machine and we can let all you guys get your guns out. Just make sure you shoot out over the sea, not towards the house."

"Great idea Dad," said Ed. "I can't wait to get my guns out again. Haven't had a chance to since the rodeo."

Ali agreed, then he said, "Ed, as soon as lunch is over, let's get our new bathing suits on and go down to the beach there."

The two young couples decided they would go for a walk together on the beach and were discussing what they could wear that would let them experience the beach and still be proper. They decided the men could wear pants, rolled up a bit, and loose shirts. After all they were married. The women had a bit more of a problem. Fashion dictated long flowing skirts and tight shirtwaists buttoned to the neck. Sally said, "I don't care, I am going to get rid of all the slips and tuck my skirt into my belt, and the bottom of the shirt will not be tucked in nor will all the buttons be done to the neck. I am with my husband on our own beach and I want some enjoyment from that. I want to walk on the beach and in the sand. Some day soon I will also want to try on those scandalous new bathing outfits we got in New York. I want to enjoy this summer. God knows I will be shut away soon enough." Then she realized she had said too much and shut up.

Mel had caught it though. She leaned over and whispered to Sally, "Are you pregnant too, I thought it was only me?"

"You too? Have you told anybody else yet?"

"No, its supposed to be unlucky if you say anything before the third month so I haven't even told Mag yet. Looks like those honeymoon suites in New York did the trick for both of us," said Mel.

Brent and Mag saw the two women whispering, and Brent said, "Wonder what they are talking about?"

"Probably when they are going to tell us that they are pregnant."

A shocked Brent gasped, "You think they are both pregnant, at the same time?"

Mag said, "I don't know what you did in that suite in New York, but I know what we did, and that is how women become pregnant. They have some stupid idea about luck, and they have to wait till a certain time. You know, you can't have sex four or five times a day for a week without expecting it to happen."

Brent was blushing, "Four or five, you too, I thought we were just being indecent."

Mag laughed, "No, I think we were perfectly normal, it's just this stupid society we live in here, in the east. God, I hope it's better in the south when we get there in the fall."

The two men went over and sat with their wives. Brent said, "So, are you two gonna tell us?"

"Tell you what?" asked Sally.

"That the two of you are pregnant, both about two months," said Mag.

"Shh, it's not lucky to talk about it too soon," cautioned Sally.

"Mel, there is no luck involved. All of us were doing the exact same thing at the exact same time and almost in the same place. This is just what happens and both us guys are delighted."

Carl was watching this conversation from across the terrace and when he saw the two couples hug each other, he said to himself. "Knew it, you can't put two healthy young couples alone in a hotel suite without that being the result. Perfect."

The three older boys had taken a walk down to the beach and returned, seeking him out. Des said, "There is a dock down there with a nice sailboat. Is it ours?"

"Yep, but I don't want the three of you trying to take it out until someone teaches you how to use it. Actually, that is why Fritz is coming over. Apparently, he is quite involved with the classes at the local yacht club. We will see if he can set you three up with lessons." Shortly after, Fritz Von Stedding arrived in a small buckboard. The Montroses had rented one too, as well as several saddle horses and a couple carriages. There was a small stable on the property with its own staff.

When Fritz heard about the sailboat and the need for lessons, he was almost eager to help. He had the boys take him down to the dock and inspected the boat, in the end saying it was "yar". "That means it a good boat and will be perfect for the three of you. Big enough, once you can sail, you can take your Dad or your little brothers out with you."

When they went back up to the back terrace and sat with Carl, Fritz said, "Look, our house is way out on the other side of the bay so my Dad keeps a couple of rooms at the yacht club for me and my crew. They won't be down for a couple of days so one is standing there empty. If you three want to come down there, we can take my boat out in the morning, about seven, when there is a light but strong breeze; and I can show you all what to do, how to sail it. We can spend the day. It's not hard and I am sure you will know what to do by the end of the day."

The boys looked at Carl. "It's okay by me. I'll give you some money to handle the meals and you can go, as long as you are back by five. Thing is though, you will have to take a couple of the Pinkertons with you. Don't worry about them, they will likely just sit in the lobby, but they can give you three a ride back. They can take our buckboard. Go pack what you need and tell Woody and Frank they are going with you."

After they left to gather their stuff and gear, Carl said to Fritz, "This is nice of you, to give up your day for them, but won't your parents mind, you not being home all day?"

"No, they won't mind. I think they are happier when I am out of their hair anyway. This is the second year Dad has had the rooms down at the yacht club for me." The boys returned with a small bag each and Carl gave each of them a hundred dollars in twenties to get them through the day for meals. "This is much more than you need but you can keep the extra for the summer. We haven't worked out an allowance for you, but this looks like an expensive place. We will talk about it tomorrow night, after you get back." He showed them out the front door and they crammed themselves into Fritz' buckboard, then headed down the drive followed by the two detectives.

When they arrived at the club it was pretty deserted. "Pretty early in the season yet," explained Fritz. He showed them upstairs to the rooms. "Mine is the one at the end of the hall, you three can use this one, there are two beds in it." After they stowed their stuff, they went out to the docks. Fritz showed them his boat, and they spent some time learning the lines for when they went out the next morning. When it started to cool off, Fritz suggested they go back to the clubhouse and get some dinner.

After a few bowls of New England chowder, the four boys went into the lounge where there was a fire and they sat around it just talking. Fritz asked them if they wanted a beer, and the surprised boys said "Yes, but how, they were too young."

Fritz said, "Let me see to it. There is no one here to complain and they usually give me what I want." Fritz came back with a tray of beers and set them on the table beside them. "There are two here for each of us." He took two and set them on the table beside Des. "These are yours." Then he took two more and sat beside Des, saying, "Those four are for you two." The four young men sat around the fire talking about the usual thing teenage boys talked about, women, or more precisely, girls.

Des said, "I heard Mel and Sally whispering. They are both two months pregnant, they are waiting to get to the third month before they tell Dad."

Fritz said, "They were both married when you got to New York."

Diz said, "They were both married within an hour of each other and had honeymoons the same week in New York."

"Wouldn't it be something if they each had a baby within an hour of each other?" said Chuck.

Fritz and Des laughed and Fritz said, "I don't think the nine-month thing is that exact. They might be weeks apart, assuming it happened the first time they did it."

Des noticed that Chuck looked a bit reflective and kinda quiet. "What's up Chuck, you seem kinda quiet over there."

"Just thinking about something. Mag was sixteen when he had the twins, wasn't he? And he has been a good father?"

"Yes, on both counts, but why are you thinking of that. You aren't about to become a father, are you?"

"No, I ain't. We never done it. But still, I can't forget about her, my mind just keeps going back there. She is a person I can see having a family with and if Mag can be a father at sixteen and be happy, why can't I?"

"If it's the right person, I don't think age matters. You just have to be sure it's the right person," said Dizzy.

The four boys finished their beers, chatting about other items. When they were done and started to rise to go up to the rooms, Des found the room was reeling about his head and had to sit down. "Jeez guys, I don't think I can walk out of here on my own, the room is spinning."

"Why Des, we all only had two beers and the rest of us are okay."

"Guys, you have to remember, all of us react differently to alcohol. Maybe Des here is a one beer man. Now, one of you help me on the other side and we will get him upstairs," said Fritz. By this point Des seemed almost half asleep. When they got to the top of the stairs Fritz said, "Put him in my room tonight. My room has its own bathroom in case he has to barf. You have to go all the way down the hall from the other room."

"Sure, if you want to deal with our puking brother have at it," said Diz. They got Des in Fritz' room and on one of the beds. By that point he was asleep. They removed his shoes and socks and Fritz drew a cover over him and said, "He can sleep like that. It's okay you two, you can go to bed; but remember, we have to be up at seven if we want to catch the winds." He ushered them to the door and out, then he closed the door and snapped the lock behind them. He turned and looked at Des muttering, "Finally, got you to myself. The condition you are in I can do whatever I want with you, and you will likely not even remember." He went over to the bed and drew the cover back, then he knelt and unbuttoned Des' shirt. He struggled a bit, but he got Des' arms out, and he pulled the shirt from beneath him, throwing it to the floor. Fritz then undid the belt, loosened the button and drew the pants down and off. Then he drew the under-alls down. At this point Des roused a bit, "What yer, what doin?"

"Take it easy old man, just getting you ready for bed. You had a bit too much to drink. Just go to sleep." Fritz released the shorts at that point and looked down at the totally naked Des. He was satisfied with what he saw, a beautiful young man, lean and muscular. He could hardly wait. It was worth the extra twenty he gave the man at the bar for whatever it was he put in the two beers.

Des roused a little and muttered, "Ccc Cold." Fritz drew the cover over him again. Then Fritz removed his own clothes and crawled naked into the bed beside Des.

In the hall Frank and Woody were talking. "I wonder what happened to Des. He only had two beers like the rest of them and they are okay," said Woody.

Frank said, "You know, people react differently to beer, but still, I wondered if I saw the barman drop something into two of those beers, it was so quick I wasn't sure."

"Funny you mention that, I wondered too, but why would someone do that? I thought they were all friends."

In the room, Fritz had rolled over on top of Des and was running his hands all over Des' body. Then he started kissing Des' neck while he rubbed himself against him. Fritz was fully aroused and he could feel Des responding to him. "Oh, this is gonna be good," thought Fritz.

Just then Des roused a little, becoming aware of someone on top of him, kissing him, and that it was Fritz. He could feel him hard against him.

"NO. Stop. Stop it! GET OFF MEE!" Des struggled to free himself and Fritz tried to pin his arms to the bed.

In the hall, Frank and Woody heard the call. "That's Des, there is something wrong here. Come on." The two ran to the door and tried it, then they put their shoulders to the door, and it splintered as they burst in. They saw the two struggling on the bed. Their efforts had dislodged the cover, and both were clearly naked. Fritz was pinning Des to the bed as he struggled to subdue him. Frank strode to the bed and gave Fritz a backhand slap to his face that flung him from the bed into the corner. Des looked up at him, wide eyed and shocked. "He was, he was, he was trying to…" Then his head fell to one side and he was unconscious again.

Frank said, "Come on kid, it's time you went home." He leaned down and took the cover from the floor, then wrapped Des in it and lifted his unconscious body from the bed. Woody stood over Fritz and said, "You are lucky we don't beat you to a pulp you bastard." He turned, grabbed Des' clothes from the floor, and followed Frank to the door.

Diz and Chuck were standing there, drawn by the noise, and Frank said, "Get your stuff, you all are going home, NOW." The boys raced into their room and gathered their stuff, cramming it into the bags and within a few moments were back in the hall. They all went down the stairs and out the back door where the buckboard was. Frank sat in it, holding Des, while Woody and the boys hooked the horse into the traces again, then they made a rapid trip back to Sea View. Frank carried Des up to his room and put him into his bed. Woody went off in search of Carl and returned a few minutes later. Carl strode to the bed, drew the covers back to look at his sleeping naked son; then gently put the covers back on him. He turned to the other four and demanded, "The full story, now."

Diz explained, "We had a good day, went to the boat, learned the lines, went back to the club, had supper, then went in and sat by the fire. Fritz asked if we wanted a beer, then he went out and came back with a tray. There were two for each of us."

Chuck continued, "He took two and gave the   m to Des, took two for himself, and left the other four for us. When we were done and it was time to go up, we were all fine, but Des was a little dizzy, so I helped Fritz get him upstairs. When we got up, Fritz said to put him in his room as there was a bathroom in the room in case he had to puke. We put him in one of the beds, took his shoes and socks off and covered him. He was asleep. Later we heard a crash in the hall and came out. Woody and Frank were in Fritz' room and the door was crashed to pieces. Frank came out carrying Des, Fritz was huddled in the corner naked, and had a bleeding nose."

Frank took over, "We were sitting in the hall outside the rooms. We were talking and both of us were surprised Des seemed drunk. He only had two beers, and all the others had the same and were okay. It was when we were talking, we both said we wondered if the barman had put something in the drinks, two of them. Then we heard Des yell, "STOP, NO, GET OFF," and we broke into the room. We found both of the boys, naked on one of the beds, Des was struggling to push the other one off, but Fritz was pinning him down. I went over and threw Fritz off. Des passed out again. I wrapped him and got the others, and we came home. Des seems to be sleeping, breathing okay. I checked several times. Must be some kind of sedative."

Carl said, "Frank, Woody, thankyou. You did a good job tonight. It is a hard job guarding teenagers, giving them the space that they need while still protecting them. We all know what would have happened had you not been there. That is all for tonight. There may be more we have to attend to tomorrow, but you two can go to bed, again with my gratitude."

He then turned to Diz and Chuck. "Dad, we are sorry, we had no idea, or we wouldn't have left Des there with him," said Diz.

"Boys, again, you did nothing wrong. There was no way you could have known, I saw Fritz almost as much as you did and I had no idea, so how could I expect you to know any more than I did? You guys are learning some hard lessons this year, most of them the hard way. Des is okay, nothing happened to him that he can't sleep off. Now you two go to bed and we will talk more tomorrow."

The two boys left, and Carl sat beside Des' bed, just watching him breathe. After a few hours Des awoke and found his father sitting there. "Dad? I am at home, why am I at home?" Then he reached under the covers. "Dad, why am I naked under here?"

Carl said gently, "What do you remember of the evening?"

"We had dinner, went in by the fire, Fritz got us some beers, only two, but when I tried to stand up, I was dizzy. After that it is very fuzzy. I remember me being put to bed. Then I woke up, Fritz was kissing me, and touching me, and he was pushing himself against me. Dad, he was hard. I started fighting him and yelling when I realized, then it got all fuzzy again. I remember a crash, then Frank was there, then I was here. Dad, why was Fritz like that? If I was a girl, I would say he was trying to rape me, but we are guys."

"Des, I guess part of this was my fault. You boys have had sheltered lives. There are some men who like to have sex with men. I guess Fritz is one of them. He must have worked something out with the bar keep to put something in your drink, to make you sleep, so he could have you. You struggled enough and made enough noise that Frank and Woody heard you. They came in, threw Fritz off, and brought you home."

Des considered this for a few minutes, then said quietly, "Dad, you know about Lacey and me, that I know how two people have sex. I am not like Lacey, how did he expect to have sex with me?"

"If you think about it, there is only one way isn't there?"

Des thought for a few more moments then said, "Dad, that really is nasty, I am really glad Frank was there."

"I am too son. Now get some sleep. We will work something else out for the sailing lessons, and I think I will have a talk with Lucas, and with the barman."

The next morning, before the boys were up, Carl hunted up Frank and said, "Frank, take one of the rigs and go down to the harbor. We need someone to teach the boys how to sail that boat. We want someone who knows his stuff and who the boys can relate to. Find out what the going rate is and offer three times that, plus room and board for the summer. There is still space on your floor."

Frank returned with a sturdy young fellow, about fifteen years old, slightly built and of thin frame, but who seemed solid as a rock. He was from Maine, and named Marcus Wellstone.

Carl said, "Marcus, we need someone to teach sailing to three boys a little older than you. Can you do that?"

"When Frank there asked me if I could sail, I asked him, sail what? I told him I could sail schooners and ketches, even up to three masters. So, I guess I could teach your boys."

"What's your history Marcus?"

"My mother died when I was young, but I had a Dad and four brothers. We had our own boat. There was a storm and the boat sank, I was the only survivor. I was eleven. The town looked after me then, made sure I had berths for every fishing season, and a place to winter. This year, I decided I wanted to see a bit of the world. I was just sitting at the harbor looking at the boats when your man Frank came up and offered me so much money for a couple month's work, I thought he was crazy."

"No Marcus, he's not crazy. I think you will be perfect for the job, so we will offer you a berth for at least the summer, maybe longer, and you can stow your gear and start today, whenever my worthless sons drag themselves out of bed. Frank will show you your room. Then he can take you down to the kitchens where they will find you something to eat. I will come and find you when the boys are ready."

About an hour later, the boys wandered in, yawning and stretching. They sat at the table with their toast and coffee, and some with juice. "Are you three older ones awake yet? I found you a new sailing instructor, name's Marcus Wellstone. Been sailing for ten years, knows his stuff, was shipwrecked and survived, but lost his family in the wreck. He was twelve. Strikes me as an independent young man."

The boys were looking at each other. That was more nice things than they had ever heard their father say about anyone, including them. This must be one hell of a sailor. Carl had left the room in search of the inimitable Marcus. A few moments later he came in accompanied by a sturdy young man about their own age. But, when they looked closely, there was a toughness to his manner and there was the experience of life glowing in his eyes.

Carl invited Marcus and his three sons down to the dock to inspect their boat. As they walked along the dock, Marcus pointed out. "You see this dock is about 300 feet long and way down there at the end there is the little boat-docking slip. You ever wonder why? I bet you bought this house from someone big."

Carl said, "The house was built by the Astors."

"That explains it then. The Astors had yachts, steam yachts, and this dock was built to accommodate them. You could easily tie a two-hundred-foot yacht up on the left side of this dock. That was what it was built for."

They arrived at the end of the dock and looked down at the sailboat. Marcus began to laugh. "This isn't a ship, even a boat. This is a dinghy with a sail on it. I can teach you to sail it, but you can't go very far, not even out of the sight of land. There isn't even a compass."

Carl was a little miffed at Marcus assessing the sailboat as a dinghy, but he said, "It is a starting place, besides, I am not sure I want them sailing in a boat that goes out of the sight of land." Carl left the boys to it and headed back up the dock. He was thinking to himself, "I was wondering why the dock was so bloody long, now I understand. I also think we need a bigger boat."

When he got to the house, he hollered up Deeds, Frank, and Woody. "Get us two buckboards, you two will need one and we will need the other. Deeds, get my check book. We are all going to town, to see a bar man, the Von Steddings, and a yacht broker." Ten minutes later they were off, and the first stop was the yacht club. The four men went in and Frank pointed out the barman in question. Carl went up to him, "I am the father of the boy you slipped the mickey to last night. I want you to listen very closely. My lawyer here, Mr. Deeds, will help you write up a complete description of the events of last night, and you will sign it. Don't bother denying anything. Then, you will have one hour to leave town. My two friends behind me will give you a hand, and a ride to the station. If you would rather stay in town, you may, but every day after today they will come down here and beat you to a pulp, and there will be no help for you at the local constabulary after I lay charges over what has occurred. I doubt if that was the first time so I will set a squad of detectives to find other victims. You will be lucky to get less than twenty years. At some point, I just may get tired of it all and shoot you myself. You won't be the first man I killed. I really am leaning that way as it is." The barman quickly began writing. When he was done, Deeds witnessed the confession and Frank and Woody ushered him out the door. Carl told them when they were done, they could find him and Deeds in the harbor.

Then, he and Deeds drove over to the harbor and stood looking out at the boats anchored there. There were several that looked like what Carl was thinking of. He turned and spied what he was looking for, a Ship's Broker. He led Deeds over to the office. The broker was named Lucius Drafters. Carl said, "I want to buy a ship, a yacht, say fourteen to twenty passengers plus crew. Sail and steam. What do you have out there that meets my requirements?"

Mr. Drafters looked up. "A boat like that needs a dock, do you have one?"

"Yep." said Carl.

"It would need a crew of at least four, including someone who could captain it."

"Got all that," said Carl.

There are two that might meet your needs here at the moment. One belonged to the Astors, called Sea View Too. And…"

"No, Sea View Too, that's the one. Show her to me."

They went out and down the dock. The Sea View Too was moored second ship, out board, beside a bigger yacht so Deeds and Carl had missed her when they surveyed the harbor. She was about a dozen years old but looked like she had been well cared for. The broker led them across the other boat and onto the Too. He pointed out the teak decks and what great condition they were in, and the shiny brass works. "One hundred eighty feet. This ship is in good shape, no one will have to spend hours on her, and she is sail and steam, now let's look inside." He unlocked one of the lounge doors and opened a couple of curtains so they could see. It was a beautiful room, many soft chairs and a bar in the corner with sparkling crystal glassware. The floor was wood, teak again and the trim around the windows was mahogany. The room sat about twenty. Beside it there was a large dining room, again a table for twenty. Under that was a galley, and towards the bow, on the main deck, there was a wheelhouse and the captain's cabin. Below decks there were about a dozen cabins of different sizes for passengers on the cruise, and then to the rear there were the crew quarters, to accommodate about a dozen, and the engine room, with a coal fired steam engine. Carl noticed that in addition to the engine there was a dynamo so when they went back to the upper decks, he checked. The boat had been electrified and there were some electric lights in the cabins and the main rooms. "She is complete, down to the dishes and glassware. She is sound, a surveyor has gone over her, and the boiler has been inspected, ready to go. She can be managed with a crew of four."

Carl puled out his check book and said, "Price?"

The broker said, "Four hundred sixty-five thousand."

Carl said, "Four oh five, fifty-five now and the other three fifty when you deliver her to my dock at 4:30 this afternoon. The property is Sea View, and I imagine it was her home dock, she will like going home... I'll arrange a couple cabs to bring the crew back here at 5:00." With that, Deeds and Carl crossed back to the dock and went back to their buckboard. They found Frank and Woody waiting there. "He's gone, train to New York."

"Good, follow us to the Von Steddings."

When they got there, the two wagons pulled up in the drive, and Carl told Frank and Woody to wait. "We have your sworn and witnessed statements and I hope that will be enough, but you are here just in case we need you. Lucas is mild, I don't think you have to worry about him attacking me."

Carl and Deeds went up to the door and were admitted by a maid. They were shown to the library and soon joined there by Lucas.

"A surprise, but glad to see you."

"Lucas, my son Des was brought home from the Yacht Club last night totally sedated by a drug put in his beer at the prompting of your son Fritz. Read this, that bar man confirms it."

Lucas read it quickly. "And the barkeep?"

"He is on the way to New York, with the warning that if he comes back, I will shoot him."

"Would you shoot him?" Lucas asked.

"He's lucky I haven't already," Carl said simply. "Now read these two statements. The men are outside if we need them, but I am just trying to get through this as quickly as possible."

Lucas read the statements then said, "Carl, I am so sorry, I had no idea he was that way."

"Lucas, let's all be honest about all this. You had an idea, that is why you are thinking of changing his school, that's why you like him out of the house and don't question him all that much, that's why a sixteen-year old boy has rooms at the yacht club. You had an idea, but I think you did not know how to deal with it so ignored it. Just be honest."

"You're right, things have been hinted at. This is the first that blew up in the open."

"Lucas, I believe when a boy goes this way that is his nature, how he was born, and no one, least of all him, caused it. Nothing you and Marte did caused this either. This drugging and force are way too far though. Fritz needs a place where there are likely more people like him that would be willing participants in this sort of thing. You have to make it clear to him that the drugs and force have to stop. You need to find him a place where he is more likely to feel he belongs."

"Where would that be and how do I do that?"

"Lucas, you have the summer. Book a boat for the three of you and go to England. I understand the private schools there are rife with this. Find him one where he feels comfortable for the next three or four years, with a college associated with it. You and the family can go over summers, and they have special programs for the other holidays. You can do some business at the same time." He handed over a small piece of paper. "This fellow is in London, but he is doing a lot of investing in India. You said you were looking for a place to invest, talk to him when you have Fritz settled."

"I do have a brother there. They could take Fritz for Christmas and the spring holidays, and we could go over summers. You might have a solution here."

"Thing is Lucas, he is not to go near my sons, or I guess me. Honestly, if I see him, I will shoot him, just because of the pain he has caused Des. Then it all will hit the fan. So, I really would appreciate it if you got him on the first ship over."

"I think you could be a dangerous man, Carl Montrose, and I think I should take that warning. The last thing we want is for someone to get shot and have this whole thing blow up in our faces. I will send for a shipping agent as soon as you leave. Thank you for being so understanding."

Carl said, "I don't know how understanding I am, but I am a realist. There are some things that just are, and we have to learn to live with them. Now, I think Deeds and I will go."

Fritz had been listening at the top of the stairs and when Carl and Deeds came out, he sank back into the shadows. He was not displeased. Maybe it would be better in England, and at least it would get him away from his insufferable parents for most of the year; and eventually they would stop coming over summers too. Sure, he would put up a fight when his father brought it up, but that was only to make sure he got enough money to live on over there. His father would do as he always did, try to buy his agreement.

Carl and Deeds returned to the house. They prepared the check for the ship broker. Carl wrote a letter to his house builder telling him to build a three-hundred foot jetty at the bay by Oakside, and to have it ready for September first.

Out on the water, the boys had had an interesting afternoon. Marcus was strict, but he knew his stuff; and by the end of the afternoon they did too. When Marcus knew that, he backed off a bit. "You know boys, your dad is an interesting man. When he wants something, he gets it. He wanted you boys to know how to sail, and you are almost there. Now what am I supposed to do for the rest of the summer?"

Des said, "Dad wouldn't have hired you for the whole summer if he didn't have something in mind for you."

"Yeah, Dad is always thinking. Nothing gets by him. He has something in mind for you," said Chuck, "And whatever it is you might as well just agree, there is no changing his mind once it is made up."

The sailors came in about 4:30 and Marcus oversaw the setting straight of the boat and all the lines. Ten minutes later, they were all distracted when the Sea View Too entered the bay under steam. Marcus commented, "Boys. There is a real boat, classy, steam and sail. I would give my eye teeth for the command of a ship like her." Carl and Deeds had wandered down to the dock and they stood there with them as they watched her steam up the bay. Of the six watching, four were astonished when the yacht changed course off the end of the dock and pulled in. When it was clear it was going to dock, Marcus rushed to put over the bumpers and helped the two men who jumped off to moor her. The broker alit and strode up to Carl and Deeds. Carl said, "Marcus, check her out now and let me know if there is anything wrong before I complete the purchase. Take your time, we will wait."

Twenty minutes later Marcus came back up and swung himself over to the dock. He came up beside Carl, "She is fine, ten or twelve years old but well taken care of, in fact the boats were better made then, than they are now. She is a good boat and she rests easy here."

"Thankyou Marcus. Deeds, take them up to the house, the signed check is in the desk, complete the paperwork and the transfer and put them all in the cabs we ordered." After they all left the dock, Carl turned to his three sons and said, "Alright, I know you are itching to, go take a look."

After they had left Marcus said, "Now, Mr. Montrose sir, you didn't do this because I said your boat was a mite puny, did you."

"No Marcus, I've wanted to do this for a while, but what held me back was who I could get to look after it for me. When I met you, I knew I had the man."

"But sir, I am only fifteen. Don't you think you need someone better than me?"

"Marcus, when I judge a man, I do not do it by years. I do it by their heart and what they know. You are my man on both counts. Now Marcus, you are the Captain of the Sea View Too, and I hope you can teach my sons to sail her. I think maybe you should go into town to find someone to handle the boilers and that dynamo though."

The boys had returned by that point and Des heard that last comment, "I missed that Dad, you mean she is electrified?"

"Yes boys, she is electrified. I am having a dock put in for her at Oakside, at the bay shore, and when we go home at the end of the summer, some of us will go in her, so you guys better know how to sail her by then. And when we go to Florida and along the Texas coast, we will take her. The rail car will just follow along for side trips if needed."

Diz edged up to Marcus and said, "See, we told you, always thinking and you have to just go along for the ride."

The next morning, just as Marcus was about to go to town in search of a stoker for the engine room, Carl drew him aside. "While you are in town stop by this address and have him put together a uniform for you as captain." Carl cut off Marcus' protests. "Look son, we will start using the Sea View Too to entertain, for business purposes, dinner at sea type things. We will have some very rich people on board, and it is just a matter of confidence that they see you looking a bit more like a captain. A pair of dungarees and a singlet just won't count with an Astor, a Vanderbilt, or a

Whitney. Don't worry though, when it is just us, you can wear what you want." Marcus found his person to look after the boiler, and he got his uniform, with a white hat. He looked quite dashing in the uniform.

At least once a week Carl had a dinner party at Sea View and Carl noticed a pattern. After dinner, during the dancing, Des and Diz would slip away with a girl each, and Carl noticed, soon three girls for the two of them. They would wander down to "Look at the boat" and would invariably go aboard for a closer look. A couple hours later the group would return, holding hands, and sometimes Marcus would be with them, in his white hat. Marcus never went into the house with them but would split off and enter the house through the servants' quarters and go to his room by the back stairs. Carl also noticed that the supply of condoms steadily had to be restocked. He drew the inevitable conclusion about what the boat was being used for but was impressed by the steady supply of new girls that seemed to be only too willing to take part.

One day, Carl drew Marcus aside and said, "Marcus, I know what the boat is being used for when we entertain in the house. I've seen the boys and the young ladies going down, and all of you coming back later. I can imagine what goes on in between. Now Marcus, I would hate to think my boys have corrupted you."

"Corrupted?"

"You know. Started you doing that sort of thing. You are only fifteen."

"Started? No sir, they didn't start me. You remember how I told you they fished me out when the boat sank? I was so cold, they put me in bed with their cook. She was a nice lady, not all that old. Well, that night things happened, that was when I started. After that, when I was on the boat, well you know sailors when they come to a port? They took me along and usually treated me to one of the ladies. So, your boys never started me. Though, I have to admit, until I came here, I never used any of those fancy things the boys bring, to make sure the girls don't get, you know. One thing though, you made it much easier to convince them. They go wild over that white hat you got me."

Carl laughed and gave him a shoulder hug, "Oh Marcus, you are a treasure. I was so worried they had corrupted you, and you started years before them. I am glad to hear you all are using condoms, and most of all I am pleased I was able to help you along with that white hat you didn't want. Christ, I wish I was twenty years younger and could join you all."

"Oh sir, there are twelve staterooms, we don't do it together," Marcus said seriously. This got him another hug from Carl and a deep laugh as he walked away.

Occasionally Carl would announce at breakfast. "We have dinner guests tonight, but I think we will dine on the boat." He enjoyed seeing the crestfallen looks on Des' and Diz' faces as they realized that they couldn't play their regular games.

The two expectant mothers had announced their good news to Carl. Mag said, "I still don't know what I am doing, but soon I will be a father of at least three, maybe more."

"What do you mean maybe more?"

"The doctor says there may be three, he thinks he can hear three different heartbeats."

They each were sitting on the terrace holding one of the twins. Carl looked down at Lou, the one on his lap, and said, "Well, you might have three younger brothers, or worse, sisters. Have to have a talk with your dad or you might have more brothers and sisters than there are stars in the skies." He glanced up at Mag who was blushing deep red.

Carl gently said, "Son, when these are born, maybe you should start trying some of those condoms in the desk. Don't get me wrong, I love all the little ones, more the merrier, but infants are hard on the mother. Wouldn't want to ruin a good marriage by having too many little children all at once. And for you, as a Dad, five children turning fourteen or fifteen all at the same time will drive you absolutely mad." He then went on to tell Mag what Des and Diz were up to with Marcus.

"Marcus? I thought he was only fifteen?" said Mag.

"Marcus informed me he had his first encounter when he was twelve, and has been frequently involved ever since."

"Twelve? Jesus, five kids are more than enough if I have to start worrying about them at twelve, and God I hope there are no girls."

"Seeing how easy it has been for those boys to come up with three girls every time we have a party, I have to agree with you."

Ed and Ali were having an interesting summer. Western riding parties were popular in the Hamptons too. They got lots of invitations. One young lady was especially fond of Ali, and she had repeated riding parties, usually managing to get Ali off by himself. It would usually progress that the horses would get tired, usually by some small stream, and they would be tied to some convenient log to water while the riders sat under a tree and talked. Talked was euphemistic for kissed. Ali and the young lady were getting pretty proficient at the "talking" part. One day the girl said, "We've been doing this for a month now, I expect I will have the baby in eight months, whose house are we gonna live at? Yours or mine, after we are married?

Ali replied, "I dunno, I'll talk to my Dad tonight," His head was still reeling with the number of things that had just been decided for him. Having a baby, perhaps moving, in any case being with this girl somewhere, and he had thought they were just kissing. That evening he went into his Dad's study and shut the door then sat across from him, sighing mightily. Carl was immediately alarmed. This was his eleven-year old son and he thought there was still a few years before these man-to-man discussions would be needed. Yet here was a serious boy, clearly with something on his mind.

"Ali? Do you have something we need to discuss?"

"Yeah Dad, Sarah asked today where we would live after she had the baby in about eight months,"

After recovering from almost fainting, Carl asked, "What exactly have you and Sarah been up to?"

"Just kissing a bit when we go riding."

"Ali, have all you been doing with Sarah is kissing? For sure? Nothing that includes taking any of your clothes off?"

"Our clothes off? No Dad, that would be embarrassing. We have never taken any of our clothes off. All we have done is kissed."

"Then Ali, I can safely say if all you have done is kissed and you have never taken your clothes off, any part of them, then the two of you are not about to have a baby. There are quite a few steps between kissing and having a baby and they involve a lack of clothing. Now, I hate to go into these steps too early lest you feel the two of you want to try them. So, Ali, are you okay with the just kissing part right now?"

"Sure Dad, that is all I want to do right now. I don't want a baby, and if I can avoid that by keeping all my clothes on, that's all I need to know for now. But, when I think I need to know more, can I come back and talk?"

"Definitely Ali, as soon as you feel you want to go past kissing, you and I have to talk, and Ali, maybe you should suggest Sarah and her mother should have a talk about where babies come from, I think she needs some more information."

Then there was the time Ed and Ali got shipwrecked. Carl had arranged to have a morning meeting and lunch on the Too. They would use both the engine and sails, so the older boys had been pressed into use as crew. The passengers were a group of tobacco buyers from England and Carl was eager to pin them down as customers for the crop that had been growing all summer on Oakside. Ed and Ali were on the dock when the group boarded, and Carl knew they were waiting to be asked to come along. He knelt in front of them and said, "Boys, most other times I would ask you to come along, but your brothers will be busy with the sails and can't watch you, and I will be busy with these people. We all know what happens if the two of you get bored. Now, you only have an hour until you see Mr. Travis, and if you ask him really nicely, you might be able to convince him to have your class on the sailboat. He knows how to sail. We should all be back just after lunch." He gave each of them a hug.

As he stood, Ed said, "Can we take out the boat then, just for the hour?"

Carl turned back, "I have been talking to Marcus, and he says you two are getting really good at it, but he doesn't feel you are quite ready. Hear me clearly, you are not ready to take that boat out by yourself. So, don't."

After Carl was on board, Marcus backed the Too away from the dock. He, and the three others all waved at Ed and Ali, standing there on the dock in their swimming suits. The yacht slowed and turned, the sails were unfurled, and she sailed down the Sound.

The two boys watched her sail out of sight, then Ali turned to Ed, "Come on, let's sail. We got an hour before we have to meet Travis."

Ed hesitated, then as usual, agreed. The boys jumped down into the boat and let loose the lines, pushing away from the dock. They pulled the sails up and were a little surprised at how strong the wind was. Soon they were speeding down the bay with the boat heeling heavily to port. A couple times they tried to tack and return but the wind was too strong, and they were driven further down the bay. The two boys were getting a bit worried but tried not to let each other see their concern. They were sailing with the centerboard down because of the strength of the wind, the water was choppy, and suddenly the board caught on something under the water, the boat slowed quickly, then shuddered to a halt, leaning ever more sharply to port as the wind tried to push it. The boys rose and tried to lower the sails, but they were thrown into the water as the boat flipped and slowly slid under. The boys found themselves all alone in the middle of a lot of water. There was no shoreline visible to swim too. There were a few large rocks jutting from the water over to one side and the two made for them. Ed and Ali struggled but they did manage to clamber up on the reef. Soon they were sitting there in the sun, which seemed to get hotter as the swim suits dried. As his suit dried, Ali pulled at it. "Damn these things. They are made of wool and cover you from your knees to your neck. God it's itchy."

Ed agreed and said, "Looks like we are going to be here for a while, I am gonna peel the top part down at least." He undid the buttons and peeled the top part down to his waist. He continued, "There are a lot of rocks here now, but when the tide comes in, we are going to lose some under water. Do you think there will be enough left?"

"Sure, there will, I've seen rocks here abouts before," Ali said doubtfully.

On the Too, Carl was telling his guests. "The whole plantation, Oakside, was planted with brand new tobacco plants in the spring. From all reports those plants have flourished and should be ready to pick in a few weeks. We have several mechanical pickers to try. We have new drying houses, and since the plantation is electrified, the drying houses have fans. The whole process will be speeded up because of that. We expect to have our first shipment ready by the third week in September, and have a shipment ready every week after that. There is a new three-hundred-foot dock, this boat will be moored on one side of it, but the other side will be kept clear for your vessels. The dock has also been fitted with electric hoists to help with the loading. So, gentlemen, I will commit ninety percent of the crop to you, the other ten percent I want for a project there on Oakside, an automatic cigarette factory. Who knows, maybe next year you will be taking the crop in the form of cigarettes."

The group was receptive. Contracts were signed, and the deal was made. A schedule was set up for ships to shuttle back and forth. These buyers were English, and there was no tobacco in England. They appreciated a new firm supply. After the negotiations were done, the brandy came out. Carl had brought one of the footmen from the house and he handled the pouring. A short time later a cold lunch was served, meats, salads, and some pastries. About 1:30 the Sea View Too pulled back up to her dock. The boys swiftly secured her. Carl was surprised to see Mag and Brent, and several of the Pinkertons on the dock, waiting for them to tie up. He went to the railing and Mag said, "Dad, by any chance are Ed and Ali there with you? We have been looking for them all day, ever since they didn't show up for their class with Brent.

Carl glanced over at the slip where the sailboat was kept as he said, "No, they are not with us. They were on the dock when we set off, and they wanted to take the boat out, I said no, they had a class in an hour. God, they must have taken the sailboat out, despite what I said. Deeds, can you see to our guests and help them get cabs? Marcus, spin this thing up again and bring a chart to the lounge. We have to figure out where they may have gone. Frank, get some more of your guys down here, we can use all the eyes we can get to look, find some telescopes too, there are about a dozen in the house."

Marcus was quickly back with a chart that he spread on the table. He had gotten rid of his hat and jacket. Marcus pointed to the map. "The dock is here, and when we left about ten the wind was coming from this direction. That would have driven them down here, this way. It was a strong wind and they would have had no control. They were not ready to make a tack, a turn, in that kind of wind so it would have kept driving them this way, until they got here, the shoals. In that wind, the center board would have been torn off and the boat upended. These shoals are fifteen miles long, they could not have missed all of them. There was no way they could have swam to land from there. If they are lucky, if we are lucky, they may have made it to those rocks. Thing is though, there are only a few of those rocks above water when the tide comes in. We better get over there. I'll have the ship under way in five minutes. By the time he was ready, the detectives were back and arrayed around the deck. Marcus and Carl were in the wheelhouse with Mag and the three older boys together on the bow with a couple of the telescopes.

Marcus headed immediately for the shoals. He constantly urged the man in the boiler room to give him more speed. After about half an hour, the lookouts started to find items in the water. Marcus stopped while one large piece was brought aboard. It was clearly part of the sailboat. Marcus set off again for the shallows they were concerned about. Finally, they reached the shoals. Marcus slowed, in one direction there were no rocks visible at all, in the other, far far away they could see a few rocks. Marcus headed that way, that was their best chance. As they neared, Des yelled out, "There, to port, I think I see something."

Marcus bore that way and he and Carl both held glasses to their eyes. They both saw the same thing. The boys were standing on a rock, a not so large one, holding each other. Occasionally a wave washed over their rock, and they struggled to maintain their footing, helping each other. The tide was fully in now, so there were many waves for the boys to contend with. Marcus got as close as he could and dropped anchor. The detectives were struggling to get one of the lifeboats free.

Des and Diz looked at each other, and Des said, "Look, they cannot hang on much longer, we have to…"

"Go and get them. We are the best swimmers." The two stooped and removed their boots, pants, and shirts. Frank was removing a section of the railing for them and when they were ready, they jumped together. Carl and Marcus joined the others at the railing and cheered them on. Just as they reached the rocks a wave finally dislodged the two. There were now four in the water. The littler ones positioned themselves on their brother's backs, arms around their necks, and the older boys headed back to the ship. It was a lengthy swim and took a while. They stopped a couple times to rest, treading water. Finally, they neared the Too, and a rope ladder was dropped over the side. The little ones were sent up the ladder first. As each of them came over the side Carl grabbed them and checked for broken bone or serious cuts or scrapes. When he was done checking the first, he turned to the second just coming on the deck and repeated the process. When Des and Diz each came on deck, they each got a long hug and a heartfelt thankyou. Then Carl said, "Marcus, home please, and you two, it is time we talked." He grabbed Ed and Ali by the scruffs of their necks and manhandled them down the stairs to the cabin level. The door to the owner's cabin was closed firmly behind him. Des, Diz, and Chuck each looked at each other with a slight smile. There was the sound of the anchor coming up, and of the engines at full speed as the Too returned to her dock. There was no sound from the cabin, at first.

Frank said, "I would have thought there would be some yelling by now."

Des replied, "Dad never yells. He just talks, and reasons with you, and makes you feel guilty, that's worse. I would have rather he yelled."

"Then you have been hauled off by the scruff of your neck then," said Frank.

"Yeah, we all have at one point or another. Would rather have been shot."

In the cabin, Carl was sitting on the edge of the bed, the two boys standing sheepishly in front of him, swimsuits drooping down around their waists. "Well?" said Carl.

"We didn't mean nuttin," tried Ali. There was no response.

"Yeah, you left us behind," said Ed

"So, it's my fault?"

"Well..no, it's Ali's fault, he is older, and bigger, and he made me do it," tried Ed.

"Ed, you two have been like twins for four years. You do everything together. If either of you had objected, the other would have given in. You did this together and no one objected, am I right?"

"Well, yes, dammit. Sorry Al, I lost it."

"It's okay Ed, I understand. Dad, you know we never meant for this to happen and we are sorry."

"Sure, I know all of that, but the two of you have to understand something. You did something I expressly told you not to. You risked your lives, and almost drowned, would likely have in another hour. In addition, two of your brothers risked their lives to get you. I could have lost four sons today. In the past, I have gone to extreme lengths to avoid losing any of you. That was why we moved to the north, to get you all away from a war. I don't know how I could adjust to losing any of you, let alone four at once. The way of nature is that you all bury me, not the other way around. Now who is first?"

"First for what?" asked Ed suspiciously.

"Boys, you know what is going to happen here. There are some very big lessons here that you have to learn, that you can have absolutely no doubt of. Like when you are expressly told not to do something, you don't. That you think of the consequences before you do something. That if you decide to do something, you are also prepared to take the consequences of what you have done. Now who is first?... No volunteer, then you first Ed."

Carl reached over, took Ed's arm and folded him over his knees. "Nice of you to be partially prepared." Carl reached down and moved the swimsuit so it sank around Ed's ankles. Carl started his task, administering twelve smart slaps to his son's bottom. When he was done, he said gently, "Okay son, we are done. You can stand." Ed stood and pulled up the swimsuit to cover himself. There was no crying or wailing. There was a bit of a tear at the edge of his eye, but he had taken his punishment like the young man he was. After all, he had helped repel Indian attacks.

Ed stepped back, and Carl looked at Ali. Ali stepped forward and dropped the lower part of his suit then knelt over his father's knees. Carl administered twelve measured strokes. When finished, Ali stood, pulled up his suit, and stepped back. He looked directly in his father's eyes but said nothing.

"Okay, you two, this is over. Go find some clothes in your cabin, we will be at the dock shortly. Make sure you talk to Des and Diz."

In the lounge those waiting heard the slaps and winced with every one of them and they heard the door open and close as the boys left and went to their cabin. Carl came up to the lounge. He looked the others straight on and said, "Now we go on. Hopefully, we will move on to new problems. Gentlemen, raising sons will never be problem free. Some of you are about to find that out." Later, once the Too had docked, Ed and Ali came up and they thanked both Des and Diz for coming and getting them. Ali said, "We acted like little kids, and it could have lost you two your lives. That was wrong of us." The four boys came off the Too together and went up the dock towards the house. Carl saw the four and was satisfied, that was the most important part of all that had gone on.

About the middle of August, Carl decided he had to come to terms with some of the outstanding problems. One of them was the issue of Chuck and the girl in New York, Abbie Somers. He called him into the study and said, "Okay Chuck, the summer is almost over. I did see that you didn't take part with your brothers in the games on the boat, in fact you have been pretty quiet all summer. I trust you have been corresponding with Abbie, what has happened on that front?"

"I have felt the same way all summer, but here is a letter I got today."

Carl read the letter, the most important part was in the last paragraph. Carl read, "So while I do love you, I have learned something this summer. I don't love you enough. I couldn't get through the summer without you and stay true. No, I haven't had sex with someone else, but I thought of it, and I flirted with other boys. I am sorry Chuck, our relationship is not strong enough. It should have been. It would have been if we were truly meant for each other. So, I do wish you the best and I hope you can find a person who deserves you. Love Abbie."

Carl looked at Chuck. "Son, I am sorry, I hoped this would work out differently, but I am not surprised. True love takes a while to develop. You can see that with Mag and Louise, and with Sally and Brent. It usually doesn't happen in two months like we had in New York. It is not due to anything you did or are, it is just a fact of life. What you have to do is just carry on with your life. You will meet the right person at some point."

That evening Carl had one of his last parties of the summer. He was standing by the window when he saw some movement on the lawn below. There were three boys and four girls on their way to the boat at the dock where Carl assumed Marcus was waiting. "Jesus, I had better buy the condoms by the case if there are going to be four of them dipping into the desk drawer, actually five when Mag starts after the babies are born."

The next weekend, Carl had a meeting with all the family and Marcus. "We have to decide on the process for the end of the summer, for the move to Oakside. Marcus, here is a chart of the Chesapeake, with Oakside marked on it, and the Potomac. The dock is finished, and I had them check the seabed. There is a shelf that goes out 10 or 12 feet from shore then it drops off to at least forty feet. The dock is well over two hundred feet long, almost three. I trust that will accommodate the Too. The way the hoists have been installed is to service the left side looking from the sea in, so you will dock on the right side, going in. During the day the dock will fly two green flags over one red one, and at night there will be two green lights over one red one. For you Marcus, there are two questions. We want the boat delivered to Oakside. We would like you to stay with us and the boat but if you want to move on or go back to Maine, that would be the time. Come and talk to me privately and let me know what you have decided. Secondly, your fireman, or stoker, or whatever he is called. I assume you want him for this trip. Then you can let him go, we'll give him a train ticket back here. There is no sense keeping him for the winter as the boat will not move far for at least three months, and just for your information Marcus. Then, we will want the boat to go south to Florida and the Gulf coast for the winter. I hope you will be with us for that. We can get a stoker from the plantation when we need one, train him a bit."

"Now for the trip to Oakside, we will have the boat and the rail car. On the way to Oakside, I have to stop in Washington for a couple of days, the Washington LePrad. So, we have to decide who goes which way. Who is coming with me on the railcar and stopping in DC, and who wants to go by boat. I do feel I have to say, if all the kids decide to go on the boat and all the adults want to go on the train, I would have some concerns." There was a lot of general discussion.

Finally it was decided. The three older boys would go on the boat, after all they were Marcus's crew. Mag and Mel said they would go on the boat, but they would send the babies on the train with Imelda. Brent and Sally said they would like to go on the train. Deeds said he would go on the boat. Carl looked at Ed and Ali.

"What? We are waiting for you to tell us, we know you won't let us make our own decision," said Ed.

"No, you can decide. I assume Mag and Mel, and Deeds, are willing to take responsibility for you if you chose the boat. What would you rather do, boat or train?"

Ali said, "We have spent days on the train. We would rather go on the boat."

A cook and a footman from the house were engaged to go on the boat. They would be given a train ticket back and a cash bonus. The detectives would be split. Marcus said the voyage would take three or four days, depending on the weather. They would leave Hampton Bay and sail southwest to the Jersey shore. The hope would be to get to Atlantic City or Ocean City on the first day. The second day would see them cross Delaware Bay and follow the Delaware coast south, until it became Maryland and eventually Virginia again, and they would continue, rounding the tip of the Virginia Spit into Chesapeake Bay. Then it was northwest across the Bay to the vicinity of Mathews and Oakville where Oakside was located. Oakside was a big plantation and had about twenty miles of coastline on the Chesapeake. There couldn't be that many three-hundred-foot-long piers jutting out into the bay. Marcus went over the charts with Carl who agreed to the plan and told Marcus, "If need be hole up in a port on the way down, it really doesn't matter how long it takes. Be safe. With the rail car it will take a day from here to D.C. A day and a half in the capital, then half a day by train to Oakside. So, if we are lucky, we should all get there about the same time."

Carl had a side conversation with Deeds and thanked him for going on the boat, saying he felt better there was one of them on the yacht. They had a short discussion about how much cash Deeds should take on the boat.

Marcus also came in for a private talk. "Sir, I would like to stay with you. The idea of taking the yacht to Florida and the Gulf really excites me. And actually, I feel really comfortable here, and I get along well with the boys, almost like brothers. I haven't felt so comfortable anywhere since my family died. Just not sure what you want me to do for three months."

"Marcus, we are glad you feel that way, we are all fond of you. As far as what you would do, there will still be maintenance on the boat, you have to keep it in shape for when we want it, and it isn't going to be parked for the three months, we will use it in the bay. Then you might find something that interests you on Oakside, maybe in the new cigarette factory. You are quite mechanical."

Chapter 12

By Land and By Sea

So once again the Montrose Family was on the move. The car was ready on the siding, and Imelda and the babies were installed on it. Carl, Brent and Sally had come down to the dock to see the others off. The Sea View Too was backing out by steam so all of the boys were gathered on deck waving good bye. Deeds and Marcus were in the wheelhouse, and Marcus gave the steam whistle a little toot. They all seemed eager for their little adventure but Carl was very disquieted. His whole family had never gone off like this without him and he didn't like the feeling. It wasn't that he felt they were in danger, but it was the separation from them. The three returned to the house and Carl had a brief talk with Mrs. Langley. She said, "The summer staff is twenty-one. You took two with the boat and will release them when you get there. I will release another twelve tomorrow. That will leave us with our winter staff of nine, including me. This is a big house and still needs cleaning over the winter."

"I know Mrs. Langley. Get some carpenters in and there are a couple of things I want done on the second floor to the bedrooms, God know there are enough of them. I want two of the rooms joined together to make a large nursery with cribs and everything for up to 7 or 8 babies. Take a room to one side of the new nursery to make a big play room, and equip it. Most of the kids will be one, two, or three next season, but that will have to be upgraded every year. Set up a bedroom on the other side of the nursery for a nanny. Now the big thing. I will be sending a crew here this winter to electrify this place. They will wire the house for electric light, perhaps some electric stoves in the kitchen, plug ins all over the place, and there will be a lot of new lamps. They will make a mess of some of the walls, and I want you to get plasterers and painters in so that when we come next year there will not be any evidence of their even having been here. They will build a new building somewhere in the yard for a power plant. And, they will be doing the whole house, including all the floors. Now next year, staff up for the start of April and go until the end of September. We are skipping Chicago and New York next year. So, plan for a long season, not sure of the numbers but I will let you know. Oh, you know the big room on the back of the house, the one with the balcony? That will be Captain Marcus' next year. Get him a big telescope for that room so he can keep an eye on the Too will you. Now have a couple of the people take the Travers and I to the rail car, and then you can just keep on carrying on until next year. You did a marvellous job this summer so here is a little thank you from all of us." He handed her an envelope and the last three left. As the carriages exited the gate, she glanced into the envelope. There was a ten-thousand-dollar bonus in it, more than a year's salary. She was astonished.

When they got to the rail-car, Carl told the detectives they could station two men in the private car, there were lots of extra rooms. The rest would be in the second car. Imelda was pleased to be back on the train. She liked the little room she had with the babies, who were now quite active, almost four. Sally spent a lot of time helping her with them.

At lunch that day, Carl said, "I am glad you chose the train. Means you will be with me when I tour the Washington LePrad. Apparently, that hotel is a disaster, lots of problems. You are both very perceptive people. Go on the tour with me and keep notes, I want to know what you see, and any suggestions. That hotel should be triple A, it is costing a fortune to run but the customers are always filing complaints. We should get there about three, so we will have a chance for a little look around before we have dinner. We will just see what we can nose out. You two don't mind, do you?"

Brent said, "No, we don't mind, we are just surprised you care what we think that much."

"Look you two. You have grown up in places like these, you are more likely to spot something than I will. I get caught up in looking at roofs and boilers, and plumbing. There is far more than that needed at a luxury hotel. You are two brilliant young people and I value your opinions very much."

After lunch, Carl filled them in on more of what he knew about the hotel. "It runs with a cost per guest that is twice as high as any of the other hotels. There are 7 times more complaints to head office about this place. The occupancy rate averages 54%. The lowest rate in any of the other hotels is 92%. In most of the other LePrad hotels, the large rooms, the ballrooms and the meeting rooms, are rented 63% of the time, in Washington, 26%

of the time. Per guest day this hotel has 37% more staff. Maintenance costs per room are 48% higher for D.C., and it is less that ten years old. As you can see, I know lots about this hotel, I just don't know why."

When the train pulled into Washington and was sited on the usual siding, there were no carriages and wagons to meet them. One of the detectives had to set off in search of both, and returned in a half hour or so. Carl appeared calm but Brent knew he wasn't. They arrived at the hotel and there was no doorman. One of the bellhops who had just put his guests in a cab, came over and opened their door, helping Sally down. "Good evening ma'am. Welcome to the Washington LePrad. My name is Holly." He whistled up several more bellhops to help the party. Carl led the group into the lobby and up to the desk. A desk clerk was a bit distracted but eventually looked up and smiled at him. "You name sir?"

"Carl Montrose."

The desk clerk searched her card file, then a book, and then she said, "Mr. Montrose, sir, there does not seem to be a reservation here, and we are fully booked for tonight. I am sorry sir."

Carl, a pleasant smile on his face, said to her, "I want to see the manager of this hotel right here, right now." As he was waiting, Carl looked around the lobby, and saw the head bellman in a corner behind a potted palm, a newspaper in his hands. The door man was in a corner too, sleeping. About five minutes later, a fat man with a florid face arrived, a bit out of breath and out of sorts too, for having his presence demanded. "Now sir, what can I do for you.? I am Edger Flood."

"Do you have a hotel detective?"

"Benny? Sure, we have a hotel detective. You want to see him? Liza, ring Benny." Benny was there in ninety seconds. "Yeah Liza, where is the problem.?

Carl spoke up. "I am Carl Montrose. I own this hotel. You were notified of my arrival, but no one saw fit to have the new owner met at the station. Now Mr. Flood, you were the manager of this hotel, you are now fired. Benny, remove him from my hotel, and when you have him out, get rid of the doorman sleeping in the corner and the head bellman behind the potted palm with the girlie magazine."

Benny gulped, and started to show Mr. Flood out. Carl turned to Liza, "Now, let me see the register. This hotel has not been over 54% occupancy, so I want to see how this hotel is now mysteriously full of guests. There are 197 rooms in this hotel, let me see 197 guests."

He looked briefly at the register then motioned Brent and Sally up beside him. Carl took a red pencil from his pocket and used it as he read through the register. When he got to the end, there were 47 names with a red check beside them. "Liza, these ones with the red checks. They all have a red EF after them. What does that mean?"

Those are Mr. Floods complimentary rooms."

"Complimentary? You mean he gives them out for free?"

Liza whispered, "He says they are free, but I have seen him pocket money when he shows the guests up."

"The man who was the manager of the hotel showed people to their rooms and collected money from them. Benny!"

Benny was their immediately. "Yes sir."

"Benny, in the ledger there are 47 names of people who have rooms at this hotel. They are to be evicted immediately. My security men will help you, all but one, Frank. Frank, you stay here by me and make sure I don't shoot someone. I am very close to doing that. Holly!"

Holly was their immediately. "You are now head bellman. Organize your people and have them meet the guest's carriages immediately, and Holly, you just got a raise, your old salary times four. You sharpen up the bellboys, they are the front lines of this hotel. Between guests, get this lobby smartened up. Now Liza, you still have a job, but you are on probation. Get me the head housekeeper."

Benny and the Pinkertons were emptying the hotel of a third of its guests, and they were not happy about it. Keys were being dropped on the desk by the dozen. Sally and Brent slipped behind the desk to organize the keys and make a list of the newly vacated rooms. The head housekeeper arrived, a simple and evidently hard-working woman. Carl said to her, "There are forty-seven rooms being vacated right now, my two friends here are making a list. They all have to be squared away. Call in extra staff if you need to, I want those rooms as good as any other rooms in this hotel, to the LePrad standard, and I want them as quickly as you can get them done so I can rent them again tonight. Now Liza, are there any assistant managers? I want to see them now, and the accountants, the head custodians, and the maintenance people. Everybody, all department heads and their seconds. Now, in that meeting room over there."

"For your information, the manager, head doorman, and the head bellman have all been fired. Holly, is there an owner's suite in this hotel, and is it empty?"

When told yes on both counts, Carl said, "Have your boys take all of our stuff there, find me later and give me a key. Liza, give my security men rooms, two per, and then all the rest are available for rental as housekeeping is done with them. Sally, you okay staying here with Liza while Brent and I take a walk around this place before the meeting? Good, Benny and Frank come with me too."

The tour started in the basement. They checked the furnace and the water systems. There was a very clean and neat area near the furnace. Most of the rest of the basement was filthy. Carl checked the desk drawer and there was some mail there addressed to a Fred Haver. "You know who this is?"

"Sure, he is one of the custodians, a young guy. Keeps to himself."

They then went into the kitchens. The kitchens were modern, spacious, and well equipped. They were also clean and efficiently run. Carl muttered to himself, "At least this part works." They wandered through the ball rooms and the meeting rooms. They checked out the cloakrooms and the locker rooms for the employees. Then they went upstairs and saw some of the guest rooms. The rooms were simple but quite luxurious, quality furnishings, and top-grade linens. As he went through the guest rooms, he noted that the hotel had been electrified but wasn't using it. There still were gas lamps. Then they headed down to the meeting with staff leaders.

When Carl and Brent entered the room, the assembly quieted. Carl said, "First the kitchens. A core to a hotel. The kitchens here are fine, and the food tastes good. All the people here involved with those operations can leave and continue as before. Staff from housekeeping can also go. You are doing a good job. Problems are centered elsewhere."

"Now the staff in charge of the facilities, the furnace, the water, the general plant. I noticed some of the inspections are not up to date, the fire extinguishers have not been charged in over a year. There are leaks in several places in the water system. There are several rooms taken off line because there are problems with their bathrooms, and their gas lighting. A fortune has been spent electrifying this place, but it has not been completed. Could the engineering staff please rise so I can see where you are. There were about seven men who stood. One was a young fella, the rest older. Carl spoke to the young man, "You Haver?" The man nodded. "You are now the head of engineering and facilities. The rest of you are dismissed and may go. Haver, I am afraid you will have to work tonight, and tomorrow build your staff up with people like you, young and honest. The new managers will talk salary with you."

"Custodial?" several men stood. "Look, this place is filthy, all the common areas, and all the area back of the house, the locker rooms and the cloakrooms and the staff areas, the areas you are in charge of. You are all on probation, and have three months to get this place in order or you too will be dismissed. Now go. Now the guest services, the accounting, the office staff and so on. Accounting, you knew what you were doing, the information was there, no one cared enough to investigate. Guest services, I have already made some changes. You have a new head of the bellmen, Holly. He is bright, friendly, and outgoing. He is eager to help. I have fired the head doorman. He was sleeping in the lobby when I got here. He did not value his job. Clean house out there, use Holly as the model. They are the face of this hotel. We want the young and the bright, courteous and helpful and eager to please. Get rid of those who aren't. Everywhere, from the front desk to the person who carries the bag, to the one who brings your room service. The manager has been let go as are the two assistant managers. They knew what was going on and chose to let it continue. None of them showed any loyalty to the company. Okay, that's it. There will be new managers in place as of tomorrow."

That evening, as Carl, Brent and Sally sat around the owner's suite, which was very nice, equal to the one in New York; Brent said, "Carl, you came in here, shook this place up and ejected all the debris, or at least most of it. This place should be a snap to run now."

"That's good, because that is what I want the two of you to do, manage the hotel. You are bright, ambitious, and organized. You know what the clients who use this place will require and expect. You are ideal. Take the combined salary the two of you earn and multiply it by four. That will be the base salary of each of the two of you as the managers. In addition, you get this suite to live in, free use of hotel services, and the hotel will provide you with a nanny when you need it, and Sally, you can work then to whatever degree you wish to as delivery approaches. Lastly, as a bonus, you will be paid five percent of the net profits this hotel earns under your leadership, and I have a feeling that can be a lot of money. You and your children will always be welcome at Oakside, when you want a break from this place. You are part of the family now."

Sally said, "We were wondering what we should do, and where to live. We knew we couldn't be tutors forever, and my condition was going to make it hard to work at anything. With this we are settled. I can work as much as I want when I want."

Brent said, "Carl, this is an ideal solution; but somehow, I have the feeling you didn't just come up with it. We appreciate it and agree to it anyway."

"You're right, I have been thinking of it for a while. When we were all choosing how to go back to Oakside, I was praying you would choose the train. I didn't want to have to tell you to. I knew the key here, once it was shaken up, would be leadership. I have seen your leadership at work with the boys. There is no way the boys could have handled the year without that leadership." They spent the next few hours talking about the time Brent first, then the two of them, spent with the boys. The conclusion was that it was far from easy, but that it was always interesting.

The next morning, Carl took them down and got them settled in their new offices, then he said, "Okay, I'm going. You have some good people here, use them. Above all, enjoy yourselves. If, a few months from now, you are not enjoying this, drop me a note. I will slip over, and we will work something else out."

Carl went up and rousted out the Pinkertons. They went to the station and the two cars were soon on their way to Virginia. At about two, the rail cars were dropped at the siding at Oakside. Carl and the men dismounted into a green clearing beside the tracks. The sun was shining, it was warm, and the birds were singing. Woody and Frank stood together. Woody said, "This is perfect. What are we gonna guard him from here, rabid chipmunks?"

Frank said, as he pointed to Carl, who was now wearing a holster at his hip, "When was the last time you saw him do that? He knows this all isn't as perfect as it seems. Keep sharp."

Carl said, "A couple of you come with me, maybe Frank and Woody. The house is about a mile to the west. We will send a couple of wagons back for the luggage." The three walked down the road slowly. Carl was distracted, his mind adrift in the memories of life here before the war, when Mag and Des were young. They were happy for those first ten or so years. It was a wonderful place to raise a family. The South before the war was in many ways a paradise. Oakside, under Carl, was not devoted to cotton so did not have the big demand for slave labor. When he got control of it, there were a few slaves, but he never added any and even then, he treated his people well. They were never mistreated physically, they were allowed to have families, and family units were never broken up. They had food and clothing, and they were paid. Even then that made him unpopular with some of his neighbors. Carl was always searching for the best crop he could grow, with the lowest labor input and the highest profit. He had experimented a bit with tobacco, and it grew well. The problem was with the harvesting.

The key to growing tobacco this time around would be the mechanical pickers they would try, and the fact there was much more of a market for tobacco now. It would be especially good if the tobacco could be processed there on Oakside and the cigarettes be sold. They arrived at the gates, two big black iron gates that closed under a wide white archway of wood with the name Oakside carved into the wood and painted black. This was just like it was before the war, and even on the day they left. Carl could remember getting down off the wagon on that last day to close these gates.

The three opened the gates enough to squeeze through, and then closed them again. The purpose of those gates, and the white fences that seemed to stretch in all directions, was to keep something in. Before the war, he had closed those gates in the hope of keeping the evil out, the cries for war. It had not worked and when his wife had died it had been her wish to get all the boys away from this, but it had been his desire too. If things had been different and she survived, he still probably would have wanted to leave, despite his love for Oakside. They walked down the avenue towards the house, under the big oak trees that reached across to each other. It was shady and cool there. He remembered putting some of those trees in, and he loved the memory of playing tag with Des and Mag around the trunks of those trees. They came up a little rise and the vista opened before them. The house was there, again as beautiful as it had been before the war, the broad white gallery on the front, the eight tall white columns, the house three stories high with an attic above that, and the grey slate roof. A little behind the house were the new large stables and barns he had ordered for the reincarnation, and the miles and miles of fences for the new paddocks. There were several outbuildings, more than there had been before, and they all were new and white. There still was the old smell of the south, a mix of the trees, the grass, and the crops. You could still smell the cotton. There must be some neighbors close by raising it. But, you could also smell his crop, tobacco. There also was the smell of horses. He had sent detailed instructions on what was to go into the stables. He had ordered there be a good mix of the strong old southern lines, to be a core of a good new stable; as well as a few of the general use horses. There was also to be several ponies for Ed and Ali. All the tack was to be of the western variety. He had also had a half dozen of the Texas longhorn cattle, and a few of the western horses, shipped in to remind him of Arizona. He craned his neck a bit to see if he could see them and there they were, in one of the far paddocks.

Frank and Woody were agog at what they were seeing. They had no idea what the old south was like until they saw this house. Now they were mute with amazement. They followed Carl up the stairs to the door which Carl pulled open yelling, "Hello the house," as they stood in the front vestibule. It was a wide room, with a pair of curved stairways up to the second-floor gallery. There was a huge crystal chandelier that hung down from the ceiling two storeys above. Under it was an antique mahogany table, circular. There were a few more chairs and tables by the walls. The kitchen in these houses was below the dining room, and Carl's hello had elicited some action. There was some loud laughing and pounding on a set of stairs at the back as some one raced up them. A large black woman appeared, holding up her skirts as she ran. "Oh, Mr. Carl, it is so good to see you after all this time." She swept over and Carl disappeared in an enormous hug and a cloud of petticoats. When they released, Carl noticed the two little boys standing behind Mama Clarisa. "Are these yours?" he asked.

"Well, in a way, they are my grandsons. I got them when they were four, they are nine and ten now. Their parents did not make it through the war. The taller one is DJ, and the shorter one is CJ. As you directed, we have a little house out back, with 'tricity too, and indoors, you know."

"The house is amazing. I have only seen a bit, but it is exactly as it was before. Right down to the woodwork." Carl then introduced Frank and Woody. "They are a couple of the men from the family security team. The rest are at the train. We need some men and wagons to pick them up. The children will be here tomorrow. They are bringing the boat up to the new dock."

"DJ, CJ, run out to the big barn and tell Clem and Zion to bring two big wagons up to the house. There are people to pick up from the train at the new track." The two boys scooted away. Carl said to Frank and Woody, "Have a seat on the porch until they get here and then go with them to the train and get the stuff. They will be too shy to go without you. When they get here, just get in the wagons and tell them to go to the new track. Talk to them a bit, they will open up as they get to know you. Clem and Zion are Mama Clarisa's sons. Blacks in the south normally say very little around white folks."

When the wagons arrived, they were driven by two tall dark teen black boys, eighteen or nineteen or so. Carl was standing on the porch and they waved at him, grinning broadly. With Frank and Woody aboard, they set off down the avenue between the trees towards the gates at the front. Carl went back inside and up the stairs to the master bedroom. He went in. Even the furniture was like it was before. He sat on the bed and it was almost as if she were there still. He muttered, "Hon, you will be so pleased. They are so big, and so sure of themselves. The two you never got to know are amazing. Watch them closely. I added two, no really three to our little brood. You would have picked them too. But hon, the sex thing, don't be mad at them, or me. It is so different out there now than it was for us. And Mag, he has a wife now, expecting in the spring, likely triplets and he has two already, but that's another storey. This is going to be a happy place again. Hon, I do miss you and it is not getting any easier."

Carl heard the wagons returning and he went back down and met them at the front door. The baggage was unloaded to the front porch and Clem and Zion were released. Carl talked to the detectives. "Take your stuff in and up to the third floor. You all can take the third, for you and the ones on the boat. There are eighteen bedrooms on each floor so there should be more than enough for all of you. You don't have to leave a room for Marcus, we will put him on the second with the boys. There is a kitchen, a staff dining room, and a lounge in the basement and stairs at the back of the house. Get settled, get something to eat, then go for some walks. More than any of the other places, there are lots of outbuildings here that you must get to know. A big barn, a stable, a powerhouse, and some houses for staff, and a whole bunch of little things. Tomorrow morning, we will take a couple of wagons and explore the property. I want to see the boat dock, the tobacco, and the cigarette factory. A word about risks. The rebs hate me because I left before the war."

"They hate me even more now that I have come back and built this up again. That really galls them, that they are poor as mice and I could do this. The other plantation owners hate me. This always was a cotton county and they hate the fact I have tobacco. Then there is how I treat the black people that work for me. There are no slaves now, but there are share croppers, about the same. The black people that work here are employees, not share croppers, and they have good quarters and good pay. A lot of people hate that. Then there is the KKK, and a few old family feuds. If you ever thought you were needed anywhere we lived, you certainly are needed here. You will need patrols 24/7, and you will need to always have arms. If you go into town, you will be shunned, so it is not something to chose to do lightly."

For dinner, Carl went down and ate with the Pinkertons. "Damned if I am going to have dinner at a table for twenty-four by myself. Never thought a man with seven kids could be so lonely. Never should have let them all go on the boat." After dinner, Carl took a tour through the house. There was the dining room above the kitchen with its enormous table. There was a butler's pantry, a smoking room, two large lounges, a man's and a woman's, and a library as well as a plantation office with its own outside entrance and outer office. The telegraph station was in the library. There were two big bathrooms also, one for men and one for women.

The second floor had eighteen bedrooms, a few less than in the original house because each bedroom had its own bathroom now. One of the bedrooms had been set up with an adjoining nursery, for Mag and Mel. The third floor was much like the second, except for the fact every two bedrooms shared a bath, but the baths were a bit bigger. The fourth floor was attic storage. Second floor bedrooms had radiators and fireplaces. Third floor bedrooms had radiators. All the main floor rooms had at least one fireplace, sometimes two, and radiators. The whole house was electrified, and Carl tried out several of the lights and chandeliers. Carl went out on the porch, to have his nightly cigar, and he noted there were yard lights all over the place, also in the staff housing area. He was glad about that. The forces of evil in the south did not like light.

The next morning, he again ate downstairs. Clarisa had called in some extra staff for the kitchen and the bedrooms now that the house was full of people. There were three younger black girls introduced to him, Zelda, Zinia, and Corrie. They would help with the meals and then during the day, the housework. Carl arranged for Clem and Zion to hook up a couple of wagons and drive them around the plantation to see the outer parts. There were about five thousand acres of land being farmed and another 14000 acres of forests, shoreline, a gravel pit, and a rock quarry. Then there were the drying sheds and the cigarette factory. At the factory and the sheds, Carl got out and had a good look. He was glad to see there were about twenty houses built for the staff of the factory, when it was completed and assembled. About half the drying sheds were full and their fans were running to circulate the air and speed the drying. The factory was big, and full of equipment but none of it was assembled. He decided he would have to get at that. When they got to the tobacco fields, Carl was impressed. They seemed to go on forever. There were a couple of crews using different kinds of picking machines. That was where he met the plantation manager for the first time. He was a tall middle-aged Quaker from Pennsylvania, Zeb Klien. You could see he was liked and respected by the men working in the fields, all black, and all living on the estate. He got down and watched each of the two machines work. He talked to the crews and asked for their opinions. The upshot was that the crews had tried five machines and decided three of them were junk but these two worked quite well. They recommended that Carl get a couple more of those. When the tour got to the new dock, Carl again got out and walked along the dock, looking out to sea. Nothing was visible. When he got back in the wagon, he said to CJ and DJ. "Look, here is ten dollars for each of you. Once we get back to the farm, I want the two of you to get Mama to give you a lunch, then the two of you get on that old mule and go down to the dock. When you see a boat, a big boat, big enough to make smoke, one of you get on the old mule and ride to tell me, then you go get Clem and Zion to bring the wagons down. I will have a horse ready and I will ride down. You don't have to wait to see if it is the right boat. There aren't any other boats that will come up here yet, though there will be." The boys were happy with the job and soon set off for the dock.

Carl had a meeting with the Pinkertons. Their headman was saying. "Even with the double allocation, it will be difficult to provide security for the family. It will be impossible for us to provide security for the whole operation. You need your own small private army."

"I saw that today. Soon as Diz gets here, you can wire your boss and get another twelve of your people out here. As for the private army, you have any idea where I can get one of those?"

"Actually sir, I do. Lots of Federal troops are being demobilized, whole units at a time. Why not find a unit of southern men, maybe even Virginians, that fought for the blues? They won't have much to go back to. Bring them in here as your security force, build them a little village for their families, and you solve a couple problems, your security force for your facilities and some friendly neighbors. I understand the demob is being done in Baltimore, that is near here isn't?"

"That is an excellent idea. We can do it down by the docks, and protect them too. The rail spur goes right down there so it will be easy to move the men and materials in. And there is all the timber around for the building. Some of their families can even get jobs in the factory, it is close by. With Diz on the telegraph key I can get that organized in twenty minutes."

Just then DJ came riding up on the mule. "Boat sir, coming up the bay. Carl and Frank grabbed horses that had been saddled and hitched by the porch. Carl called, "Send Clem and Zion with the wagons and a couple carriages, and a few of your men. Now this place will really come to life."

Carl and Frank got to the dock just as the Too was starting to pull alongside. Cark was shocked. There were chips in the paint and there were grazes on the teak decks. The glass in the windows had been shot, but not broken, evidently, it was special type of glass that did not break. The Sea Vista Too had been attacked and Carl fretted whether there had been any casualties. Frank had his gun out and stood with his back to the boat. As soon as the boat was moored, Carl boarded and entered the lounge. Deeds was there, a bandage on his head, and an arm in a sling. Mag was sitting close to Mel, who was clearly upset. Ed saw his father and said, "This was better than fighting the Indians. Good thing we had the trunk on board with the guns."

Carl sat and said, "What happened?."

By this point Marcus had joined them and he started the story. "We were coming through the narrow parts at the end of the spit. I had slowed and all of a sudden there were about ten boats around us. I blew the whistle and asked them to get out of the way, and they yelled back they were not letting any tobacco buyers in, let alone Yankees. The county was cotton, nothing else. I said we were not buyers, just family, the Montroses heading for Oakside, then all hell broke lose. They started firing, I think at first just to scare us, I sped up and forced our way through some of their boats, and I yelled for the boys to get their guns. We are lucky, most of the boat is steel, and the glass is special too. We had lots of fighters on board who could shoot, I don't think they expected that. We got a few nicks, Mag on the leg, Des in his butt, Chuck got one in the leg that might need a doctor. They lost a couple of boats, one drowned I think, and a good dozen and a half winged. We were far better."

"Thank you Marcus. The wagons are here now, so let's get you all and the baggage up to the house. Diz, which arm got shot, the telegraph one or not?"

"No pop, I can still use the key, good as always."

"Good, you are gonna be busy for a couple of hours. The rest of you, I am proud of you, and I will be honest, I am so happy no one got killed here. I could not have abided that. Now let's go. Make sure all of you have your guns, just like back on the ranch. These woods are filled with savages too, only thing is, they are not so easy to recognize."

Carl led the boys outside and saw they all were accommodated in the carriages. He then ordered half the Pinkertons to stay and have the baggage from the Too loaded in the wagons. "Better leave a couple of your people down here on the boat, just until I can arrange for some other men."

Carl rode with the carriages with the family and and some of the detectives up to the house. As they came over the rise on the avenue, there were sharp intakes of breath from several as they saw the house for the first time. Mag and Des remembered it, but Ed and Ali had been too young when they left, and the rest had not seen it. At the house Mama Clarisa was waiting with Zelda, Zinia, and Corrie. She made a big fuss over all the boys, especially Des and Mag who she had helped raise. They both remembered her. The men unloaded the wagons to the porch and the detectives spread out around the house.

Carl said, "Now each of you grab a bag and we will get you to your rooms on the second floor, Marcus, you too, second floor. The girls will bring the rest up to you." At the top of the stairs, Carl said, "This room here is mine, you all settle into the others, there are lots, all with their own baths, get your stuff in your rooms from the hall here. Then come downstairs and you can explore the rest of the house. Des, Mag, Marcus,

Diz and Deeds in the library downstairs in ten minutes. Diz your fingers are going to be sore before you are done."

The boys quickly sorted the rooms out. Ed and Ali shared, and all the rest chose their own rooms. Mag and Mel were pleased with theirs and even more with the nursery where they were glad to be reunited with Imelda, Lou and Les. When Mag went down, Mel was sitting in a rocked singing to the two little ones. Marcus stood in the middle of his room and looked about in wonder. Diz, Des, and Chuck all checked out the views from their windows, their baths, and their closets. They all also checked to see if there was a route they could use at night to climb down from their rooms undetected. The boys met in the hall on their way downstairs as directed by their father. "Nice digs eh," said Marcus.

"Pretty much like it was before we left, except the bathrooms, there were none then," said Des.

"Yes," said Mag, "Isn't it amazing."

The boys joined their father, Deeds, and Werner, the head of the detectives in the library. Carl sat Diz at his telegraph key. "Okay Diz, first to the President of the Grand Trunk Railway, New York, from me, you know the drill. Nod when you are ready." Diz nodded and Carl dictated. "Len, I need a favor. I need a train sited at the depot in Baltimore by eleven tomorrow, and for my use for an indefinite period. The train is to be composed of, an armored engine and tender, a baggage car, four armored coaches, ten box cars, five horse cars, and a caboose. The train will proceed to my spur at Oakside Plantation, Virginia, with the passengers and cargo that will arrive at the station and await directions." The message was sent and acknowledged with a yes sir.

"Now Diz, to the president in the White House. To, from, you know. Message as follows. Mr. President, my family was attacked today on my yacht sailing to my estate, Oakside, Virginia, by a group of rebels and 'seshonists; and barely escaped with their lives. Imperative order be maintained here. Suggest the federal garrison in Oakville be trebled. In addition, am willing to hire a unit of newly demobilized federal troops, preferably Virginians, at my expense, and use them for security at my facilities. Request that you despatch such a unit to a train that will be waiting for them at the depot in Baltimore at eleven tomorrow. Unit should be complete with horses, weapons, ammunition, tents and all necessary provisions. Bill me for all.

Unit should also have a federal warrant so as to preclude interference by local sesh authorities."

"Also request that demobilization sell to me six of the small armed steam coastal cutters, fully manned by demobbed seamen all of which will then be employed by me to guard shipping in and out of Oakside. Seamen too are to have federal warrants for the same reason as stated prior. All costs shall accrue to me and I will employ the seamen." It took about ten minutes, but the White House agreed.

"Now Werner, message your boss in New York and get another twelve men on that train in Baltimore." The message was sent and acknowledged.

"Now Deeds, complete that deal we have been working on with Remington for purchase of 55%. Then instruct them to have twenty cases of their latest repeating rifles, with ammunition, on that train by eleven tomorrow." When that was done, there was another task for Deeds. "Contact that contractor in Baltimore. Tell him to get all his men and equipment on that train tomorrow. He has to return and build a new dock for the cutters, and a settlement at Oakside Landing for all the soldiers, seamen, and their families, about forty houses." That task too was completed.

"Now boys, a couple of things for you. Do not look for or expect to find any friends in the locals. We are hated for the fact we left before the war and prospered during and since. They resent our wealth and you saw today how they would like to deal with us."

"Now, a couple projects. Chuck, I have one for you which you will see in a minute. The rest of you, the cigarette factory, led by Marcus and Des who seem the most mechanical. It is in boxes and has to be assembled and tested. It has to be functioning before we can hire the staff for it. You can start tomorrow, one thing though, none of you can go there unless you have at least six of the detectives with you, and of course your guns."

"Now, let's go see Oakside and let Chuck see what fate awaits him. They toured through the barns and saw they were first rate operations, well designed and staffed. Then they entered the stables. "Chuck, this will be your world."

"Back to the stables dad?"

Carl spun Chuck to face him, "No Chuck, we have grooms and stable boys for that. For this job you use your head and all that knowledge you have of horses. You supervise the breeding and training of the Montrose line, horses for racing and personal use, riding, carriages. In a few years, we want to be known for the best in the south, maybe the country. I have bought the best of the remaining breeding stock in the south."

"Sorry Dad, I shouldn't have said that."

Carl gave Chuck a hug, "Son, I would never send you back to the stables, you do know that, don't you?"

The next morning, Carl had Dizzy man the telegraph station at ten thirty and there were several messages. First, the rifles and ammunition were aboard. Then the message came the contractor was aboard, soon followed by a message that the Pinkertons were on the train. Then the final message came, the cavalry and all their equipment, including horses, were aboard. Departure in ten minutes. Arrival on the siding at Oakside Landing would be at about 2 PM.

"Okay Diz, we are done. What say we go see what is happening at the cigarette factory?" They went to the stables and got horses for the them and the ever present two detectives. Chuck said, "Dad, do you mind if I come with you? I have been looking at blood line charts so long my head is spinning." Carl readily agreed and the five set off for the factory. When they were a quarter mile from it, a shot rang out from the woods and Chuck was knocked from his saddle. The two detectives were off their horses in a flash and into the woods after the ambusher, Diz and Carl knelt over Chuck.

Chuck looked up. "Damnit Dad, the same leg as on the boat and that hasn't healed yet." Carl and Diz were tying a tourniquet just as the other boys arrived from the factory in a buckboard and with guns drawn.

They all loaded Chuck in the buckboard and Carl said, "No two ways about it, we have to take you to town and find a doctor."

Just then the detectives came back with a ten-year old kid, who looked a little the worse for wear after being pursued and cornered by the detectives. "Tie him up and put him in the back beside Chuck, we'll drop him off with the army when we get to town."

On the way, Chuck said to his ambusher, "Why did you shoot me, I never saw you before?"

"You're a Yankee carpetbagger aren't ya?"

"I ain't no Yankee. This is the first time I've been west of the Mississippi in my life."

"And we ain't carpetbaggers. Four of us were born on this land. My mother died and is buried on it, ya dumb kid," said Des.

"And I hope the army shoots you, ties you up to a tree and shoots you, seven times," said Ed.

"Nah," said Ali, "They's gonna hang im, why waste seven bullets."

"I hope they do both," said Chuck, kicking at the kid with his good leg. The boy was considering his two suggested fates and was a bit worried about both of them. As the group entered the town, they saw a house with a doctor's shingle in front of it. They stopped and Chuck's brothers carried him in. The detectives stayed with their captive who was still worrying about whether he was gonna be shot or hung.

Inside the house, a girl about fifteen showed them into the doctor's office and they put Chuck on the doctor's table. She showed the others back to the waiting room and said the doctor would come out as soon as he saw the patient. Then she turned to Chuck. "Looks like you got yourself shot, twice, a couple of days apart. How dumb do you have to be to get yourself shot twice, in the same leg?"

"Well, I didn't do it on purpose. I can't help it this country is full of people who want to shoot me," Chuck said indignantly.

"Suppose, so let's get those clothes off," she said as she pulled his shirt over his head, and his pants down. She threw them over the chair. "Now these," she said as she reached for his underwear and pulled at them to remove them.

"Hey, stop that, the doctor can see the wounds without your removing these too," Chuck exclaimed as he held onto the waist of his drawers to preserve his modesty.

"What, you think I have never seen a man before? They all have the same equipment. You can't mean a girl has never seen you naked before?"

"Yes, no, dammit. Yes, working in a place like this you have probably seen a man before. Yes, they all have pretty much the same equipment, and yes, if you must know, I have been naked with a girl before, but no, you have not seen this equipment, and no I do not wish to show it to you. I don't think it's proper."

At that point the doctor came in and said, "Okay Nan, you can leave now."

"Yes Daddy," as she left.

"She.. she tried to remove my clothes, all of them," sputtered Chuck.

"I know, that's her thing. You should feel complimented, she only tries that with the cute ones, the ones she likes. You would be surprised at how many handsome young men come in here with a sore throat and end up sitting there naked, on my table."

"Jesus doc, that ain't proper, is it?"

"Probably not, but if I was your age, I would find it kinda exciting. Now tell me about the leg. Looks like two wounds a day or so apart." Chuck explained.

"Son, I'd say you are either lucky or a cat, and if you are a cat you only got seven left, and if it was luck, a person only has so much luck, and I would recommend against any further gun fights. Now, this is gonna hurt, but I got two bullets to get out of you."

About twenty minutes later the doctor came out. "Mr. Montrose? I am Dr. Stephen Fellers. Actually, your son is lucky he got shot today. If he hadn't, he likely wouldn't have come in and he would have died from the first wound where the bullet was left in. A couple of your other sons can go in, help dress him and help him out."

Carl nodded to Des and Marcus, then he said, "Thankyou doc, we were lucky you were free to deal with him."

"Sir, I am usually free. I doctored for the north in the war and this is a southern town. I don't get much business."

"We are going to be living here now, at least for most of the year, and I have six boys. I am sure we will be bringing you a lot of business. Thanks again," and he handed the doctor a hundred-dollar bill as he opened the door for his sons to exit."

As his brothers settled him back in the buckboard Chuck winced and said, "I hope they shoot you but they don't kill you, and that they go in and get their bullets so they can use them again, on you." The ambusher paled a bit at the thought. The group left in search of the army. A bit further down the road they came to a compound where there was a US flag waving in the wind. They all pulled in and Carl went in a door that said Commandant. It was a small room with two people, a clerk and a captain. The sign on his desk said Capt. H. Green.

"Captain Green, I am Carl Montrose."

"The same Montrose that got my unit multiplied by four?"

"Probably. My family was attacked, and I was mad. I am friends with the President, and I suggested if you had four times the men, you then could root out the rebs."

"That didn't make my job any easier. Now they will expect me to do that. You probably expect me to go after the men who attacked your family."

"Me? No. I bought myself a troop of cavalry and half a dozed de-175mobbed patrol boats. I want them to come after us again, and they will be slaughtered. No one plays with the Montroses. I will deal with them."

"You know, you can't take the law into your own hands."

"All my men have federal warrants, just like yours."

"So then, why are you here?"

Carl beckoned him over to the window and said, "That kid there took a shot at us, wounded my son. We have just been at the doctor to get the bullet removed. Thought we could turn him over to you."

"I thought you said you took care of your own problems. If I take him, I got two choices; shoot him, or let him go, and given he is ten you know which one it will be. You deal with him, if anyone asks, I never saw him. Shoot him, hang him, up to you. No one cares about him. His dad was a reb, killed in the war. He had a mom, but she died a year ago. He just hangs around town on the streets. Every once in a while, someone gives him a meal. Name is Tully Devers."

Carl said, "Fine," and slammed out of the office. He returned to the wagon and mounted his horse saying, "Captain says we can look after it ourselves, whatever we want. His name is Tully. Back to Oakside."

That started the debate among the boys over what to do with Tully. Carl listened as he rode beside the buckboard.

Chuck said, "I vote we take him up to the attic and throw him out the fourth floor window."

"How about we drench him in chicken blood and throw him in the hog pen?"

"Why don't we use some of the tricks we learned from the Indians?"

"Yeah, tie him to a wagon wheel and roast him over a fire."

"No, scalp him."

"I got a better one. Remember how they cut the little slits all over the body and let them bleed to death over five or six hours, screaming."

"You remember how they stopped the screams. They cut them off and stuffed them in the mouth."

Ed looked at Tully, "He's kinds puny. I don't think he would live through many of them, just maybe three."

Tully had been listening to all of this and said, "Look guys, I never meant to shoot anyone, just shoot at you. I am just a poor shot. First time I shot a gun. I went in the woods searching for rabbits for something to eat. You came by and I just reacted to the talk in town." By this point they were back at the house. Carl told Des and Marcus to help Chuck in, take him to the dining room and make him comfortable. It's almost noon." Then he grabbed Tully by the scruff of his neck and urged him towards the house. "No, No, I don't want to be thrown out of the attic, and I don't want to be fed to the hogs, and I certainly don't want them cut off and stuffed in my mouth, no, stop."

Carl dragged Tully up the steps with Tully's feet only touching two steps of the eight. The boys followed, looking at each other and grinning. Carl dragged Tully into the library. Slamming the door behind him. He undid the ropes then sat, pulling Tully over his knee and pulling down his drawers all in one motion. "Now, young man. You have to learn some lessons from this. You never aim a gun at someone unless you really mean to kill him. Guns are not toys. People hurt when they get shot." Carl then administered fifteen very sharp slaps to Tully's bottom. The boys sitting in the dining room waiting for lunch winced at every sound slap. Chuck however felt increasingly satisfied. When he was done, Carl stood Tully on his feet. "Pull up your pants son," he said as he stood and strode from the room to the dining room. A few minutes later Tully followed and stopped in the doorway.

"What do I do now?" he asked.

"Way I see it, you have two choices, you can run out that door and go back to living in the woods or where ever, or you can come and have some lunch."

Tully looked at the door, which was open, just with the screen on the outside. He could be gone in five seconds. Then he looked at the table with all the boys around it, looking at him, and he said, "I think I would like to have some lunch."

"Okay then, there is a space between Des and Ed, come join us."

Tully came up to the table then he said, "Is it okay if I stand?"

Des said, "Sure thing kid, been there," and he reached down and pulled the chair out of the way so Tully could take his place at the table. As lunch finished, Carl said, "Tully, since you got Chuck in the position he is, I think you should be his fetcher until he can get around again on his own, don't you?"

After lunch, Des and Marcus helped Chuck to a seat on a couch in the lounge. They helped him bring his legs up so he could lie down. Tully came and sat on the floor beside him, legs crossed, head resting on his folded hands waiting to be needed. Chuck closed his eyes. Ten minutes later, he opened his eyes to find Tully sitting in the exact same spot watching him. Chuck said, "Christ kid, I feel like a mouse being watched by a cat. Why don't you go sit on the porch for a bit while I sleep for a couple of hours?"

Tully was standing on the stairs when Carl, the boys, and some of the Pinkertons came around the side of the house on horses. They stopped, and Carl urged his horse forward. "Tully, where's Chuck?"

"He's having a nap on the couch. He said I was making him nervous just sitting there watching him in case he needed something. Told me to come out here while he had a sleep for a couple of hours."

"That's okay then. Here, give me your hand. You can come with us. We are just meeting a train." Carl reached down and drew Tully up into the saddle in front of him. It amazed Tully at how easily he had done that and somehow he felt more secure at that moment than he had for many years.

The spur at Oakside had been set up so that there was a space closer to the house where the private car was parked, and then the spur went by the factory to the dock area. The engineer was instructed that on this day he could deliver the whole load to the dock area. Carl had chosen this because there were large clear areas where the crews could set up camp, and also due to the fact that the army unit could provide security for the contractor. It did mean they had a couple of wagons with them for the new detectives to get their baggage back up to the house.

When they got to Oakside Landing, as it would be called, the train was not there yet, but they could hear that it was coming and there was some smoke visible over the trees so they dismounted, tethered the horses and waited. All of Carl's boys were armed. They wandered down to the dock and the boat, looking at some of the damage. Carl thought to himself that was something else he had to see to.

Just then the first of the train cars appeared from the woods. The train had been re-arranged and the engine was pushing the cars in. The boxcars arrived first, followed by the passenger cars, then the baggage car, the caboose and the engine. The train crew would drop the others and leave with the caboose. Carl stood to the side and waited for those in charge to approach. The Pinkerton chief approached him first and was told to load his men and their baggage in the wagon then go and join the others at the house. "But, make sure you take one of the crates of the new rifles from the baggage car." The next was the engineer. "I see why you ordered the armored engine. Several people took pot shots at us in the last twenty miles or so. Now, we will drop these, and I will head out. No hurry to get them picked up is there?"

"No they can stay until things quiet down a bit. You all be careful on your way out."

Next to approach him was the contractor, Drew Sanderson. "My father-in-law sent me out with the crews. He just had a heart attack, probably due to when he was out here the first time. So, what are we up to now?"

"I shall have the army set up their camp over in the large clearing and you should set up over there too. Part of their job is to protect you. You are building a village here, Oakside Landing. Lay it out as you see fit, water and sewer and with full electric. Each house is to have an indoor washroom. Total houses fifty, plus a main street, a hotel, two general stores, room for maybe ten other stores with living quarters above them, couple of restaurants. A church, a school, a bank, a saloon, and a jail. And a town office. Leave some slots in the main street for fill in. The houses are to be three bedrooms, master on main and two kid's rooms above. Sidewalks on the main street. There will have to be a livery, a big one to handle the army and the general population, several pens. Then there is another dock, nothing like that one. Make it six slips, against the shore, boats 20 or 25 feet long, those armored patrol vessels that were everywhere in the war. They only need a draft of about ten feet. Do it ASAP because the town is for those guys camping in the field with you. Cut down the trees you need here and mill them for lumber, and there will have to be a road cut out to the nearest one. Also, the captain of the cavalry may have you build a few concealed firing positions. And then, before you leave, over by the cigarette factory, clear the land and mill the trees, just stack the wood. I expect we will call you back to build a couple of other factories when we are sure what they will be."

"Okay, got the idea. Will put a crew on the dock first, then the houses, with a hotel and a restaurant. Sort of phase it because you don't need all the businesses til you have the people."

After he left, a captain and a lieutenant came up to Carl. "You Mr. Montrose, Carl? Captain Fassert and Grady. You have some pull Mr..., we went through Demob in less than an hour and were told we were hired as a group and sent here with all our gear. So, what's the story?"

"I needed a private army and you are it. I will hire all of the men and you, army pay times five. That contractor there is going to build a village here, and each of my employees shall get free use of one of the houses so they can bring their family from where ever. I asked for mainly Virginians who fought for the north, thought they might find it easier to relocate here."

"The job is to protect the estate, about twenty thousand acres, fields, tobacco processing, cigarette factory, and the house; although there is a large group of Pinkertons assigned to the personal security of the family. There also will be regular shipments of tobacco from that pier that will have to be protected in and out of the bay. If your hometown is anything like our nearest town, Oakville; you guys probably don't have a friendly place to go to. As much as anything else, this will be a chance to build a little bit of the New South."

"It all started when we moved here. I came by train, the family by that boat there. It was attacked by a bunch of Rebs out there in the bay. They fought them off. The locals see me as a Yankee carpetbagger I hear. I lived here before the war and left before it started. The locals resent that, and above all they resent the fact I was able to come back after the war with enough money to buy back the property and rebuild it all. The other plantation owners resent the fact I am going with tobacco. This was a cotton county before. The local feds seem afraid to do anything. Now, when I got you guys, I had the president extend your warrants. We won't have any problems with local kangaroo courts. There also are a half dozen or so armored patrol boats due tomorrow. Their crews and families will share the village with you. Any of you, or from the families, who wants to work in the cigarette factory will be given preference. It is just being assembled now. So, when this place quiets down you still will have jobs, and if any of your men are craftsmen, there will be places in the operation for them too. You guys won't have to be an army forever. There is lots of evil out there, not the least of which is the KKK, and we likely will have to face them all down before this is done, but then I think this will be a real nice place to live. So, talk it over with the guys. If any of them want to leave, I will give them two weeks pay, at my rate, and their horse, for their trouble. One last thing, there are several crates of the newest Remington rifles in the baggage car. Give them out to your best men."

"Okay then, we will set up camp, and we will look after our contractor friends tonight. Then I will talk to the boys and let you know what the decision is tomorrow," said Captain Fassert.

"I'll be over tomorrow to meet the boats," said Carl. "Leave you all to it then."

Carl gathered his sons, and the detectives, and they all headed back to Oakside. Once again, Tully was with him. When they got to the house and the horses were turned over to the grooms, Carl reached up and pulled Tully down from the horse, tucking him under his arm.

"Tully, we have been particularly close for the last couple of hours, and boy there is something you need badly."

"No, not another whuppin. I ain't done nothing."

The other boys were following up the stairs and they were grinning.

"No Tully, you have been very well behaved today and I noticed. You should learn, spankings are fairly rare around here, and if you do get one, you really deserve it." By this point he was turning into his room and then into the bathroom. "No Tully, you need a bath. When was the last time you had a bath?" Carl asked as he set Tully down on the floor.

"A real bath? Like in a tub? That was before my mother died, a year and a half ago. I had swims in the summer though."

"Tully, it's fall. You really were going to go to next summer before you had a bath again?"

"Well, I guess so, less it rained."

Carl had turned on the tub and was mixing the water, hot and cold. He poured in some bubble soap and threw in a couple of washcloths. Then he turned to Tully, "Well, you have to take your clothes off, what are you waiting for?"

"I usually don't take off my clothes in front of other people."

"Tully, that is a good rule, will keep you out of trouble, but in case you hadn't noticed, this house is full of boys, all ages, and they all come equipped pretty much the same way, besides, a couple hours ago I gave you a spankin' and saw it all. Get in the tub boy."

A few minutes later, Tully was sitting in a tub of hot soapy water almost up to his neck. "One last thing, really two, see this clock. You can't get out of that tub til this big hand here on the four gets up there to the twelve. When that happens, there are towels over there. I'll see what I can come up with for clean clothes." Carl then reached over, put his hand on top of the boy's head, then pushed him under, holding him there for ten or fifteen seconds. Tully came up sputtering, "Hey, what was that for?"

"Tully, a bath means all of you, including your hair and behind your ears. Do it right, you don't want me to put you back in there and get a scrub brush."

Carl went down stairs to the lounge where the boys were sitting. "He's in the bath, for forty-five minutes. We as a family have to talk. What should we do with him?"

Des said, "Dad, we know what you want to do with the little assassin, just tell us his story."

"His father was a reb, killed in the war. His mother died a year and a half ago. Since then he was on the street alone, living in abandoned houses. Every once in a while, some one gave him something to eat. The last bath he had was a year and a half ago before his mother died, apart from the occasional swim, or perhaps a rain."

"Okay dad, what do you want to do?" said Mag quietly.

"This reminds me, I have been lax with some of you. I think of all of you as my sons, that included Diz, Chuck, and you Marcus. I want to know if all of you would be okay with making that formal, adoptions and name changes, and a place in the will. Frankly, I would like to include Tully. He isn't a bad kid, he just needs a family."

Chuck said, "I am the one to have the most against him, but I sort of like him too. He is a bit rough by our standards now but we all can work at that, and I would love to formally be a Montrose, dad."

Mag added, "I think the kid needs a chance, I am just glad you don't want me and Mel to take him on. We are gonna have somewhere between three and five kids soon."

Des looked at his brother, "Five, man you are a glutton for punishment. I don't care if you are married, if the result is multiples you better put a cork in it, but, with Tully, sure, give him a chance."

Everybody looked at Marcus, "I am surprised you even want my opinion and I am flattered to be considered a brother. I would like to have a family again, which is how I would think Tully feels. So sure, take him in."

"I know how relieved I was when you took me in, away from where I was. I loved being one of the brothers, and how it was us against the world. Give Tully a chance," said Diz.

Then attention turned to Ed and Ali. "You mean we have a say? Someone is interested in our opinion?" said Ed.

"You all know this will affect us the most. We are the same age. He will hang out with us. In fact, dad, I bet you are about to ask us to get him something to wear."

Carl nodded, "I was. But there is another option. We can send him to Sally and Brent in DC to be a bellman."

Ed said, "Aw gee Dad, the old guilt trip? We know when you do that."

"It works doesn't it?"

Ali answered, "Yes it does dammit. We all vote yes.

A few minutes later Tully appeared in the doorway, wrapped in a large fluffy towel. He had stopped on the stairs and heard part of the conversation. Carl invited him over beside him. "Tully, we have all talked. We all want you to join the family, totally, name change, everything. Would you like that?"

Tully burst into tears. "I can't, I don't deserve it. There is something I haven't told you, that I should have but I didn't know you."

"What is it Tully?" asked Carl gently.

"You know how I said I heard things in town. People talked and just ignored me, as if I wasn't there. In the bath, while I lay there thinking, that was when I decided I should tell you."

"What is it Tull," prodded Carl.

"They are gonna attack tonight, the KKK. I heard them talking. They want to burn the tobacco, the drying sheds, and most of all the houses you have for the people working for you, and they want to chase your people away. I heard them a couple of days ago. That's where I got the idea, I should be against you too. I'm sorry for not telling you sooner."

"It's okay Tully, you are just getting to know us. Now Ed and Ali will take you up to their room and find you something to wear."

As the three boys went up the stairs the rest of them heard, "You know Tully, we have these knickers with these shirts you might like."

"Des, can you get a horse and ride over to the dock? Tell that Captain that I need to see him right away, here, in the study. Marcus, can you run upstairs and tell the Pinkerton head I need to see him in the study now, and Diz, get that telegraph whipped up. I need to talk to that fool captain in town." Then Carl turned to Mag, "Looks like we go to war again, son."

The two stood and headed for the study, as did Deeds who had sat there quietly during the last conversation. Carl said, "Go ahead with the legal steps, for all four, Tully, Marcus, Dizzy, and Chuck. Do it in New York, or Washington, not here in the south."

With the detective head and the Captain present, Carl went over what he knew of the KKKs plans. He pointed to a map of the estate. "If they want the fields and the drying sheds, they will have to split their forces. There is only one place where they can access the fields from a public road, here. You can't get to the sheds from there, so a second force will have to attack from here too. Now, if they also want to attack the hands, burn their houses and drive them away too, they could carry on from the sheds, but more likely they will take a third force down this little lane and attack from back here. They need all three targets. They want to stop the tobacco farming, and above all they resent the fact my hands are living better than they are. They like to wait until late, to make sure their victims are in bed. I will move my people into the basement of this house, but have them leave some lights on low. In the south you cannot have the blacks involved in a shoot out with the whites. The blacks get hung. No, we will let them get in there with their torches and open fire from the trees and the attic of the house. With three teams of detectives we can handle that. You and your men Captain, you deal with the raid on the fields, and on the sheds. I will let you devise your own strategy. Now, all of you, we don't want a slaughter out there, but we want them badly hurt. Let's try for arms and legs, not heads and guts. Dizzy, telegraph this message to that fool Captain in town. 'Hear there are going to be raids on Oakside tonight. Suggest you have men on all the roads to apprehend all the fleeing attackers on their way back to town, likely a little after midnight. Montrose.'"

At the dinner table that night, the boys were quiet, anticipating the events to come. Carl had talked to them and told them this was not like with the Apache. Unless someone was directly attacking them, they were to shoot to wound, not kill. That was an added responsibility.

They sat around the table eating quietly. Suddenly Chuck said, "Damn, I forgot my diagram in the lounge. I wanted to study it as I ate."

Carl looked at Tully who said, "Just a minute Chuck, I'll be right back." And he was off like a shot. The others grinned. A few seconds later, Tully handed the diagram to Chuck who said, "Thankyou Tull." Tully beamed, making all of them feel a bit better...

They took up their positions a little after ten. There were Pinkertons sprinkled in the woods around the houses and in the shadows by the mansion, front and back. Carl's farmhands were in the basement with the lights down low. Carl and the boys were on the third floor and in the attic, looking down over the group of little houses. They all had new repeating rifles, as well as their older ones. They also had their revolvers and several of the preloaded cylinders to slip in.

Tully looked at all this and said, "Gee, you guys are really ready for this." Carl said, "Tully, you never want it to come to this, and you try to avoid it, but, if it does, you want to win."

They waited quietly and at last about eleven they could see white blurs on the far side of the clearing. Finally, there was a signal and the shadows became brilliant white as about two dozen torches were lit. One of the figures carried a cross which was also lit. The line advanced toward the houses chanting, "Out, Out, Out."

When the line was well out into the clearing, Carl fired the first shot and that set all the others off. The Klansmen were fired on from all directions, and above too. Most of them were soon limping or crawling back into the darkness, some helping others. As per directions, the firing stopped and the men were allowed to escape, knowing that if it had been desired, they all could have been killed.

Carl said to the boys, "Good work, no corpses, just a lot of men who will be limping for a long time. Now, let's go down and have a snack then go to bed. The detectives will keep watch tonight in case anyone wants to take this further."

After a quick meal, two of his brothers helped Chuck upstairs, into the washroom, and to bed; then they left. A few minutes later, Tully came in wearing one of those long frilly shirts. Chuck looked at him and said, "Did Ed and Ali give you that shirt? You go right back to them and tell them I said to give you the proper under-alls."

A few minutes later, Tully was back with the proper clothing, but with a rabbit. Chuck looked at him and it. Tully said, "I thought it was stupid, but they said da...Carl, expected children to take animals to bed until they were twelve. They both had bears. Now, where do you want me to sleep in case you need anything overnight?"

Chuck threw him a pillow, a blanket, and said, "You can use that couch over there. Now, turn off the light." The light went off and Chuck heard Tully settle himself on the sofa. But, there was the sound of constant tossing and turning from the direction of the sofa. Finally, Chuck said, "Tully, what's the problem over there? You are making it hard to sleep."

"Sorry, this sofa is horsehair, and it's itchy. Hard to fall asleep."

There was a pause, then Chuck said, "Okay Tully, come over here and crawl in with me." He held up the covers and his new brother crawled in with him. Chuck put his arm out and helped the smaller boy curl up beside him. "It's okay Tull. You are my brother and you should sleep soundly now."

The next morning, Carl was up early, ready to receive a report from the captain. He glanced into Chuck's room before he went down and saw the two snuggled together, and believe it or not, there was a rabbit too. Carl thought to himself, "Well Tull, looks like you made a direct hit on another heart. Two down, five to go."

The Captain gave his report to Carl and Deeds, in the library over a cup of coffee. "You were right. They split into two groups, about fifteen in a group."

Deeds commented, "You had thirty, we had twenty-four. That's almost sixty men, significant opposition."

"The men at the tobacco field seemed to be older men. They lit their torches and then hesitated a bit. As soon as they made to light the field, we opened fire. We could have killed them all, those new rifles are amazing. We shot to wound, and we let the wounded ones get away. From what I could see, there may have been one killed at the tobacco field."

"They were likely the other farmers. They would be older, and they would be reluctant to fire another man's crop."

"At the drying sheds, it was a bit different. The men seemed younger, they were more excited and running around. When they started to fire the sheds, we opened fire. Some of them had pistols and fired back. They took casualties there, I'd say maybe six or seven. When they fled, we let them go."

Carl said, "Casualties about ten percent. Not bad when compared to the rates in the war. However, these men are at home. They have mothers and wives who are gonna tear a strip off them for going out, doing stuff like this, and risking getting killed in what is not even a war, so maybe our sixty is pared down to forty. Now Captain, what was the decision of the men? How many did we lose.?"

"We started with two officers and twenty-four men. We lost two but they asked if they could stay in the village at the landing. One was a parson before the war and said that since he was no longer fighting for his country he would rather not. The other one offered to run the livery. He just wants to get on with his life with his wife and kids. The rest were eager to go on. They see a future here though, and like the idea of bringing their families here to them. All of the men, including the two, took part last night."

"Tell the parson we are building a church and it will have a parsonage for him, and tell the other one he can run the livery and have the house closest to it. They both sound like good men, the type we need if we are going to prosper here. Now, are you okay to proceed with the twenty-two or do you want to try to replace them?"

"We will go on as we are. We trust each other, that is the most important."

"Good, the boats will arrive today, and I expect the next action will be on that front. I will be over later to meet them. Now, you take care over there. They are mad and want revenge, and I can see them putting snipers in the woods. I would not be gentle with snipers."

Carl and the boys went over to the landing after lunch so as to be there for the arrival of the patrol boats. They first went down to where the new docks were. The area on the land by the docks had been cleared back for about fifty feet and a series of small buildings had been constructed. The docks were not all side by side in a row but spread out over a large section of the shoreline. Carl questioned the contractor about this. "Why is everything spread out like this? Wouldn't it be more efficient to have it all together?"

"The Captain pointed out to me that it might be more efficient but it all could be taken out by one person with a bomb in the right place. That's why we spread it all out like this, for security."

"That's good, the Captain is right. Continue to listen to him, he is the professional in all this." The new docks were finished even down to the cleats the boats would be tied to. When the boats rounded the point to the north, several of the contractor's men waved them in. There were six boats and six slips finished. The boats fit almost exactly.

When the boats were tied up, some of the men disembarked and gathered around some of the soldiers on the docks. The soldiers pointed to

Carl and the Captain and six of the men walked over. One stepped forward and five stayed back a bit. "You Montrose?" asked the one who was a bit forward. "I am Captain Dan, Dan Bevers. They put our squadron through demob in an hour and then told us we had a job to deliver the boats to you, and a job with you if we want it."

"That's right Dan, at five times your current pay. And, each of you can have one of these new houses to bring your family to. The captain brought 24 men with him and 22 have taken the offer. The other two will settle here too, one as a parson and one running the livery. I recently moved back here from the north, and I have a lot of opposition. Sixty KKK's attacked the estate last night. The captain's men and my Pinkertons drove them off. We showed them mercy last night because they were attacking property, but we wounded almost all of them. My idea was that some of the men's families would rein them in. Further opposition will not be shown that mercy. They will be out to kill us, and we will act accordingly. You see the yacht there. My family was on it and they attacked. Luckily, they were able to fight the attackers off."

"The opposition is rebs and KKK. They hate me because I left before the war, returned after it with enough money to rebuild this place, have hired many of my old workers back and pay them a good wage and give them decent lodgings. On top of that, I planted tobacco, rather than cotton. I have sold ninety percent of that crop to English interests and ships will soon start arriving to get the crop. It will be the job of you and your men to protect them, meet them out there and escort them in, and then escort the fully loaded ships out to safety."

"I have chosen to build a new settlement here at the landing because I think you will find Oakville, the nearest town, is as unfriendly to people who fought for the north, as any other southern town. I asked for Virginians in the hope they might find it easier to move here."

"Now, take the information to your men and discuss all this Let me know the decision. If your men decide to leave, I can likely get a train in here to take them back to Baltimore. There will be trains bringing materials for the town. If some don't want to fight, but would like to stay, let me know what skills they offer, and I will consider their request."

Dan returned to the boats and the seamen gathered around. There was a lengthy discussion then Dan returned to Carl and the captain. "There are six boats, four men per boat, and we have one extra crew; a total of 27 men.

Two of the sailors would like to stop fighting. One of them is a baker and would like to know if your new town would like one. The other is a factory superintendent. One of the soldiers told him you were starting a factory, thought you might need him. So, you have six fully staffed boats."

"Thank you Dan. Tell the baker to talk to the head contractor and tell him I said to get him a shop with some ovens, I think all of you would like some fresh bread. Tell the factory man I will use him, and the boys will come find him shortly. They are the ones struggling with the machines. The army here will find your men a few tents until the houses are ready. All you men can decide among yourselves which families will get the first houses. I am sure some of the single men can share houses to get out of the tents. I will give you the rest of the day to settle and I will come back tomorrow to make a plan. The boats from England will stop in New York first. I thought we could send the shipping agent a series of co-ordinates out there where we could meet them and bring them in, something like that, and we can use the yacht too. Fill it up with soldiers. Everybody, get settled."

Carl gathered the boys and they headed back to Oakside, with the ever-present detectives. They had left Tully to fetch for Chuck, and when they went in the two were sitting on a sofa laughing. Chuck looked up when the others came in and said, "Good, you guys are back. As a family we have a job to do. We have to take Tully in hand. He doesn't know anything. He can't read, or write, or do sums. He has never ridden a horse. The time he shot me was the first time he had a gun, and we saw how well that went. Rather than playing games with him with shirts and rabbits, we have to pull together and get him shaped up."

Tully said softly, "I like the rabbit, first toy I ever had."

That got the attention of everyone. Carl motioned Diz into the library. "Send a wire to that gunsmith in Tucson. We want another set of double holsters as soon as possible. Tell him to take them to the hotel and they will send them to me by train. Send a wire to the Peters and tell them to rush me a complete western wardrobe for a ten-year-old boy, including a hat, and to include an assortment of toys, games, and books. Send it on the first train." Diz was grinning as he worked the telegraph key. Back in the lounge the boys were splitting the tasks up. Ed and Ali said they would do the shooting and riding. Des said he would do the reading, writing and sums. Marcus said he would show Tully how to steer the yacht and to use charts and maps to navigate. When Dizzy came in later, he said he would show Tull how to send and receive on the telegraph. Carl said, "I guess I get to teach him manners and table etiquette."

Tully said, "Guys, remember I am only ten. My head might explode with all of that."

The next week was a busy one. Carl met with the sailors and they worked out a set of meeting places for the boats, which was sent to New York and the shipping agents. Carl introduced Marcus to Captain Bevers so they could discuss tactics for the use of the yacht. The cavalry men shot and killed three snipers in the woods by the settlement, all before they got off a shot. That seemed to dissuade any others. The village at the landing came along quickly and some of the new residents managed to make arrangement for bringing their families in the following week through Baltimore and the supply trains that were coming in twice a day. The railcars on the siding were being switched frequently. The cavalry men were patrolling Oakside on a regular basis. The boys helped Des to uncrate the whole cigarette factory and the factory manager got involved in the set up. By the end of the first week, the pieces of a cigarette factory were in at least the right order. A shed was constructed at the landing large enough to hold a full shipment of tobacco, and it was filled ready for the first ship.

By the end of the first week too, someone seemed to always be teaching Tully something. Chuck was getting around on his own and he brought up the idea with Tully of the need to get him a permanent room of his own. The need became all the more pressing when the shipment of items for Tully arrived from the west. There seemed to be enough to fill half a boxcar, let alone a room. His pistols arrived at the same time, and his own small horse from the ranch, along with several spares, as the population of Oakside had increased so dramatically. Tully was shocked into silence as it all was loaded into the room he had chosen, beside Chuck's. When Tully came downstairs wearing cowboy boots, his holsters and a cowboy hat; he got a round of applause. The family was pulling together to make Tully a part of it.

The night after everything arrived, while he was curled up beside Chuck in bed, Tully said, "Chuck, now that I have a room full of stuff I guess I will have to start using it, but you won't mind if I come in here with you once in a while will you? I like these times at night when we talk, before we fall asleep."

"No Tull, I won't mind. You are welcome here anytime at all. I like these times too."

Finally, it was time for the first tobacco shipment. Carl took all the boys down to the yacht. It would go far out to sea and get the cargo ship. The gunboats would surround the two as they came in to the landing. In addition to Carl and the boys, there were twelve cavalry men on board all out of sight...

The gunboats were all steam, made a racket, and a lot of smoke. Anybody watching the landing knew when they started to make steam. When the yacht did the same it was clear something was up. The southerners made their own preparations. The meet up was set for 11:00. At ten, the yacht pulled away from the dock and idled just offshore as it waited for the patrol boats to join it, then the little flotilla set off down the bay. At a certain point the little boats left the yacht and just milled around in a circle while the yacht headed directly out to sea. An hour later it was back with a large steam packet following it, and the patrol boats formed a circle around the larger boats. The whole little flotilla headed for the dock. That was when the southerners attacked, from all directions and in all types of boats, from dinghies to larger steam fishing trawlers. The patrol boats had small cannons and immediately began using them. The shutters on the yacht were dropped to form firing positions and all the riflemen opened up, as well as shooters on the patrol boats. Marcus found a small steam yacht crossing his beam and he ran her down. The engagement lasted for about fifteen minutes with about two thirds of the southerners destroyed. Carl gave a couple toots of the whistle on the yacht, and the remaining rebel craft were allowed to pick up a few survivors and flee. There were no injuries on Carl's craft, and they all tied up in appropriate spaces at the Landing docks. At the end, shortly afterwards, Carl was wandering around the Too, finding and bemoaning new blemishes. He ran into one of the cavalrymen doing the same.

"I, and a few friends, used to work in a shipyard, making yachts like these. We all went to war. This is a shame; she is a beautiful boat."

"Why don't you write any of those friends that are left. I am willing to give you a piece of land on the bay here so you can start a new shipyard, and you have your first commission right here. We want to take her south around Christmas, to Florida and into the Gulf, and I can't do that when she is looking like this."

"I'd like that sir. All this nonsense has to end sometime, doesn't it?"

"I sure hope so. You pick out a spot, and get your friends together. Plan, then come talk to me, just make sure that any new people you want to bring here, to the landing, will fit in here. The village is blue, and I want to keep it that way."

Then Carl left the yacht and crossed the pier to the freighter. The captain was on deck and Carl asked, "So? Everything okay? Anybody get hurt?"

"No, we did as you told us, battened down the hatches, closed the storm shutters, and followed you in. That's the beauty of these steel ships. Now, I have to look at the tobacco before we start loading it. It shouldn't take us long, what with your equipment and ours."

The two went across the docks to the tobacco warehouse, and the quality of the tobacco was inspected. The captain was satisfied, and the loading began. As they were finishing, the Captain said, "Can we leave tonight? We can load in an hour. There is still enough light to get through the bay and into the ocean. Do it as fast as we can. The freighter and the yacht both have speed."

Carl said, "It might be an idea. The opposition won't expect that. Let's go talk to the other captains, Fassert, Bevers and Marcus. The other two agreed it was a good idea, but Captain Fassert had a caution. "If we do it that way, you have to understand one thing. We can likely get the freighter out almost by surprise, but coming back in, all the opposition would be centered on the yacht. Marcus had a suggestion. "How about, the two of us slip out, and after we are gone, you start getting yours ready to sail. I'll take the freighter about a half hour out then turn back. By that point you should be out in the bay and I'll bring the yacht in fast. Make a run for you. Just make sure you leave a space for me to get through."

That was the agreed to plan. The cavalry men went back to the yacht in twos and threes so as not to tip off any watchers. The gunboats loaded their wood so as to be ready and the rest of the cavalrymen were close to the dock, ready to board the gunboats when they were ready. The tobacco bales proceeded down the dock at a steady clip. Clem and Zion had come over to do that and the hoists on the ship as well as the electric hoists on the dock worked together efficiently. Mama Clarisa had sent over several boxes of sandwiches and fruit for the boys on the boat and by 5:30 everything was ready. There were a few bales of tobacco on the dock, looking like they were waiting, but when the boat was gone, they would be moved back. Carl and the three captains met for a moment and Carl said, "Let's go."

It took five minutes then the Too eased away from her dock, and a minute later the freighter was away to. The yacht led the freighter out at full speed, and they were well away from shore before the opposition was out in the bay, but out they were swarming like angry hornets, although not as many as there were that morning. When they detected the smudge on the horizon to warn of the returning raider, the patrol boats formed a picket and moved down the bay. Marcus had gone to full speed and the yacht knifed through the water. The Southerners tried to move in on it, but the patrol boats opened up with their cannons. The gunfire from the yacht was also directed at the attackers. The picket opened a space and Marcus turned for it, catching two of the opposition off guard and running right over them. Marcus went through the space and the picket closed. The opposition got the point, and faded away. The others returned to their docks at Oakside Landing. Carl and the three captains were standing on the dock when the fireman staggered up from below on the Too. He reeled up to Marcus, "Hey boss, I thought you wuz going to fire me and send me home?"

Carl went over and said, "I understand, we have worked you hard, so how's this. I understand you are a cabinet maker and have a family. When this is all done, we will give you a shop in the village center and a house for your family so you can ply your trade, and one more thing, you can have tonight off, we will have someone else fill the coal bunkers on the Too."

Just then Des and Dizzy came out with Chuck between them. Carl said, "Chuck, not again."

"Dad, can't believe it, same leg again. Dammit ."

"Okay guys, get him up to one of the wagons and we will go see Doctor Fellers again. He sent the other boys back and said he and Des could help Chuck into the doctors. The Pinkertons were split between the two parties. When they got to the doctors, Carl and Des helped him in and onto the table. Then Carl went out the door in search of the doctor as Nan came in. Chuck whispered to Des, "Don't leave me alone with her, all she wants to do is take my clothes off."

Des glanced at Nan, then leaned down and whispered, "What are you complaining of, she's good looking and she is getting half the job done for you. Now the two of you can work at getting her clothes off." Nan was getting something out of the cupboard, but she heard the conversation and smiled. As Des left the room, he winked at her and she smiled back. Then she approached Chuck on the table.

"Well, you're back, shot again, in the same leg. Won't you ever learn? Well, better get you out of those clothes. She helped him off with the shirt and the pants. Then she reached for his under-alls, and this time Chuck did not resist. Then Nan pulled a sheet over him. She leaned over and whispered into his ear, "Once we get you fixed up, we are gonna have to talk. You seem like a real interesting fella to me."

Doctor Fellers came in, and pulled back the sheet to see the leg. "I see, Nan has been up to her usual hijinks, but she must like you, she gave you a sheet. Now the leg, third wound, same leg, you aren't a bank robber, are you? These are a lot of wounds for one fella in a week. The first two are healing well though. Now, I have to go in again, and you know the drill." Ten minutes later Dr. Fellers was done, and a pale Chuck was quiet on the table. Dr Fellers patted Chuck on the shoulder and said, "You are a brave young fella. That one was deep. Same as before, stay off your feet and rest the leg, it should heal okay. Now stay there a minute and I will send your brother back in to help you get dressed. Right now, you don't need any more of Nan's hijinks."

The doctor went out and sent Des back in. He slowly got Chuck dressed, with many winces and pauses. Carl was in the hall talking to the doctor. "This one was pretty deep, one of the old mini balls from the war. In the war he would have lost his leg because by the time he got to a doctor he would have been gangrenous. I like doing medicine this way better."

"Doc? may I call you Stephen? Are you still having trouble attracting patients?"

"Yeah, even with all the hijinks you guys have been having out your way, I never saw any of the casualties."

"Then Doc, since I am your main client, I would like to have you and your daughter come out to Oakside for lunch tomorrow. Then I would like to show you the two settlements that are developing on the estate. Doc, if you chose a site, I will build you a house with an infirmary attached and I would like the two of you to move out there. Right now, we have about seventy men on the estate, and soon fifty of them will start bringing their families, and I have a daughter in law who seems to be having triplets. I think we really need a doctor out at Oakside."

"Be glad to come out for lunch, and look at your operation. Frankly, if yours is where the future growth is going to be, maybe that is where we should be too, should warn you though, I think Nan has set her sights on your boy, the one who somehow keeps getting shot. I would hate to think he keeps doing that to see her. Now for Chuck, try to keep him off that leg for at least a couple days and out of the wars if you can for a while."

Des and Carl took Chuck home and when they got there the other two boys got him upstairs. Tully brought him a sandwich and a glass of milk. He went to his room to get the rabbit and a few minutes later came back and crawled into bed with Chuck, "Just in case he needed anything overnight."

"Thankyou Tull, I appreciate that."

Chapter 13

New Arrivals

The next morning at breakfast, Carl mentioned that Doctor Fellers and his daughter Nan were coming for lunch, and that he was trying to convince them to move to the estate in one of the villages.

"What!" said Chuck, almost falling off his chair. Tully, who was sitting beside him, reached over to steady him. "She, they, are coming for lunch? Are they both gonna go look for a site for a new office?" asked Chuck innocently.

Carl was looking closely at him, as were several of his brothers, especially Des. Carl said, "I expect she might like to check the places we are offering as she will be living in one of them. What else would you think she might like to do?"

"I dunno, just maybe she might like to…rest, that's all, uh maybe around here."

"With you!" said Des triumphantly. "You are hoping she will choose to stay here with you alone, aren't you? Chuck, you are in no shape to look after a girl alone, you can hardly walk. Maybe one of us should stay to help you."

"No! That's okay. We could manage without help. Really guys, if she decides to stay here with me, I really want it to be alone. Frankly, I like this girl and I want to get to know her a bit. Dad, really, if I can convince her to stay with me, can you make sure all the other galoots go with you."

Carl said, "Okay boys count on it. Mag and I, and the doctor, will be going on a tour of the two villages to look for a site for a new infirmary. Your brother would like all of you to go with us so he could be alone with her. So, Des, Diz, and Marcus, along with Ed, and Ali, you will all be expected to be with us. Now Tully, in your capacity as fetcher you will remain in your room in the house, you have lots to put away still, but you will not bother Chuck and Nan unless one of them calls you. Now Chuck, is that okay? You do realize though that Mam and the girls are still downstairs and there are Pinkertons all over the place, its not like you will be alone."

"Just trying to remove a little of the competition Dad. I can live with Tully, **IF HE STAYS** to his room."

Dr. Fellers and his daughter arrived about eleven. They had a tour of the main floor of the house and both were convinced it was a hundred years old, and were very surprised it had been finished for less than a year. "Yes, I had the original plans and I gave them to the architect and the builder. They tried to keep the changes to the bath rooms, and electricity. I think they did a pretty good job," said Carl. "All the new houses on the estate, including the field hand's, all have both too, so if you decide to come here you will also." After lunch Carl took the Dr. in the study and showed him on the map where the two settlements were being erected.

When they came out, Carl said to the boys, "Go and get horses for all of us, and the doctor will use his own buggy. And Nan, do you want to come with us, or would you rather stay here with Chuck there." Nan was quick to see an opportunity and she quickly said she would stay with Chuck, who was glaring so fiercely at his brothers they wisely chose not to make any comments.

Tully kept himself busy in his room for a good fifteen minutes before he came across something new, a telescope. He had never had one before, but Marcus had shown him the one on the Too. Tully started scanning the horizon at the front of the house, which was where his room faced. His attention was drawn to the trees along the avenue to the front of the house and after about ten minutes watching he ran downstairs to Chuck with the telescope. He burst into the lounge and ran up to Chuck, who said, "I thought you were supposed to stay in your room?"

"I know, but this is important. There are men in the trees on the avenue, best I can make out is about ten. Every ten minutes they sneak a foot closer."

Chuck took the scope and watched for several minutes. Finally, he said, "Buzz for the Pinkertons," which Tully did; and soon there were three or four in the room. They looked thru the scope and the head one said, "Thirty or forty minutes before they get here. There is less undergrowth as they get closer, that will slow them down."

Chuck said, "First thing, send DJ and CJ to warn Dad and the soldiers, the Landing and the factory. They can go out the back and thru the woods without being seen, they know them. Then get the rest of the staff out of the house and hiding back in those woods too. Then we want to keep them moving closer so you can get your men in behind them. How about if Nan and I and Tully went out on the porch to sit. Tull, you put on your guns, with bullets in them, but also bring rabbit and a couple of those cap guns, your boots, and your cowboy hat. After watching you shoot the rabbit with caps, they will assume the other two guns are cap guns too. There are already rifles clipped to the back of the seats out there, we just have to make sure we get one of those. Maybe that will draw them closer, hoping maybe to take some of us as hostages. How many men are there in the house?"

"There are ten, plus me, and there are six outside, probably closing in from the other side."

"Good then, we are not going to be over-run when it hits the fan, we'll spend some time on the porch and maybe they will see us as harmless and approach. We will try to stall for time until the others get back, and then when the others get the message there will be many more, if we can hold out long enough.

The three went out on the porch, Nan and Tully both being needed to help Chuck out. Then Tully lay on his stomach shooting his cap gun at the rabbit, who he tried sitting up in various positions. Out of the corner of their eyes they watched the rebs inch closer and ignored them. Nan even took advantage of the situation and kissed Chuck at least twice. It was a very innocent sight, at least to the rebs, who finally just stepped out of the trees and strode towards the house. They were holding their rifles, but were not aiming them.

"Who are you guys?" said Chuck. "You need some help? Lost or something? There is a well around the side if you need water."

"Why are you hobbling around?"

"Someone shot me the other day, on the yacht. Hadn't even left the dock, can you believe that?"

"We lost a lot of people that day too, more than just shot in the legs," the man with the rifle said bitterly. "I lost my brother."

"Never understood what all the ruckus is about. So, we sell our tobacco to England. What difference does it make?"

"Not supposed to be tobacco, should be cotton."

"Why? Can't sell cotton now. You guys got cotton? I bet it ain't selling that well."

"The price of cotton will come back soon," said one of the other men.

"My Dad, he lived here before the war, and he said that is what everyone would say. Cotton price was low, but everyone said it would come back. It never did, or if it did, that was only the years something was wrong with the cotton crop and people didn't have any cotton to sell."

"Some truth in that," said another one of the men. "Cotton always was a mean crop, never enough money, even on a place like this."

The first guy spoke again. "Say, what did you mean when you said your Dad was here before the war? Thought he was just a rich carpetbagger."

"My Dad owned this place years before the war. Four of my brothers have their mother buried in the graveyard under those trees over there. We are not carpetbaggers. You know what was left here after the war. Don't you think what is here now is better? Carpetbaggers come looking to buy something cheap and sell high. They don't invest anything. That is not what this is, just look around." The group looked around, taking in the barns, and the stables, and the fields. One of them even noted the crazy looking cows. Then Chuck said, "Have a seat on the stairs fellas. Nan and Tull, go get the guys some lemonade and some glasses. We can talk this out."

When CJ and DJ caught up with Carl and the boys, there was a great deal of excitement. Troops were quickly assembled, and they raced down the road towards Oakside. They swarmed up the avenue. Carl was concerned there was no firing and wondered if they were too late. When they crested that last rise and saw the house, sitting there peacefully in the sun, and all the boys sitting on the stairs, around Chuck and Nan, Carl put a hand on the Captain's arm, and he yelled out to slow the troop. Carl said, "Take your men over to the pen beside the barn there and let them dismount. The boys and I will get off here and send our horses over. I have a feeling something good happened here today."

Carl dismounted. Mag and Des were with him. The others had been at the factory. The doctor was coming slowly behind in his buggy, expecting to have a lot of work. The three stood as a group at the bottom of the stairs. Chuck looked up.

He was laughing. "Dad, everybody here is a McCall, but there are three families. Lots of cousins. I am afraid I don't know most of the names yet, but this one here is Fred and this is Elroy. We have been talking about tobacco farming. They want to know things like how hard it is, and how much money was in it. Their families do cotton and they are having a hard time."

"Be glad to pass on what I know, but this is my first season with tobacco. Before the war I experimented with small patches of different tobaccos. There were four or five that did well here in our soil. I grow all five and I blend them. The buyers like it that way. Truthfully boys, they paid a very good price, the English. At the moment there is a tremendous demand for it there and they have no other source. I got many times more than I ever did for cotton, even ten years before the war. It is less labor intensive, and it can be picked with machines. I am also experimenting with my own factory making cigarettes. In fact, you all can try some of the first off the line." Carl reached in a pocket and handed out several cigarettes to each of the boys. Between them they found matches. Carl went on, "I think this is the future. Premade cigarettes. Even women will smoke them. We are going to start packaging them in packs of ten. Sell them in every little store, not just smoke shops. Any of you guys want a job, go see the manager of the factory. We want to set up a group of sellers. Fill up a big set of saddle bags and send people out in all directions to find those stores and sell them. We sell a pack to the stores for a nickel, and they sell them for a dime. Cost us 2 to make, we get 2 of the five and the guys who takes them out to the stores get the other cent. You sell 500 packs a day, that means you earn 5 bucks a day. Once they get more popular, we will push the prices up, but we will keep the same ratio."

The general consensus was that the cigarettes were pretty good. Several of the boys said they would talk to their fathers and asked if they could bring their dads back. Carl said "Anytime, just tell them not to make it when we are being attacked." A few of the boys blushed at that. Carl said, "I don't know what went on here today, but this is what it should be like, neighbors talking and helping each other. If any of your parents want to try tobacco next year, I will share my contacts. They would have taken twenty times what I had this year, and when I get the factory up to speed, I may not be selling any tobacco."

When the group left, they left happy and smiling, and welcome to return as friends. After they were gone, Captain Fassert came over and said, "The first hopeful thing I saw since we got here. I was afraid this little war of yours would never end."

Carl said, "Its not over, but there are ten less soldiers next time. I think one or two more rounds and some of your guys can start looking for something else to spend their time at. Get your guys to start thinking that way. We want them and their families to stay too."

Stephen Fellers arrived in his buggy and was glad to see no blood had been shed. Nan came over to them and the two hugged. "Well?" she said. "Are we moving?"

"There is a nice lot, at the landing, and we will be able to look over the lot when they take the trees out. I gave a sketch to the builder and it should be done in two weeks. And you, did you get to meet your young man a bit?"

"Oh yes Dad, and I think he saved several lives today, at least ten, likely more, and I think he likes me too. He is very definitely a good young man." Then she saw Chuck wave her over to meet one of his brothers and excused herself. Stephen looked at Carl and said, "And in-laws should live close to each other, shouldn't they? Now our problems begin, keeping them apart, so to speak, until we can get them married."

Nan and her father stayed for dinner and took part in the discussion of the afternoon's events. It was a hopeful conversation although Carl did warn them, "Don't let your guards down, you have to remember there will be die-hards. I fully expect one more set of attacks, at least with the boats, so we need a new ploy for that, but each time there are fewer and fewer. Therefore, it should get easier. It has to stop soon though, Chuck is running out of places he can be shot safely." The whole table laughed at that. After dinner Nan and Chuck went and sat in the far corner of the porch and talked quietly. Tully went over to see if they needed anything and Chuck had him move one of the potted plants to give them a bit more privacy. Tully came back grinning. He said to Ed, "Chuck is toast, gone, married. That girl got him."

That night at bedtime, Tully and the rabbit came into Chuck's room. Tully checked if he needed anything, but Chuck was okay; then Tully crawled in beside and said, "I know, I won't be able to do this much longer. You know Nan wants you don't you, and I think you want her. That's good though, I think the two of you are a set."

"What do you mean by a set?"

"A set is two things that belong together, neither one of the things is right without the other. You two are a set and it is only right you belong together. But that means the two of you will be together at night and we won't be able to have our talks like this."

"Well, we'll just have to find other times to have our talks. You know, I think you were brave this afternoon when we had those rebs out front. No one could have told you knew they were there. But, I know if it had gone bad, you would have been there to help me."

"That's what brothers are for, aren't they?"

The next morning at breakfast Carl said, "Boys, we have another boat today and even though we cleared away a bit of opposition yesterday we know there is still some left out there. We are gonna go over to the landing when we are done and try to come up with a plan for this one. We have some special guests on this trip, the head of the tobacco buyers' group and his daughter. So, we really want to make sure nothing goes wrong this time."

Later, at the landing, the four captains got together with Carl to see what they could come up with. Marcus asked, "Do we know where their boats come from?"

Captain Bevers said, pointing to a map, "We think they come out of this little bay. You can't see it from here, or even from the bay until you are right on top of the entrance, see how it curls back."

"They can't fully man it all the time. What if we took the gunboats down and shelled the hell out of everything, sank the boats, killed whatever men are there. Fill the yacht deck with marksmen, and I'll nose in there too, give the gunboats cover."

Captain Bevers agreed it was a plan. He offered one suggestion. "The yacht is big enough. We can take a couple of bigger boats, tow them, then land some men on the beach this side, they can go through the woods and fire on their base from there. We can have some sort of signal, they back off and go back to their boats, row out, and we will pick them up on the way back, just abandon the boats. That was the adopted plan and they enacted it immediately. It took about thirty minutes to get the steam up on the patrol boats, but the yacht was up in twenty. The patrol boats were loaded with their crews of four and an additional four gunmen. The yacht had the Montroses plus an additional twenty-four marksmen ranged over her decks. Chuck and Tully were in the wheelhouse with Marcus. The yacht was towing two extra boats. At the agreed spot she stopped and twelve of the men off loaded, six to each boat, and they immediately rowed for the nearby shore. The seven steam boats continued on. The gunboats entered first and immediately started shelling the rebel's tied up boats. They were taken by surprise and there really were not that many crewmen there, just a few and some pickets. The Too followed them in, as far as she could go, and her cavalry men opened up on those on shore. The patrol boats continued to shell the moored boats until they all were sunk or in flames. Any who fled into the woods were shot by the marksmen from the boats. The Too reversed and backed out of the little bay, stopped to pick up the men from the rowboats, then headed out to sea to escort the tobacco ship in. The patrol boats roamed the bay during the whole period, meeting no opposition. The new ship was loaded in the afternoon, and was escorted out at four PM, again with no opposition. The Montroses were home for dinner by six, but no one was very hungry.

The problem was, they had all seen several of the men killed that day were some of the boys on the front steps that afternoon. None of the Montrose's had fired a shot at them, but they had seen the result when others did. The one who felt it most was Chuck, as he had had the greatest contact with them. Chuck sought out Carl that evening in the study.

"Dad, was that right, what we did this afternoon? I can't help but feel there was something wrong about us going in there like that. I can understand it when they attack us, we are fighting back. But today, we just went in and wiped them out. What if they weren't going to attack today? What if those boys we knew had just gone in to quit? What if…..?" His voice just died out.

"I know. All of what you said crossed my mind. The only thing I can say is that you know every one of the soldiers in the boats, and your brothers. If we had not done what we did, I am sure they would have attacked, and odds are we would have lost some people. Now, who of your brothers or the soldiers would you be prepared to let be those casualties? This is a war, declared or not. If these people were willing to let us carry on with our lives, there would be none of this. I suppose we could return to Arizona but then we would have to kill Apache. We could go to New York or Chicago and probably not have to kill anyone, but I don't think any of you would like that very much. I hope now that they have lost all their boats they will just give up and that will be the end of it."

As it turned out that was pretty much what happened, at least as far as the tobacco shipments were concerned. It was not the end of the problems though. There were some good developments, Dr. Fellers and Nan moved onto Oakside at the landing, which was a blessing for the growing community. Many of the soldiers and the seamen had their new houses and had their families moved in with them. The church and the parsonage were done, and the new church was full every Sunday. Several of the soldiers had also moved into businesses in the new community. No one protested, but it was clearly understood they would return to duty if needed.

There were a total of eleven tobacco shipments to England that summer and the last of the crop was in the drying sheds and would be used in the Oakside factory. The cigarettes, called Oaks, were by the end of the summer being sold all over the country and were very popular. There were thirty thousand Oaks a month sold in Virginia. Nationwide, by the end of the summer, sales were approaching a million a month. A second cigarette factory was ordered and representatives of the Oakside factory were trying to procure contracts for other tobacco supplies. The staff of Oakside were working on a planting schedule for next year's tobacco crop.

The workers at the new shipbuilders, and Marcus, were working on returning the Sea Vista Too to her proper condition. It was still the plan for the family to head south in her in the winter. Carl was leaving Captain Fassert and Captain Bevers in charge of security for Oakside. After the last battle, the raid on the cove and the destruction of the rebel boats, there had been incidents of growing seriousness. It started with unexplained fires and shots from the woods. Then one of the soldiers was shot while on a patrol. A seaman walking home from the harbor was shot in the back. One of the Pinkertons patrolling by the house was similarly killed. There were changes in patrolling methods, no more single patrols and increased vigilance.

Then Zion and Clem were killed. They had delivered a load of tobacco to the drying sheds, and were on their way home. Someone shot both of them in the back, leaving them slumped in their wagon. The horses quietly plodded back to the house, headed for their barn. They were stopped by the closed gates but just stood there waiting for someone to come and let them in. They were found by a passing patrol an hour later. Mama Clarisa was grief stricken when the boys were brought up to the house. A few days later DJ and CJ were hunting in the woods and were shot at. They both escaped. Then there was an incident at a church picnic at the landing.

There had been a picnic at the beach. A wagon had been brought so the youngest of the children did not have to walk home. A shot from the woods killed the driver and the horses bolted. There were ten children in the wagon when it sped away from the following parents. It spilled on the beach, throwing all the children out. Seven of them were killed, all under six.

Feelings were high in the community at the landing, but Carl and the parson cautioned them. It was not clear that any of the people from the village were involved. It might be someone totally unrelated. Captain Fassert had to admit, he had seen that during the war, people who enjoyed the killing and would kill for no good reason, just for the satisfaction it gave them. The whole situation came tragically home to the people at Oakside one afternoon.

Tully liked to play Cowboys and Indians with Rabbit on the porch. He would set the stuffed animal up on a railing or a chair, with a cap gun. Then Tully would try to sneak up on the rabbit. Sometimes Tully would shoot Rabbit with his cap gun, other times Rabbit would get the draw on Tully who would die dramatically on the porch. With all the problems, the adults at Oakside had agreed to try not to leave any of the younger ones alone outside. Mel was sitting on the porch with Tully that afternoon, knitting. Most of the adults were now immune to the pops of the cap gun, but three blasts from a rifle were impossible to mistake. Mel looked up and saw Tully laying in a pool of blood on the porch deck. She screamed, and when she rose to go to him, she was in turn hit with three bullets. She fell to the floor clutching her stomach. Carl, Des, Mag, and Deeds were just inside the house and came running, guns drawn. They each fired several times at the woods which drew further assistance from the house and several Pinkertons to come running from the side. They descended on the woods. By this point Mag was cradling Mel, and Carl held Tully. Carl yelled, "Get Dr. Fellers, immediately, the rest of you help us get them in.

When the doctor arrived ten minutes later, he found people holding compresses on the wounds and the bleeding stemmed. He took a quick look at each of them and then ordered Mel taken upstairs to her bed. She had the three wounds to her stomach. He then checked Tully. There was a wound to an arm and another to a leg, neither terribly serious, but there was a graze to the side of his head. The doctor was worried about that one. He ordered that Tully be spread out on the dining room table and the wounds bared so he could get the bullets out, and then rushed upstairs to look at Mel. Clarisa was there when he got to the room, as was Nan, who had been at the house that afternoon. They both looked worried. Nan said, "I think she is miscarrying" The doctor checked and saw his daughter was right. He did what he had too in order to save her life. He handed a covered container to Clarisa, "Keep these, they might want to have a funeral." He then went out in the hall to tell Mag. He and Des held him as he sank to the floor. "Mag, Mel will survive, and I would guess she may even have more children. I am so sorry son, now I have to go see to Tully." He left the two brothers holding each other leaning against the wall in the hallway.

In the dining room Tully was ready, he looked pale and he still was unconscious. Dr. Fellers quickly dealt with the arm and the leg, finding the bullets, stitching and bandaging the wounds. Then he turned to the head wound. It was a graze, but a deep one, and there was no bullet to remove. Dr. Fellers gently lifted the eyelids to look at the eyes, he tried some stimulus with a light. Then he turned to Carl who was standing there with the rest of the boys. "Carl, I am not sure yet, and I hope I am wrong. I think Tully may be blind. The other wounds are okay, but the graze is deep.

Carl was stunned speechless. Ed said, "No, it can't be, Tully blind." He clutched Ali. Chuck, who probably was the closest to Tully, was shaking from suppressed anger. "How could someone do this to a child like Tully? This is so evil."

Captain Fassert had been drawn to the house by all the excitement and when he came through the door, Deeds filled him in. Fassert's face became stone hard. Carl turned and saw him, then came over. "Carl, I will get every man I have out, but frankly he has evaded us so far. I am so sorry."

Later that evening, Chuck was sitting in Tully's room waiting for him to waken. Then he heard a small voice from the bed, "Anybody there? It is so dark in here I can't tell."

Chuck leapt from his chair and went to lie beside Tully, pulling him close, as they normally slept. "Tully, there is a light on in here. I am afraid one of the bullets grazed your head. Dr. Fellers is afraid it may be permanent. You might be blind forever."

Tully considered this for a few moments then he said, "Chuck, I am afraid. How can I get by if I am blind? How does a blind person manage?"

Chuck gently said, "Tull, it is normal to feel afraid when you face something new. We are all here for you. The brothers and I have talked, and one of us will be here at night with you as long as you want it. And we will work with you in the day, help you, but one thing, you must try, you have to try to do as much as you can when you can. It would be really easy to sit back and let people do everything for you. That would not be good."

"I know Chuck, I will be as brave as I can, but I am a kid. It is hard to be brave like you. Chuck, where is Rabbit?"

Chuck reached behind him to the table and got him, "Here Tull, here's Rabbit. I knew you would want him, especially now." Tully hugged the rabbit to him and settled back against Chuck's chest and closed his eyes.

Carl was leaning against the wall in the hallway, tears streaming down his face. Finally, he stormed down the hall to Deed's room and in. "Lionel, I need you to go to New York in the morning. Come with me while I get Diz up to send a message." When the three were in the library, Carl said, "Diz, first to the railroad. Tell them to have an engine here in the morning at eight and they are to hook up to the private car, which is then to be taken to New York. Mr. Deeds will be aboard, and the engine is to wait for him while he attends to business and bring him back here. Have no idea how long that will take but it makes no difference. They wait."

Deeds was looking mystified, but he waited. He knew Carl would tell him what he wanted. Carl walked to a shelf in the library and took down a book, The Directory of Private Schools. He paged through it then passed it over to Deeds open to Baxter School for the Blind, New York City.

"Lionel, I want you to go there and get an instructor for Tully. We have no idea how to help him. Also, tell them that I want to open The Virginia School for the Blind, here, on Oakside; and I want to have it built by next spring. I want their help in setting it up and staffing it. For their assistance right now give them a donation of three hundred thousand dollars. When the school is built and operating there will be a further half million-dollar donation."

"Diz, to the Baxter School for the Blind, New York. Representative, Lionel Deeds, arriving tomorrow morning on matter of gravest importance. Please accommodate, sign my name."

Lionel was on his way the next morning by 8:30 and was back a little after five. He was accompanied by a young lady, who immediately asked to be taken up to Tully. He and Rabbit had been confined to his bed all day because of the bullet wounds. His brothers had cycled through, but he was still bored. Tully heard the rustle of the skirts and called out, "Who's there?"

"Hello Tully. My name is Jennifer Baxter. I am here to help you, and you know what, I think we are going to get along. I brought my rabbit too. I'll show her to you later."

"How can you help me?" said Tully a bit sadly.

"Well, Tully, my parents run the Baxter School for the Blind. They are both blind. I know what you are going through, I have seen it hundreds of times. You seem like a bright boy, I am sure you will manage."

At first they just talked about the kind of things they would do. After a couple of days, Tully was pronounced fit to get out of bed. Jennifer brought some clothes over and sat on the bed beside him, the clothes between them. "You want to make sure when you get finished your clothes are right, not inside out and not front to back. So, feel them, make sure you can tell the difference."

Finally, Tully said, "Okay, I think I have it. Now, you have to go."

"Go?"

"I am a guy, you ain't, it ain't proper for me to change with you here."

"Okay Tully, I'll be out in the hall. Call done when I can come back in."

A few minutes later Jenn heard "Done" and re-entered. She sat on the bed beside him. She looked down at the floor where the clothes he had taken off were thrown. "Okay Tully, what happened to the clothes you took off."

"Uh, I guess I threw them on the floor."

"Before, that wasn't a big deal, you just looked and picked them up. Now, you have to find each. Use your foot, find it, then drag it over here. Then you have to bend to get it. Now, when you bend, keep one hand on the bed. When you are blind and lean over it is easy to fall over, that is why you keep a hand on the bed. Helps your body to know which way is up." Tully accomplished the task.

"Now, this is one of the hardest lessons for young boys. You have to learn to be extremely neat. Everything you have has to have a place and you have to learn to put it back so the next time you want it you know where to go. For example, where's Rabbit?" Tully looked agitated.

"Rabbit? I can't lose Rabbit. Last time I had him was in bed, by the pillow." Tully began frantically feeling around and at last found it. He lay there while he calmed himself.

Jennifer said, "Now, when you wake up, before you get up, you put Rabbit away, then you will know exactly where he is. There is a shelf above the head of your bed and I cleaned it off. Reach up and put him away." When that was done, she said, "Now we will go down and get something to eat. You take my arm for now, and we will go down. Stand with me. You know where the door is, count the steps, and remember. When we get to the door, turn to the stairs and count again. Don't worry, I won't let you go to far." At the top of the stairs she said, "Okay, I am on your left. Reach your right hand out and hold the bannister. Count the stairs and remember." At the bottom of the stairs she reviewed, "Now, lets review. You stood and turned to the door, how many steps, just think it, you don't have to say it. Then you turned to the right, how many steps to the top of the stairs, think it, then how many steps down?"

"Now, point to the dining room door, and tell me how far it is, in steps."

"Nine, maybe."

"Let's see." They walked and stopped. "See, you were right. Now I see a table. Do you have a space at it?"

"Yes, my seat is between Chuck and Ed, third down."

"Okay, I see it, maybe Chuck can move down one space just for today, and he can watch what we do and do it for you tomorrow. Now, let's go to your seat, you have done this a thousand times, just let your feet take you."

Tully arrived at his seat perfectly. Jenn said, "Slip in. This is where your family can help you. You have to have an area in front of you to work in, where you know there is only your stuff and you will not knock anything over, but you will, don't worry about it. If Ed there leaves his orange juice in your space that's his fault, not yours. Now, I am moving everything out of your space except your plate, knife and fork. Now, can you tell time?"

"No." Jenn shot a sharp glance at Carl. "Okay then, you know top, bottom, left, right, and center. Show me those parts of your empty plate, and say it as you do it." She waited while he did that. "Now, we will put some food on that plate, and when I do, I will say where, you have to remember. Tomorrow maybe Chuck can. Toast at top, eggs, scrambled, at the bottom. On the right I will put the bacon. Now for the toast you use a hand, and it looks like all your brothers use their hands for the bacon, so you can use them too. That means you only have to use the fork for the eggs. Use your fork and get some eggs on it."

Tully did that while his family watched wordlessly. "Okay, now the scary part. I bet you are scared you will put the eggs in your nose." There were several grins around the table. "Just think about it. You have used that fork and that plate a hundred times to eat eggs, and I bet most of those times you were talking to your brothers and not even watching. If you do make a bit of a mistake, what is the worst that will happen? One of the brothers will laugh at you, and if they do, we will make them eat a meal with a blindfold on and see how well they do." She glowered at the other boys as she said that. "Now, let's have some eggs." They all watched quietly as he made his first try, and he did it perfectly. There was a murmur of approval around the table.

Carl said, "Good Tull, at least we know you won't starve to death."

Jennifer said to the others, "There are some secrets to all this. Things have to be kept neat, and the things that Tully uses have to always be in the same place. No stuff left on the stairs, or the floor. You will soon see Tully is the neatest person in the room. He has to be. Now, why can't he tell time?"

"Tully just came to us a few months ago. Before that he was on his own after his parents died. All the boys have taken on tasks to teach him. I guess we forgot time."

"Now, the reading, the writing, the arithmetic, I will have to teach him as they have to be done in Braille, but there will not be stuff to be unlearned, so it will be easier."

"Uh Jenn,"

"Yes Tully, I just did something we all have to be careful not to do. Blind people tend to be forgotten, talked over and about. If we do that again demand to be heard. Now Tull, what do you need?"

"Well, I am sorta thirsty."

"Today, I will pour it for you, but I will teach you how to do that too. Would you like orange juice or milk?"

"Milk please."

"Okay Tull, I will pour the milk and put it beside your plate half way between top and right, that would be two on the clock." And that was how the re-education of Tully Montrose began. The family watched closely as Jennifer worked, the way she did it, slowly and methodically, building little gains on little gains. It would continue for a while as, academically at least, they were starting from near zero. There were occasional mis-steps, but as long as everyone kept a sense of humor about it, they all made their way through. The bonds between Tully and his family were firm, and that was what was needed for success."

After a couple of weeks Carl had a family meeting and included Jennifer in it. "We have to decide on the calendar for next year. The tobacco crop here is in and the schedule in place for next year. The new factory is on the way, and we have staff here to look after it. There is enough of our crop to run two factories until a new crop is in. The yacht is ready and the rail car. The idea is we will all take the yacht and the car will follow us. We can then use it for side trips where the yacht can't go. There will be a full team of Pinkertons with us on the Too, and two more with the railcar for when we go on land. We will sail south along the Carolinas, Georgia and Florida so that we can Christmas in Florida. We will stay on the boat unless there are La Prads to stay in. When we find one we like, we will stay in it as long as we want to. We will sail up the other side of Florida, eventually past Louisiana, Alabama, and Mississippi to Texas. In all of those states we have major oil interests which I want to make the boys aware of. There is also a big new ranch in Texas, which I want to show you all, and some more hotels. Electrification has started on the ranch and the hotels in the south. Then at some point, we will reverse and come back, first to the Hamptons, then to Oakside; hoping to get here in the spring. By the time we get back Jenn, your new school will be finished, on the estate here and within sight of the house, although not next door to it. Your parents have agreed to come down when it is ready and help get it open. I even have an idea for the next year, an around the world cruise."

"In the Too?" said Marcus. "I think she is a little too small."

"I know Marcus, that's why at some point we will meet the people from Newport, and you and I and Deeds shall sit with them to design and commission a new steam yacht, steel, and capable of worldwide travel for next winter. We want it tied to the dock when we return from this trip next year. I have to admit; Arizona is sending us a lot of money but I really have little desire to live there again. I like Virginia, and I hope to like Texas, and when we do that world trip, I want to see California, because I think there may be parts there that may be appealing. We have gold, oil, and agricultural interests in California. I feel those will be the main areas for our family in the future.

Mag spoke up. "Mel and I had hoped for Oakside to be our forever home, but with what has happened it will be difficult for it to be a happy place for us in the future. We look forward to Texas."

Jenn said, "I will enjoy the trip this winter, but I imagine I shall settle in the end with the new school."

"Marcus, for the trip this winter we will need a new permanent stoker. Check first with the patrol boat crews or the soldiers. There may be a young fella among them who is unattached and would like to get away for the winter."

"There is one other thing we should discuss. This murdering madman that has come to the fore this summer. When we leave, he will still need to feed his need and I imagine he will then turn to the people of Oakville. Should we warn them?"

Chuck said, "With what has been going on, I can't see the general people of Oakville being supportive. I think we should warn them though."

So Carl talked to the parson in the little church in the village at the landing, and the parson in turn talked to the reverend at a church in Oakville. A Sunday, a short while later, Carl and his sons went to church in town. He left the Pinkerton men at the door. The Montroses were accompanied by Dr. Fellers and Nan, as well as Jennifer Baxter. The reverend met them at the door and showed them to a pew at the front. The congregation was aghast. The reverend then said, "Mr. Montrose asked that he be allowed to speak to you today about something he feels is very important to you. Mr. Montrose."

Carl went up to the pulpit, "I won't take long, then we will leave. We do not want to disturb your worship. My family and I shall leave next week for Florida and points south and we won't return till next year, but we will return. My crop next year will be tobacco, but it shall not be sold. My whole crop will be processed in my own plants." He held up a pack of Oaks. "You may recognize these. We sell them in the county for ten cents. Everywhere else we sell them for a quarter, 70 000 a month in the state, a million a month nation wide. The second plant will produce a new brand, Tulls. If any of you wish to produce some tobacco next year, see the manager at the cigarette factory for a contract. My experience has been it will do well on marginal land, land not good enough for cotton."

"But that is not the main reason we came. When we started our little wars on the bay this year, I saw some honor in what we were doing. Both sides were fighting for something we believed in. When those wars died out something evil persisted. There continued to be isolated murders, a soldier here, a sailor there, a few Pinkertons. All of these were brutal but may be understandable, given the hostilities. Then two of the young black men from Oakside were shot in the back as they returned to the estate from the factory. These were two totally harmless young men I knew all their lives, very shy, very polite, men who never spoke in the presence of a white person. Those boys were delivered to their horrified mother at Oakside after the horses returned to their barn. Then there was the incident at a church outing for its parishioners at the landing. A wagon had been brought to the beach to take the toddlers back. Babies were carried by their mothers but those a little older rode the wagon. A shot rang out from the woods that killed the driver, and a couple more shots to spook the horses. A half dozen children under six were killed that day. Most recently there has been an incident at Oakside. Some of you may remember Tully here. He lived among you after he lost his parents. Anyway, he heard the talk in the village early in the summer and decided he should help too so he got a gun somewhere and came out to Oakside. When my family rode by he shot and wounded one of my boys. My son lived, but Tully got two things from me that day that he sorely needed, a spanking since no nine-year-old should be going around shooting people, and a bath, which he hadn't had for a year. We kept Tully with us, and he became part of the family, legally too." There was bit of a gasp in the room at that. "When Tully came to us, he got his first toys, a stuffed Rabbit and a set of cap guns. About ten days ago he was playing Cowboys and Indians on the porch with Rabbit. He would prop the Rabbit up somewhere with one of the cap guns, then try to sneak up on him. Sometimes Tully won, sometimes the rabbit. With all the problems we tried to never leave the youngest outside alone. My daughter-in-law, Mel, was out there with Tully, knitting. Mel was due to have what they thought would be triplets in a few months. Shots rang out from the woods. Tully was shot three times. When Mel rose to go to him, she was shot three times also, in her stomach. We believe it was on purpose as her condition was readily apparent. Mel lost the three children. Tully will recover from the shots in his arm and his leg, but he is blind from the graze on his head. We believe all of these incidents were the same man. One of my people, Captain Fassert, said they saw this during the war. Some men got to enjoy the killing, did it for fun. We couldn't go, taking away his main targets, without warning you. You have this man living with you who loves to kill, and when we are gone, he will still have that need. He will turn to you, to some one who slights him or offends him, and satisfy his needs. One other thing, while we are gone, there will be some construction on Oakside, the new Virginia School for the Blind. I am afraid it will look a bit like a fort, but we have to make sure it is safe for the children, no windows on the outside, nothing overlooking it, built on a central courtyard. Just didn't want you to think we were building a castle. The school shall serve the state so if you are aware of any blind children get the word out. The school will be free. That new brand of cigarette, Tulls, will have all its profits devoted to the school. A blind child's world is dark enough, they don't have to be shut away. That's all we have to tell you so we will go now and leave you be."

Carl walked over to the first row and lifted Tully's hand to his arm. "Let's go Tully, you are on my left. He and Tully started down the aisle, the other boys falling in behind. By the time they got halfway to the door the whole congregation was clapping their support. Several of the women were in tears as they saw Tully go by. From that day forward there were no problems between Oakside Plantation, Oakville, and Oakside Landing. Before they left for the south, the Montroses were visited by several families from the town. Regrets were expressed over all that had happened, and Mel had several tearful conversations with some of the women from the town. She and Mag felt a bit better about Oakside as a place to live.

One night, Captain Fassert was awakened by loud pounding on his door. There was a group of men from the town, about seven of them, and they had one man with his arms tied behind his back. His face was a bit the worse for wear.

One of the townsmen said. "We wondered if we could borrow one of your patrol boats, we have some garbage that has to be dumped in the bay. We want you to know we dealt with the problem. He tried to murder one of us tonight, but we were waiting to make sure. I don't know about you, but we don't think he deserves a trial."

Captain Fassert nodded and accompanied them down to the dock. Captain Bevers joined them, drawn by the noise. When the steam was up, the boat went a mile out in the bay. There was a loud splash and the boat returned to the dock. The townsmen said thankyou and carried on, one less than had gone out. Fassert commented to Bevers, "Well, southern justice is fast and sure." The other man nodded.

By the end of August, the Sea Vista Too was being prepared. Her bunkers were loaded with coal, but Marcus fully intended to use the sails too, and had warned Des, Diz and Chuck of that. Jennifer had spent several days acquainting Tully with the boat, and he was as comfortable in it as he was now in the house. Clarisa, DJ and CJ had agreed to come along to prepare and serve the food and they were settled in the crew quarters along with ten or so Pinkertons. On the passenger deck, Carl and Deeds each had their own cabin, as did Jenn. Chuck would share with Tully. Ed and Ali would share, as would Des and Dizzy. Marcus would use the Captain's quarters. Mel and Mag, the babies and Imelda had two cabins. There were still four cabins left, and, at the urging of Chuck, Carl invited Dr. Fellers and his daughter Nan along. Relations were now good enough between the plantation and the town that he felt secure in going on a vacation, knowing his patients would be cared for.

Chapter 14

Sailing, Sailing

One early morning, late in November, the Sea Vista Too let go her lines and backed out in the bay, leaving the little graveyard on the plantation with three new little souls gathered around their grand-mother. The passengers were in the lounge or on the deck watching the land recede. "Hard to believe all that happened in just a few months," said Carl to Deeds. They were both standing on the deck watching the land fade away.

"You paid some heavy costs for this visit to Virginia, the babies and Tully."

"Yes, but we found Tully too. Wouldn't have done that if we hadn't come," said Carl stubbornly. "The first LePrad will be in Charleston. Until then we have several days at sea to enjoy the peace and quiet."

Once out in the Atlantic, Marcus had the boys deploy the sails. Des, Dizzy, and Chuck enjoyed that. They liked having something to do that taxed them physically and emotionally. Marcus loved having the feeling of a real sailing ship under his feet. At the end of the day, Marcus ordered the engines started and the sails furled. He then nosed in towards land in search of a safe anchorage for the first evening. The shores of North Carolina there were quite wild. And when they were anchored, they spent the last few hours of daylight watching the birds on the shore.

When it was dark, everyone retreated to the lounge. Jenn had taught Tully how to use the braille cards and he was always in search of someone to play with him. He was merciless though, and people soon learned to stop losing to him because they felt sorry for him. Tully would have none of that. He wanted to know that if he won, he earned it, and if he was beaten, he was content. That first day out, Jenn had spent most of the day with Tully and a checkerboard designed for the blind. There were marks on the discs to tell whether they were red or black. And the board was marked too. One thing that was readily apparent when Tully started to work with the board, it was clear he had an excellent memory. Occasionally, he had to reinforce his "View" of the board but then he could go several moves keeping the board clear in his mind. That night he convinced several of his brothers to play with him, and in the end they all won, but they were not easy wins, they had to work surprisingly hard at them. As Des turned his place over to Marcus he said, "Better enjoy winning while you can. Give him a couple of days with this and we won't be able to beat him at it either, just like the cards."

Jenn was sitting with Chuck and said, "I see this all the time. People lose a sense, like sight, and all the other abilities get that much sharper. Tully is a very bright young man who never had much schooling, his mind is like a dry sponge, just soaking up the knowledge. When you are talking with him don't be afraid of going into deep things. He likes to talk about them. We talked an hour today about whether there really was a God, and why things happened the way they did. For a ten-year old he clearly has thought about things."

"You have to remember he was absolutely alone for the better part of two years. And, I think he had a lot to think about. He saw all the townspeople living their lives totally ignoring him and his needs. He must have wondered at the fairness of that," said Chuck.

"He is a wonderful boy, and with the blindness I think there will be parts of him developed that are very special, and that you never would have normally seen. Now, how about telling me something about yourself."

"I came to the Montroses when I was thirteen or so. I had an uncle who abused me, made me work in his livery stable, live there almost. I guess I was much like Tully, except for the fact my uncle liked to teach, so I knew how to read and do sums. Dad, Carl, came in one day when my uncle was beating me and stopped him. Took me with him then and there. Carl bought the livery and my uncle disappeared. I went to live on the ranch and had a bunch of new brothers."

"You weren't one of the originals then?"

"The only originals are Des, Ed, and Ali, and Mag of course. The rest of us were added."

"You all are a family now, as close as any I have seen. What about a girlfriend?"

"Girls are a rather rare commodity in our world, but I do think there is something special between Nan and I," Chuck said, looking across the room at where Nan was laughing with Ed and Ali.

Jenn said, "Well, it is a nice warm clear evening. A perfect night to take someone special out for a walk on the deck, I would think."

Chuck grinned at her, then he rose and went over to Nan and the boys. A few minutes later they went out on deck.

Carl, Deeds, and Stephen Fellers noted this. Stephen said, "See, I told you. The problem will be keeping them apart."

"Well, we are on a boat. There are not many places for them to go, and no place to hide. And really, when the sails are being used, the four of them are pretty busy," said Carl.

"Oh, they will find a way, mark my word. But really, I am not worried. Chuck is a nice boy, just has a propensity for getting himself shot that he has to work on. Nan is a good girl. When she is sure he is the one, then nothing further will happen, until it should happen."

Out on the deck, Nan and Chuck were embracing, occasionally kissing. At that point they both knew, but were a little afraid of telling the other, in case the feeling wasn't mutual. They continued looking at the stars and relished the closeness. Finally, Chuck broached the subject. "Nan, I feel special here like this with you, do you feel the same way?"

"Chuck, I do, from that first day I saw you, I knew it then, I knew you were the one for me. You do know, Dad was kidding about me and the boys. You were the first boy I saw totally naked."

"Really, if I had known that then I really would have been embarrassed."

"Why? From what I saw you had nothing to be embarrassed about."

"I dunno, I never compared myself with the others."

"Chuck, if we are sure about each other and we both know what we want, then why do we have to wait?"

"Nan, while I would love to do it, I don't think that would be right."

"No silly, you ain't touching me until we are married. That's what I mean, why can't we get married? I turned sixteen last week."

"I turn sixteen next week. Down here in the south people do get married before they are sixteen, but I think we should be sixteen."

"Okay then, next week we get to Charleston, and we will be there a week. If we really want to, that's when we could do it. The question is whether we should do it, do we really want to get married? Do we love each other enough? Is it real love? Will it last or is it just passing with our age?" said Nan.

"As you said all those questions, the answer was yes. I do want to get married. I think it is real and will last. I think the love will last and we should get married. The thing is, can I offer you enough? If we got married, my job at Oakside is running the horse breeding program. Dad and I never talked about a wage, so I don't know what we would have that way. Dad told us all we were in the will, but you can't plan a life on that. Mag said when he and Mel got married Dad gave them a lot of money, I suspect he would do the same with us. From what Mag said the idea was they would have the money for investing in what they wanted to do. What I want to do is work with the horses."

"Well maybe you could buy a few horses of your own, then sell them, make some money of your own that way."

"Do you mind the idea of living at Oakside?"

"Chuck, how could anyone mind living at Oakside."

"So, what should we do?"

"Chuck, what do you want to do?"

"I think I want to tell them we want to get married when we are in Charleston. I don't want to go through this whole trip, months and months, wanting you and not being able to have you."

"Then I think that is what we should do, and we should tell them right now, get it over with and let them get used to it. Somehow, I don't think they will be surprised. I think everyone knows how we feel about each other," said Nan.

They had another kiss, then they entered the lounge and walked over to Carl, Deeds, and Dr. Fellers. They sat together on the floor before their parents, and Chuck said, "Dad, we have to tell the two of you something. We both want to get married, next week when we are in Charleston. We are sure what we want, and we don't want to spend the whole trip wanting to be together and not being able to."

"Dad, remember I am sixteen now and Chuck will be next week," added Nan.

Carl and Stephen looked at each other, then Stephen said, "We are not surprised, in fact we were just talking about the two of you. Thing is, we really didn't see it happening next week."

"Look Dad, why not? If we start sneaking around about this, that would not be good. We both would rather be up front about this. Chuck knows what he wants to do, work with the horses and he is already doing that at Oakside. I am okay with that, I want him to do something that makes him happy."

Carl said, "We don't doubt you love each other, even that you will get married, but why next week?"

Chuck said, "If we decided we wanted to do it this week we would have to let Marcus do it, as Captain. That doesn't seem right though. We know we are stopping at Charleston for a while and that seems about right." Then Chuck noticed the room had grown quiet as everyone listened to what was developing. As Chuck looked at his brothers, he realised they did not look shocked, just amused. Chuck said, "See Dad, look at the rest of them. They aren't shocked or surprised. Most of them know what it is like to be young and in love. Sure, we could wait, but why?"

Carl looked at Stephen and said, "I guess he is right, why make them wait. It won't make them any more in love, just more frustrated."

Stephen nodded. "Okay Nan, I will agree, and it sounds like Carl will too. When we get to Charleston, we will get you a dress. I assume you just want a small family wedding. Church or in the hotel?"

"Hotel Dad, just the families."

Tully had moved down the sofas, "Jenn?"

"Yes Tully, here, sit beside me." Once he was settled he said, "This is when I miss being able to.."

"To see," Jenn said quietly, "Why?"

"If I had always been, then I wouldn't know how people showed how they felt, showed in their face. I would love to see how Chuck looks now. Is he happy?"

"Yes Tull, he looks very happy. I really do think the two of them are meant for each other. They should be very happy."

"I hope they are. Considering how Chuck and I met, he has been very good to me. Really, he is my best friend. The only time I really feel safe and comfortable is at night when I curl up with him. I am going to miss him."

"One day, you will meet someone like Nan, someone for you. Then you will feel comfortable."

"Me? Like this? Who would want a blind guy? I don't think that will happen."

"Tully, the person for you will choose you for the kind of person you are. How each of you looks to the other will not mean anything at all. You are unbelievably bright, and you have a heart a mile deep. There is someone out there that will be attracted to that. Who knows, next year you will go to our new school. Maybe you will meet someone there."

"Another blind person? How could that work? There would not be anyone to look after the other."

"Sure, why not? The purpose of the school is to make you totally self-sufficient. If one is self-sufficient, two can be too. To a degree. Remember earlier today when I told you not to go out on the deck alone. That is part of what you have to learn. It is good to be self-sufficient, but you can't be foolish. When the ship is at sea, and moving, it is just too dangerous for you on the deck alone. That's what I mean about not being foolish. Now if you met some one who was blind, the two of you could be perfectly happy, as long as both of you recognized there are just some things that are too dangerous to do without some help. Like for example jumping off a cliff into the ocean. You might be a perfectly good swimmer, but if you got disoriented in the dive, you could drown if you didn't know which way to swim."

Just then Des came and sat beside them. "A bit of a surprise eh? I knew they liked each other, but to the point of getting married? At sixteen? That I didn't realize."

"What part Des, the sixteen or the getting married? I have the feeling you like girls, enjoy being with them but that you see them more as toys, to make you feel happy. Some day maybe, if you let yourself, you might meet a girl that completes you, makes you happy by just being with her. That you find you need to be with. That perhaps challenges you. That doesn't fall over just at the bat of your eyelashes. That kind of girl might be worth having, even at sixteen. You have to realize Des that even smart rich pretty boys like you have to grow up and put away the toys. Now, I am gonna go and congratulate the couple."

Jenn rose from the couch leaving a shocked Des sitting there. Tully said, "Des, I am only ten, but I think you were just told you were a spoiled kid, and should grow up."

"Yes Tull, you may be blind, but that is what you saw. It is a bit of a shock when you realize how other people see you."

The brothers were gathered around Chuck and Nan. They were a happy lot. Deeds and Carl stood to the side and Carl said, "When we get to Charleston, send some wires and move things around a bit. I will do the same for these two as I did for Mag and Mel, a hundred thousand cash and a draft for a million. You see to it, will you please?" Deeds nodded.

Later that night, when they were in bed, Tully said to Chuck. "I am glad about you and Nan, but I am gonna miss this, the time before we fall asleep and talk. You are my best friend, I don't know now whether I can go to sleep alone."

"Tull, I told you before, one of the others will be here for you, all you have to do is ask."

"That's the point Chuck, I never had to ask you. A couple other things happened today that I wanted to tell you. Jenn told Des to stop being a spoiled kid and grow up. He didn't like that much."

"No, I don't imagine he did, but she was right. Up to this point Des has been a bit of a user, of girls at least. I imagine Jenn was telling him that if he hoped to find the happiness Nan and I have, he has to change his attitude a bit. You said a couple of things, what was the other?"

"Jenn also said that someday I would find a girl that is meant for me. That surprised me, especially now. I really thought that now I was blind that would never happen for me, that I would always be alone with someone to take care of me. Jenn said the whole purpose of the school was to get me to a point I could manage by myself, on my own; and that someday there would be a person, and that we could manage together. Maybe even the other person might be blind too. I never thought of anything like that. That would be almost a normal life."

"Tull, that is what I want for you, as normal a life as you can have; and you can be sure that is what Dad wants too, that is why he is going to all the trouble of starting the school. That school will fill in the things you don't know, having not been to school. But, more important, the school will teach all of you how to manage, to do the things you have to do. That part is even more important. But as far as the general school stuff, you are really smart. Look how you have mastered the cards and you have almost got the checkers. You just put in a little effort and you just might end up the smartest person in the house."

The next morning at breakfast, Marcus asked if they would like to stay where they were for the morning. "I was looking through the telescope. The shore seems a bit wild, sand dunes and drift wood, but if some of you would like to stay a while and explore, we can leave after lunch and find a different spot to anchor for the night. No one says we have to steam past everything. We can lower a couple of the lifeboats if you want."

That is what they decided to do. Tully was carefully seated in the middle of one of the lifeboats, with a strong brother on either side as the boat was lowered, and Jenn spent the morning with him. He even explored the sand and the driftwood with his hands on the beach. She found some crabs, and clams. Tully had never had contact with either and was totally intrigued when he felt them in his hands. Des attached himself to the two of them and thoroughly enjoyed himself. He found he was closely watching Jenn and wondered why he found her so enchanting.

They all went back to the boat for lunch and all sat at the dining table. Des was on one side of Tully and Jenn on the other. Des said, "Tull, lunch is a buffet. I'll get a plate for you, I know you find that hard at a buffet. There is potato salad, and it looks like corned beef, what say I put that on a bun, two dollops of mustard right? Milk?" Des came back about five minutes later and put the plate in front of Tully. "Okay Tull, here is your plate. Now that you can tell time, the bun with beef is at 9, the potato salad is 3 to center, your milk is at the top of your plate at 12, and I put three dill pickles on your plate at 6. Okay?"

"Yes Des, thanks."

"Good man Tull, I'll be back in a minute after I get mine."

After he had gone, Tully said to Jenn, "What's up with Des today? He is being especially nice."

"Oh, he's just trying to get me to notice him, impress me, I know that."

"And, are you noticing him?"

Jenn whispered, "Tull, I noticed him the first day I came to Oakside, but he was far too sure of himself. All the other girls he has met have made it too easy for him. He needed to be knocked down a couple of steps, smarten him up. But yes, I am noticing him, but don't you tell him that."

Tully smiled to himself smugly and thought, "Maybe two of my brothers will be married before we get back to Oakside."

They continued down the shoreline like that, stopping to spend time when something on shore interested them. It took them about six days but finally they reached Charleston harbor. Marcus sought out the city dock and tied up. The Pinkertons split themselves into three shifts and spread over the deck and the dock. They would leave some of them to protect the boat when the rest moved to the hotel. Doctor Fellers took Nan and Mel, the Maid of Honor, ashore to find a wedding dress. Carl took Chuck and Tully, who would be Best Man, to find a set of rings and suits.

Deeds took all the rest and the luggage, and they went to check in at the Charleston LePrad. The others would join them there later. Deeds also had been ordered to arrange for a minister, and also for the Honeymoon Suite for a week. He also had to go to the telegraph office and a local bank.

That afternoon they had the wedding ceremony at 3:30. Chuck was extremely nervous until he saw Nan. Tully was grinning broadly. When Nan appeared, a vision in white, Chuck immediately calmed, as if he had been afraid she would leave him at the altar. Chuck slipped an engagement ring and a wedding band on Nan's finger, and she slipped a wedding band on his. They were irrevocably joined; and they sealed that with a long kiss. There was a wedding dinner served in the suite and it was a merry affair. Deeds slipped Chuck the key to the suite and told him it was one floor down and was his for the week. Carl slipped Chuck an envelope and said, "A hundred thousand cash, and your wedding gift, a draft for a million. Invest it, and when you see your dream you have the money to get it. The two of you have to take some time and think about that. It's not like you don't have a job. By the way, that job, with the horses. You earn fifty thousand a year plus five percent of sales and winnings on our horses. If you get some horses of your own, you get all their profits."

The newly weds held out til 5:30, when they excused themselves. When they arrived at the suite, they found a chilled bottle of Champagne. As he popped the cork, Chuck said, "You better look at this envelope before you have too much bubbly. Our wedding gift from Dad. A hundred thousand dollars cash and a draft for a million. Dad says to invest it, so we have the money when we see our dream. He also told me about the job, with the horses. Fifty thousand a year, and 5 percent of profits and winnings, and all the profits on any horses I buy on my own."

"Hon, I think that means we are already rich doesn't it?" said Nan.

"Yes it does. Dad said he doesn't believe in making us wait until he is dead for our share, so this is how he does it. I'll have to ask Deeds about how to invest it til we need it." Then the two adjourned to the bedroom, where they pretty much stayed for the next week, at the end of which, although she didn't know it yet, Nan was pregnant.

The rest of the group enjoyed the week in Charleston. It was a lively city. Des attached himself to Jenn and Tully and they explored the city together, joined here and there by one or two of the other brothers. Carl did his inspection of the hotel, and found it was in good shape and well run. This was what he expected from all the reports he had read. There was no need for him to intervene.

That first night, the day Chuck and Nan were married, Tully was in his bedroom with Rabbit, trying to go to sleep. He heard his door open and felt someone get in bed behind him.

"Son, I thought you might be having trouble getting to sleep so I thought I might join you, hope you don't mind."

"Dad, you are right. I was feeling a bit alone. This feels good though. Anytime you want to, it's okay." Carl became a frequent visitor, as did the other brothers. Ed and Ali came together, and on those nights the three of them would squeeze into the bed.

Finally, the week was up. Nan and Chuck emerged from their suite looking very satisfied. Marcus had made a couple trips to the dock during the week to make sure the yacht was refueled and ready to go. Mama, CJ and DJ had visited the markets and all the food lockers were restocked.

It took a couple days to clear the coasts of South Carolina and Georgia. Carl was taken with a part of South Carolina called Hilton Head, the beauty, and the large trees. Then they got to the coast of Florida. Carl was amazed. It was so beautiful and so wild, but there were not many people. There were groups of native settlements and a few villages with white people. The beaches were broad and white, the vegetation lush, and the wild life varied and beautiful. A man called Flagler was starting to make noises about building a railway and resorts, and making Florida the destination vacation spot for the northeast. Carl said to Deeds, "He is right, that is what Florida will be. Get the word out, we want to buy coastal land, lots of it. It will be cheap now, it won't be later."

They sailed past miles and miles of beaches on the east coast of Florida, occasionally stopping to spend an afternoon on one of them. These were joyous occasions. Clarisa would pack them a picnic lunch and sometimes she, CJ. and DJ would go ashore with the rest of them. The littler kids, black and white, would play in the surf. That was when Carl felt the sorriest for Tully. He could go down and sit in the shallow water, but he couldn't rough house with the others, at least he couldn't if he didn't want to be the one always being dunked as he couldn't defend himself. One day, Carl went down and sat on the edge of the beach with him.   "Tully,   I know this is hard for you, you can do many things but occasionally there will be things like this that you cannot do."

"Dad, it's like I have had to give up a part of the things I should be able to do as a kid. It is making me grow up too soon. I wasn't ready, I was just starting to like being a child."

"I know Tully, it isn't fair. Some of the things that kids would do you can't and if you had started out blind you likely wouldn't realize. You used to do what all the others did so you know what you are missing. Thing is though, as you work more and more with Jenn, you will learn how to do some things that you never knew about and some of them might be even more fun. You are only starting the transition, it's only been five or six weeks at most. Now, you want to go for a walk along the beach with me? This place is really amazing, I'll tell you about what we find."

When he saw some little lizards on the sand, he had Tully kneel and put out his hands, letting the lizards cross his fingers, then he caught one and had Tully cup his hands to hold it. This was a new experience for Tully, and he appreciated the fact Carl was taking this time with him. They came across some orchids and Carl picked one for Tull to smell. This was another new experience.

"You know Dad, I have held flowers before, but I don't remember them smelling so good then."

"Tull, Jenn told me that when a person loses a sense, like sight, sometimes the other senses get sharper to make up for the loss. You feel more with your fingers, hear better, and maybe your sense of smell gets sharper."

The two spent another hour or so exploring the beach before they headed back. "Thanks Dad, this last couple of hours have been special, I enjoyed that. It was something we never did before."

"You know Tull, I did too, and likely if it had not happened, we never would have done it. We will do it again."

Des and Marcus had stayed on the boat that day, and were sitting on the deck with their backs against the wheelhouse wall, on the shady side. They were watching the others on the beach. Marcus said, "I have seen you trying to make Jenn notice you. How has that been going?"

"I've been trying. No other girl has given me such a hard time. Honestly Marcus, usually I just have to be nice to them and smile a bit, but that doesn't work with Jenn. She seems to be trying to tell me something, or learn something."

Marcus said, "Des, maybe you have to learn how to be yourself. I have seen you two together, and I think she is interested in you, but that is the real you, not the one you trot out to impress the girls. You had it too easy with the other girls and they didn't ask that much of you before they gave you what you wanted. This one is a very special girl, there is a lot to her, and she is not one you discard after you have had a roll in the hay. You are chasing this one, but do you really want to catch her? This one, once you catch her, will expect you to be there for her forever. You are my brother, and I love you dearly, but can you give this girl what she wants? You have to think of that, and if you make any sort of commitment, you better mean it. Jenn does not deserve to be played with like all the others."

"I know that. That is why I am interested. The other girls were shallow, they had their uses but none of them was a person to share the rest of your life with. When I met Jenn, I knew she was different. She was the first girl I met that I could see doing that with."

"Have you tried telling her that?"

"What! Admit that. Isn't that the last thing you are supposed to do? Isn't the guy supposed to be so tough he doesn't need anyone?"

"And where did you learn that?"

"That is sorta like Dad is, tough."

"Des, your Dad is tough because he has to be, to protect the ones he loves. Inside he ain't so tough. Look what he has done with us, me, Diz, Chuck and Tully. There was no way he had to take us all in, but he did because he really does have a soft heart in there. He took all of you out of the south before the war because of a promise he made to your mother. Your mother knew what he was like or she wouldn't have asked him to do it. You can be sure he and your mother were totally honest with each other, like you should be with Jenn. What is the worst that could happen if you are honest with her?"

"Maybe she might laugh at me."

"So what? She might also appreciate you are finally being honest with her, and show some honesty in return, and you might be surprised, and pleased, with what she tells you. I think she is worth it."

That evening after dinner, Tully was beating several of his brothers at cards, and Des noticed Jenn was missing. He went out on deck and found her there, just looking at the stars. He went up beside her. Jenn said, "The stars look so big out here at night, with nothing else around. They are so beautiful."

"Yes, they are. Jenn, I don't normally do this with girls, but can I be honest? Can I tell you something with out you thinking I am stupid or weak? Usually I just tell girls what I think they expect to hear."

"I bet that hasn't worked so well up to this point. I don't see anyone hanging there on your arm. Des, I want to hear what you have to say, the real you. Now, what would you like to tell me?"

Des took a gulp, then said, "Jenn, the first time I saw you I knew you were special, I felt something special for you. Did you feel anything special for me? Do you?"

"Des, I will be honest. The first time I saw you I thought you were something special, but I also saw you knew it. I bet you had the girls falling over each other to get to you in New York and the Hamptons. Now, be honest."

"Jenn, honestly, there was a girl in New York. I thought I cared for her. We were together a lot and at the end of the summer she said I had made her pregnant. Thing is, she had another steady boyfriend at the same time, before too, and the doctor said she got pregnant a month before I met her. I was just the rich kid who would be her meal ticket while she carried on with the other guy. Dad busted her. After that, in the Hamptons, there were lots of girls, none for more than one night, and none that I ever cared about. That first one hurt too much. Then I saw you and thought again that maybe there might be a real relationship between me and someone else."

"I believe everything you just said. I could tell that was the truth. The girl in New York tried to pull a dirty trick, but I assume you learned something from that because you had a summer in the Hampton without any further children."

"Honestly? Dad clued us in. He hadn't done it before because he hadn't thought we were there yet. He had a talk with each of us, one by one. Frankly, when he had his big business parties, we found a girl and slipped down to the boat."

"What? All of you?"

"Diz and I, and we took one extra for Marcus. That white hat he wears as Captain, it drives the girls crazy. Chuck never went. He wanted a better relationship, one that would last, and he has it."

"Well, it's nice to know you had an enjoyable summer," Jenn said dryly.

"Thing is Jenn, I didn't. Sure, sex was sex, and I was a fifteen year old boy. None of it meant anything though. When it was over, it was over. Same with the other guys. It's not like we had to try very hard to get the girls to the boat. Jenn, we were prime meat, with a rich Daddy, who probably had twenty times as much money as their Daddies did. If they could have snagged one of us, they would have made a perfect catch."

"So, is that what all of this is about, the fact I am not chasing after you makes me more attractive?" said Jenn angrily.

"Come on Jenn, it's not like that. True, I want you to want me. But more important, I want you. As I said, I knew that as soon as I saw you the first time."

"Well, I don't have anything interesting to tell you about my past, no legions of boyfriends, actually not even one, a girl with two blind parents doesn't have much freedom. I know I am a bit bossy, might come with being a teacher. Now, are you gonna kiss me so we can see whether there really is something, or are we deluded teenagers?"

"Yes ma'am. I like it when you are bossy." Then they kissed deeply and for a long time. Afterwards they stood together looking at the stars. "Well Ma'am, I would say from that kiss there is definitely some chemistry. Now we have to decide what we are going to do about it," said Des.

That night, Tully was bit surprised when Des came in and crawled into bed with him. "Hey Tull, you spend a lot of time with Jenn, just you and her. Has she ever mentioned me?"

"Yes."

"So, what did she say?"

"She told me not to tell you."

"Awww, Tull, we are brothers aren't we? Brothers tell each other everything."

"No they don't. You never told me about the girl that tried to trap you into marrying her, you never told me about all the girls you and Diz and Marcus took to the boat, you never told me nothing, and now you expect me to tell you something I was told as a secret and not to tell you. I am not dumb you know, just blind."

"Tully, where did you get all that. I never told anybody all of it. Only Dad knew. Dad didn't tell you that, did he? You are too young, he should know better."

"Des, don't be stupid, you did tell one person, tonight."

"You mean Jenn came and told you!"

"No stupid. I went to the bathroom. When you are blind you don't bother to turn on the light. You were standing right outside an open porthole."

"Why, you little con artist. Eavesdropping like that."

"There have to be some advantages to this, I finally found one. Now as far as Jenn, she pretty much told you what she told me, she did notice you right at the start, but she thought you were too sure of yourself, that the other girls had spoiled you. That's pretty much what she said to you tonight isn't it?"

"Yeah Tull, she wanted to see the real me"

"I get the impression she saw you and liked you. I stopped counting at 180, that's three minutes."

"What's three minutes? What were you counting?"

"How long the kiss was, I gave up at the three minutes."

Des said, "Tully, you may be blind now, but you don't miss much do you?" The two curled up together and Des rather enjoyed it. It became something he did frequently, for a while.

After the Too had sailed almost the whole East coast of Florida it came upon a small village, some natives and some white people. It did have a dock and a coaler, so Marcus moored and replenished the coal stores. Carl went ashore with CJ and DJ, and got some fresh vegetables for Mama. Marcus talked to a few of the guys lounging on the dock. When everyone had returned to the boat, Marcus met them in the lounge. "I was talking to the guys on the dock, and I looked at the charts. Soon we will be at the tip of Florida, and we can head west, or we can continue south along the keys to the end, Key West. The guys on the dock said it was interesting. We can anchor there for the night, or take a space at the dock if there is one. Then, tomorrow, we can head north again and there is a little village on the other side called Naples, a lot of Italians there. So, I thought I'd give you the choice. Key West is as far south as the country gets."

The group agreed to head south to Key West, after all they had no set schedule. The keys were fascinating, little islets that seemed to just rise out of the sea, beautiful white sands and a few palm trees. They got to Key West in the late afternoon, and found a typical small fishing village. There was a space at the dock so the Too tied up to it. The group decided they would go out for dinner at one of the outdoor cafes as the weather was balmy. Tully was a bit hesitant as this would be the first time he had eaten in public. Jenn said, "It's okay Tull. We will help you, and for sure there will be something other than soup. Now, take my arm, and enjoy yourself."

They found a nice café overlooking the docks and the Gulf of Mexico, and they took a large table. Jenn sat on one side of Tully and Des on the other. The waiter came with the menus and put one down in front of Tully. Jenn reached over and slid it under hers then opened hers between them. She read the list aloud to him and said, "Tull, they have spare ribs, which you eat by hand, you might like them, and they have whole corn, on the cob, which you also eat by hand and they have that new southern soda, root beer, it comes in a big mug."

When the order was taken, the three all had the ribs and the corn, as well as the root beer. Several of the others had fish and rice, or ribs too. The waitress put the root beer down in front of Tully, and Des eased his hand over Tully's and slid it over to the mug. When Tully had his hand in the handle, Des said softly, "Now put it where you know it is, just make sure you leave room for the waiter to put down the plate." When Tully's plate arrived, Jenn turned it slightly and whispered, "Ribs across the top from three to nine, corn at six. That was all Tully needed. He enjoyed the rest of the meal and relaxed. Everybody joked and talked, and it was a happy time. Tully's dark glasses were not even out of place as it was still quite bright out. At the end of the meal, Jenn gave Tully's face a little swipe and said, "Missed a bit of sauce hon," in a perfectly natural way. Carl paid the bill and the group made their way back to the boat, trailed by the ever present Pinkertons. Other than Marcus, the group stayed awake fairly late in the lounge with the cards. As was becoming the practice, Tully was beating them all.

The next morning, early, Marcus set sail. A couple of the Pinkertons helped him cast off as most of the Too's passengers were still asleep. Carl awoke and came out of his cabin, surprised to see they were at sea. He went into the wheelhouse and Marcus said, "I was talking to one of the fishermen on the dock last night. He said there was a big storm coming tonight, from the south, so I thought it best we leave early and get into the port at Naples. These old fishermen are usually right."

"Good idea son. Out there at the end of the keys you are a bit exposed to any big storms that come in. You think we will make port okay?"

"Yeah, I think so. There is no sign yet of anything behind us." By about noon, you could see the dark smudge of a storm on the horizon astern; but you could see the coast of Florida ahead and to the right. As the afternoon progressed the seas got rougher and the waves higher. Jenn made Tully sit in one of the big chairs in the lounge and she sat with him. The others circulated in and out of the lounge to and from the deck. It was an exciting afternoon, and even though relegated to a chair, Tully shared in the excitement.

Jenn said, "Remember when I told you there would be times when safety and common sense would dictate what you had to do, this is an example of one of them. With the boat moving the way it is, you are safer in that chair. Actually, some of your brothers are being rather foolish. If any of them go overboard, there is no way we could get to them."

About five thirty Marcus sighted Naples ahead and about an hour later pulled into the port and found a space to tie up at a crowded dock. By eight, the storm had taken hold and the boat was moving considerably even though she was moored. Marcus had the lines doubled up. Mama Clarisa did not start dinner until the boat had docked and even then, dinner was sandwiches and fruit. There was no way something could be cooked in the galley with the boat moving the way it was. The family spent the evening in the lounge together and Des and Jenn sat on a sofa side by side, holding hands discretely between them. Carl did notice however. By about 9:30, the storm had abated enough so the family could go to bed. Carl said he would stay in with Tully in case he needed to get up or needed something. Tully did not object, he enjoyed the little talks he had with his father as they were falling asleep.

Carl said, "You spend a lot of time with Jenn, are she and Des getting close?"

"Dad, they are close. I wouldn't be surprised if we marry off another brother before we get to Texas."

"Do you think they are meant for each other? Are they a set?"

"Dad, I have heard them together. Des is different with her. With other girls he is all, I dunno, braggy, sure of himself, all trying to be someone. With her he is gentle, and calm, and a little unsure. It is good for Des to be a bit unsure of himself. You are more likely to find the real person when he is not so sure of himself. They both have told me separately they saw the other that very first day and were interested."

"Tully, how did you get so wise at ten?"

"I spent a lot of time alone with nothing to do but think, I guess."

The next morning, at breakfast, Carl said, "We get to Tallahassee in about a week. There is a LePrad there. I am sending the railcar North to get the naval architects from Newport. They have laid the keel for the Three but there are some final decisions that have to be made now. Dr. Fellers will be going north with the car. I have convinced him to come with us when we do the world trip next year, so he figures he should go back for a while with his patients. Now is the time to tell me if you want anything from the north, while the train is going there."

Carl noted that after breakfast Des and Jenn were deep in conversation, as expected and intended. They came to him. Des said, "Dad, can we have the Baxters, Jenn's parents, on the car when it comes down to Tallahassee? We want to get married. You probably think it is a rush, but we have known for a while. We are sure."

Jenn added, "Maybe they can bring me a dress, my dress dummy is still at home."

"I am not surprised. I knew from that first day, and Des, if anyone can make you grow up it is Jenn. Jenn, you make him face the world. He has a lot to offer it. Before we leave Naples, we will check to see if it has a telegraph. I know the next place, Miami, does. We will send the railway a wire telling them they have to go to New York with the car in addition to Newport, and you can compose what you want to tell your parents." They can go back with the car when it goes back with the shipyard people. We can send Deeds with the car when it goes North, to make sure everything goes right. He has some business to attend to for me anyway." Naples did have a telegraph line and Jenn's parents were notified of, and invited to, their daughter's impending wedding. The railway was notified, and the car was to be in Tallahassee five days hence and would go north to Rhode Island and New York, south to Tallahassee then north and south again over a period of a week or two. Carl requested an engine and crew be assigned to the car for a three week period. The railway was also notified the engine and crew would be required again in Texas a few weeks later for transportation to a private siding at the new ranch. Deeds was given private instructions by Carl to arrange the same wedding gift as Chuck and Mag had received, cash and draft. Des asked Deeds to see to a set of rings when he was in New York, assuming correctly his father would pay for them.

The Too then left Naples and sailed north for Miami. On that leg, Dizzy made a point of hunting up Carl for a private conversation. "Dad, on the Three, you should make sure they put in a radio room. I have been doing a lot of reading on this. There is this man Marconi, who has plans for setting up radio stations all over the world. Ships will be able to talk to each other and to anywhere in the world as easily as we use the telegraph. You should make sure we have room for that on Three, a room 12 feet by 12 feet would be big enough. It has to be on the top deck, close to the bridge, an aerial, and it has to have lots of electricity. Something else Dad, I have decided, that is what I want to do, work somehow on this communications thing, for boats, and more. I haven't figured all that out yet."

Therefore, two days later, when the Too pulled into Tampa Bay Carl was thinking of a lot of separate topics encompassing all the boys. This was all immediately replaced by one overwhelming thought, "Boy, this place is beautiful, amazing beaches and lush vegetation." Deeds was standing beside him. "Remember, I said to invest in Florida real estate? This is where I want a large part of it, as well as on the other side, Miami. I can see these small towns some day being major resort areas. Buy as much as you can get. In fact, I want a LePrad resort hotel in both within three years."

Tampa was large enough to have a good tailor, and as soon as they docked Carl took Des there to be fitted for a wedding tuxedo. They would pick it up the next day, before they left. The two days there were used to explore the little town. His brothers made a point of including Tully in their adventures, and protecting him when necessary from the prying eyes of the townspeople. By this point, Jenn had taught Tully how to use the white cane and he found it so freed him he didn't care what people thought. In fact, all the brothers had to keep an eye on him as he tended to set off on little explorations of his own, with little regard to passing wagons or horses. Just as Des had finally decided he was ready to face the world and a new set of responsibilities, Tully had decided he was ready to face the world also, despite the fact he couldn't see it. Jenn saw this and mentioned something to Carl that got him thinking.

"You know, they are starting to work with dogs in New York as aids for the blind. The blind person has the cane and the dog on a short harness. The dog acts as the eyes for the blind person, making sure he doesn't step out in front of a wagon or something." There was another item for Deeds to see to when he was in New York, and two more passengers for the rail car on the way back.

The Too pulled out of Tampa Bay two days later and headed north again. Four days after that the Sea Vista Too pulled into the landing near Crawfordville, as close as they could get to Tallahassee. Some of the Pinkertons were put in charge of the yacht, and instructed to see to its provisioning. Everyone loaded into a couple of carriages, with the luggage to follow, and proceeded to the LePrad hotel in Tallahassee.

They were expected at the hotel and Carl had a word with the manager to ensure the honeymoon suite was kept available for the duration of their visit. Deedsmadehiswaytothetrainstation,locatedtherailcarandsetoffforthenorth. Carl and the rest of the party settled into the hotel to await the return, meanwhile, little excursions were organized around the city.

Chapter 15

Weddings and Texas

Deeds returned from New York in about three days, with the Baxters, a dog and handler, and a whole bunch of people from Newport. After a few hugs and hellos, Jenn left her parents to interrogate Des and went with Tully and Carl, as well as the dog and its handler; gathering in a field out behind the hotel. Tully had been introduced to the dog and had his face washed in return. Now the handler was showing Tully how to walk with the dog and to recognize his cues, how the dog would lead him around obstacles and stop if there was danger. These dogs were trained in protection and would growl if someo0ne approached in a threatening manner. They could fetch some small items if trained to. The dog's name was Cleo, and the two soon became a pair. She took a while to approve of all the brothers, and she seemed at first determined to keep Des and Jenn from sitting together. Des looked suspiciously at Jenn's parents wondering if perhaps they had arranged something with the dog handler.

Jenn and her parents had a private conversation to insure she knew what she was doing. Then they had a long conversation with Jenn and Des together, trying to determine what they wanted to do. Jenn confirmed that she intended to go through with the new school at Oakside, and Des said he was agreeable to work with her on that, handle some of the administrative duties and perhaps teach a class. He had been well educated by tutors.

The Baxters pointed out this was going to be a residential school, which means someone would have to stay each night in the school with the children. "We assumed we would live in the school, not Oakside, although we want to include the children at Oakside activities, for examples picnics or holidays. It is a rural setting. There will be lots of time outside and we will have our own fields," said Des.

Jenn's father said, "Des, I mean this kindly, but you are buying into Jenn's dream, running a school for the blind. If you had never met her you wouldn't be doing that. It concerns me for the long term, for your happiness."

"True, I was searching for the future before I met Jenn, but not that hard if I am honest. Frankly, I was more interested in the girls. Now that will be taken care of, and the fact is that at some time soon we may have a family of our own, I have to settle down. The school is at Oakside, and all of the potential of the estate is there for me. My brother Diz, and his new wife Nan, are going to settle there because he will work on breeding horses, all different kinds of horses. As well, part of this trip is to show us boys some of my father's other interests. He is hoping me and my brothers will settle on parts of the "Empire" so to speak. I may, but I know it will have to be something that can be run out of Oakside, because that is where the school will be, and my wife and children."

"We would have preferred that the two of you have greater direction, but when we were your age, we didn't either, we just knew we would be together, just as you are. I can see your father is actively exposing his sons to his investments hoping for some matches, and I hope he is successful. The new school will be a good base, but Des, I think for you to be happy you will need something more. From what I can gather, you have led an exciting childhood and you will need something that challenges you. However, Jenn's mom and I can see the two of you have something special so we think this marriage will work."

It was agreed the wedding would take place the following day at three. Tully would again be the best man, he had the experience and the suit. Mel would again be Matron of Honor. Carl had engaged a local minister recommended to him by the hotel manager when he had gone down for the Honey Moon Suite key. He also scheduled his inspection of the hotel for a couple days after the wedding."

Carl also had a quiet talk with all the brothers. "Tully now has Cleo, and Cleo is a dog, which means she has to be taken out several times a day. We are lucky with this suite as we have a big terrace and I expect Tully will be able to use that. On the boat, I will get DJ and CJ to do it and clean it up. However, if he decides to take the dog for a walk outside, can you all make sure one of you goes with him? The dog is amazing, but if someone decides to mug a blind kid I doubt if the dog could stop him." The boys agreed. Carl also had a talk with the Pinkertons, who had had their numbers supplemented with the joining up with the rail car.

Jenn's parents, the Baxters, turned out to be wonderful people, lively and amusing, with wonderful senses of humor. Dinner that night was a roaring event. The Baxter's listened carefully as first Mag and Mel told about their first meeting and how they knew immediately they were meant for each other, but Mag admitted it took him a couple of years to work up the nerve to ask Mel to marry him. Chuck and Nan talked about how they met, how Chuck kept getting shot. "I had to do something, couldn't just keep getting shot to see her." said Chuck.

After dinner, the Baxters made a point of sitting with Tully and gently asking how he was doing. Tull was honest. "I think it would have been better if I had never known what it was like to see. Now I know what I am missing and what I can no longer do. There are many times when I hear the others, they try to include me, but there are just things that I can't do anymore which were so simple before, like say Baseball. I would love to go swimming in the pond again, and ride a horse like the wind through the fields. Some things are just too dangerous now. Sometimes I feel so alone. I actually am looking forward to the new school because at least there will be some more people like me who understand completely. At least I have a family who go out of their way to include me, I guess a lot of people don't have that. They must just get shut away in a room."

"You are right Tully. That is why these schools are so important to get those children out of those rooms. The school your Dad is building will take children from all over the state for free. Those cigarettes with your name on them, they will pay for all of that."

That night Des came into Tully's room. "Thought I would sleep here tonight, will likely be the last time for a while. You understand that Tull, no hard feelings?"

"Sure Des, wish I was old enough and had someone to marry, I would do the same. You and Jenn are good together, I hope you two are happy, and maybe you will have lots of kids to drive you crazy like we do Dad. Remember, Mag almost had triplets, so it can happen all at once."

"You just said that so I wouldn't sleep at all tonight, you little rat," and with that they tussled on the bed awhile laughing. Then they curled together and after a while Des said, "Tull, what do you think I will be like as a Dad. It scares me a bit, that I might not be good enough."

"Des, with me you have been great. That is all I have to go on, but I wouldn't worry about it. The way I see it, the first couple of years it is mainly the mother, so you have time to learn. Then you have to do the next sixteen or so."

"Jesus Tull, you are not helping a lot here you know."

"I know Des," said Tully laughing.

The next day was pretty much taken up with preparations for the wedding. After breakfast, Carl met with Tully and Des to make sure their suits were okay, and they had everything they needed. Des gave Tully the two wedding bands and made sure they both knew where they put them in the suit. No one wanted lunch, they were too nervous.

Jenn and her mother went downstairs and had their hair done. They shared a few quiet moments, and then helped each other dress. At 2:30, they all met in the lounge and Carl introduced them to the Reverend Small who would conduct the ceremony. Promptly at three Rev Small began the wedding ceremony and by three fifteen Jenn and Des were the new Mr. D. Montroses. There was a wedding dinner afterwards and people were hungry by then, over their nervousness. Carl knelt beside Des and handed him an envelope and a key. "Some cash for the week, a place to stay, and something more for when you two find your dream. In the mean time, Deeds will help you with the investing if you want. Then Carl slipped away as Des checked the envelope. $100 000.00 in cash and a draft for a million. Des was surprised by that amount, and the cash. What were they supposed to do with that in Tallahassee? He had no intention of leaving their rooms anyway. Des and Jenn got increasingly nervous and by 5:30 they were on their way to their suite. Carl said to Jenn's parents, "I'm surprised they lasted that long, you could tell they were dying to get out of here for an hour." The Baxters smiled, "We remember, we were young once."

Carl went on, "Tomorrow I meet with the shipyard people and the day after the train will go back. I hope that doesn't inconvenience you too much." The Baxters said that would be fine.

Downstairs in the suite the newlyweds were already in bed, but Jenn was a little nervous. "Now Des, you have had some experience at this, but I haven't. Is there anything I should know."

"Hon, don't worry, I know enough to get us started and after that nature takes over; and if we don't get it right the first time, we can do it again. We have a whole week to get it right."

A half hour later they were laying together. "Des, that was so good, but I think we can do better. Can we try again?"

"At your service ma'am. My aim is to keep you happy." That was exactly what they did for seven days and nights. And, as Carl hoped, but no one knew at the time, he was going to be a grandfather, again.

The next day Carl, Deeds, Mag, Marcus and Dizzy met with the people from Newport. The naval architects reported, "We laid the keel, and we have completed the hull. Her length is 254 feet and she has a beam of 34 feet. We will have two steam engines and two propellers. There will be a total of four decks as it stands. You have the main deck with two large lounges, a dining room and a service pantry, some washrooms and a study. Above the main deck you have the wheelhouse, a chart room, Captain's quarters and two mate's cabins, washrooms, and a couple extra cabins. "

Here Carl cut in. "Those last two cabins, put a hatch joining them. One will be a future radio room, and beside it the quarters for the radio man. There has to be lots of power to that room." Dizzy was beaming. "My son here, Dizzy, has been studying up on this, these radios are very close to being readily available and we have to have the room when they are."

The naval architect went on, "The first deck below is the owner's quarters and the staterooms for guests, all with their own baths. That level also has the main galley, with dumbwaiters up to the dining room, and down to the crew's mess. The second deck below is for the staff that serves the owner as well as the ship's crew for the deck and the engine room, and since the ship is so complex, a chief engineer, for the engines and the complex water and waste systems."

"Now you have to make some decisions. The original concept was as a coal burner. We would like to take out some of the coal bunkers and put in some oil tanks, making one of the boilers oil only. Standard oil is putting in oil at all the coaling stations world wide. It's cleaner and takes up less space. The ship will be lighter and faster too. At some point in the future you can convert to total oil for steam."

"Look, if the future will be oil, and you are sure we can get it anywhere, then that is the way we should go, all oil. The ship will be lighter and faster, and cleaner. It will need less staff to run it. We want to use this ship for at least twenty years, likely more."

"Fine, that is the direction we will take then. As far as accommodation, there will be sixteen cabins on the owner's deck, and the crew's deck can have eighteen, two or three per cabins. The staterooms on the owner's decks are much larger, each with their own washroom. That is because the second deck below has to accommodate a crew's mess and the engine room while the owner's deck only has to allow for the galley."

"Now propulsion. Do you want sails or is this going to be only a motor yacht? We can still put in a couple of masts, just for cruising, but you can't get the full treatment unless you allow for a whole lot more crewmen. It would take a lot of crewmen to sail a ship this size."

Carl responded, "Skip the sails and that will cut back on the crew a bit. Now, what about the special package I requested. Did you get what you needed from the Secretary of the Navy?"

"You have the permission to be an armed motor yacht. We can put in a cannon in the bow, one in the stern, and two on the top deck, one fore and aft. Then heavy machine guns, nine around the ship. We will put the gun mounts in, and the guns stored nearby, ready to drop in. We can put armor around the wheelhouse and in the walls, all around the upper deck, bulletproof glass in all the windows, even the portholes. We are upgrading the plating on the hull, and the deck below the teak. This thing will be more bullet resistant than most warships. You will be faster too, about 13 knots, maybe more. We have a well armored hold for the ammunition with a system to flood it if it were ever hit. Now for all this ordinance you have to have people to man it. You will see that we have allowed for a mess area for the marines, accommodates two dozen, and their officers can take some of the crew cabins."

"So, for staffing, we have the engineer, two firemen, two seamen, two mates, and the Captain. Then there are a dozen Pinkertons, two dozen marines, two or three officers, and then you have to look at the service staff, a cook, two or three stewards, an assistant cook or two, and perhaps a couple of maids. We have thus allowed for a crew of about five dozen. This would all depend on where you are sailing. For example, in the Gulf you likely could do without the marines, and if the capacity of guest passengers was low then some of the cleaning or serving staff could be reduced. But we have to allow for the max, in the worst location."

"To sail world wide you are building a small ship, but you have to meet almost all the needs of a large one. This actually is large for a yacht."

Carl sat back and said to Deeds and his sons, "Well, is there anything else we need?

Mag said, "Remember that a couple of the cabins have to be made to accommodate children, upper and lower berths, and maybe a berth for a nanny, and if this is a world-wide trip for a year there will have to be a tutor or two, likely with cabins on the owner's level. Also, it looks like there will be a doctor on this trip. Shouldn't there at least be an infirmary?" Carl agreed to all the suggestions and they were noted by the people from Newport.

"Dad," said Marcus, "I can handle the Too, but this is much more of a ship. Don't you think maybe we should be looking for a real captain?"

"No, you will be the Captain, but there will be three mates, and we will look for some experience there. In addition, that month or so we spend ashore at the new ranch, I have hired a master mariner to join us and brush you up on your navigation and chart skills. One of the things we are going to look at in Texas, Galveston, is a shipping company. I am looking for that company to be a source for us of the seamen, engineer, mates and whatever else we need for the Three. When we get back to Oakside next summer, the Three will be there. We can get our crew up from Texas, and you and them can take her out for a few practice runs before the cruise, and then we may take her to the Hamptons before we set off. So, again, you are the Captain as far as we are concerned. And maybe, in the next few years, when we have long periods ashore, you can do a couple voyages in our ships from Galveston." Marcus nodded. That suited him to a tee.

Deeds said, "I have to admit, you surprised me Carl when a yacht turned into a small battleship. Where are we going that we need all that, although I must admit this family does attract opposition."

"The Middle East and the Far East, the Philippines, Sumatra, Borneo, parts of China. They are all still quite wild. You know we are going into oil. There is oil in the Middle East and the Far East. Malaya also has rubber. I want to see some of those rubber plantations. Oil and rubber will be the mainstays of a modern industrial economy so I think this family should get their piece of all that."

Carl turned to the people from Newport and said, "Do you have what you need? I want her finished and tied to our dock in the Hamptons when we get back early in the new year. By the end of next August, we will be getting ready to go, and by the next Christmas she will be in Europe and the Med."

"We just need her official name," they said.

"I thought you knew. She will be called Sea View Three officially, register her in New York. We will call her The Three."

That evening the Montroses and the Baxters ate in the suite. Jenn managed to slip away from Des for a half hour to say goodbye to her parents and promised to see them again at the new school the next spring. Carl agreed, saying they would stop at Oakside on the way to the Hamptons in the summer.

The next morning, the Baxters, the dog trainer, the people from Newport and Stephen Fellers all boarded the private car and left for the north. That same morning Marcus went out to the Too to see if she had been provisioned in order to leave at the end of the week.

Tully and Cleo were constantly together and grew very close, as they were supposed to. The dog knew Tully's habits and anticipated his needs, even picking up the odd lost piece of clothing from the floor and finding the wayward shoe. One of the others observed dryly, "Tull has the mother he has been missing for the last few years." But Carl noticed how protective the dog was of Tully and one night he went with Tully to walk the dog around the block, before going to bed. Cleo seemed nervous that night, so Carl was not surprised when three tough looking men assailed them on the street behind the hotel.

"Hey, it's the blind guy with the dog, and a friend. We only want some cash; you guys seem to have enough of it. Let's say twenty bucks each, now is that asking that much? One of the men pulled a knife from his waistband to stress his request. Cleo leapt at him, surprising Tully and wresting her halter from his hands. Carl also reached in his jacket, pulling out a pistol which he leveled at the two still standing, the third having a snarling dog standing over him, prepared to tear his throat out. At that moment two Pinkerton men also emerged from the shadows behind them, also with their guns drawn.

"So fellas, do we turn you over to the police or give you ten minutes to get out of town? I don't feel like giving the dog a bath tonight, otherwise I would let him go ahead, but it makes a mess of his fur."

The men begged to be let free and the Pinkertons made sure they were disarmed then let them go. Carl returned Cleo's halter to Tull, who had listened closely to what had transpired. He said, as he praised the dog and rubbed her ears, "She really would have protected me, wouldn't she? And you Dad, packing a gun again? I was beginning to wonder why we had all the Pinkertons around, but I see why again. The rich are targets, and so are the blind. I guess people think I am both."

"Yes Tull, I am afraid you are both, rich and blind. So, that means you have to be extra careful. Just another lesson you have had to learn."

That night Carl glanced into Tully's room. He was asleep, laying on the bed, one arm down to the floor where Cleo slept. Poor Rabbit was still on his shelf, looking a bit miffed, Carl thought.

At the end of the week, Jenn and Des emerged from the Honeymoon Suite and joined the others for the trip out to the Too. They sat together in the corner of one of the carriages holding hands. They were quiet, almost serene. Carl saw them together and knew he had been correct in going along with the marriage. Des seemed to have aged a couple years in the week, and seemed more mature. The first night after they left, the TOO anchored off Point Saint Joe.

It was a quiet calm evening, and everyone spent some time on deck watching the sunset over the Gulf of Mexico. When it got dark, they all moved inside to the lounge. Jenn and Des were seen in a corner in deep conversation with Deeds. Carl asked him about it afterwards and was told, "They are taking this investing thing seriously. They told me they wanted to invest the million ninety thousand until they figured out what they wanted to invest it in permanently. We talked about the different kinds of investments they could make that would be safe but still have the money available easily if they wanted it. In the end, they decided they would invest in government bonds. I think you better allow for a whole day in New Orleans so they can go to a bank. I was impressed by the two of them. Des never seemed so serious about anything."

"Having a family does force a boy to become a man, doesn't it? I think another nine months from now he will also be a father, around the beginning of the summer. About a month after Mag and Mel, although they haven't told me yet, probably that three-month rule thing."

That evening Carl noticed DJ and CJ as they performed their new duty. Carl had talked to them and they had agreed to follow Tull around the deck twice a day when he walked Cleo. They each carried a pail of soapy water, and when Cleo was finished and moved on, the boys would use the water to flush her deposits overboard. Tully made a point of thanking them, and said that occasionally he would let them walk the dog. The boys liked that idea as they were fond of Cleo; a feeling that was mutual. Dogs seemed to always like young boys.

The next morning, Marcus weighed anchor as soon as he could, well before the others were awake. He wanted to get to Pensacola that day, and to cover that distance in one day would be difficult. He advanced the speed indicator to full and the yacht knifed through the waves. He even had Des and Diz unfurl a few of the sails for the added speed. When Carl awoke and came on deck, he couldn't help being excited by their rate of progress. Just after dinner, the Too pulled into Pensacola Bay. The Bay itself was beautiful, just as the sun was starting to set. Des and Jenn stood by the rail, holding each other and watching the sun set. They both agreed this was one of their favorite places from the trip so far. Marcus did not bother pulling up to the dock, as it would be easier in the morning to just slip away. He did set two anchors though, in case the wind came up over night.

The next day was an easy sail. They quickly sailed past the small coastline of Alabama, then Mississippi as far as Gulfport, where Marcus took a spot at the city dock. This put them right in the middle of all the action, the fishermen and shrimpers, as they came in at the end of the day. There were a couple of Pinkertons stationed on deck as usual every time they tied up at a dock. Tully had taken a seat in a deck chair and pulled a hat down over his eyes. Cleo sat there beside him, looking over the activity on the dock. Then she started to growl and the Pinkertons came over to see what was bothering her. They looked down and saw there was someone trying to get one of the portholes open from the outside. They yelled and the man dropped a package and ran. One of the detectives chased him while the other checked out the package. The town constable had been attracted by the excitement and he was looking over the detective's shoulder as he opened the package carefully.

"Hey, that a …" said the town policeman.

"Yeah, it's a bomb. He was trying to get a porthole open. If he had succeeded, he would have lit it, dropped it in, and ran. A bomb this size would have done a lot of damage, maybe even sunk her. There are lots of boats around, he could have chosen any of them, but he chose this one. He must have had a reason."

Marcus and Carl had been summoned and joined the detective and the policeman on the dock. The detective said to Carl, "He was trying to get one of the portholes open, if he had, he would have lit it and dropped it in.

We heard Cleo growling, and we saw him. My partner chased him, haven't seen either of them since."

"The Too isn't made to handle the amount of water that would have come in. That likely would have sunk her." They were interrupted as the missing detective staggered through the crowd. "I caught him, but he had a knife." With that he sank to the ground and the others gathered around. The town policeman sent one of the crowd to get a nearby doctor who, when he looked at the man, said, "Dead, knife wound." That news shook the gathering up. The town policeman had to get involved and he asked the other detective to come to the police station to give a report. Carl sent one of his sons to get the head Pinkerton and bring him out. Deeds also appeared and Carl directed him to see to having the body prepared and sent home to New York. A wire was sent to the New York Pinkerton office to prepare them to meet the body. Carl asked if the dead detective had a family and when he was told there was a wife and a child, he said to Deeds, "Have one of our people in New York see the widow. Give her a hundred thousand and help her find a job if she wants one."

Several more detectives were sent topside and Carl said, "Marcus, as soon as our man gets back, let's go out in the bay to anchor. It's too late for us to leave today but we can get some space between us and the shore, and we can leave first thing in the morning." Then he went up the gangplank and said to the gathered boys, "I want all of you to get your pistols from the trunk, and keep them loaded and handy. I have no idea what is going on here, but whoever made the bomb intended it for us. We are going to move out into the bay as soon as our man gets back."

It was an uneasy night. They felt a little better after they moved out offshore, but no one really rested that night. In the morning, Carl had Marcus pull up to the dock. Several detectives were arrayed around the ship while Carl and Deeds went to the police station. Carl talked to the detectives to see if they had any idea who was responsible for the attack.

"You are a rich man with lots of interests, and that kind of man makes enemies. There are also people who are jealous of the rich. So far, we don't have a culprit, but there has been a murder. We take that seriously. Do you have someplace you can be reached after you leave here?"

Deeds gave him the address of a firm of lawyers they were using in Galveston. "They will know how to reach us all the time we are in Texas. When we go east, they will know. You can send us a wire in care of them."

The two then returned to the boat and Marcus set sail for New Orleans. It was a relatively short trip and in the early afternoon the Too headed up the Mississippi to a berthing space on the waterfront of New Orleans. There was a LePrad hotel there, so the family moved into it. Carl told the manager they would likely be there for about a week, and that he would do an inspection the next day. The Pinkertons were stationed in the halls of their floor. Several had been left on the ship. Des and Jenn slipped out and across the street to a bank where they purchased almost 1.1 million dollars worth of government bonds. Deeds went in and talked to them. Fifteen minutes later Des came out and handed him a slip of paper with the serial numbers of the bonds on it. Deeds had told them that if the serial numbers were kept separately from the bonds, they could be replaced if they were physically destroyed, like in a fire or something. Carl then had a meeting with all the family.

"I have had the railcars and an engine brought here. Louisiana has a large role in the family's investments. There are several LePrads in addition to this one. There are others in La Fayette, Baton Rouge, and Shreveport. That's a total of four. There is also a lot of oil along the coast. There are some places it just bubbles out of the ground, mostly in the southern part of the state, but there are a couple in the northern part of the state that look promising too. We have property all over the south of the state and oil options on many more areas. An option means we have the right to explore, drill and extract oil on the properties in question. So, the plan is for me to inspect this hotel today, and have a few meetings. Tomorrow we will all load the railcar and take a tour of the state, brief pauses for the other three hotels, we won't check in and those of you that wish may stay on the car. The real reason for the tour is to eyeball some of the lands we have purchased. Be prepared for a long day on the train, bring your toys and games. I am not prepared to leave anyone behind, given the guy with the bomb, and boys, I still want you to keep loaded guns handy. We still don't know who is mad at us now or why, but it would be reasonable to assume it has nothing to do with Oakside. It has to be something to do with our new Southern investments; Louisiana and the oil, Texas, the oil, the shipping and the new ranch. So be alert, keep together, and Des and Jenn keep an eye on Tull, he can't shoot now but that dog of his seems to be able to spot trouble."

After Carl and Deeds left on their tour of the New Orleans Hotel, the brothers sat around talking. Marcus said, "I haven't seen him so edgy since the start of the Oakside difficulties."

"Once before," said Mag, "When we first went out west and encountered the Apache. Dad has a good nose for trouble, and I would suggest we listen to him. There is something up. People don't just go around trying to blow up yachts for fun, and remember, whoever it is has already killed."

The tour of the hotel was going well. It was an old-style southern hotel, large galleries and balconies on the second two stories, big walk out windows. The rooms themselves were all large, mainly to accommodate the heat in the summer. The electrification of the hotel had been completed on the first floor and in many parts of the second and third. The manager was saying, "The guests with the electrified rooms were a bit leery at first, but they soon got to like them. The electrified rooms all have a big ceiling fan and the lights and lamps of course. The electricians are working on the second and third floors now. After the tour of the facility, Carl said, "You are doing a good job here and it is a nice well-run hotel. Just keep up the good work and get the electrification of the hotel finished. The guests like it. I will be checking on the other three tomorrow, and a day or two after that we will be out of your hair."

Early, the next morning the whole group was on the train and heading west. After about Morgan City, you could see the gulf to the left side of the train. "This is where our land is, between the rail tracks and the gulf, all the way from Morgan City to New Iberia. Some of the lots go right down to the shore, and some even go five miles out under the Gulf. Word is they will soon be able to erect platforms over the water that they can drill for oil from. The Montroses may not get this oil in my lifetime, but they will in yours. This, and some of the other investments, will be your future."

When they pulled into Lafayette, only Deeds and Carl got off. The hotel was across the street from the station, and it was only two stories tall. Carl was back in an hour with Deeds in tow. He was saying to Deeds as he came in, "Nice little hotel, always full, as are the restaurants. That is what happens when you have a good location." The train then pulled out and headed for Baton Rouge. The hotel in Baton Rouge was much larger and again by the station. Carl and Deeds left the car and walked outside. Carl looked across at the LePrad. It was three stories tall. There were groups of people gathered in front of the hotel, along with solitary women who seemed to be patrolling the block. Carl turned back to the car then walked in and sat, surprising the others who thought he would be gone at least the hour. They looked at him for an answer. Carl said, "Deeds sell it, I don't want it. Ruffians hanging out in front and hookers. That is not the type of hotel I want to be associated with. You can send a wire to the real estate brokers when we get to Shreveport." Carl was mumbling under his breath then said to his sons, "Boys, there is the reason we are doing this inspection trip. A rotten apple like that one can spoil the barrel as they say. Up to this point all the hotels have been excellent, or at least redeemable, like Washington, where Brent and Sally went. This one was not worth the effort. I could see it as soon as I took my first look. You guys remember that. There are occasions when the best decision is to cut your losses and not spend any more effort at all."

The conductor came up to Carl for instructions. Carl said, "Ready to go. Get this show on the road to Shreveport." He then added for the others, "Our properties are mainly between Pineville and Couchella, assorted lots on both sides of the railway. And we have some industrial land in Shreveport near the railway for a refinery when the wells get here. Everything we have in the South, to do with oil, is owned by the Montrose oil company. If you see a big green M and a small red O, then it belongs to us." That started the count the signs game, and by the time they got to Shreveport the total number of signs spotted was 39.

Carl commented, "That last big sign in the really big industrial lot is the one for the refinery, it will take a bit for that to be fully developed, but we will start on it."

Mag commented, "You really have done this for the long term, for us, haven't you Dad."

"Wait till we go on the world trip and we stop in California. There is some real potential there for the future." Carl then suggested they all go to the Shreveport LePrad and have lunch while he did his inspection. The family readily agreed. At least they would get a taste of upstate Louisiana. Cleo was left with the Pinkertons, much to her protestations, but everyone knew there would be problems if they tried to take her into the dining room. Several cabs were ordered, and the group set off. The hotel was in the center of town, away from the rail-yards, which pleased Carl. There was a genteel southern atmosphere to the hotel, and when they entered the lobby it was rather hushed. Carl did note however that the chandeliers had been electrified so that process had at least started. Carl introduced himself to the manager, who had arrived at the influx of such a large group of evidently wealthy Northerners. He seemed a bit surprised to be face to face with the owner, but he gritted his teeth and graciously showed the family into the dining room and saw them seated in a large alcove. He motioned and there were quickly several servers tending to their needs. Carl then told them that he and the manager would do an inspection tour while the family ate. The manager looked a bit suspiciously at the several men standing around the room and Carl said, "My Pinkertons, we had someone go after the yacht with a bomb recently, so they are rather vigilant, but we just try to ignore them."

The tour of the hotel went well for the manager. He ran a tight ship and Carl noted and commented positively on it. "You have a very well-run establishment here. I am proud to say I own it. I didn't feel that way about the Baton Rouge hotel and I ordered it sold."

The manager said, "But, that is the state capitol."

"I am not saying we don't need a Baton Rouge LePrad, but we don't need that one. Now, if, or rather when, we decide to build a new LePrad there; would you be interested in moving there to oversee its construction and then to run it? Or would it be too much of an imposition on your family? Our new hotel will be totally modern, fully electrified right from the start, and about twice the size this one is. There would be a comparable adjustment in your salary. Frankly, this is the best run hotel I have seen in the South, even better than the one in New Orleans. There will be a new corporate structure in the future with a system of regional vice-presidents. I can see you getting one of those positions."

The manager of the hotel was a bit flustered. When he came in that day, he had done so without any idea of perhaps having to make the biggest decision of his career. "Mr. Montrose, I would be happy to serve in any place and position you need me. There is only my wife and I, so we can move where required."

"Okay then, it may take a while, but your next move will be to Baton Rouge for the new hotel, and after that we will see. It still hasn't been decided where corporate headquarters will be, but at some point, I will bring you there. I am thinking perhaps Washington though."

They returned to the dining room where the family was just finishing what they said was an excellent meal. Carl gave the manager payment for the meal, despite his protestations. "I should pay for this. If I didn't the cost would be reflected in you balance sheets, in a very minor way, but still. And, give the servers ten dollars each. They did a good job too." The family moved toward the front entrance and stood out side as they waited for the cabs to be prepared. Then a shot rang out from across the street to be met by a hail of bullets from the Pinkertons. The family dropped to the ground, but several heads poked up with pistols raised and ready.

One of the Pinkertons ran back and searched out Carl, "It's okay sir, we got him, but I am afraid he can't talk. He has a few too many bullet holes for that now." Carl then rose and checked out the family, "Okay then, everybody OK?"

Chuck called out, "No Dad, they got me again, same leg. Can you believe that, four times in one leg? I must be some kind of bullet magnet." The family helped Chuck into the manager's office and he sent for a doctor who arrived quickly. When he was ready, the family escorted him out to the cabs and sped them all back to the train. The hotel manager was a bit relieved to see them go, although he had several broken windows and a couple policemen to satisfy.

Chuck was propped up in a corner of the sofa with a brandy "for the pain". The engineer was told, "East, then South to Baton Rouge and New Orleans as fast as you can." The engineer went to the telegraph office and sent a wire. From that point on the train had priority for the right of way, and they arrived back in New Orleans about five PM. The Pinkertons rounded up some more cabs and they were taken back to the hotel. The next morning, the whole group moved to the yacht and sailed for Texas, Galveston. On the way Carl mentioned that there were over a dozen LePrad hotels in Texas. This elicited a series of groans from the family. "No, we are not going to inspect them all. We are going to Galveston, and there is one there where we will stay for a couple of days, while I have a few meetings about the oil, and the shipping line, then we will take the train north to Rockwell, where the ranch is, and where I have had a spur put right into the ranch. By the way, the ranch is 15 000 acres. On the way, we will go through Houston, San Antonio, Austin, Fort Worth, Dallas, Rockwell, and home. Look on the map, we will cover a third of the state in one day. I will pass six of my hotels without stopping so you better not complain about the train ride."

"Does this ranch have horses and cows?" asked Ed.

"Sure, there are about a thousand cows and likely a couple hundred horses. There are a couple dozen horses at the house, assorted sizes as I ordered, so each of you should be able to find one that fits. There are also about three hundred iron horses."

Ali said, "What do you mean iron horses, and why so few cows on 15 000 acres?"

"This used to be a working ranch with many more cows, but they found oil. Those iron horses are oil wells, you'll see. Once they find the oil, they take the derricks down and put these iron pump things in. The thousand cows are really, I guess, for atmosphere. This ranch is a home, and a source of oil. There are a few cowboys left to take care of the horses and the cows. The oil pays for the ranch. But, there is lots of space to ride and do the fun part of ranching. That does not have to pay the bills. There are no Apache. By train, it is maybe two days to Oakside, and a day from that to the Hamptons where we will keep the new yacht, or alternatively a day to Galveston where we can also keep this yacht, the Too. Then two days west could get us to Arizona and the Hacienda if we wanted to go there, and a day after that by rail to California. We seem to be pretty well situated here in Texas at the Triple CCC, that is the name of the ranch. Mag, I want you in on the meetings with the oil people, and the shipping people, you will see why. and Marcus with the shipping people. Now Chuck, Des and Dizzy, has any of this interested you?"

Dizzy said, "Unless we are gonna communicate with the cows by radio or telegraph no, but when we can put the radios on the ships maybe."

Carl said, "By the way Diz, there is a telegraph line in to the ranch too, so you can listen to your hearts content. As of this moment, Diz, you are the vice-president of Montrose Communications, and Mag, the vice-president of Montrose Oil, and Marcus, the vice-president of Montrose Shipping. Des you come to the meetings too as a consultant. Now Des, do you see any involvement here?""

Des said, "Not really Dad, but I do think I have a direction, the law. I am gonna read the law with Mr. Deeds. I can do that and still help Jenn with the school."

"Okay Des, you are now the junior partner at Deeds and Montrose, so you will attend the meetings too, as these companies will be your firm's main clients."

Everybody looked at Chuck. He said, "Sorry Dad, Nan and I are still looking at the horse breeding program at Oakside, but there may be some way of working the ranch here in too. I don't see, however, any way to link it to the oil company, or the shipping company; thank God, or you would have me going too, shot or not."

Chapter 16

Corporate Foundations

After a short trip on the Two, the family arrived in Galveston. They tied up at one of the docks that already had a new sign on it, 'Montrose Shipping'. On the dock, there were several cabs waiting for them and a couple of wagons. There were also a couple of ex-executives from the company that used to own the docks before the whole operation was folded into the new Montrose firm. As the baggage was loaded and the family settled in the cabs, Carl talked to the two men.

"Let everyone know, we will meet at ten tomorrow. The shipping people and the oil people for the new ships." Then the family went off in search of the Galveston LePrad, which turned out to be a good well-run hotel with about a hundred rooms.

After diner in the rooms, the family was sitting around in the suite's lounge. Carl and Lionel were going through a huge stack of newspapers, everyone that was available in the news shop in the lobby. Carl seemed to be getting increasingly frustrated and finally said, "This is ridiculous. The news in these papers is three days old, at least. This copy of the New York Times is eleven days old. There are no up to date financials. How do these people manage their investments? In three days, there can be wars, disasters, anything can happen. We might as well still be using the pony express."

Diz had been listening to his father and then he had an idea. "Dad, I have it, I know what we can do that I am interested in. The financials first. Am I right that the prices and sales pretty much take place in New York or Chicago? Would it be of interest to you to know about what was being bought and sold in those two places as it happens?"

"Knowing what was happening would be good, but it would be better if I could buy and sell too. Immediately. That was why I wanted our own telegraph, so I could send messages to my bankers and have them do that."

"What about if we made it possible for all investors to do that. You already have some banks in the east and are putting up banks in the west.

What about if each of those banks had an investment room. We put an operator in each room, and some in New York and Chicago where these sales are made. The operators in New York and Chicago record all the sales and transmit them. The sales are read in the banks and displayed for the investors. If they want to buy or sell something, our operator transmits their message and we have people on the floors of these exchanges who can do that for them, for a commission of course. We already own miles and miles of lines all over the country and we have trained ninety percent of the operators out west."

"You know Carl," said Deeds, "He has a good idea here. That could become a big part of our banking houses, the investment arm. Cost almost nothing to put a separate room in the bank, make it like a men's club, a little posh where the guys could hang out, perhaps smoke a cigar, and watch the figures. Have big black-boards on the walls for the different exchanges and kids writing the numbers on them. The men watch for trends of interest to them and make purchases or sales based on what they see. The banks could even provide advisors to help, for a fee of course. And the bank would take a small percentage, say two percent, of all trades. That would be to cover the costs of the operation. Now two percent is not much to the individual investor, but when it becomes a share of all the trades, it will add up. Call them brokerages or something."

Dizzy added, "We would be using the technology we have now, the telegraph. Over the years there will be faster things and we would have to keep up with those. That would be my job with the communications company. To keep it all modern and fast with the latest of technologies. I hear someone is working on an automatic Morris Code reader that displays the messages on a tape."

Carl had listened carefully, considered for a few minutes, then said, "We own enough banks, and parts of banks, we could do this all over the country and it wouldn't cost much to set it up. Deeds, send a wire in the morning to our new bank in Denver and tell them we will send the car to them next week. We will have a few of them down to the ranch and start this up. Some from the other banks too, rent some more rail-cars. Montrose Communications will be in charge of the technical side of things, good idea Diz."

Dizzy went on, "Why don't we do something the same with the news. Get some of the reporters for the big eastern newspapers to write us stories about important events happening there, or around the world, and put them on a telegraph service that comes out in newspapers all over the country? Those papers could take stories as they come off the service, no need to rewrite, and print them. Those little papers could put important things on the wire too, say about a new gold discovery in the wilds of California, as it happens."

"How would that be paid for?" asked Deeds.

"Each newspaper would pay a monthly fee to get the service and a fee for every story they take and print. The papers and reporters would get a part of the story fee. If they put a story on the wire and no body takes it, then they don't get paid. That would encourage them to do a good job on the story and the originating papers could use the money they get to pay part of the cost of their news people. Again, our part would be to set up the lines, the operators, and to run it. When there are faster technologies, we use them too," said Diz. "Then there would be no need for three-day old news and people might buy more papers if they know they are current. Some day there may be faster ways of getting the news out and we can own some of them too."

Carl considered for several moments then said, "Deeds, find some people to work with him on this, people who can go around the country and sign papers up. We might have to buy a few papers in major markets to show people how it works. If we always had the latest news, they would have to buy into it or be blown out of the water. Find some operations we can buy lock stock and barrel on the condition they go into the service, they can carry and print the financials too, so they can use the other service also. Diz, these are your babies and you will manage them. For now, we will set you up here, but later if you want to relocate to New York or Washington, we can look at that. I can see Montrose Communications being a power in the years to come. You are young, you have fifty years to work with all this. Communications are important and changing everyday."

The next morning at ten, was when the meeting was scheduled with the men from the shipping company, and the ones from the oil company. It was also the meeting where Mag, Marcus and Des had been ordered to attend. At breakfast, Carl had a couple words with his sons.

"Now, I know you are not eager to attend this, but this meeting involves the areas of our assets that you each are going to be in charge of in the future so you might as well start coming up to speed. In addition, two of you now have the titles of Vice-President, which means you are being paid, and even Des there, as a junior partner in the law firm, will get a share of the profits, so you all are being paid. Now, the people attending the meeting are the sharpest ones left at the companies we have taken over, all the other ones have been let go. They will all be sizing you up to see if you are threats to them, so, if you have nothing bright to say, keep quiet, that will keep them guessing, and that is good."

The meeting was at the shipping company by the dock where the Too was moored. There was a large boardroom and when the Montroses arrived with Deeds, there were eight people waiting for them. There were two from the shipping company, four from the oil company and two from a local shipyard. Carl, Deeds and the three boys made the total thirteen. Carl noted that, because it was an unlucky number and he wondered for who. He sat and called the meeting to order.

"The new company, Montrose Oil, has oil wells, lands, and leases all over four states, Texas, Louisiana, Mississippi, and Oklahoma. We have one refinery, in Houston, and storage facilities almost everywhere. There is a new company headquarters ready to open in Dallas, and will as soon as we get there. Montrose Shipping is centered here, in Galveston, but we have new docks all over the coasts of three of those states I mentioned, and we have a facility in Tulsa where we load that state's oil on rail cars and bring it to our refinery in Houston. It would seem we are reaching the capacity of that refinery. Therefore, I want to start immediately building the new refinery in Shreveport, and also to start the planning for the doubling of the capacity of the refinery we have in Houston."

One of the oil company men asked, "Why are we doing a new refinery in Shreveport and also expanding Houston? Why not just expand the one we have? Or, if we have to have a new one, why not in Corpus? And why did we build the new headquarters in Dallas?"

Carl was not used to having his decisions questioned but he tried to be patient. The boys looked at each other. They knew Carl did not do patient well and did not like questions from those he employed. The three of them sat back waiting for the fireworks.

"The reason for the headquarters in Dallas is quite simple. I have a ranch nearby and since I am paying for the building, I want the headquarters near me. All of the major operations will be connected by telegraph anyway. Now, as far as why a new refinery, as opposed to expanding the one we have, there is a saying, never put all your eggs in one basket. Refineries do catch fire, frequently, and I don't want all of our production taken out if we are so unlucky. As for Corpus, I considered it. Problem is all the hurricanes you have down here and the fact that Corpus is frequently hit by one of them. Houston has access to the gulf but is not right on the coast. Shreveport is away from the hurricanes but near the oil. Now, Mr. ah.."

"Fedders, sir, Frank Fedders."

"Well, Mr. Fedders. There is something you have to learn about Montrose Oil, and you might as well learn it today. I own it and I run it. My sons will someday. It is not a democracy. I make the decisions and I have the likes of you around to carry out my decisions. If I ever want your input, I will ask for it, but that is not likely. Do you understand me Mr. Fedders?"

"Yessir," said Frank, realizing he was lucky he still had a job. The boys smiled at each other.

"Now, to get back to the task at hand. With all the added production, we have to have a better way to move it. There is not, and will not, be enough rail capacity for it all. We shall have to move it by water in a new fleet of tankers, which is why Montrose Shipping exists and the shipyard people are here today. The Shreveport production will be sent by rail. The Houston production will go by sea. Now the people from the shipyard will show us what the new ships will be like." After a detailed twenty-minute description of the new boats and their features, the men from the shipyard sat.

"Well, I would say we know all we ever need to about oil tankers now. What we still need to know is how much and how fast. We have to make sure we have the production on line to fill them and places for the oil to go. Now, I want one of you Montrose people to head up the marketing of the new oil, one to head the construction of the new refinery in Shreveport, and one to head the expansion of Houston, the fourth can deal with all of the old business. You decide who does what and each of you will keep in touch with company headquarters and the division heads there. Mag is head of Montrose Oil, and Marcus heads Montrose Shipping so communications are to be addressed that way. They will bring items to me as required. This all is to coincide with the schedule the shipyard people give us for the new ships, twenty-four new ships over the next year and a half. Any questions?"

There was an immediate chorus of, "No Sir."

"Very well, you all may go and start, except for captain Hayes, who I would like to see for a few minutes. We will see all of you at the opening of the new headquarters in Dallas the day after tomorrow, 1 PM."

All the men left, except for a tall distinguished looking man in a naval uniform. Carl asked him to move up the table closer to where the five of them sat.

"Now Captain, this is Marcus. I talked to you about him. I would like you to take him out in our yacht this afternoon so that you can see for yourself, he is a marvellous sailor. When you come back, I want you to sit with him and develop a schedule to fill in any gaps the two of you feel there may be. Send the talent you need by train up to the ranch for a few days at a time and change your tutors as required. There are no restrictions on cost. He will captain our new yacht next fall on an around the world voyage and he is concerned there may be some gaps in his knowledge. When the two of you are ready, take him on some trips with you on Montrose ships. I really see this as a building of confidence issue. Now the rest of us will leave the two of you to the making of your arrangements and Marcus, we will see you for dinner tonight. There are a couple Pinkertons staying with you and they will arrange transport."

After the others had left, Captain Hayes looked at Marcus, "Around the world eh?"

"Yessir."

"You will have some experienced mates?"

"Yessir, three."

"There are no ways to make him reconsider any of this?"

"Absolutely none sir."

"Then, I guess we had better get busy son."

"Yes sir."

The next day, the family left for the ranch at Rockwell, just outside of Dallas. Their route took them through many of the large cities in the state. They left the Too at the dock in Galveston, and crossed to the mainland in a small boat provided by the shipping company. The railcar had been spotted onto a siding and was waiting for them attached to a steam engine with a couple other cars. Ten minutes after getting settled, their train left. They had priority and journeyed through the state without any stops in any of the cities. Generally, the cities were new and vibrant, separated by miles and miles of flat prairie. They saw many cattle, many oil wells, and it seemed thousands of the "iron horses". Carl pointed the first few out to the boys.

"See, those are the iron horses we talked about before. They just go on all by themselves pumping the oil into pipelines. I imagine many of them belong to Montrose oil." Ed and Ali started to count them but gave up after they got to forty, they were everywhere.

When they went through Austin, Carl reminded them it was the state capitol. "If you look, you will see there is not much here in the way of industry. The government is the industry. The people that hang out here, the politicians, are a bunch of lying deceitful crooks. They will shake your hand and smile to your face, seem like your friend, meanwhile they are trying to figure out how to use you to their profit. As long as you realize that, and keep your wits around you, you have to learn to use them. They are predictable and handy to have in your pocket, and they really are cheap to own. You just have to pick the ones that can help you the most."

"Do we own any of them here yet dad?" asked Ed.

"Yes son, a herd of them," replied Carl.

When the train arrived in Dallas, it made a ten-minute stop as ordered, on a private siding. Carl called the boys over to the left side of the car. "That building there is the Montrose Building, the headquarters of Montrose Oil, Montrose Shipping, Montrose Communications, and the location of Deeds and Montrose. There will be offices there for all of you. Montrose Shipping operationally will have to stay in Galveston, but you can have offices here connected by telegraph. There are some empty floors for the others when we find out what they are interested in." The boys looked at the building with mixed feelings. It was a nice building, six storeys tall, big windows and faced in granite. It looked solid and dependable. The bottom floor was a branch of the Western Fidelity Bank that Carl owned most of and there was a fair amount of traffic. However, the boys couldn't help but feel the building formally represented their transition from boys to men, and all that implied.

The train carried on and then slowed, stopped for a moment, and was switched to a siding. "Everybody, we are now on our ranch, the Triple CCC. Everything you see belongs to us, including those oil wells. The boys, especially the young ones, were looking out the windows. Ed said, "Dad, I see more of those oil well things than I see cattle or horses. What kind of ranch is this?"

"The best kind son, the kind you don't have to work your butt of on to make it pay, and believe me, those oil wells pay a lot. There are no Apache out to slit your throat, but you still must keep your guard up. There are snakes, rattlers, and two-legged kind. Texas fought for the South and didn't come out of the war very well. Same as at Oakside, there are people here who are not fond of us. But, we have 50 000 acres to separate them from us, and I bought several neighboring ranches. We use them to gather the breeding cattle for Arizona, although now we will send them by rail. They also will raise cattle for Armour."

After a few minutes they entered a valley and steamed along beside a small river. Eventually, they could make out a house on top of a butte above the tracks. The train stopped below it. The house was painted white, two storeys with a large attic above them. There were many large windows that offered a wonderful view of the valley and the range. They could see a wide verandah on the front of the house, and it looked like it went all the way around. There was a gentle path up from the tracks to the house with some shrubs and bushes on either side of it. Just then, the front door of the house opened, and two people came out and down the path. When they got to the group, the man introduced them.

"This is Selma, the housekeeper, and I am Paul, the foreman. Come on up to the house, I will send some men down for the baggage."

Selma was about forty, with dark hair that was graying a bit. She had a broad open face, a wide smile, and a hearty laugh. Selma was the type of person that was immediately friends with everyone and when she saw Mag and Mel each holding a three-year-old, she immediately went over and made a fuss over the little ones.

Paul was tall and thin, with an air of authority. He was the type of person that demanded attention and got it. Paul shook hands with all the men, and nodded to the women, as Carl introduced them, and he even shook hands with Ed and Ali, with a wink. When he was introduced to Tully, with his dark glasses, he knew immediately that he was blind and said, "Tully, I think we will put some ropes around the porch, waist high as a railing, so you can come outside, just until you are familiar. Wouldn't want you to tumble down the hill, would we."

The group went up the hill to the house and in the front door. They found themselves in a wide hallway that went from the front of the house to the rear where there was another wide door to the yard. There were wide stairs to the second storey on the right side of the hallway. All of them could immediately smell the aromas of someone cooking and an older, somewhat plump, lady bustled from the kitchen at the back of the house to be introduced.

Selma said, "This is Rose, our cook, and she has been hoping all day you would get here in time for dinner. By the smell, I would say we were in for her chicken and dumplings, and her home-made bread and pies." She put a hand each on a shoulder of Ed and Ali. "I would guess that Rose's main purpose in life now will be to fatten these two up."

There were two large parlors at the front of the house, one on either side of the hallway, and Paul led the family into one of them and urged them to have a seat while he saw to the baggage, then he hustled away. Selma explained the layout of the house. "In the center part you have the two parlors across the front, and at the back, a dining room and a kitchen to the left and a large ranch office to the right that has its own door to the porch. There is a wing to each side of the house at the back. The one behind the kitchen is the house staff wing with about six bedrooms and a small staff lounge and dining room. We have rooms there, so does Paul and there is space for more staff if you need it. The wing at the back at the other side has a billiards room, a smoking room, and a big playroom for the children. There are modern washrooms over there and in the center part of the house for you. Upstairs, the second floor goes over the whole house, center and both wings, and there is another set of stairs in addition to these ones here in the hall. There are fourteen large bedrooms, and each has a bath of its own. Sir, the master's bedroom is just up the stairs to the right. There are two bedrooms that adjoin and one of them has been set up for the little ones as you asked, with two children's beds and one for an adult. Mr. Reynolds, who built the house, had seven daughters. He said a man with seven daughters could never have enough bathrooms. Out back are the barns and stables, and the cookhouse and bunkhouses for the staff. We have cleared out one of the bunk houses as you directed, for your Pinkerton men. They will have their own kitchen with one of the cooks assigned to them. Both bunkhouses have their own area for the men to gather."

Just then Paul came in with several of the ranch hands, burdened with mountains of luggage which they put in the hallway on the floor. Paul sent the men back for a second load.

Carl said to the family, "Okay, get your bags and go up and choose your rooms. Take some time to get cleaned up and settled, then come back down here. That should be about time for dinner. I am going to have a little talk with Paul after he gets the Pinkerton men settled in their bunk house."

When Paul came back he took a seat opposite Carl who asked, "Did you get them settled alright?"

"Sure, they said they would be comfortable there, and the cook was already starting supper for them. For city fellers, they seem okay, but there are sure a lot of em, two dozen or so. Are you 'spectin a range war or summin?" Paul asked shrewdly.

"How many hands do you have here Paul?" asked Carl.

"Ranch hands come and go. We run this place with six or eight. There are not that many cattle, Mr. Reynolds just liked a few for show, same with the horses. The money here is in the oil wells."

"Okay Paul, you deserve an answer to your question. When we were out in Arizona, we fought Apache. In Virginia, we had to fight a whole town of rebels. On the way down here, we had muggers, a sniper, and a bomber, who got away. This family sorta attracts trouble, haters and people who are jealous of what we have. When we go into town, we will take at least half the Pinkertons with us, and the other half will stay here to protect the family. The two young boys are just itching to get out riding the range and when they go, I want you to assign two men to go with them, as protection. The Pinkertons are good men but they don't do horses well. I also want you to slowly increase the number of your men, to at least three times what you have, but I want the right type of men. Totally trustworthy and good with guns. They should also be good with horses. We will not get more cattle but we will be doing horses on the property in Virginia, and will do some here too, perhaps many. If you need another bunkhouse, have it built. When we have enough force here on the ranch, I will send some of the Pinkertons back to our plantation in Virginia. They are a bit more suited for there and I think in the spring some of the family will move back there. The rest of us will move between the two places."

"Okay sir, I think I understand. You should remember though, Texas was with the south. I don't think I can find a couple dozen Yankee cowhands, of the right sort."

"Paul, I don't care if the people you get were rebs, just that they are over that now. When we left Virginia, we had made friends with the townspeople.

Paul, I lived in the south before the war and if I hadn't promised my dying wife that I would take the boys away before it started, I likely would have fought alongside them. I didn't have any slaves, didn't believe in it, but they were my people and I likely would have stood with them. Thing is, the war is over, and we all have to get along now, and work towards the future. So, I don't care if they were gray or blue, just as long as they are good dependable men and they all can get along.

After the discussion, Paul left, digesting what he had been told. There was clearly more to Carl Montrose than there would appear to be. He was not a rich spoiled northerner.

Shortly after Paul left, Des strolled in, looking a bit troubled. "Dad, you got a minute? I need to talk something over with you." The two sat in chairs facing each other. "Dad, how is all of this supposed to work. Oakside, the school, Jen, me a lawyer, the law firm here?"

"Des, I know, the school is back in Virginia and you and Jen want to be back there for when it opens in the spring and you will likely live at the school. Chuck and Nan want to live at Oakside and do the horses. They likely will go back when you do in the spring. Tull needs the school, although he doesn't have to go back there until it opens, and I would like to take him. Mag and Mel will likely settle here and do the oil, they don't feel the same about Oakside after losing the babies there. Marcus has the shipping company and I expect he will spend some time at sea, at least until he finds someone, and perhaps he will settle in Galveston, or perhaps Oakside, it is on the sea. Diz will work out of here, but I think he will be on the road a bit, at least until he finds the wife he is looking for, and then who knows. Now, as for the law bit, you will read with Deeds until you are ready. If need be, he will go back with you and stay at Oakside. You both will be working in house and you can do that anywhere. When you are ready, the law firm can have two branches, one here with Deeds, and one in the east with you. Ed, Ali, Tull and I will move between all the places and I will get them another tutor to travel with us. Summer in the Hamptons will be for whoever wants to come, and depending on the number of students, you might even bring the whole school for a while, we do have the rail car which would make them easy to move. The cruise will be strictly voluntary, and I can perhaps see you not doing that. Now, does that set your mind at ease?"

Des was sitting there slack jawed, mouth open. "Dad, how did you do that. It will take me hours to remember all of it and tell Jen, and you just rhymed it all off. Amazing."

The family gathered in the dining room for their first dinner on the new ranch and it was a joyous one. They were alone as a family and thoroughly enjoyed one another. The food was the best they had had for months and all the diners complimented Rose. Imelda had fit right in on the ranch, and when she wasn't busy with the babies, she helped Rose and enjoyed it. The Montrose women had been comparing notes and it looked like all three would be mothers in the new year.

After dinner, Carl and the boys took a walk out to the barns. Ali and Ed were ecstatic, there were ponies there for them, four of them. Carl sat them down. "Now boys, I have some news for you, and I am afraid you will not like all of it. First, we have the horses for you, but you cannot just jump on them and ride off over the range. Since the Pinkertons don't do all that well on horses, I have had Paul assign two of the hands to you, Tex and Fargo. You don't have to ride with them if you don't want, but they will tail you. If you try to lose them, or leave with out them, you will lose the horses and also get your hides tanned royally. Now, don't look so glum, that is just the way it has to be, accept it. Oh, one other bit of news. The Birches will be down here next week, and Roger will be with them. If you want, we can ask his parents if he can stay a couple of weeks. Glad to see that cheered you up. One more bit of news, I am getting you another tutor, he will be here in two weeks." Another wave of despair crossed the two young faces.

The next day was the official opening of the new office building in Dallas. Carl, Deeds, and the boys all went, accompanied by a dozen or so Pinkertons. They took the rail car to the siding by the building and then crossed the street. The bank was busy, but they didn't go there, instead entering the lobby to the right of the bank. In the lobby, they stood looking at the directory for the building. The bank, the lobby, a restaurant, a smoke shop and a news stand took up the first floor. The second and third floor were taken by Montrose Oil. The fourth listed Montrose Communications and Montrose Shipping. The fifth was vacant and the sixth listed only C. Montrose, and Deeds and Montrose. They all went up to the sixth floor where there was a gathering of local and state politicians in the reception area, and an open bar. When Ali and Ed edged towards that bar, they felt a firm hand on their necks and were guided to the other side of the room by Carl. "Forget it," he said firmly. "Stay right by me."

Carl tapped the side of his glass and began a short speech for the locals. "The Montrose family is glad to welcome you to the new headquarters for several of our endeavors. Montrose is heavily invested in Texas and has high hopes for the future of this state. We are betting that the future of this state is golden, for you and for us." There then was a half hour of general mingling in the gathering where Carl kept firm control of Ed and Ali. When the event was over and the politicians all left, Carl led the boys through the reception room past a couple of secretaries to a door that simple said C. Montrose. He ushered them into a room that took up a quarter of the floor. Two sides were windows. There were eight desks gathered together in a group. To one side was a large billiards table and a comfortable seating group of chairs and sofas by a fire place.

"Boys, this is the place where the real work will be done. There is a desk there for each of you and space for more when we need them. This is where you and I and Deeds will discuss matters and make decisions. The offices downstairs are where you will meet new people you have to impress, they are what is expected, and they give the aura of stability and power. This is where the real power is. When you leave your offices downstairs and come up here, you will have one person who knows where you are and can contact you here, if they need to, by use of one of those speaking tubes over there and the pneumatic tube system beside it."

The boys settled at their desks for a general discussion of business matters, and Ed and Ali took over the billiards table. Tully, who couldn't play billiards, sat at the collection of desks and listened intently. Every once in a while, he would make a comment or ask a question and the others listened intently. With his blindness, Tully had become very perceptive and wise beyond his years. He had been a bit like that even before, given the life he had been forced to lead and the time he had spent alone, just mulling over different things. His input was valuable and always listened to, to the same degree as each of the older brothers. He had a permanent spot at the grouping of desks that determined the future of the Montrose interests. Ed and Ali were too busy playing to merit a seat there yet.

On their way out of the building, the boys toured their other offices and met their staffs. The quarters were indeed grand, and staffed by capable people. Each of them had an office that was truly a showcase, meant to awe and impress. None of them wanted to work in them though. As they got on the train Carl said, "Those offices are like tools, each with a specific role and to be used when need be for their purposes. However, we are a family and will make the important decisions as a family, in the office on the sixth floor."

After they had been at the ranch for a week or so, Carl went out on the veranda one morning and looked down at the rail spur. Five private cars had been spotted in to it overnight, one of them being theirs that they had sent to Laramie for the Birches. The others had the representatives from the big Eastern and Mid-Western banks. They would all have a meeting that day to tie down Diz' idea about the investment houses and the telegraph service. He went back in the house and rousted Diz with the order, "Get up and get dressed in that new suit, and roust out those guys that have been helping you. It always looks better when you show up with a staff. We meet at ten in the men's parlor."

Then, he went in to Ed and Ali's room. They were awake, and just about to get up. After all, it was 7:30, and they didn't want to waste a day away. Carl said, "Okay, he is here. You can go down and wake them, invite them up for breakfast, but for God sakes make sure you get the right car, our car. The others won't want to be woken up yet and they all have Pinkertons, you might get shot. You two and Roger have a good day, get him a horse and you can go riding, just make sure you take your two hands with you. They won't bother you, they will just ride a quarter mile behind." There was no grumbling, they knew it was either that way or stay in the house. When they got to the CCC ranch, Carl had made that clear, that a couple of the ranch hands would follow them around. As he left the room, the boys were scrambling to dress, wanting to get their friend Roger from the train. Just outside the door, they found Tex and Fargo sitting there on their horses, with three more for the boys, all saddled and ready.

It was only a two-minute ride down to the rail spur and when they got there, Roger was already hanging out the window waving and yelling. When Ed and Ali arrived at the back platform, Roger was standing there with his father, Charles Birch. Ed said, "Dad says to come up for breakfast when you are ready, there will be a surrey here in a few moments with one of the hands. We have a horse here for Roger now. We will take him for breakfast then we will explore. Those two galloots back there are Dad's version of Pinkertons in the west and they will be with us all day, although I still don't see what danger there is out here, other than snakes, coyotes, and mountain lions, which we all could handle on our own, but, that was the deal. Them, or we stay in the house. They are kinda nice guys anyway. Rog, make sure you bring your guns."

Roger looked up at his father who laughed and said, "Okay son, looks like Carl has thought of everything, and these two tails he put on you look capable enough, but I want to see you at dinner tonight up at the house." Within ninety seconds, they all were gone, and he went in to do the most dangerous thing he would have to do all day, wake his wife and tell her they were invited for breakfast. Cynthia did not like to get up before eight and even then, she needed time to adjust to the new day. Telling her she had to be beautiful and bright at breakfast in half an hour was not likely going to go well, he thought.

The breakfast with the Birches and the Montroses did go well. Some of the Montrose women were not good at early rising either so they just zoned in on breakfast and let each other be as they woke up and gently cruised through the morning. Charles commented to Carl that it had not taken the boys long to disappear and Carl agreed. "My two have been on the moon ever since they heard Roger was coming. Be prepared, they are all gonna want to extend the visit a couple of weeks and once they start asking, they won't let up."

"If I agreed, how would he get back?"

"When it is time, Deeds and I, and a couple of Pinkertons, could bring the boys back in our private car. It's only a little over a day, and you could show Deeds and I the new bank. The only downside is that you would have the pleasure of our two for a day before we headed back."

"That would be nice, I will agree to it when they get to me, after a little fight of course."

"Of course, we must never give into them easily, we might spoil them."

At ten thirty, the rest of the bankers came up from the cars and the meeting about the investment rooms began. Carl thanked the men for coming and said he had an interesting proposition for them. The men at the meeting represented the ten or so banks Carl had a controlling interest in.

"My son Diz came up with this idea and we discussed it. We all decided it would be a perfect match for a bank, not in its lobby, but in an associated room, like at the back, or upstairs in your building. It would be like a clubroom for investors. You would tailor it to your clients. A bank situated on the Golden Mile in Chicago would have a much posher room than a bank that deals mainly with farmers in Kansas. They all would have some essential elements provided by Montrose Communications. I will let Diz explain the rest."

"Gentlemen, as you most likely are aware, the trading of 95% of the stocks, corporate bonds and securities takes place now in five locations in the country, four in New York, and one in Chicago. If you live in one of those cities you go and trade, or send a representative and make your purchase or sale. Some of the really wealthy station men at the exchanges to watch trends and report back. If you live in places other than those two cities, you watch newspapers and if you want to invest you write a banker in New York or Chicago and ask him to invest for you. By the time all that is done, whatever news caused you to take your action is long gone. Montrose Communications will run two telegraph lines to each exchange and station two operators and a broker at each site. One telegrapher will send out all sales as they are made. The other will take in orders to buy or sell stock as they come in from the client. He will pass the order to the broker as it arrives, and the trade will be made immediately. The order will show up on the line as soon as it is completed. The other end of the systems are the investment rooms. The rooms should have large blackboards on the walls where the last ten purchases or sales for any of the companies in the exchanges are listed. The people watching in the rooms are looking for trends, and when they see one, will invest or sell. When they want to buy or sell something, they will approach one of the brokers who write up an order and sends it to the broadcast telegrapher, and again, if it is completed, it will show up on the tape. The bank provides the clients, the room, the boards, and the runners who write the quotes from our people as they come in. You can provide investment counselors, your costs, your fees, but you must provide a broker to write up the orders and give them to our operators. We provide the information and facilitate the trades over our equipment. Each trade through the system has a three percent commission, one to Montrose and the other two to the room. There also is a monthly fee for the service. As business expands, you can add more brokers, counsellors and a second line out for orders. As methods of communication improve, we will use them to keep the system as fast as it can be. Presently, we have lines to all cities east of the Mississippi, and all cities west of the Mississippi where any of you have banks. Notify us of future branches and we will be there when you open. We are not offering the same guarantee to your competition. In fact, for the first year, we shall offer the service only to your banks. One last thing, these rooms will likely be for the big investors. We would suggest there are many other people out there with a little money who would like to invest if we offered them a way. Consider some small storefront operations in the bigger cities staffed by just the broker, a board boy, and the two operators to serve the general public."

Carl added. "People who get in the habit of using these investor rooms would likely also use your institutions for the rest of their banking needs. We can give the people the ability to make investment decisions and act on them instantly. Montrose Communications has the equipment and the people to allow you to provide that service. Now, despite the fact I am the majority shareholder in all of you, we are going to give you an hour to discuss the concept, then we will come back and finalize this, one way or another."

When they returned, all the banks bought into the concept without further encouragement from Carl. They all saw the potential for profit. An hour after the meeting, the visiting rail cars were picked up and on their way. Charles Birch and Carl were sharing a cigar in the smoking room when Diz came in with a package of Tulls, and sat with them. He said, "Dad, that felt good today, having all those important people listen to me and buy into the concept. I liked that." He offered one of the cigarettes to his dad and his guest. Charles made note of the name.

"Yes, we put out this brand after Tully, and all the profits go to the new school for the blind on Oakside. You would be surprised how well they are selling nationally, and people don't even know anything about the profits. People like variety and we shall be putting out two more brands next year, in addition to the Oaks and the Tulls, just slightly different blends and tastes. People, especially the women, like the cigarettes. We are making an absolute fortune. Likely put up another factory next year too."

Charles laughed. "Does everything you do turn to gold?"

"Almost Charles, almost."

Chapter 17

West Again

About three weeks later, Charles Birch had long gone home leaving Roger for a visit of "two" weeks. Carl and the family were at breakfast three weeks later and Carl said to him, "Well Roger, we have extended your stay by a week, I think it is time we started to see about getting you back to your Dad. We have to make a trip to Connor and Tucson the day after tomorrow and we will take the train car, I also think that will be a good time to take you home."

There were immediate groans from the three but Ed added, "Dad, if you are taking the rail car, and going to Laramie, then Connor and Tucson, then why can't the three of us go, you have to go back through Laramie anyway?"

"We are going to pick up Roger's Dad and take him to Connor and Tucson, we are adding our banks there to Western Fidelity but Roger will have to ask his Dad." The three rushed away to determine the best arguments to use on Roger's dad and get another week they could be together.

Carl looked over at Mel and Mag. "Mel, if you have made a decision on that offer Jessops has for the hotel, we can complete that for you when we are there."

Mel said, "Well, it makes sense to sell it. We never want to go back there to live, and we might as well sell it and invest the money in something else. I have good people there now running it, so ask the new owner to try to keep them on if he could, but the price offered seems fair. Mag and I have talked about it. I did enjoy running it though."

Tully said, "Who all is going on this trip? Can I go? I never was in Connor."

Carl said, "Deeds and I have to because of the banks, likely Roger's dad too, so he can see the new banks he is getting from us, Diz to run the telegraph. We have one in the car now you know, just need someone to climb up a pole beside the track and we are connected. I expect the boys

will talk Charles into going along and that way get another week together."
He was looking over at the older boys and Des got the message.

"Why don't I go too, me and Tully can hang out, and I can say good
bye to Conner and good riddance. Tull, really, Connor is not anything
special, you haven't missed much."

There were a few telegrams sent to alert Charles Birch of the plans, and
Roger sent seven or eight, a new one whenever he came up with another
reason he should be allowed to go with the group to Tucson and Connor.
There was none from Charles back saying Roger could stay with the group,
much to the disgust of Roger, Ed and Ali.

Finally, the train was ordered. Carl had asked for a car for the Pinkertons,
a dozen or so, and a couple cattle cars for two dozen horses, for them and
the Pinkertons. That was so they could take a horse along for everyone,
including Tull, Roger, and Roger's Dad, Charles. Tex and Fargo were asked
to go along and look after the horses, as well as the three younger boys if
they managed to get off on their own. The railway provided a cook and a
steward. Everyone was told to wear their gun, and the trunk with a further
arsenal was added to the baggage. The train left heading North and West,
arriving in Laramie in a day and a half.

They were met at the station by Cynthia and Charles Birch. Cynthia
grabbed her son and hugged him, despite his protestations of, "Awww
Mom, not in front of the guys, Maaa."

Charles asked them if they wanted to go back to the house, but Carl
said, "No, I think we will head right out. We can be in Connor by dinner
time. Have you decided whether you want to come with us or not? You
really don't have to, a bank is a bank."

Roger said, "Dad, you have to go or else I can't."

His mother said, "What do you mean go, you haven't been back for
five minutes and you want to go somewhere already? If I had known it
would be like this you would not have been an only child."

"Huh?" said Roger, missing the point entirely. "Daaad, they even
brought a horse for me, and you."

Charles turned to his wife. "Cynthia dear, we will only be gone for two
days, three at the most. Connor, then Tucson and back. Two new banks. I
really should at least see them, I have seen all the other new ones."

"Charles, you are just like Roger. You want to go off and play with the
boys. I thought coming back here from the east would be enough for you

but apparently not. You want to take off with the boys at the drop of a hat. Fine, but what are you going to do for clothes?"

"I have a bag in the buggy," said Charles quickly. "I had a feeling Carl might want to leave right away." He rushed off to get the bag and Cynthia turned to Carl.

"I knew he was going to do this, but it is my job to rattle his cage, both of them. There has to be at least one adult in the house. I guess I can manage for three more days. At least they are in your train car, not out on the roads. Okay Roger, three more days, then you go to school."

She stood on the station platform waving as the train pulled out. The three boys stood on the rear deck of the car and Charles stood in the doorway. After she was out of sight the three boys entered the car and Roger closed the door behind them. "Gees guys, she almost said no. You guys are lucky you don't have a mom to foul things up." The other two looked back at him doubtfully.

The steward came in to see if they wanted anything, and Carl told him to get a cognac for Charles, Lionel and himself; and he looked at Des questioningly. Des shook his head no, he still didn't like to drink in front of his father. Ali tried, "We three will have one, whatever it is."

"Like hell you will," said Carl, "I find any of you three near that cabinet and you will be whupped within an inch of your lives," stated Carl emphatically. The three boys smiled slyly at each other and Carl knew.

"You have been at the cabinet, haven't you? When you sneak away after dinner, I bet you have snuck on the car and explored it. Do I have to put a Pinkerton on the car to protect it from you three? If I do, I will tell him to shoot to kill." The three looked back at him innocently, never admitting anything, just as Carl would have at their age. "Really Charles, these kids grow up too fast these days." A few minutes later he said, "Okay boys, go get your guns from the trunk, and bring out ours for the rest of us. Sorry Tull, but when we are in Tucson, I am gonna take you to see Sam the gunsmith. There might be something we can get for you."

"But Carl," whispered Charles, "Tully's b…"

Tully said, "I can hear that you know. I may be blind, but I am not deaf, especially when people yell like that."

"Yes Charles, we have noticed, Tull's hearing has grown remarkably acute since he lost his sight." Charles Birch was blushing with embarrassment.

The group arrived in Connor about 4 PM and their train was shunted onto a siding beside the station. There was a corral there for stock, so Carl told Tex and Fargo to get the horses off the train, let them stretch in the corral, and to feed them. "You shouldn't have any trouble getting someone to help you when you say who you are, just about everything you see, I own. The rest of us will go down to the hotel and we will get you a room. I'll send a couple of the Pinkertons back to keep an eye on the stock overnight and you two can come up to the hotel when they get there. I will keep an eye on the brats. By the way, did you guys know they have been dipping into the bar on the rail car?" Tex and Fargo shook their heads no, but after Carl was gone, they grinned at each other.

He had sent a telegram from Laramie to reserve a dozen rooms, so they were ready for them when they got there. Carl took two adjoining rooms for himself, Charles, and the three boys, Des and Tully shared a large room with Diz, Deeds got a room of his own and the rest were told to sort themselves out but to be sure they left a room for Tex and Fargo, and that someone had to spell them. The Montroses and the Birches dropped their baggage in their rooms then met in the dining room.

As they were eating, Jessops came in with an older man and joined them at their table. He introduced the man as the prospective buyer for the hotel. "We heard you were in town. News travels fast in a place like this. Mr. Saunders here wondered if Mel had come to a decision on the hotel."

Carl reached in his pocket and drew out the signed agreement. "She has agreed and the two of you can get together with Deeds after dinner to complete the sale. If you complete it tonight, Mr. Saunders can be the owner as of tomorrow. I will have Mel's possessions packed and put on the train tonight. Mel did ask that the new owner be considerate of her employees, they have done a good job for her while she has been away. Charles wants to look at the bank anyway since it will be part of Western Fidelity." After dinner, Deeds, Jessops, Charles Birch and Saunders went over to the bank to complete their business, and the Montroses and Roger, along with half a dozen Pinkertons, took a walk down the main street and ended up at Peters' General store. They went in and the boys spread out. Carl went to the counter where Louise was standing and they gave each other a hug.

"Carl, it is so nice to see you. I heard you were in town, you know how these small places are. What brought you back?"

"The bank here, and in Tucson, are becoming part of Western Fidelity, and Mel is selling the hotel, I brought Deeds back to complete both of those, and I wanted to check on the ranchero."

"I am sorry to hear Mel will not be back. I hear she and Mag got married."

"Yes, they are, but they have had some bad luck too. She was going to have triplets but she lost them in Virginia. They are trying again next spring."

"How are Lou and Les?"

"They are wonderful boys Louise, Mag sent you a picture of the two of them." He reached in his pocket and pulled the photograph out then handed it to her. She stood there looking at it, stroking it gently.

"They are so beautiful, and they look so happy."

The bell on the door tinkled and a man strode in. He crossed the room to stand behind Louise, embraced her and kissed her on her neck. "Beautiful boys, who are they?" Carl noticed the look of panic in Louise's eyes and he said, "They are my grandchildren," and he reached for the photo, putting it back in his pocket.

Louise said, "This is Greg Lerner. He works at Wells Fargo and we are good friends. Greg, this is Carl Montrose."

"Mr. Montrose? In a way, I work for you. Everyday my men and I go to the mines and get the gold and silver. We put it in the Wells Fargo safe or the one in the bank. Once a week, we take the lot into Tucson. Actually, in a couple of days we are to go into Tucson, get the month's worth and take it on the train to Laramie. We try to keep that a bit of a secret."

"That's a good idea Greg. I already have had a couple of gunfights over that gold. A month's worth of it must be quite a draw for certain types." Greg nodded. Carl called out to the boys, "Hey guys, time we got back. Bring whatever you have found and get it checked out. Then we will head back." As usual, Carl paid the bill.

At the hotel, just before bed, Carl, Deeds, Charles, the older Montrose boys and Tex had a quick meeting with the head detective about the following morning. "Tomorrow, in the morning, we will check out of the hotel and go to the car. I want to go out and check on the ranchero. Those that don't want to go, can stay on the car until we get back. When that is done, we will load the horses and go into Tucson. We will split the Pinkertons, but the rest of you let Tex here know in the morning what you want to do so they will know how many horses to get ready."

The next morning, there was quite a large group that rode to the Ranchero Grande. Carl, all of his sons, the two Birches, Tex and Fargo, and almost a dozen Pinkertons rode into the courtyard. Carl was shocked. The plaza was filthy, there were a few of the old workers sitting around doing nothing and they looked up in shock when they realized who the new visitor was, then scuttled away. Carl dismounted then strode into the house. He found all the furniture was dusty, the floor un-swept, and it was clear no one was taking care of the house. He entered the kitchen and found it deserted. He headed out to the stables and found there were no animals, but he thought that was a good thing. If there had been, they would have been neglected. He gathered his party and they rode out back to the bunkhouses.

There were some cowboys there who leapt to their feet as he entered. Mason Fellows, the foreman, was there and Carl motioned him to take a walk with him.

"Mason, I was just up at the house. It is a disaster. Filthy."

"I know sir. When you left and took Imelda, there was no one over there to keep them in line. Some of the old workers have drifted away, and I guess the others are just hiding on you. I went over and got all the animals out of there, they were being neglected. If someone had asked me, I would have told them, but no one did and I didn't know how to reach you."

"Okay Mason, in the future if you ever have to reach me just go to the bank, they know how to get in contact. Now, get some men and turf the lot out of there. Tell them they are all fired. I will get someone to move in and look after the house. You keep on with your end of the operation, at least that is going okay. Have your people keep people out until I get someone out here. Do you remember Louise from a couple years back? I am gonna see if she wants to live here in return for taking charge of the place."

Carl gathered the group again. The boys had visited their old rooms and taken a few items. They were a bit disturbed by how the house looked now. On the way back to town, Carl talked to Charles. "I have to get someone to take charge out there, I think I'll try Louise, the lady at the store, and see if she will move out. I don't think we will ever move back here, but it is an asset and has to be protected. I should have realized that they would let things go if they thought no one was looking. When you get back, set up an account for the house in the Connor bank, to cover maintenance and staff, and I will let you know who can draw on it."

At the train, Carl told the others to get the horses loaded while he made one last stop. He, accompanied by three detectives, went down the main street to the store. He went in and Louise was alone at the counter. She looked surprised when she saw Carl. "I thought you were gone," she said.

"There were three matters I had to talk to you about. First the picture, did you want it? I have the feeling you have not told Greg anything about them. I can understand that, but I also think you are very fond of him. It is not good to base a future together on a lie. Just think about it before you do that. Greg seems like a nice guy, don't underestimate him. The main reason I am here is the ranch. You probably know Hose died and we have Imelda with us. The people we left out there are not doing the job. The place is filthy and run down. We are not going to come back here but I can't sell the house as it is in the center of all the other stuff, the mines. We did a surprise visit today and I fired the lot of them. They are being turfed out right now. Would you like to live there and take charge of the place? I have set up an account at the bank for staff and maintenance. You could live rent free in return for looking after it, just the house. If you and Greg do get together, he could live there too. In any case, hire whoever you need."

"Carl, it is a beautiful house, and I would love to live there. I have this job though."

"I am not suggesting you give this up, but you have to live somewhere. It really is not that far, remember the kids came in for school everyday. As for staff, get as many as you need, from house staff to yard and stable staff. They need to know there is someone living there checking up on them. When there wasn't, they just stopped doing the work but took the pay. Think about it for a couple of days and telegraph me. I won't look for anyone else until I hear from you."

Then Carl returned to the station and saw they were just finishing loading the last of the horses. The engine was attached to the cars, just waiting. Twenty minutes later they were steaming for Tucson. Carl, Deeds and Diz were sitting in the rail car's lounge discussing the incident at the ranchero.

"I was so disappointed in the people. The expectation was the house would go on as before. There were people there who were being paid, but they couldn't be trusted, they slacked off with no one to check on them. I asked Louise if she wanted to take it over, with a staff of course. If she doesn't, then I will ask Jessops to find me a staff for out there. If I could sell it, I would, but there are the cattle and the mines."

"I saw that during the war. You have a perfectly normal unit, looks good, one or two slack off, then three, ten, all of them and you have a group of derelicts, no one has any pride, and no one sees any of the little extra jobs as theirs. It was very disheartening," said Deeds. "I hope Louise takes it on, she is a good woman."

When they pulled into the station in Tucson, there were several people from the hotel to meet them, including the manager, Jerome Monroe. Carl told him, "I have two cowboys and two cars of horses that have to be looked after, can you despatch one of your people to work with them. There are a dozen and a half Pinkertons that have to be accommodated near us, then there are twelve or so in my party. After we are all settled, I want a quick tour of the hotel and then a little chat with you."

When they were gathered in the owner's accommodations Carl spoke to the assembled group. Diz was already listening on the telegraph set in the suite. "Since you all ate on the train, you can hang in for an hour. I need half an hour in the hotel and maybe Deeds and Charles can keep a lid on things until I get back. When I do, they can go to the bank and the rest of us can drop in on the Peters and Sam the gunsmith. A couple of the detectives have gone with Tex and Fargo, a few will go with Deeds and Charles, a couple will stay to guard the rooms and the rest will go with us." There were some groans in the room. "That's enough, that is just the way things have to be, we do not live here anymore. It's only for one day anyway, we head home tomorrow."

Carl had a quick tour with the hotel manager and was pleased. It was a new hotel and should be in good physical shape, it was. The rooms were modern and up to date, and electrified. The lobby had an air of refinement and stability. There were two elevating rooms to serve the seven storeys, each with their own bellboy operators 24 hours a day. He went through the kitchens and found them bustling and spotless. The people were friendly and respectful. The event rooms were luxurious, as were the dining rooms. There were several different sized restaurants and they all were busy. They returned to the manager's office, and Carl said, "Jerome, I am pleased, you are doing a good job. This inspection was a little more important than most. This hotel will become a LePrad, the first in any of the territories. You will receive some literature in the mail from head office that will contain the standards you have to maintain, but I don't think there is anything there you are not already doing. I have the rules here for new signs, which you can order immediately. Incidentally, you are now the regional manager of LePrad Hotels for Arizona, New Mexico, Colorado and Wyoming. You report to me for now and when I get back, I will send you details of the plans we have for out here. Start building up a good group of assistant managers that you can despatch as managers as we complete the new hotels. LePrad Tucson will be the flagship of your district."

Carl left a very satisfied hotel manager and returned to his family. Deeds and Charles then went over to the bank and Carl rounded the others up. "What say we go to Sam's first and see what is new." Now, that was something a bunch of bored young people could get behind.

When Carl and a bunch of boys entered his shop, Sam's little quiet world was overwhelmed but Sam recognized Carl and had a feeling this day would be extremely profitable. The boys spread themselves out around the shop and Carl said to Sam, "Two special needs when we are here. Rifles, what is the latest, and one of my sons, the one with the glasses, he is blind now and we want something for him. I know, he is blind, but his sense of hearing is remarkable now. Is there something we could do for him? He wants to be independent, but he is so vulnerable."

"First, let's show you the new Remingtons, they are auto-eject, you load twenty shells in, then just aim and fire. They are amazing. Let's go out to the range and let your fellas try them." A few minutes later Carl's boys, and even some of the Pinkertons, were blazing away with the new rifles. It took a little practice to get used to them, but they were soon proficient.

Then Sam turned to the issue of Tully. "Even if his hearing is acute enough to locate the general location of an attacker he still would likely miss with normal armaments. He would need something with a spread, like a shotgun. For a shotgun though, look at his size. He is still pretty young and small. I do have something though, from France. They are a set of matched guns, really large pistols, that we could put in holsters that fit him. These guns take shotgun shells, our regular ones will fit. He would only have two shots without the need to reload, but that might be enough for self defence. The range is not that long though."

He picked one of the pistols off a shelf and Carl examined it a bit dubiously. Then he called Des and Tully over. "Tull, we are going to try something here. Sam is going to fit you with a pair of guns, really small shotguns, which would mean you wouldn't have to hit the target exactly, just close. We will try it on the range here."

Des took over. "Tull, there is an image of a man down there at the end of the range. If you had to protect yourself against someone you would be able to hear them, walking, or even breathing. I will throw a small stone at the target and you will hear it hit. Then you take a gun and aim where you think the sound was. I will have my hand near your wrist, but I won't touch you unless you are about to shoot one of us. Just about all of us are behind you right now. Before you fire, say fire, and I will make sure you are aiming the right way. I will say yes, and you pull the trigger."

Des picked up a stone and threw it. It hit the chest of the target. Tully had been listening, he reached, drew, and fired. There was a tremendous explosion that surprised all of them. They had forgotten they were contained inside the confines of the firing range. Then the others started to laugh and Tull said, "What? Did I miss?"

"No Tull, you didn't miss. You got him where it hurts most, in his guy stuff."

Sam said, "Well, that may have been luck, maybe not, but there is enough there to work with and show us this is possible." Des and Tull worked together for the better part of the hour. The others were telling Carl what great rifles the new ones were, and he tried one too. Then they went back into the store, leaving Tully and Des. In the store, Carl said, "Sam, these rifles, I want all of them I can get, four dozen if you can get them, with ammunition."

"I have three dozen and thirty thousand rounds, and I can order the rest. They are expensive though."

"Sam, they are what they are, and you have never cheated me. Besides, I own part of the company and will get my money back in the end. We'll give you the evening to get it all together. Bring it to the hotel by ten in the morning and I will give you a bank draft for everything, including the ones you have to order. You can deliver those to the manager at the hotel and he will get them to me. Clean them all up though so they are ready to use. Throw in those guns for Tull, with the holsters and ten thousand rounds, it looks like he will have to practice a bit."

Then he retrieved Des and Tully, and the whole group went down to the Peters General Store where the Peters were overjoyed to see them. After the boys spread throughout the store, Carl chatted with Gillian and Stu Peters. He commented that it looked like the store was doing well and complimented them.

Stu said, "With the new hotel, and the station, this end of the town is booming, so are we. You really should raise our rent."

"No Stu, you are covering costs and you are my friends. I don't treat friends that way. We stopped in Connor and I saw Louise. That store seems to be doing okay too."

"Yes, I don't have to go up there very often. She does a good job."

They continued to chat for a while as the boys amassed a large pile of items on the counter. When they stopped finding items of interest and gathered at the counter, Carl said, "Well, I guess they are finished so total it up and we will go for now. Good thing we are on the train though by the looks of all this." They all exchanged hugs before they left. Carl took his usual jar of jawbreakers, only two this time.

At nine the next morning Sam was at the hotel. He had to wait a few minutes while the family finished breakfast. When Carl came out to the lobby, he called the head of the detectives over. "See these get to the train. Issue one to each of your men and a couple of hundred rounds each, then have the rest of the rifles put in the gun trunk. Keep someone there to guard them." Then he turned to Sam and thanked him. "I may not get out here to see you, but you will still have my business. If something new comes up you think I should know of, drop me a telegram through the hotel manager, Mr. Munroe. We move around a bit, but he will be able to get it to me through the hotel head office."

The same manager, had a telegram for Carl from Louise. "Carl, am willing to take on the house, with or without Greg. Will start this weekend, have already found some staff. Will see Jessops at the bank. L."

Carl passed that to Deeds and asked him to send a wire to Jessops telling him of the arrangement and that there was no limit on funding she required, "And send a wire of acknowledgement and thanks from me. The way Greg Lerner is standing here, I think he has something to tell me and I had better see what he wants."

Greg was indeed waiting to see Carl. "Sir, I am sorry to bother you, but your railway has made a mistake and presented us with a problem that might leave one of us sitting here in the station for five or six hours as they fix it. Both of us ordered a special train to Laramie, and they seem to have presumed both orders were the same, just duplicated. They sent one train, for you, and for my fifteen million in gold and silver, well really your fifteen million to be precise."

"To be precise, it's Wells Fargo's fifteen million. If they lose it now, they owe me." They had been walking over to the siding in the station as they talked, followed by the rest of the group, boys, detectives, and porters with luggage. Greg was right, there were two trains on adjacent sidings but only one engine. Carl invited Greg into the private car and called to Diz, "Is your telegraph still hooked up?" When there was a nod yes, he said, "Get Central Despatch for the railway and see how long it would take them to get another engine here. State exactly this. Your majority shareholder is very unhappy. Either they have forgotten about him, or his fifteen million worth of gold sitting on the siding beside him. Send second engine immediately."

Carl was smiling as he turned back to Greg. "I would say that should get their attention. Diz was listening to the wire and keeping up a running commentary. 'Despatch is wiring the railyard in Connor. No train there. Now the railyard in Laramie. No engine there. Now he is asking everyone if they have an unassigned engine. No answer. Now the issue is being sent up the line with everyone wiring the person above them in the pecking order and asking what they should do. Now it is at the President of the railway. The president is bawling them all out and says if he gets fired today so will all of them right down to the guy in the despatch office. They must not realize we are listening to them. Now he is messaging us. He is wondering if, because both trains are going to Laramie, and since after all it is our bullion, would it be terribly inconvenient if we all went as one train, and shared the engine."

Carl said, "Send back, Policy of railroad is to not send bullion shipments on trains with passengers because of the potential risk to them. I feel that is a good policy and question your willingness to throw it out the window just to cover up some one's incompetence. Just this once, and it had better not happen again, or both you and the fellow in the despatch office will need new jobs, but just this once we will share a train. The bullion is too much of a target sitting here and I want to get home. Give us priority, Tucson to Laramie. Remember, past Laramie the engine is mine. Montrose."

Carl was smiling as he turned to Greg, and the conductor and engineer, who had joined them. "Okay Cecil, make up one train, the armored engine, it is an armored engine isn't it." The conductor nodded. "Then after the engine, tender, regular baggage car, freight cars with the horses, then the armored bullion car, the Pinkerton car, then this car at the end, no caboose, you and the brakeman ride in here. If we had a caboose any attackers would just take it over, you guys are not armed, and they would use it as a base against us. Now, you are the engineer? Highball it to Laramie and stop for nothing as long as there is track before you. Any robbers will likely try to stop the train so they can board it easily, so if there are barricades on the tracks just barrel through them, don't worry about the engine, I own it, or most of it. If we can keep moving, they will have to work to board us and that makes them easier targets. Keep the train moving and keep your heads down. Now Greg, am I correct in assuming this is a larger than usual shipment, I thought we were only shipping four or five million at a time?"

"Yes, we had to miss two weeks because of equipment problems with the railway, so this is a three-week shipment."

"That means it is three times as big and will attract three times the attention. One of you boys run and get the head detective, the rest of you get your guns from the trunk and the new rifles too. Greg, I think you have a dozen men, there are a dozen and a half Pinkertons, and then us. Once we are set up, I will send any extra of the new repeater rifles up to you, twenty shots without a need to reload. If anyone is foolish enough to try something, we will have lots of fire power on the train, but this is no way to run a railroad. I will have some words with our ex-president."

The train was put together and pulling out of the station in ten minutes. Carl gathered his people about him, and the Pinkertons gathered in a circle around them. "Look guys, there is no certainty anyone is going to try to rob the train, but if anyone were to go after a train this would be the one to try for. So, we have to be ready just in case. Everybody, including Tully, gets a new rifle, load them now, then find yourself a shooting position with good cover. I think we have a little time, I doubt if anyone will bother us until well past Connor. I want the detectives spread out between the two cars. Des, can you stick with Tull? Tully, make sure you know how to load you rifle by touch, and if anything starts you can just stick the rifle out the window and shoot. You might not hit anything, but you will count as one more gun, Charles, I will show you and Roger in a moment. Now boys, one last thing. If someone attacks, they are not Apache, but they are desperate and out to kill you. They will not hesitate, so you must not either. Shoot to kill."

The atmosphere in the car was quiet, and icy calm. Most of the boys had faced the Indians and were not new to the need to defend themselves.

They got themselves settled, usually in pairs, and found a place to shoot from, some water, a bit of food and they were ready. They talked quietly among themselves and waited.

Greg came back from the other cars to check on things and was impressed with their preparations. He sat with Carl for a few minutes. "Your boys are ready, aren't they? I have the feeling they have done something like this before." Carl told him about the trail drive to Laramie. "Well, some of them look young but they aren't really if they have faced all that. Carl, if this goes badly, can you tell Louise I was thinking of her? She is a good woman, but there is something there between us. We seem to go so far and then her armor comes up."

"Greg, I can safely say that she does love you, and she would like to see the two of you together. She is afraid something from her past, if you found out about it, would finish the two of you."

"You mean the boys, the ones in the picture? This is a small town and people talk."

"The boys are my grandchildren and their father my son Mag. He acted like a spoiled child, with no care for others, and the result was the children. The two of them did make one good decision though, and that was that Mag would raise them. He now is married and as far as they will know, Mel is their mother. Louise was just the friendly lady in the store who spoiled them a bit, but she was okay with that because that was better for them. She could have pushed the point and Mag would have married her, but she said no, she wanted a husband and a real marriage. She is afraid though, about how you will feel about the boys. I told her a good marriage doesn't start on lies. You know Greg, there is such a double standard with regards to what is acceptable for men and women. All the boys were sexually active at about fifteen, and generally that is acceptable, but girls, a totally different story. In the Hamptons, they all had different girls every night. I think this whole attitude is in for a change among the young people."

"I thought it might be something like that. I know Louise and the kind of person she is, that is why I like her. I think we need to have a good talk about all of this. What I am interested in is the kind of life we can have in the future. There are some things in my past, I am not all that proud of either. "

"You should know that I asked Louise to live at the ranchero, get some staff to look after it and supervise them. No rent, there just has to be someone in the house. I would love if it could be her, and you, and a family of your own."

Greg nodded but looked grave, "First, we have to get through this little predicament. I think we are safe until we get past Connor, after all, there are army patrols between Tucson and Connor, if I was a train robber I would wait until well past Connor. There is a place where the rails get steeper and there are mountains. I always get nervous in that section, it is about half way between Connor and Laramie, just after we cross a long trestle. We reduce speed for the trestle and then come off it into the upgrade. The train slows down quite a bit and the terrain gives them some raised areas to shoot down on the train. Once we get past that area it all flattens out and the train can pick up speed. From that point on, any train robbers wouldn't stand a chance of getting aboard."

The train steamed on. It went through the station at Connor at almost full speed, surprising the stationmaster there. He barely had time to wave. Greg returned to the Bullion Car and made sure his men were securely sealed in. Carl made the rounds of his car, and the detectives' car, encouraging his men and telling them to be ready as soon as they crossed the trestle, as that would be the most likely spot for an attack. As the trestle came into view the engineer gave several short whistles to alert them, then he gave the engine more steam and they rumbled across the bridge and started up the other side. When the engineer spotted a barricade ahead on the tracks, he again tooted the whistles and poured on the steam. There were several men sitting on the barricade, expecting the engine to stop and they had to leap for their lives as the train barreled through. There was an immediate volley from the train robbers as they realized their job that day was not going to be easy. Their shots were returned from the train ten times over, from all the cars including the fancy one at the end.

The thieves ran for their horses and many galloped down the track in pursuit of the train. Some went overland to try to catch the train as it rounded a bend. Carl and Deeds opened up from the back windows of the car and picked off about five thieves between them. The robbers decided they might be better off approaching from the side of the train and left the tracks. They approached on either side through the trees. The train continued steaming along as fast as it could so the riders had to struggle to close on it. They were firing on all of the cars and by that point all the windows in the private car and the coach in front of it were broken.

The boys were for the most part crouching below the window sills just peaking out but when a target came into view, they would alert each other and rise together blasting away. The target was usually killed. By ten minutes into the melee about a dozen of the train robbers had been eliminated, with only four or five of the first group left.

The train rounded the bend and came upon the part of the group that had gone overland. They did not try to stop the train again as they knew it was futile, but they raked the train with fire as is passed between them. There were a few casualties as this fire was not expected. The robbers also managed to get a couple torches into the bullion car as it went by.

Shots from the bullion car slackened as its occupants had to fight the fire at the same time dealing with the smoke. A couple of the Pinkertons were killed as their car went between the attacking thieves but Carl heard the shooting early enough to yell to his people to "duck".

The robbers were again approaching the train on horseback, their numbers reduced to about half of their original three dozen. They came up on either side of the steaming train and Carl had ordered his group to hold their fire and stay hidden. When most of them were beside the rail car he ordered, "Okay boys, get em." They all stood and opened fire. All the ones on either side of the car were shot, for the most part killed, or at least knocked off their horses, wounded. One did manage to get on the platform at the back of the car unseen. He pressed himself against the wall of the car and slid over beside the open window. The boys and Carl were gathering in the center of the car, jubilant in their victory. Tully hung back a little, not sure of what was happening as he could not see it. The train continued steaming along.

The robber edged to the window. Des, with the group, noticed a slight movement behind Tully and yelled, "Tull, behind you, ten o'clock." Tully reached for both his holstered guns at the same time as he turned. His guns roared at the same time as the robber fired. The thief was hit by the blasts from both guns and thrown backward off the train, dead. Tully collapsed to the floor, blood streaming from a wound to his head. Carl and the boys rushed over, and an anguished Carl sank to his knees beside Tully, holding a napkin snatched from the table against the wound on his head. Tully slowly regained consciousness, then he said, "Take my glasses off, Dad, take them off."

Carl did so, and Tully blinked his eyes several times then said, "Dad, I can see, I can see. I got a headache, but I can see." Carl removed the napkin to check the wound, then said, "Tull, it's another graze. We will have a doctor look at it in Laramie, but boy, I would say God has something in store for you, he has given you another chance to do, or be, something great."

"Maybe dad, but can I just be eleven for a while. I missed being eleven."

When the train pulled into the station in Laramie, Cynthia was waiting and was absolutely shocked at its condition. When the train pulled to a stop at the platform, a Pinkerton detective rushed off in search of a doctor and Cynthia rushed on. She found several people gathered around a prone Tully on the floor, but she saw her son and husband off to the side. She rushed over to them. "You two, you said you were going to look at a new bank, and look at this, it looks like you all went to a war. Can't I even let you out of my sight. Charles Birch, you are the top banker in the city, not some sort of, of, ...of..."

"Shut up dear, we are okay," said Charles and gave her a hug. The other older boys were smiling knowing they would get exactly the same treatment when they got home.

The doctor that was summoned examined Tully and said he was not sure what had happened, but that Tully seemed cured. He dressed the wound then treated a few other minor scrapes and wounds among the boys. There were several wounds among the detectives and two fatalities. The bullion car had one casualty and a couple of wounds. The doctor took an hour to finish his rounds among the cars. The local sheriff was called, and he and his deputies helped deliver the shipment to the Western Fidelity Bank, accompanied by Charles Birch.

Roger said goodbye to Ali and Ed, "Bye guys, best time I ever had in my life. We have to get together again. Soon." Carl gave him a hug goodbye before he left. A glazier was called to fix the windows in the car before they could go. While he was working, Carl took the rest of the group to lunch at a nearby restaurant.

Just as they were finishing, Greg came in. "I was just over at the station. The windows are done in your car, a new coach has been found, and they have the train rearranged for you. There is some nervous guy pacing back and forth on the station platform, someone said he was the president of the railway."

"Ex-president," corrected Carl with a smile.

Greg went on. "I want to thank you. Without all your people, we never would have made it through. The sheriff went out there and they counted twenty-nine bodies. This made one thing clear to me, I could have been one of the casualties here today. The first thing I am gonna do when I get back is have a good talk with Louise, and then I am gonna ask her to marry me. We want to start on our future, at least I do."

"That's wonderful Greg, and I look forward to knowing the ranchero will be full of kids again at some point. If you don't have to work it for a living, it could be a wonderful place to raise a family. One suggestion though, you need a different job. We were lucky today, and you can't count on that type of luck forever, that is why we are moving back east. When you get back to Connor go to see Jessops at the bank. I am going to send him a wire and we will find you something to do that you like, but that still will allow you to become an old man someday and enjoy a family meantime. One thing I know we need is a town Police Chief, and a force of about ten. Since I own the place, I can offer you that. Think about it, and let Jessops know. If you want something else, we can arrange that too."

"I think you are right. If Louise accepts me, then I owe her a future, don't I? That Police Chief thing does sound interesting. Thanks Carl."

Chapter 18

Christmas In Texas

On the way back to Texas, Carl pulled Ed, Ali, and Tully aside. "Boys, when we get back to the ranch, the new tutor will be there, and he will work with all of you. He is a fellow from the west who went back east to school and then came back to Texas after the war. So, he isn't a greenhorn. Word is, he is kinda tough, was in the army during the war, in fact by the end of the war he was a lieutenant. His name is Hank Carter. I expect you guys to behave yourselves and learn what he has to offer. There will be consequences if you three get up to hi-jinx and I hear about it." The boys were distinctly unhappy at the idea of another tutor, Tully especially.

"Dad, I just got back my eyesight. Can't I have a little time to myself to have a little of the fun I missed?"

"Tully, you have no idea how happy we are, all of us, at that. You should realize that the things that are the most fun are with other people. Now these two will spend four hours a day with the tutor and will not be available to have fun with you. As they are your likely fun partners, I think you are gonna have to stay with them. I will tell Mr. Carter to try to find things to do with you all that are fun. You other two have gotten into enough trouble this summer with Roger, you don't deserve any more fun." The three boys were in a distinctly glum mood after their talk with Carl.

Des noticed and commented, "Dad, what's the problem with those three. They look like you killed their dog."

"I reminded them there is a new tutor waiting for us when we get back. None of them is too happy about that. The one that will struggle is Tull. He did not have much schooling before he lost his sight, remember we were all working with him. Then after the shooting, what education he got was as blind person and largely how to cope with that. Now, he is sighted again and needs a general education. I am wondering whether he needs a tutor of his own. I think I will talk to Jenn about it when we get back."

When they arrived at the ranch, the engine left the two cars on the siding, the private car and the coach the Pinkertons were using. The people in the house wandered down as Carl and the boys were getting off the train. Some of the cowboys came down with a wagon for the baggage and to help with the horses. The horses were still skittish after the gunfight and they were difficult to handle. Tex and Fargo appreciated the help from the other hands. Several of the people were looking at the car and all the bullet holes. Jenn looked at Des, a question in her eyes that demanded an answer and clearly indicated it better be a good one.

Des stammered a bit then said, "It wasn't our fault. They had to put the bullion car on our train and some people tried to steal it."

Just then Tully came off the car, without his cane or his glasses, a big bandage on his head. He came over to Des and Jenn and said, "Hi Jenn, never knew what you looked like, but you are as beautiful as I imagined. I can see why Des fell for you."

A speechless Jenn just reached over and hugged him. After a few moments she said, "Tull, what happened? How?"

"No one really knows. There was another graze on the head, and I could see when I came to. Jenn, I can go on being a kid again for a while."

Carl joined them just as Jenn said, "That is wonderful Tully, but now you have a whole bunch of new stuff to learn, don't you?"

Carl joined in then. "Jenn, I wanted to ask you about that. Do you think he can join the other two with their new tutor or should we get one for Tully by himself?" Tully looked aghast at the very thought when it was mentioned.

"Tully, don't look so upset. Having a tutor of your own would allow you to learn so quickly. You really are very bright, your only problem was that you haven't been to school. Carl, that would be wonderful, and I know who would be ideal. I can have mom and dad send us out a tutor, just for the winter until we go back east. By then, Tully should be able to share a tutor with Ed and Ali."

"Deeds is going east with the private car, the day after tomorrow. Send a wire to your parents and the tutor can come back with him."

Dinner that night was a joyous affair, because of Tully, and because the rest of them had made it back with only a few minor scrapes. The boys that had not gone were envious of the others and the adventure they had missed. Their wives were just thankful their husbands had not been at risk, and vowed to keep them even closer in the future.

That night, at bedtime, Carl swung by Tully's room and lay down on his bed beside him. "Thought I would visit you tonight, at least until you fell asleep. He pulled Tully over beside him and the boy snuggled in. Carl was surprised to see he was holding Rabbit. "I see you brought Rabbit out of retirement."

"Yeah, I saw him sitting there and sort of missed him. Cleo won't mind."

"You know Tull, you can't go back and get that year you lost, you have to go on from where you are now. You are not the person, the kid, you were back then. Too much has happened to you and you have learned so much. You have matured, you had to. You already were older than your years, and this last year made you much older yet. You are an old eleven-year old, but that is okay, you will fit right in with Ed and Ali who, although a bit older than you, rarely act their age. There are still lots of things you can do that are fun."

Carl had intended to only stay with Tully until he fell asleep, but Carl himself dozed off and spent the night, something Tully was very happy with. That was something he never did with Ed and Ali anymore.

The next morning Ali and Ed met their new tutor. He did not live on the ranch with them, but rather had a house on a neighboring one and rode over every day. Carl showed Hank Carter into the study where the two boys were waiting. As soon as they saw him, the two boys knew the jig was up. He looked more than capable of handling the two of them and they realized they would not be able to get away with anything. Just out of principle they would have to try, but they had little hope of success. Carl left the three together smiling slightly at the boys' and their discomfort. As he went through one of the parlors Jenn and Tully sat on one of the sofas working at his reading. She was using the printed versions of some books he already could read in Braille, which made it a bit easier for him.

One morning, a couple days later, Tully was on the veranda with Jenn and Carl when the railcar was spotted into the siding. Lionel Deeds was back from New York with the new tutor. Deeds came down the stairs first, then turned back to help the tutor down. Tully gave a big gulp. His tutor was a young lady, a very pretty young lady. All at once all Tully could only wonder was whether he was old enough, for what he was not certain, but he knew he wanted to be old enough. He told himself he had to make sure Rabbit was not left on the shelf for anyone to see who passed by. His tutor would have a room just down the hall from his, after all.

Deeds and the young lady came up the path to the verandah. Carl rose at their approach, and Tully did too. Deeds said, "Gentlemen, this is Denise Warner, Denise, this is Carl Montrose, your employer, and Tully Montrose, your student. You already know Jennifer I believe." Carl stepped forward and shook her hand. Tully was speechless and frozen to the spot he stood on. Jennifer rushed forward and gave Denise a big hug.

At diner that night, Carl sat back and watched bemusedly as Denise was the center of attention for all of the unattached Montrose males. The three younger ones sat in a row across the table from her, watching every move and hanging on every word. Occasionally, she flashed a dazzling smile at them and they all blushed beet red. Marcus and Dizzy had managed to seat themselves on either side of her. While the younger three looked at Denise adoringly, Marcus and Dizzy were having trouble hiding the lust in their hearts. Denise, who was used to all of these reactions, artfully played with all of the boys and withstood all the efforts of Marcus and Dizzy to charm her. Carl had the feeling that Tully would not be the only person learning a few lessons in the near future.

Despite anything else, Denise was a good teacher. She soon got Tully over his initial infatuation, toning it down to the point where they could work together, and he made rapid progress. The two enjoyed working with each other. Tully had not had that much time with someone who could mother him a bit. She found him an adorable child, bright, inquisitive, and cute as hell. When she started Tully was working at a grade 2 or low 3 level. By the end of the winter she felt she would get him to a grade 7 level, where his brothers Ed and Ali would be. That would mean the three could be tutored together, which was what Carl was aiming for.

Ed and Ali were jealous of Tully for the tutor he had. Their tutor, Mr. Carter, was a good teacher but he put up with no nonsense from them. They were under his thumb for four hours a day, getting away with nothing, and unlike Tully's tutor, Hank Carter was not anything special to look at. When he started with the two boys, they were achieving at a grade 5/6 level and when he stopped working with them, they were at a grade 7 level also.

He had to work hard to keep the two under control and at task, but in the end, he was satisfied.

During the fall also, Captain Hayes sent a steady stream of tutors for Marcus in all areas that were under the jurisdiction of a ship's master. Ship handling, the law of the sea, celestial navigation, use of maps and charts, loading and unloading practices for ships, and a myriad of other topics were covered. By the end of October, Captain Hayes had Marcus down to Galveston and on several short voyages with him. Hayes saw what Carl already had, Marcus was an excellent sailor despite his youth, the crewmen quickly saw that and came to trust him and his judgement. The Captain slowly came to believe that Montrose shipping was not going to lose its new owner on some dimwitted voyage around the world the following year.

Carl and all the older boys boarded the rail car every day for the short trip into Dallas and the headquarters. The car had been repaired so it didn't show any of the scars that had been there after the trip out west. Occasionally, they had to take a regular coach if the private car had been despatched elsewhere on a task, perhaps with Deeds to New York or elsewhere. The only one who didn't go was Chuck as his job was on the ranch and at Oakside.

At the ranch, he worked hard to establish a line of western horses that were both fast and sturdy, up to the tasks they would be required to do on a ranch in the west but also beautiful to look at and as fast as a second rate race horse. He was selecting horses for certain characteristics and cross breeding them to accentuate those characteristics. He was planning to go to Oakside for the spring but when he came back to Texas in the fall he hoped he would find several colts running in the fields with the characteristics he was breeding for.

In Dallas, Marcus split his time between the tutors in his private office, the general outer offices where he got a feeling for Montrose Shipping, the shipping business in general, and the specific practices of Montrose. The people in the outer offices, who were asking themselves what the head office of the company was doing in Dallas, were amazed by Marcus' determination to learn all he could about the shipping company and how quickly he mastered it. Marcus soon became very popular with all the people in the office, male and female.

Mag was finding it a little harder going in the Montrose Oil offices. It was a big company, growing bigger every day. There were a lot of people in the offices on their two floors of the Montrose Building and Mag struggled just to learn who each of them were, and what they did. He made several day long excursions out to the oil fields with engineers, geologists, and tough hard talking field bosses to see how the oil was discovered, wrestled from the ground and brought to the refineries then made into products that could be sold. The people that at the beginning just thought of him as the spoiled pretty boy brat of the boss came to realize there was much more to him. They came to like and admire him as he got a firm grip on the affairs of Montrose Oil.

Des came in and read daily with Lionel Deeds in the offices of Deeds and Montrose. They discussed all the matters that came to them, largely from the various parts of the Montrose empire. They had business from all the divisions. When they discussed issues, Lionel was surprised, and pleased, to hear Des' views. When the whole idea of Des joining the firm with him had been put forward by Des, Lionel had been privately sceptical. Due to his friendship with Carl, Lionel had agreed, but he hadn't expected much. He had been pleasantly surprised. Des was a bit of an obtuse thinker and came at things from viewpoints Deeds had not seen, but he also often saw issues that Lionel had missed. He would be an asset to the firm and Deeds looked forward to the day he would be a full partner.

Diz was fully involved in the day to day business of Montrose Communications. What they were doing had largely been his idea. He was smart enough to search out and employ the people who could bring it all to fulfilment. There was no need for him to actually go out, climb poles and string lines. He also had people to order those poles and make sure they were delivered to the appropriate places at the correct times. He had people who could approach the banking houses all over the country and close the deal with them. Diz wisely saw his job as the maestro of the orchestra, bringing it all together. In the end, it did, the brokerages were connected, and the system ran flawlessly. It was well received by investors all over the country.

The four boys made a point of getting together with Carl for a couple hours a day up on the sixth floor. It was through them that Carl kept a grip on the various divisions. Issues would be brought up and discussed by the group as a whole. A couple times a week Tully, with Denise in tow, would join the others as they boarded the train and Carl had set aside an office for him where he and Denise could work on his lessons. However, on the days he was in town, Tully would join the others in their meetings with Carl. He expressed his views as much as the others and his opinions were valued equally. He often came up with things the others had not thought of.

This all was as Carl had wished and expected. He wanted the Montrose companies to be governed as a group and for everyone to be aware of all the business, all the problems and all the solutions devised by the group as a whole. The only flies in the ointment, as it were, were Ed and Ali. Any time not spent with Mr. Carter, they were determined that would be their playtime and Carl felt it was still necessary to despatch Tex and Fargo to make sure they didn't get into anything too dangerous. They were a year older than Tully but seemed to have half the common sense and ambition, if he was generous in his assessment.

As soon as their four hours with Mr. Carter were finished, Ed and Ali would head for the stables where Tex and Fargo would have their horses saddled. The four would head out onto the range. They rode as a group by that point. The younger boys realized it was silly to make the older two ride a quarter mile behind. It became the routine the four just hung out together. From Tex and Fargo's viewpoint, they were being paid to just hang out and horse around.

As far as the younger boys were concerned, the conversations, the language, and the subjects discussed, were all older than what they would have participated in. That is not to say they were more mature. Young cowboys can be rather childish when they are allowed to. Ed and Ali were learning a great deal about women, and what cowboys did with them, from these conversations. Cat houses, whores, and poker were among the subjects discussed. One day they all rode to a remote section of the ranch where there was a stream and, since they were hot, all went skinny dipping. As they came out, they all ribbed Tex because he had a hard on. That led to a circle jerk to see who would be the slowest to cum, last the longest. The rules were simple, they all had to get themselves hard and then the timing would start. It would be cheating to slow the hand action and they would be called on it. Surprisingly, the one who lasted the longest before he came was Ali.

That night the two were discussing the events of the afternoon and they heard Carl go by. They stopped talking until they thought he was out of range then continued. Carl had noticed them quiet as he approached so he stationed himself against the wall by their doorway, out of sight, and listened.

"So Ali, how did you win that circle jerk this afternoon. You were going as fast as the rest of us, but you lasted the longest. I came first, then Tex and Fargo, but you still hung in there after all of us, and when you came there were four spurts, I counted."

"It was damn hard Ed. I had to force myself to think about something else. I did times tables in my head. But Ed, it felt so good when I let myself go at the end. I wonder if that is how it feels when you do it with a girl."

"Maybe we can find out soon. Fargo told me that the next time Dad goes away for a couple of days he will take us to a whorehouse. There is one two farms over, but we need a whole day to go and get back."

"Tex did say the girls would take us if we paid enough money, even though we are only twelve and thirteen."

"Maybe we can get a real drink too, not just that wine from the rail car."

"Fargo said we have to make sure dad never finds out about any of this, he is afraid dad will shoot him, and us."

By this point Carl was angry. He strode into his room and grabbed one of the new rifles, checking to make sure it was loaded, then went down the back stairs and out the door to the bunkhouse. As he neared the door he yelled, "Tex, Fargo, get your worthless hides out here."

Tex was the first out. He was shirtless and struggling to pull on his pants. Fargo was close behind clad only in a set of long underwear. "Hey, boss, what do you need?" said Tex as he came through the door.

"You are worthless saddle tramps. You were being paid to keep them outta trouble, not get them into it. You better start running because I am gonna fill your hides with holes. Skinny dipping, circle jerks, whore houses, cards, and drinking." The two were running for their lives and had scattered a bit. Carl was punctuating his rant with the blasts from the rifle. As the two faded into the darkness, Paul, the foreman, came to stand beside Carl. "Did you hit them?" Paul asked worriedly.

"No, I didn't but you do know I could have, don't you?" Paul nodded. "No, this was just for the sake of a couple kids watching from a window upstairs. Get their stuff and go after them. They haven't got far, they have no boots on. Give them an extra couple of hundred dollars and take them over to that new ranch I bought. Just tell them to stay away from here. I have made my point here and the next men I assign will not get too friendly. Now I have to go make my point with two twelve-year olds."

Carl turned back towards the house. He saw that all the lights were on upstairs, except in the boys' room. He stomped up the back stairs and down the hall, past the older boys who had gathered in the hall grinning. Carl winked at them then stormed into the boys' room, slamming the door behind him and snapping on the lights. The two were in bed, with their covers pulled over their heads. Carl leaned over and pulled the covers back.

"Don't shoot us dad!" yelled Ed.

"Shoot you? No that would be too quick. You two deserve more than that."

Carl sat on the side of Ali's bed, reached over and dragged him across his knees in one fluid motion. He stripped the under-alls off saying, "Ali, you will go first since you were the winner today and you deserve to get your prize first. Maybe you can recite times tables to keep your mind off this. Circle jerks, whore houses, poker and drinking. You are thirteen, too young for any of that."

By that point he had completed eighteen swats. His hand was sore, Ali's butt beet red, and Ed rather pale. He let Ali go and grabbed Ed.

He pulled Ed down over his knee and began. "If you two want to start thinking about stuff like that you have to do some growing up. I am sick and tired of the two of you spending all of your time in fun and games. You have to start accepting some responsibilities like everyone else in the family has. You used to, when you were younger, and we lived on the ranchero. Now, you just seem to be determined to be worthless. Starting tomorrow, you two and Mr. Carter will come on the rail car with the rest of us. I will find you an office where you can work with him and after that the two of you will do some real work. There are 600 feet of hallways in that building that have to be mopped everyday and two sets of big washrooms on each floor to be cleaned for starters. You two will not turn out to be saddle bums like that worthless Tex and Fargo."

By that point the two of them were standing there in front of him, trying not to cry and clasping the waistbands of their underwear. "One month of this, and then you can go back to your regular routine. I will assign a couple new cowboys to look after you to replace the ones I shot. Maybe by washing all those floors and cleaning all those washrooms the two of you will decide there are some things you do not want to do, and then maybe you can find something in what we own that you do want to do. Look you two, I know you are growing up, but we don't have to do it so fast, do we? Now, give me a hug and we will start fresh tomorrow."

Ed and Ali got their hugs, and climbed back into bed, laying on their stomachs. Carl turned out their light as he opened the door and went into the hall. The boys were still there, grinning. "That should hold them for a bit," he whispered.

"Maybe a week or two, never held any of us back for more than that," whispered Des.

On the way back to his room, Carl peeked in on Tully, and seeing that he was still awake he entered and sat on the bed beside him. Tull looked up alarmed. "I din do nuttin Dad, really I din."

"I know Tull, you are a much older soul than they are. My concern with you is that you lost too much of your childhood." He reached up and took Rabbit from his place on the shelf, sticking it in bed at Tully's head. That elicited a grin from Tully and a "Thank you Dad."

The next day, a surly Ed and Ali boarded the railcar with a grinning Mr. Carter, who thought it was about time the two of them got their come-uppance. He drilled them on math tables all the way into the office. When they got there, Carl showed the three of them to a room that had been set up as a library. There was a nice long table with several chairs, a desk at the side with writing materials, books and maps on the walls, and a large globe standing in the corner. There were no windows. A big electric fan hung from the ceiling to stir the air a bit. The boys were dismayed at the sight of the room, but Mr. Carter said, "Nice room, no distractions."

After four hours cooped up with Mr. Carter, the two boys just about exploded out of the room at the end of their tutoring session. Their father was standing there with an old colored man. He introduced them. "Boys, this is Moses, the head custodian for the building. Moses, these are my boys, Ed and Ali. They are yours for the next two hours. They are looking forward to mopping all the halls, scrubbing down all the washrooms, and whatever else you can think of to keep them busy. Now you two make sure you don't make any extra work for Moses here, he has more than enough to keep him busy."

Moses led the boys into the hall and over to a custodian's closet at the far end. When he opened the door, Ali reached for a mop and Moses said,

"No, not ready for the mop. You sweep the floor first, then you use the dust mop, and then, if it is clean, you use the mop and the water, then you dry mop it and dust mop it again. Otherwise you just have mud on the floor."

The boys were looking at him dumbfounded. Ed said, "Moses, that means you go over the floor five times to just wash it."

"How many times a week do you mop the floor?"

"At least once a day six days a week. In the rainy season two or three times a day. Now we better get going. There are six halls, twelve bathrooms and then all the stairs and the first floor is always three times as dirty as all the rest. There also is the third floor, which is empty, but this is the day we sweep all of it."

Carl peeked in on them a couple of times and they were working like little tornados. By an hour later, they had completed three of the floors, half the stairways and three of the bathrooms. They were looking a bit tired though. That first day it took them two and a half hours, but they stuck in to the end. Moses brought them up to Carl on the sixth floor where the others had been waiting for them. As they came in the door the others tried to look busy. Carl said to Moses, "So, did they do a good job for you?"

"Yes sir, they worked mighty hard. Tomorrow, they will be faster, they know what they are doing now, and we only have to do that extra floor once a week."

The Montroses went out to the train as a family. The engineer was wondering what was taking so long, this group was really quite prompt most of the time. Didn't matter though, he owned the railroad after all, the train would wait until he was ready. However, the engineer was glad when he saw the group coming out, the family loosely surrounded by their detectives that seemed to always be there. When they got to the train, one of them, Diz, went over to a little box on a telegraph pole beside the engine. He sent a message, waited a few moments then called up, "Okay Trev, you have the right of way to our spur, but you wait for the number six and follow her in on the way back."

In the car on the way home, Ed and Ali were sitting beside their father. Ed said, "You know dad, Moses is a bit old for that job, and it is a lot of work. You really should get him some help."

"Well, we got him help for all the offices, they come in at nights. Maybe we should let him go and get a younger man to replace him."

"No Dad," they both said together. Ali went on, "Moses is a good guy, he works hard, and he was very patient with us. He knows his job. He deserves to be in charge over there of all the cleaning workers. "

"Boys, we are in the south. There is no way I could put him in charge of any white workers."

"Then hire only colored people for the cleaning people and put Moses in charge of them," said Ed.

"You guys aren't just trying to make your month easier are you by hiring some new people?" asked a suspicious Carl.

"No Dad," said Ali, "But when we leave at the end of the month we don't think Moses should go back to the way it was. Actually, we don't mind doing this. It feels good when we are done and look down on that shiny clean floor, it makes you sorta proud."

"Then you boys are already learning what I wanted you to. It feels good when you do a good job and have something to look back on at the end. Now, after dinner, how about you two, and I, go for a ride?"

Ed said, "Sure dad, we would like that but let's ask Tull too. We keep forgetting he can do stuff like that now. We shouldn't do that."

"Excellent, there is hope for you two. Despite all your efforts the two of you are growing up. Thinking about others is the first part of becoming a man. Hey Tull, you want to go for a ride with us after dinner?"

Tully immediately said yes, as that was one of his favorite things to do now, although they didn't do it that often. Later, when the four of them were riding, Carl said, "I have to apologize to the three of you. I don't do this as often as I should, just spend some time with you, and I feel sorry for that. I have let other things take over too much of my time and I am going to try to do better at that from now on. So, let's see who can get to that tree over there first." And he kicked his horse and took off, surprising the three of them. But he didn't win, despite that, he was just a little too heavy. Tully got there first, and justifiably crowed about it. They all got a laugh about that. Ali and Ed showed the other two the little cove with the stream.

"This is our swimming hole. Tex and Fargo showed it to us," said Ali, "There is a nice sand bottom, and it is just deep enough for swimming but not too deep."

Carl said, "You know guys, when you got into trouble the other day, it was not because you went swimming. Skinny dipping in the summer with the boys is just a part of growing up. I really don't mind that, as long as it is just you guys, no girls with fathers that are going to try to shoot you. I already killed two cowboys, I don't know if we can hide a father out there too."

Ali looked a bit worried and said, "Really dad, you didn't … did you?"

Carl was silent for a few seconds and said, "No boys, Tex and Fargo are working over at another ranch I own, they still have their worthless hides, minus any bullet holes. But, you guys have to remember something. I was really mad that night, and I really wanted to plug them with a few bullet holes each, so let's try not to get me that mad again, shall we? There is only so much self-control your old dad has, you know, and you guys used most of it up already."

At the end of the month, when the boys could go back to their regular routine and had to say goodbye to Moses; they were truly sorry to do so. Moses was sorry to see them go too. Over the month he had come to like the pair of them, their liveliness and their sense of humor. He said, "Boys, when you come in to town with your dad, you make sure to come and see me. I have an office now, down on the first floor at the back by the custodial change rooms. Your daddy made me the Chief Custodian. Got me a raise too. Now, you two wouldn't have had something to do with that, would you?"

The boys flashed him their most innocent expressions and denied everything. Moses knew though, but he did not make an issue of it. Carl also noted the interaction and on the way back upstairs to get the others, he asked, "You guys do know, if you really want to, you can stay working with him."

"No Dad, we got the message."

"We ain't stupid you know."

"You wanted us to realize it was time to start growing up, take advantage of our tutors and learn something."

"We know, given all that the family owns, there must be something that interests us, just like there was something for all the others."

"We are starting to look, but dad, we are just 'leven and twelve, it might take a while, and we certainly are not old 'nuf to start looking for wives," said Ed.

"Thank God, I am not ready for all that comes with you guys getting interested in girls," said Carl.

"Oh, we are interested in girls, just not in marrying them," said Ali. Carl just groaned and Ed and Ali exchanged winks, unseen by their father.

From that point on, when Tully went into town a couple times a week to attend the meetings with Carl and the older brothers, Ed and Ali went too. A couple more desks were added to the grouping for them and they sat in on the meetings. At first, they just listened, but when they felt secure, they started to ask questions. Surprisingly enough, they were often questions the others could not answer, which made them go back to their individual companies and develop an answer for the next meeting. Ed and Ali were learning about the Montrose empire, and they were searching for the place they belonged in that empire. That was as Carl had hoped.

Once fall became winter and the months became December, thoughts turned to Christmas, their first Christmas in Texas. Carl swore Diz to secrecy and messages started flowing west to the Peters. Wrapped packages started flowing east on the trains delivered right to their front door in the middle of December. They were stacked in the corner of one of the parlors until Carl could get a tree, which was a little scarce in the middle of the Texas prairie. Finally, Carl decided to have a hundred sent to him from Colorado, in their own freight car. He let the boys choose two for the house, and two for the bunk houses, the cowboys' and the Pinkertons', then he sent the rest into town and gave them out to the employees of the Montrose companies and the Western Fidelity Bank on the first floor. The trees and their yearly bonuses were their Christmas gifts. The cowboys and the detectives each also received a hundred dollars and two weeks off with pay that would allow each of them to have a paid vacation, something that was unheard of at that time.

Marcus had gone along with Captain Hayes on a trip to Maine. They left at the start of December, but he promised he would be back before Christmas. One evening, five days before Christmas Eve, a carriage drew up to the back door delivering a guest from town. They all expected it was Marcus, as everyone else was accounted for, so there was no rush to the door. They all knew he would come in to them. A few seconds later Marcus stood in the doorway holding the hand of a little boy about four, the spitting image of him. Marcus gave a little cough and then announced, "Everyone, I would like you to meet my son Caleb, he is four."

Everyone in the room was making rapid calculations, but Ali got to the answer first and blurted out, "Jesus Christ, Marcus, you are just about to turn seventeen, that means you were twelve or so when you made him."

Marcus gave a little cough and looked at Carl. "I told dad that after the crews on the boats adopted me, they also took me with them when we made port and they visited the local, er, houses. When I got to Maine with Captain Hayes, I visited a few of their favorite houses to see if any of the guys were in port. One of the girls drew me aside and told me a girl I had been with had a baby, but died in child birth. The girls in the house had looked after the baby but when they saw me, they knew for sure I was the father. She said he looked just like me. They introduced me and I had to admit it. I took him back to the ship and explained it all to Captain Hayes. He agreed to bring us back to Texas. I brought him with me to get my stuff and we will find an apartment in town. He is my responsibility."

Carl stood and walked over. "What do you mean a place in town? There are lots of rooms here, and there are lots of people who like little kids." He bent down and gave Caleb a hug as he introduced himself. "Caleb, I am your grandpa, and we are glad to meet you."

"Hey, leggo, I don' like hugs from friggen guys I don' know, get yer paws off."

Marcus' face was beet red as he said, "Sorry dad, he is a bit rough around the edges. You have to remember where he was raised. That was sorta why we were going to get a place in town."

Jen had joined them by that point. "Caleb, I am your Aunt Jen, and it has been my job to take some of the rough edges off of some of the other people in this family." She indicated Denise as she went on, "And this is Aunt Denise. She is a teacher too. Between us we are going to make it our job to teach you a bit so that you fit right in."

"I don't care who you are, but I don't want no friggen teachers trying to teach me any freaking things, and I don' want to fit in here. I wan' ta go home where I belong. Just because this guy visited the house and fucked my mother don' make him my father."

There was silence in the room then Jen said, "Okay Caleb, that was the last time we are going to put up with language like that. You use any of those words again, and you know which words I am talking about, you are just using them now to see what effect they have. From this point on any of those words will get you a mouth full of soap. That will be the first lesson and I would suggest you learn it now." She looked him directly in his eyes, as if daring him to utter anything inappropriate. Caleb looked back at her.

You could see he was calculating, and finally the defiance in his eyes died. He had decided she meant what she said, and odds were, he would end up eating a bar of soap. He would try with the others, one by one, and the result was always the same, he grew to hate soap.

Caleb had other rough edges that were slowly worn away. Some presented themselves that night. Caleb was used to sleeping in the nude. He liked to walk around that way too, not at all bothered by who saw him. That was how everyone in the house had been. He also was not that fond of baths. On the ship, he had slept in the berth above Marcus so it was not a problem. Here, he would sleep with Marcus in the same bed for a while, and it was decided it would not be proper if he slept that way. Jenn took a pair of Tully's under alls and made some rapid alterations with a needle and thread to make them fit. Marcus had wrestled Caleb into a hot bath, much to his displeasure, which was only eased when Tully marched in and handed him a couple of boats.

"I get bored in the bath too. These make it go faster and you can borrow them whenever you need 'em."

In the bedroom Carl and Jen were looking at the few things Caleb had brought with him. Jen said, "There is not much here. No under wear at all, no coat, only a couple of shirts and one pair of pants. I wonder what he wore when they were being washed but given the way he is comfortable in his skin, and only his skin, I suspect he wore nothing when his pants were in the wash."

"Make a list and we will get Diz on the telegraph to the Peters. They can put it all on the overnight express and we will have it by tomorrow night, maybe in the morning. We can manage for one day with what he has."

Marcus came back in the room, pushing Caleb before him. He was wrapped in a fluffy white towel, but he was spotless and smelled of soap. "Here, these are for you. I altered them to make them fit," said Jen as she held out the under-alls. "In proper houses the men, no matter how small they are, do not go to bed naked, and they certainly don't wander around that way."

"What the h...er, heck are those? People don't wear clothes to bed, besides, those are kinda girlish, ain't they?"

"Hey, what do you mean girlish? Those are a pair of mine, just made smaller to fit you. All us guys wear them, and we ain't girlish. We fought injuns and bank robbers, and killed lots of them," Tully protested vehemently, then stalked away.

Carl looked at Caleb. "He is the easy going one and you have made him mad. You say anything like that to the other two and you are gonna get a swat to the side of your head. A lesson to be learned, I would say."

Caleb reluctantly put on the under-alls. Marcus also handed him an old shirt of his. "What, I have to wear this to bed too? You guys wear more clothes to bed that I do in the daytime."

"You can take the shirt off when we go to bed. It is just like a robe while I take you downstairs and get you a bedtime snack. Then we will go to bed. I am tired. Kid, you do know, you have been a lot of trouble today and I am tuckered out."

After they left, Carl grinned at Jen and said, " I have a feeling that is going to be a tough nut to crack, and all of us are going to be a mite tuckered out. Now, let's go get Diz on the wire."

Diz was on the telegraph for half an hour sending Jen's list, for delivery the next day, and a list from Carl, to be wrapped and sent the day after. In the kitchen Caleb was saying, "In this house, do we have a before bed snack everyday? At the other place dinner for me was early and I had to stay in my room after that. Evenings were their busy time and kids were not 'lowed. Once in a while, one of the girls would sneak me a piece of cake or an apple, but usually not."

Marcus said, "Here, unless you have gotten yourself in trouble, we have dinner about six, and you also have whatever you want before you go to bed, depending on what is in the cooler." He looked and said, "Today you have a glass of milk, and a choice of apple pie or chocolate cake by the looks of it."

"Duh…er Marcus, would it be possible to have a piece of both? The girls at the house were not known for their cooking. We never had cake and pie at the same time, most of the time, neither."

Marcus laughed as he poured the milk. "Caleb, sure you can. There is no real rule about that, and I often do it too. However, after two desserts you really have to brush your teeth before you go to bed. I don't imagine you have seen a dentist yet and you never want to, believe me, I have. The best way to avoid that is to brush your teeth after every meal, but at the very least twice a day."

They ate together in silence for a bit then Marcus said, "You know Caleb, I am as new at this father thing as you are at the son thing. We are gonna have to cut each other some slack as we learn how to do this. I lost my whole family when I was about eleven, you did earlier. You did however have some people who looked after you the best they could. I was alone. The people in the town made sure I had a job, and someplace warm for the winter, but I was on my own. There never was anyone who cared for me. I have a feeling that was the way it was for you too. Now you have a family, a big family, and soon there will be lots of kids around here since three of my brothers are expecting babies in the new year. There are Tull, Ed and Ali, but they are older than you, they are eleven and twelve, and there are Mag and Meg's kids, Les and Lou, but they are just over three. We don't have a perfect fit of kids to be friends for you. You are going to have to be alone a lot and I know that can be dangerous. Kids on their own tend to get into a lot of trouble. Kids that get in trouble around here have to bear the consequences. You saw a bit of that with the soap. So, Caleb, you are going to have to try really hard to keep outa trouble. When I came here at first, I found it hard, that there were all these people watching what I did and caring about me. After I got used to it, it felt good, that there were people that cared. I hope it will be the same for you. You live on a ranch though and there are lots of things to do. There are animals and horses and we will try to get you a horse, a pony really, that you can ride. There will be other things here too that you will not like. There will be rules and manners you have to learn, and you will have a tutor I am sure, who will teach you to read and write and do sums. Your new life will not be much like your old life."

The two finished eating and went upstairs. They brushed their teeth together and when they came out of the bathroom Tull was there putting some books on the bed. "Here, you can borrow these. I remember when I was his age and I still had a mother. The best part of my day was when she read me a couple of stories at bedtime. So, Marcus, since Caleb has no mother, that is a job you will have to do." Then he left and Marcus and Caleb stood looking at each other then crawled into bed. Marcus propped himself up on a pillow and pulled Caleb over beside him, one of his arms over his son's shoulder. "Okay, choose two for tonight, we are both kinda tired. We can do three tomorrow." Caleb chose one with some pigs on the cover, and one with a dog, then he lay his head on his father's chest as he read and listened to the story as the pages turned in front of him. When he finished the last page of the second book, Marcus looked down and Caleb was sound asleep. Marcus lay back, pulled Caleb in against him and was pleased when the sleeping child settled in, both of his father's arms around him. For someone who largely grew up without a family it was nice to have one of his own, although Marcus was realistic, he knew this little boy in his arms was going to be a lot of trouble for a lot of people until he was sorted out. Still, it was nice to hold his son.

In the morning Caleb woke up first, and found himself snuggled against his father and enveloped in Marcus' arms. He thought to himself that it felt good, and he just lay there enjoying it. When Marcus started to rouse Caleb pretended to be asleep. Marcus blew in his ear and Caleb rolled over, opening his eyes. Marcus was grinning down at him. "So, you ready for breakfast. We slept in a bit today but there will be some left. Let me warn you though, the cook will love you, and she will try to feed you, almost to death. You can say thankyou, I am full though. Just be polite. You don't want to get on the bad side of the cook if you ever want to see your favorite desserts."

As the two got dressed, Caleb eyed his father out of the corner of his eye. He decided Marcus was fit and strong, with muscles everywhere, not like some of those flabby people at the other house. Caleb hoped he would look like his father when he grew up. The two then walked downstairs and into the dining room. Marcus took Caleb to the sideboard and handed him a plate, then took one of his own. The two went down the line with Marcus dishing bits of this and that on the plate. When they got to the end Caleb looked at the heaping plate a bit dubiously.

"Is this for the whole day? There is a lot of food here."

"No son, there still are lunch and dinner. Just try a bit of everything then eat what you like. Next time you will only take the things you want. It's okay, you do not have to clear your plate."

The two found two places side by side at the table and sat. The others had been watching this and smiled when the two looked up. Carl said, "Marcus, we just have a half day today since it is the last day before the Christmas Holidays. Until January 3rd there will just be one or two in each office, and a telegraph operator in my office if anyone has to get one of us. You should go in today to hand out the Christmas bonuses in the shipping office and wish your people Merry Christmas."

Marcus looked a bit worried. "I hadn't thought of that. I don't know whether Caleb is ready to be left alone yet."

"Take him with you, and let your people meet him. You can be sure word of him has passed through the whole company already and they all are dying of curiosity. Get it over with."

"I really ought to get him some stuff before we start introducing him around, don't you think?"

"All taken care of. Jen and I wired the Peters a list and they put it on the train overnight." Carl pointed to a chair in the corner of the room, almost buried in a heap of packages. "That stuff there is for Caleb. You should be able to find him something there to wear. This afternoon we will take him out and show him the horses and the rest of the ranch. He should see his new home."

Caleb had not been listening. His attention was riveted on the plate of food as he powered his way through it. He looked up at his father. "Dad, most of this stuff is pretty good. I think I am gonna like breakfasts." He looked around the table at the grinning faces. "What?" he said defiantly.

Carl said, "Cook is going to absolutely love you. She adores boys who eat her cooking the way you do, just one hint though, next time use the fork to pick up the food, not the knife. It works better." Caleb switched utensils and carried on.

A couple of the other boys helped Marcus and Caleb upstairs with the packages. Tully stayed with them as they opened and explored them.

One of the first things that caught Caleb's eye was a western hat, a black one. He jammed it on his head and Tully took him over to the mirror. "Look Cal, we are in Texas and you have to wear that hat the way a Texan does, push it back a bit and a little to the side." He adjusted the hat then said, "Now, doesn't that look better?" Caleb had to admit it did.

Then they came up with some shirts in different colors, about a dozen of them and Caleb was taken with a blue one. They set it aside on the bed. For pants, there were some dress pants but there also were assorted Levis, black and blue. Caleb set aside a pair of black ones to go with the hat. When they came to a pair of black western boots, Caleb said, "That's enough for now, I have all I need for today" He tore off the clothes he was wearing and stood there naked, only wearing the black hat. Both Marcus and Tully started to laugh and Tully said, "Caleb, around here we dress from the inside out. You need socks and underwear first."

Tully checked a couple more packages until he came to the one with both. He took some and turned to Caleb, "Here, underwear and socks first, then the shirt and pants. The boots go on last because that way the pants end up inside the boots, which is how we wear them out here." Caleb sat on the floor and put on the socks, then he stood and reluctantly put on the under wear.

Caleb looked at Tully and Marcus. "You know guys, it feels better without these things, and its easier when you have to, you know." Then he put on the pants, shirt, and boots.

Tully said, "Remember I told you the pants before the boots so the pants ended up in the boots? You also have to remember the shirt before the pants, that way the shirt ends up inside the pants. Around here they like you neat and tucked in."

Marcus had been watching all this, amused. He strode over and knelt in front of Caleb. "Just this once pal, I will help you out. Tull is right though, it is easier if you put on the shirt before the pants." Marcus undid the button at the waist, slipped the tails of the shirt inside the waist band of the pants, redid the button, then straightened the shirt. Then he turned Caleb back to the mirror so he could see himself. "There you go son, the best-looking son a man could ever want."

Caleb looked back at his father in the mirror. At that moment Marcus believed what he had said, he did have the handsomest son in the world. The other two quickly dressed and joined the rest in the hall downstairs where they were waiting. Carl's three youngest sons were joining them that day, and would go around with him as he wished the staff Merry Christmas. This was another lesson for them as they learned how to manage the family empire.

As they walked down the path to the train, Caleb said in wonderment, "Do you guys have your own train?"

Carl said, "Well we do own the rail car, we just borrow the engine from the railway when we need it, but we do own the railway, so, I guess we do own our train."

Caleb looked out the windows all the way into town and when they got there asked, "Ain't there no water here? I thought you were a captain on a ship, ships need water, don't they?"

Marcus replied, "Two very valid observations I would say. Texas is a very big place and one side of it is on water, we just happen to live about as far as you can get from it."

In the offices the mood was festive. The employees were touched that the whole family circulated through all of the offices and wished them Merry Christmas, and they all were surprised at the bonuses, which for most of the employees amounted to a whole month's salary at least. All of the young ones were a hit but especially Caleb, who was continually being hugged and kissed. Marcus could see he was starting to be annoyed by this and when they came out of the first office he stopped on the stairs and sat where he was looking straight in his son's eyes. The others were gathered around.

"Caleb, I know you don't like all the hugging and kissing, but you have to remember none of them mean you any harm. You are just so bloody cute in that outfit they can't resist you. A lot of them don't have any kids or grandkids at home any more and you remind them of the family they don't have. Try to just go with the flow and laugh it off. Someday you will enjoy it."

The group continued up to the next floor and Ali muttered to Ed, "Yeah, someday he will enjoy it, and if he is like his dad it will only be in eight years or so. Do you realize that is our age?"

"I heard that," said Carl, "And don't even think about it."

After the family had completed their rounds, they re-boarded the train and returned to the ranch. They still had a while until lunch, so Carl suggested they visit the barns and acquaint Caleb with his new home. Carl and Marcus accompanied Caleb and his three younger uncles down to the stables. Chuck was there with some of the grooms and they were discussing some of the horses that were about to foal. Chuck had identified a few that he wanted to keep the colts from as part of his breeding program. There were two new foals in a pen that he was especially interested in and he took Carl over to see them. Even Carl could see they were superior.

"Dad, these happened by accident. I am going to make sure all of our new foals are like these ones." Marcus held Caleb up so he could see in the pen and he was entranced with the colts.

"They are beautiful Dad, but they aren't that small are they, for babies."

The group continued on and they came to a corral populated by yearlings. The horses were chasing each other and playing. Some were even rolling in the grass. Carl reached down and grabbed Caleb, lifting him. He immediately began to cry and pleaded, "Don't grampa, don't put me in here, Im 'fraid." He clung to Carl's neck with tears streaming down his face.

Carl held him and said, "Caleb, I know you are not ready for that. You haven't even been here a day, and this all is very strange to you. I would never do anything to hurt you. You do understand that. Don't you? I love you, you are my grandson."

Caleb leaned back and looked in Carl's eyes. At that point Carl looked in those beautiful blue eyes with the tears welling at the edge and his heart was lost to this little creature. He knew that, while he could discipline the others when he had to, he never would be able to do so with Caleb and he hoped Caleb never found that out. Caleb looked in those eyes and saw a person he could trust whole heartedly, and he also saw love there.

Carl said, "All I was going to do was put you up here on the fence. You put your toes here and hold on to the top rail and you can see. I will stand behind you so you can't fall." Caleb was placed on the fence where he could watch the horses frolic and soon, he was laughing with the others. Marcus had seen the little drama between Carl and Caleb and he immediately felt at ease. This was where he and his son belonged, where they were loved.

As they all were walking back to the house, Caleb was running and playing tag with the older boys and Carl and Marcus were trailing a little behind. Carl said, "Marcus, he is a wonderful boy. You did right to take him out of there and bring him here where he has a chance. He is a lot like you, you know that don't you. He is a bit feisty, steadfast, but he can quickly size things up and see where it is in his own interests to go. He will try all of us a bit, like with the language, but when he sees we all stick together he will give up on that. I'll tell you, when I was holding him and looked into those eyes of his, I was lost, can't let him know that though."

"I know that dad, the same thing happened the first time I met him."

"There is one way we have to make sure he is not like you though. Marcus, at twelve, a whorehouse? Don't you think that was a bit young? I think we should try to avoid that if we can."

"Actually Dad, with the cook I was eleven." But he was thinking to himself, "First the cook at eleven, then Candy, Caleb's mother, at twelve." Even then, he looked back and wondered what he was doing, but, at the time, it all felt so right. Carl was right however, he would have to try to ensure Caleb didn't follow his father in those particular footsteps.

The next morning the engine made a special trip in, since the rail car was not going anywhere that day. The engineer dropped off several large boxes of wrapped gifts which were added to the bounty under and beside the tree. Marcus and Caleb were still asleep, so they didn't see it happen.

At breakfast that morning, Dizzy was deep in thought and absent mindedly tapped out Merry Christmas with his fingers on the table. Des tapped back Happy New Year, and they both started to laugh. Caleb caught the little bi play and asked what they were doing. Diz explained they were sending Morse Code. "People have lots of ways to communicate. We talk, you can do that. We write letters. You can't do that yet, you have to know all the letters, how to spell and how to write. Once you can do all those things you can also use the telegraph and Morse Code."

"Once I can do all those things will you teach me how to do that, use the telegraph?"

Diz, thinking that would be years from then, and that the kid would forget, rashly agreed. That was all the motivation Caleb needed. When Jen came to get him later that morning for a reading lesson, he all but dragged her into the study. When they were sitting, he said to her, "I want to know how to read and spell and write so I can learn to use the telegraph. Let's start." From that point on he was like a sponge, looking to soak up every bit of knowledge he was exposed to.

Jen said to Carl, "He is not like the others, he is so bright. The others are bright, don't get me wrong, but he is driven to acquire every bit of knowledge he can get as fast as he can get it. Be prepared, you are going to be hiring a lot of tutors, he is going to wear them out."

Marcus noticed this with Caleb too. They quickly went through Tully's books in their reading sessions at night before bed. The Peters had included some books, and they quickly went through them too. Then Caleb started reading the books to Marcus. Since they both liked these nightly reading sessions, the search was on for other books. They found some of the children's classic books, and Marcus started reading these books to Caleb. Tully saw this and started joining them just to hear the stories. No one had ever really read to him, especially real books, he enjoyed it. Marcus enjoyed those evening with the two boys and he enjoyed the books too. No one had ever read to him either. Winter in Texas can be cold, and as the boys were getting into bed, Marcus would throw a couple logs on the fire in the fireplace in his room, then join them. Sometimes, if the book was good, they would read for an hour.

They started with Grimm's Fairy Tales, some of which were a bit scary. They did Little Women by Alcott, which the boys pretended not to like, and then went on the Little Men which was more popular. Swiss Family Robinson, a massive book that took a couple of weeks to read, was an enormous hit with all of them and then they went into Jules Verne's 20 000 Leagues Under the Sea.

One day, Carl was in the library when the three came in looking for the next book for their nightly reading sessions. They were all discussing how hard it was to find the good books, that the two older ones liked to read aloud. Caleb said, "And there are all sorts of other kinds of books I would love to see, a book for kids on the telegraph, the Morse Code, who is Morse anyway? Then, I would love to see a book of maps for children. There is one here, but I can't lift it, and even if I do get it open and find a map, it's useless, there are too many names. Like in that Verne book, it mentioned several places I would like to know where they are, like Paris and Washington, but it is too much trouble to use that big atlas." Finally, they found a book called Tom Brown's School Days and left. Deeds came in a few moments later and Carl said to him, "I have an idea for the last floor in the building, a book publisher that specializes in books for kids, maybe it can do text books too. Find me a publisher and a couple editors, and set them up on third. Get a couple presses and a binder, and some typesetters. All that can go in the building we own next door. When they are ready, I want the staff to have a meeting with Caleb, Marcus and Tully to ask them what kinds of books they would like. I think they are in for some surprises. Tell the publisher all the books they produce are to be run past our little committee, before and after printing. I think this might be an area for Tully and Caleb later, when they are grown."

Finally, it was Christmas Eve. The house had two parlors, the regular one which was the one they used normally, and the "other parlor" which was the one used with guests and for special occasions. It was the one where the tree was located, and it was the one being used by the family on Christmas Eve.

The room was currently being lit by candles and kerosene lamps since the generator that powered the house had been acting up all day. Des and Diz had been struggling with it and finally they had come in and Diz said, "No use, it needs a part and we will have to send someone into town tomorrow to look for it. We are down to candles and lamps tonight I am afraid. The good news is the furnace. It is gravity fed. It has electric fans, but it doesn't need them. Hot air rises, cold air falls to be reheated. The electric feeder doesn't work though, someone will have to put the coal in every hour or so. The boys looked at each other but there were no volunteers, it was a dirty thankless job. Carl, who was standing at the bar said, "Mag, take this bottle of Bourbon and go out to the bunkhouse, get a couple of volunteers to spend the night in the basement feeding the furnace, two volunteers. If there are two, they won't get too drunk to do the job, one would. Besides, they can keep each other company, play cards or something."

That issue solved, the family turned back to the celebration of Christmas Eve. The younger boys were still young enough to be excited, but none as much as Caleb. He bought entirely into the whole Christmas thing and especially into the idea of Santa Claus. No one had ever done any of this with him before. Christmas at the cat house had just been an especially quiet day for the girls after a very busy night on Christmas Eve. Marcus and Carl were sitting side by side with Caleb on Carl's knee grilling his grandfather about Santa.

"Grandpa, why would this Santa guy go around the world giving gifts to all the kids? He crazy or something?"

"No, I told you before, he likes kids and he thinks the good ones deserve a reward at Christmas."

Caleb looked a bit glum. "Then I guess I won't get much."

Marcus said, "Why not, you have been trying really hard around here to be good. It has been at least a day since someone used the soap on you."

"Because I am evil. We stayed in the house most of the time, but on the few trips we did go out of the house the people said the girls and I were evil. Some of the stores made us come to the door at the back, in the alley."

Marcus said, "Son, you are not evil. No child of four is evil. The people that said that to you just had high opinions of themselves, but they were wrong. The women who said that likely were upset because their husbands were visiting the girls."

Carl hugged Caleb, "You are far from evil. True, your language was a bit rough, but you are getting that under control, no one ever taught you better before now. Now you are a little messy, and you tend to get dirty mighty quick, and Caleb, you tend to be a little sneaky when you think you can get away with it, I saw you sneak into the kitchen this morning for those pieces of Christmas cake, but son, none of that is evil, it is just being a boy. Now, if you was lyin and cheaten, drinking and playing cards, hanging out naked with your friends doing all sorts of indecent things, and planning a trip to a local house of ill repute, that might be evil." The last was meant for Ed and Ali who were sitting on the couch opposite and listening closely. By the end of the list they were blushing deeply and looking everywhere but at Carl. "So, Caleb, I think you are safe and Santa will make a stop. What would you like him to bring you?"

"I dunno. I would like some new books. We three like that reading time at night. Maybe some stuff to make pictures. I would like silver spurs for my boots. Then a toy train that runs around on tracks would be nice. Some cap guns maybe, and you know what, a rabbit like the one Tully has. I always liked rabbits. Any one of those things would be fine." Carl and Marcus smiled at each other and gave a sigh of relief. Between the two of them they had covered most bases and more. Tully had heard this conversation too and a few minutes later he slipped out of the parlor and went upstairs. He sat on his bed, took rabbit down from his place on the shelf above his bed, and sat holding him, looking at him. Finally, he gave him one last hug and went off in search of some wrapping paper and string. Rabbit was smuggled into the parlor and deposited under the tree with a little tag that said, "To Caleb, Love, Tully." Carl, after many years of sneaky sons, saw this little drama in the parlor but pretended not to. Afterwards, he went to the tree and found the package. He immediately knew what it was and was satisfied with what it meant, that Caleb had a brother.

Later that night Carl passed by Marcus' room and smiled when he glanced in. Marcus was in the middle, asleep with an open book on his lap. The two boys were there, one on either side and both asleep, curled against him. It was a nice sight. Carl carried on to his room.

The next morning Marcus awoke with a start to find Caleb sitting there in front of him, about ten inches from his face. "It's Christmas," he said hopefully. Marcus pulled him down against him, so they were looking at each other.

"You are right, it is Christmas, just barely. Look at the clock, it is just 6AM. I know you are excited but that is just a little too early. Now try to sleep, at least for another two hours." He held Caleb against him hoping for another couple hours of sleep but that was impossible. Caleb was continually squirming with excitement. Finally, they woke up Tully too.

He looked over at Caleb and said, "I see, Christmas morning and he can't sleep. We aren't that old are we, I can still remember what it was like. I bet you can too. Neither one of us came from that great a place."

"Yeah, I know, let's get up and get dressed, then we will go down and see if Rose is up yet. Maybe we can get breakfast. But, be quiet, we don't want to wake the others."

The three went downstairs. There was no one in the dining room so they went into the kitchen where they found Carl sitting at the table with Paul, the foreman. Rose, the cook, was serving them scrambled eggs and toast from the oven. The three took seats at the table and Rose leaned over and kissed Caleb on the forehead, wishing him Merry Christmas. Caleb was okay with that, he adored Rose, and she him.

"Well, I thought you would be up at least half an hour ago. He is four."

"We were awake half an hour ago, and I have been trying to pin him down since then, we finally gave up and came down for breakfast."

Carl grinned at his son. "It is all part of being a dad, get used to it. This is only the beginning."

Marcus grinned back at him. "As they say dad, I had the fun, now I do the time eh."

"Yeah, but honestly, you are enjoying it aren't you?"

"Yes Dad, I am. If you had told me I would three weeks ago, I would have said you were crazy, but, I do."

Caleb was presented with a big plate of eggs and bacon, toast and jam. He was happy, for the moment. Tully commented, "Good appetite, for a little kid."

"What does appetite mean?" asked Caleb, between mouthfuls.

Just then Mel and Jen came into the kitchen. "Here they are. I knew the kids had to be up somewhere. Rose, we will give you a hand and we can feed the others in the dining room," said Mel.

Breakfast was soon served in the dining room. The rest of the family wandered in. Caleb had another breakfast with Marcus wondering where he put it all, he was lucky if he was three feet tall, after all.

After everyone had eaten, the family headed into the parlor with the Christmas tree. Just then they heard the toot from the train on the siding and looked out the front windows. Their railcar was being spotted in by an engine. It soon uncoupled the car and went steaming away. Carl said,

"Good, Deeds is back I sent him east on a few errands and he is back for Christmas with a few guests. Let's go down and meet our visitors."

There was an "Awe shucks," from Caleb but the group got coats and made their way down the path. Deeds was the first off, and he turned to help two others off, Jenn's mom and dad. She rushed forward to greet them. Next off was Nan's father, Dr Steven Fellers. The last guests of the train were the Travis', Brent and Sally with two little one-year old twin boys. While Nan was hugging her father the rest of the family were welcoming Brent and Sally.

Finally, Carl said, "What say we go up to the house. We were just about to open the gifts under the tree when you arrived. We have a four year old who is about to commit murder I bet, if we don't let him at the presents."

That raised the issue of where did a four year old come from and Marcus stepped forward holding Caleb's hand and said, "The four year old is my son, his name is Caleb, and dad is right, he is real eager to get at those gifts as this is his first real Christmas."

The whole group went up to the house and ten minutes later were settled in the parlor. Ed and Ali were designated gift distributors and began the task. One of the first gifts Caleb got was the one from Tully. Carl was watching closely as Caleb unwrapped it. When he saw what it was Caleb gave a laugh of delight and looked around for Tully, who was sitting on a sofa behind him. Caleb launched himself onto Tull' lap, surprising him a bit. Caleb knelt on the sofa, his knees straddling Tully's legs and his nose about two inches from his nose.

"Tully, you are giving me Rabbit, why?"

"Caleb, I am a little too old for him and I don't play with him enough. I hardly ever take him to bed with me anymore. He deserves better, someone like you who will do all those things so now that you are here, I think you are perfect for that. You make sure you look after him or I will come and take him back though."

Caleb launched himself at Tully and hugged him around the neck with both arms, again surprising Tull, but he returned the hug. Then Caleb leaned back and looked Tully directly in the eyes again. He whispered, "Tull, thank you, but you know if you ever need to borrow Rabbit, like if you get a whupping or summin, just tell me. You can." Tull looked into those sincere blue eyes and knew something, for good or bad, he had a brother for the rest of his life, and that the two would do anything for the other.

Caleb returned to his gifts. In the end he got the train, the books, and even the art supplies he wanted. There also were many other toys and a set of cap guns. In addition, there were clothes, too numerous to mention. Marcus noted, "With all this stuff I think we had better claim you a bedroom, I don't want all this stuff cluttering up mine."

Caleb seemed quite upset at that comment, so Marcus hurriedly added, "The room is for your stuff. You can still bunk in with me as long as you want and we will still have story time, the three of us." Caleb was happy again, grinning broadly. He enjoyed the evenings with his father and Tully.

The others worked through their gifts. Since all of them had everything they truly needed, the gifts were largely superfluous. When everyone was finished, Carl said, "One more here for you Caleb." He held out a small gift and Caleb came over. He took the gift and opened it to reveal a set of silver spurs, just his size. Caleb stood looking at them, his eyes big and round. Chuck piped up from across the room, "Nice spurs, but if I ever catch you using them on any of my horses, I will tan your hide. Goes for anyone else around here if they get spurs." There was a bit of a pause, but the others laughed. Chuck had made his point though.

Carl then said, "We all have to take a walk out to the barn for your big gifts from me." It took a few minutes for people to grab coats and wraps, but the family went out to the barns. Carl led them to the stable and inside, to one of the unused stalls. In that stall, on several newly built racks there were row upon row of new saddles, each trimmed in silver, and each with a little nameplate on it identifying its new owner. There was even a small one for Caleb, and even smaller ones for Lou and Les. The three smallest ones were on a bottom rung of the rack, and the three boys were helped up so they could try their saddles.

Caleb looked up at Carl and said, "Grampa, it's nice to have the saddles but all the horses are too big for us."

"Really? We will have to do something about that won't we." He bent and lifted Caleb up, and nodded to Mel and Mag who did the same with the other two. They all walked over to the side of the stall where they could see into the one next door. There were three Shetland ponies there. Two very small ones for Lou and Les, and one bigger one for Caleb, who let out a gasp when he saw it.

"Grampa, is that horse mine?"

"Sure is, but you are not ready to ride her yet. You have to meet her and get to know her, think of a name, and when you know each other a bit your dad can let you ride her a bit at the end of a tether in one of the pens. When he thinks you are ready, he will take you riding in one of the fields. You have to promise us something, you will not try to take her out on your own until he says you are ready." He reached in his pockets and came out with two handfuls of sugar cubes, giving one to Marcus and the other to Mag and Mel. "Okay parents, take your children in to meet their ponies."

Later that afternoon, Tully was showing Caleb how to set up his trainset in the middle of the parlor floor and most of the adults were gathered around talking. One of the others asked Steven how long he would be able to stay.

"That depends on the ladies here. Once I have examined them, I will be able to be more precise. Carl has asked me to figure out when they are due and to make sure I can deliver his grandchildren, I would say though that Mag and Mel will be parents by New Years."

There were a few titters from the ladies in question and several grateful looks at Carl from the prospective fathers. Carl added, "I told Steven we would send the car to Oakside, with him and Jen's parents, when he was ready."

"Us girls have been talking. We think Nan is due mid February and me in early March." said Jenn. Chuck said, "Nan and I have been talking. We would like to go back to Oakside early enough to have the baby there. That is going to be our home, with occasional visits here to manage the breeding program. So, whenever Doc here goes, we would like to go with him."

Des added, "Jenn and I feel much the same. Oakside, really the school, will be our home. I understand the construction there is finished and the school is ready to set up. We would like to be set up there before the baby was born. I guess that means we would like to go with the others."

"Okay then, we have a direction, After Mel has her baby, we will start putting together a partial exodus to Oakside with Doc, Jenn's parents, Des and Jen, and Chuck and Nan. That will likely take place in January. Chuck, I assume you will want to take some of the horses from here, we can reserve a stock car too. Des, I had some small changes made at Oakside. I had a door put in from the estate office to the smoking room so that you can use it for an office. The estate office can continue as that and also as a reception room for you. There is already the door to the outside. There is the telegraph key there and there are two operators. CJ and DJ have been trained. Deeds is prepared to go back and forth until you are ready, but he says you are close to being ready to open the east coast office of Deeds and Montrose. You can hang out your shingle, but I wouldn't count on much business from the town. You may get some from the Landing and you will have the business from our companies. You really can't set up your practice in the school, too disruptive I would think, for blind children."

Des and Jen looked at each other and then Des said, "You have been thinking of this, haven't you dad. We had thought of the problems, but we hadn't come up with the answers yet. That should work and I would only be a couple minutes from the school if I was needed."

"Since we are staking out our futures, Mel and I have been talking. We think our home will be here, at the ranch. Oakside has bad memories for us. Dad, when you and the rest go to Oakside I think Mel and I, and the kids, will stay here. We think we might like to go to the Hamptons for some of the summer, but the cruise in the fall, we don't think so. We will come back here after the Hamptons," said Mag.

"I had the feeling you two felt that way. Maybe you will buy in on a cruise at a later date. What about the rest of you? I know Marcus and Caleb are in, Marcus is steering the boat, and, by the way Marcus, Captain Hayes is retiring this spring and he has agreed to go with us as your first mate. He has ideas for the second and third too." Marcus heaved a sigh of relief. "Ed, Ali and Tully are on board, they have no choice."

Chuck said, "I think Nan and I, and the baby, are in. I want to see the horses in Europe and Arabia, perhaps buy some stock; and Doc is going. I can set the breeding up at Oakside and here, then you have to wait a year or so anyway to see what you have."

Diz said, "I want to go. There is this fella called Marconi in Italy I want to check up on. The brokers are all set up now and we are making a fortune, 1% of every trade. And, I still need a wife, maybe I can find one."

Attention then turned to Des and Jen. Des held Jen's hand as he said, "We would like to do the Hamptons, maybe even bring a couple of students if there are any by then, but in the fall, we think we would like to come back to Oakside and the school. You will have Deeds with you so I can run the practice and tend to anything at Oakside or the cigarette factory that needs to be done. Maybe we can do a little cruise out of the Hamptons in the summer or early fall, shake the Three out. But I can't see us doing the world cruise. Sorry to disappoint you."

"Look, all of you, none of you have disappointed me in any of this. All I ever wanted was for you to find your places and be happy. If I didn't feel you had, I wouldn't have been able to take this cruise. The businesses are set. Mag can mind things here and Des at Oakside while the rest of us have our little adventure."

Caleb picked up Rabbit and whispered in his ear, "I don't know why everyone is so bloody happy about all this, it sounds like a helluva lot of change to me. I just got here, got this family, and I like it. I don't want no friggen change. I got a horse, a saddle, and all these toys. And I got my Dad and a brother, lots of brothers. That's enough change for me dammit." Caleb became aware his father was looking closely at him and he paled perceptibly. Marcus opened his hand to reveal a small well chewed piece of soap. "Aw Dad, it's Christmas fer ... Please Dad, I'm sorry, but I was just talkin' to Rabbit, and he don't talk, no harm done."

Marcus' face broke into a small smile, and he reached over to hug Caleb, "Okay son, it is Christmas and I will give you a break, just this once, consider it another Christmas gift, but we have to break you of that before we get to Mama Clarisa at Oakside. She makes her own soap out in a tub in the yard and it is God awful, even to wash with. There is no way you want to have to eat any."

Caleb let his father hug him to his chest, and that felt good, but he still had some dark thoughts, "Great, something else to look forward to."

Generally though, it was a Christmas everyone enjoyed. Caleb was astounded at the Christmas turkey, which he was sure was bigger than he was. He was sure to thank Rosa for the wonderful dinner. That earned him a big hug, and a mincemeat tart. The afternoon of Christmas Day Caleb picked the name for his new horse and called fer Flower. The two formed an instant bond, as only a child and an animal could. When Caleb asked what would happen to Flower after "the move to the other place," he was reassured when he was told, "We will just have to take her."

Chapter 19

Starting the New Year

Right after New Years the family turned its attention to the relocation of some of its members to Virginia. First, they had to get through New Year's Eve, which was a bit of an adventure in and of itself.

A little after eleven, Marcus had woken Caleb and brought him down to the lounge to see the new year in with the others. At ten to twelve, Carl handed out glasses of Champagne to all the party goers. Ed, Ali, and Tully each got a quarter glass, Caleb got a glass with a mouthful in it. Caleb protested, "Hey, why so cheap on the Champeen. I usually get a whole glass, sometimes more'n one."

He became the center of shocked looks from all the others in the room and Ed blurted out "What do you mean you get a couple glasses? When? You are not yet five."

Caleb responded, a bit defensively, "There was lots of it at the house, the men brought it when they felt like a party."

Marcus crossed the room and knelt on the floor beside Caleb, pulling him to sit on his knee. "Now Caleb, it is okay, no-one is mad at you. We keep forgetting what it was like for you growing up, and occasionally you tell us something that really surprises us. Now, Ed and Ali over there, this is the first time anyone has given them any of this to drink, although I expect they might have run across something like it on their own." The two older boys blushed as Marcus went on, "We like you as a little boy so just take your time growing up, I think you have already had to cope with a bit too much as it is."

Ed whispered to Ali, "We have to pay more attention to this kid and remember where he grew up. There likely are lots of things he saw, and can tell us about."

Later, when Caleb was sitting on the floor on the other side of the tree playing with his train set, Ed and Ali joined him. Caleb looked up at them, surprised. Ed started, speaking quietly, "Caleb, you reminded us tonight about where you grew up, before here that is. Now Caleb, we are really curious about places like that, never having been in one yet, and we wonder what you can tell about such a place."

"Like what?" said Caleb suspiciously.

"Like what goes on there? We know why the men go, but then what? What goes on before they do it? Where do they do it? Do they do it out in the main room in front of everybody, or what? Do they take turns? Did you ever see any of them doing it?"

"Jeez, you guys, I am just four. Shouldn't you be asking a 'dult about stuff like this?"

"Look Caleb, I don't know whether any of them have been to a place like this, other than your dad of course. They sure as hell won't talk to us about it. Come on Caleb, tell us what you saw."

"Look guys, I got in enough trouble with what I saw and did already. I must have eaten five bars of soap by now."

Ali took another track. "I bet you saw nuttin. You probably went to bed at dinner time, and stayed there, like a baby."

"I was sent to my room after dinner, but I didn't always stay there. Sometimes I snuck out when I got bored. There was lots going on, and when they got drunk some of them were funny. It was like a party all the time, and sometimes a couple of them would sneak off."

"Then what? That is the part we are interested in."

"Why? You two aren't ready for that, you ain't built right."

An indignant Ed said, "What do you mean we ain't built right? We are built like all the other guys."

"We got the same equipment."

"Come out back and we will show you," said Ali angrily.

Tully stepped from behind the tree where he had been listening. "No, you won't, you are acting like a couple of perverts, asking things like that from a four-year old and wanting to show him yourselves. If you don't want to be his friend and help him along, then leave him alone. Caleb, if they bother you anymore, then you just yell pervert, pervert, pervert as loud as you can until some adult comes and deals with them. If it is Dad, I think they know how he will set them straight. Now, beat it you two."

Ed and Ali paled, and then slunk away. Tully turned to Caleb and said, "Cummon, your dad sent me, he is ready for bed and if we want him to read at all, we better hurry. It is late already."

Finally, New Year's Eve at the CCC ranch settled down. Carl was just falling asleep when he heard a commotion down the hall in Mag and Mel's room, and then he heard Mag going down the hall to summon his father-in-law, Stephen Feller. The two returned whispering softly. A few minutes later Carl heard Mag go down the hall to Chuck and Nan's room, and return with them. At that point Carl decided he had best get up. When he went down the hall, he found Chuck and Mag standing outside the door whispering softly.

When they saw Carl, Mag said, "Hey Dad, Stephen thinks tonight is the night. Nan is in there helping him."

Just then, Nan poked her head out the door and said, "Chuck, go get Jen, quickly." Chuck dashed down the hall, and Mag looked worried.

"Dad? What do you think that means? Is something wrong?"

"Son, try to keep calm. At this point we do not know if anything is wrong, just that it appears there is a baby coming. Stephen is a good doctor and he will do his best."

Just then Jen dashed down the hall and entered the room, followed by a half-asleep Des who joined the other two. "Well Bro, looks like you are in the soup now. Three kids and you aren't even twenty-one."

Just then they heard a slap from in the room and a baby crying. Jen stuck her head out the door and said, "It's a boy, but there is another coming," and she was gone. A few seconds later Jen stuck her head out, "Another boy," she pronounced. Then Nan called her and she left hurriedly.

Mag started to fret, "What's going on now, are there more? Is there a problem? Dad? What is going on now?"

Carl could see that Mag was getting agitated and tried to calm him with, "All we know at this point is that you have two new sons to go with the two you already had. That is a wonderful family so try to be patient a bit longer. Stephen will be out shortly to talk to you."

Finally, they heard another slap from inside the room. This time though, Jen did not come to the door. Mag noted that and said, "Dad, Jen didn't come to the door this time. There must be something wrong. I should go in there."

"Mag, they are a mite busy in there right now, the last thing they need to cope with is a frantic father. You have two women, three babies, the mother and the doctor. Give them a bit. Stephen will come out and talk to you when he can."

About ten minutes later Dr. Feller came out. He looked a bit tired. "Mag, you have three new children, two boys and a girl."

"What? A girl?" whispered Mag.

"Yes, believe it or not, there is a Montrose baby who is a girl, but I would bet she will grow up to be a tough one, given the rest of the crew around here. Mel is doing well considering what she has been through. Three were a surprise to her too, she sort of thought there might be two. These were hard deliveries, I don't think the two of you should plan on anymore for a while."

"Doc, five are more than enough, and one of them a girl, I don't know how to raise a girl."

"Son, having raised one, let me give you a couple bits of advice. Stay out here in the middle of Texas where there are no boys who are not related, and give up any idea that you are in charge. Girls are very different from boys. Now go in and see your wife and children. You alone, the rest of them can wait until tomorrow."

After Mag had gone in, Stephen turned to Carl and said, "That was hard tonight, we almost lost the mother and the third baby at the same time. I meant what I said to him, there should not be any more children for a while, a long while."

Eventually, the house settled again. Jen and Nan stayed in with Mel for the rest of the night, to look after her and the babies if need be. Chuck and Des returned to their rooms and slept rather fitfully, without their wives. Mag lay on a couch in the hall outside his and Mel's room. He didn't sleep though, whenever he closed his eyes all he could see was his three new children, one of them a girl.

The next morning Marcus woke to find Caleb and Tully curled on either side of him. This was a common occurrence as the two often fell asleep during story time the nights before. Marcus didn't mind though, he enjoyed the closeness with his son, and found he was becoming increasingly fond of Tully too, as time went on. The three quickly dressed and headed down to the kitchen to join the others for breakfast.

Tully was surprised when they entered and the room was empty except for Rose. She quickly said, "They all was up late last night, Mel had triplets, one of them a girl."

There was a shocked "A girl?", from the three.

Later that day, as Carl worked in his study, he was visited by two of his sons, separately. Chuck came in first. "Dad, Nan and I really want to go back to Oakside when Stephen does, last night made it seem all the more important. This is our first child and we don't want to take any chances. Frankly, Nan is a little afraid of us getting caught without her father around when we need him."

"I know, that was a little frightening last night. I'll talk to Stephen and work out a schedule with him. We will make sure you all go back together, and early enough there is no chance of any problems on the way."

Next to visit was Des. "Dad, you know that move back to Oakside we were planning for later in the spring, Jenn and I were wondering whether we could move it up. Maybe go back when Chuck and Nan, and Dr. Fellers do. Jenn's parents want to go back when they do and get started on the school. Nan would like to get all that taken care of before the baby arrives too. Plus, last night showed us that things can go wrong, and we would feel better back there with Stephen."

"I thought you might feel that way, and we will try to set it up so you all go together, gonna be a bit empty around here though. Deeds says you are ready to open the eastern office. There is a project you can oversee back there for me. You know we have the two operating factories and the two brands, Oaks and Tulls. A third factory building is up and the machines on the way. A third factory manager has been hired and he will help get it all together. The new brand will be called Ladies, be a bit softer and a little more aromatic. The managers there will do most of the work but they have to know someone is keeping an eye on them, that will be you. The big part of what I want you to do is I want three more factory buildings, same size as the others. I will order the equipment, you find three more managers and they can help you with the rest. One new brand will be the Broncos, aimed at the western states and territories. The taste will be a bit rougher and stronger, like the market we are aimed at. The fifth brand will be Hyde Parks, and they will cost twice as much as any of the others. The blend will be premium, quality, and meant for the discriminating buyers. That is how we will sell it."

"Is the tobacco going to be that good, we have to double the cost?"

"The cost to us will be roughly the same but there are people out there who will think they are better just because they are more expensive. These ones will only be sold in packs, say of twenty, no singles, and the packaging will be a bit better. We won't sell as many of them but at that price we don't have to. The clients will be loyal, to a fault."

"And the sixth factory?"

"That will come on line after the others are all up and running. It will be for specialty products, pipe tobaccos, chawing tobaccos, and cigars, several brands of each aimed at slightly different markets. You should hire someone to just deal with the marketing. Doubling our capacity will mean we need double the workers. I had some extra space built in to the village at the factory but you will have to get our builders going on more. We want most of our workers living on Oakside, either in the village by the factories, or at the Landing; that way they can't be interfered with. After we have our core needs met, we can fill in with a few locals. Involve as many people from the Landing as you can, we have to transition them from a private army to peacetime. Deeds is setting up the banking arrangements for Montrose Tobacco, and you and I will be the signing authorities. Capitalization is set at twenty million. Something else, Oakside will not be able to produce all the tobacco we need. Get the managers to set up contracts with surrounding plantations, but make it clear none of the contracts are firm until they go by you. In addition, find us more land. By next year I want to be producing most of the tobacco we need on land we own."

"Dad, you said a project, this is more like a career. When are you planning on getting there to help me with all this?"

"I am looking at moving the rest of us that are going in March. That is when the new boat should be delivered to Oakside. We will go to the Hamptons for July and August, and set off from there for the cruise in the fall."

Then preparations began for the movement of part of the family. Chuck identified the stock he wanted to take east with him, and finished up with what he wanted to do with the CCC stock. Now it would just be a matter of waiting to see what his planning produced over the next year or so. He trained a couple of the CCC staff in how he wanted the new foals recorded and monitored until he returned.

Des and Lionel met and decided which clients and cases would go east with Des, and which would remain in Texas for now. "Remember Des, any questions and you can wire me, we have instant communications, better than most other law firms with branches."

Nan and Jen spent as much time as they could with Lou and Les, and the new triplets, who they both had become fond of. Nan commented, "You know Jen, this will be the hard part of this split of the family into the two locations, we will not see as much of Mag's family. They might come east for visits, and maybe to the Hamptons, but it won't be the same. And then next winter the family will be in three parts, with part on the cruise. Chuck is looking forward to the cruise, and the horses in Europe and Asia. I am looking forward to the adventure, after all, it is a trip around the world."

Jen replied, a bit drolly, "We will see how highly you think of that adventure with a child under one in tow. I am glad Des and I are not going, a new child, and a new school, will be as much adventure as I can handle for a year or two. Maybe when the child is three or four, we can go on one of these cruises."

"Yes, from what I hear about this new boat, there will be many more cruises."

When Caleb realized a couple of the women would be leaving, he had mixed feelings. He liked how things were and did not welcome a lot of change. He did heave a small sigh of relief that there would now be two less women around with their cursed soap bars for his little mistakes or lapses in language.

Tully was genuinely sad about the upcoming changes and he talked to Jen about it. "You know Jen, you were there for me when I needed someone the worst, I am really going to miss you."

"Now Tull, this isn't forever you know, most of the rest of you will be coming in a couple months and most of us will be together again for the summer."

"But then, some of us will be splitting off again for the cruise. This is just the start of a whole lot of change."

"You have to realize that this is all a part of growing up. Children grow and have their own families, you will too, eventually. Thing is, this family, the Montroses, are closer that most and Carl is doing his best to keep you all centered in a few places. You will always have family close and Des' and ours will be centered at Oakside, and the school. Who knows, maybe some day you will be a teacher at the school. You really do understand what it is like to be a child and blind." That little idea took root in Tully's mind and seemed to bring him comfort.

So, in the second week of January, a special train was assembled on the spur at the CCC ranch. There were three stock cars for the stock Chuck was taking east with him for the breeding program, an extra baggage car for the possessions of the two families, a coach for the Pinkertons Carl was sending back to Oakside, now that there would be family in residence. More would go with him when the second move took place later in the year. Lastly, there was their private car for the seven adults making the relocation, Des and Jen, and her parents; Chuck and Nan, and her father, Dr. Stephen Fellers.

It was a teary good-bye as all the people there were now family. But, they all knew they would all see each other again soon so the mood was hopeful too. However, Carl was thinking as they walked up the path back to the ranch-house, "I will never get over that part, send several of them and their families away without me, no matter how old they are. And the young ones, I am really going to miss them too."

The next several weeks were busy. Carl, Marcus and Mag made their daily trips into town to the offices. Captain Hayes had retired for the new year, and he spent many hours with Marcus in the shipping offices. He was surprised at how firm a hand Marcus had been able to take over the affairs of Montrose shipping and the two of them worked at setting up procedures and processes that could drive the company during the year both Marcus and Carl were not at the helm. Carl was comforted by the fact that telegraph lines were spreading around the word and under the Atlantic and Pacific Oceans, so he would be able to have contact with head office no matter where he was, not always instantly, but quickly.

The period was one of growth and change for Mag too. He was introduced in all the divisions of the companies in the Montrose Building as the "Go To" for an immediate answer if something should come up. If he couldn't solve the problem, he would contact one of the others. This would not be much of a problem. Diz had the communications division running like a fine watch, Deeds would still be there most of the time for legal issues, and the biggest division, Montrose Oil, was Mag's anyway. Carl had been most involved in setting up the divisions and the policies they would operate under. In any case, Carl and the others would all be easily reachable until they left on the cruise the following fall.

Early in February, a second train was assembled on the siding. Carl had decided that the rest of the family that was moving East would do so together. He didn't want to go through the whole goodbye scene two more times, he found it too difficult and when he realized Mag was ready to operate the base in Dallas on his own; he decided there was no reason to drag things out further. He announced one night at dinner, "Next week, Thursday, I have ordered a new train for the rest of us that are going East. There will be myself, Ed, Ali and Tully. Then there will be Diz, Marcus and Caleb. Captain Hayes will be going with us and staying at Oakside until the Three arrives, which the shipyard has scheduled for March 5th, a little earlier than expected. Hayes may move over to the boat when it gets there, says he likes the feel of a ship under his feet. We will bring the crew up from Galveston by regular train that week and he can keep an eye on them as the snags are worked out. A couple of the people from here will go with us on the train, to cook and clean for us on the trip; then return here by rail afterwards. The security crew for the ship we will draw from the Landing, as well as some of our Pinkertons, of course. One last thing, for you four younger ones. Neither Mr. Carter, nor Miss Warner, will be going with us, it seems they are interested in forming their own family with each other. They are both going to teach at a school in Amarillo and plan to be married in April. I have asked Jen to find us four new tutors for you, and since the new school is so handy, I have rented a classroom from them until they need it. So, you will have a real school for a while."

A shocked look was exchanged between Diz and Marcus, formed at the same instant. "How could the likes of Denise Warner settle for Hank Carter, who was, and always would be, a poor; and rather regular looking teacher, and she was so, well, beautiful beyond belief."

The four younger ones were looking crushed. They had dared to hope their current tutors would not make the trip with them, and that part of the announcement was appreciated. However, the fact that the search was already on for replacements, and four of them at that, that news was not appreciated at all. Carl saw the look and said, "What? You guys didn't think we were just going to let school slide, did you? We know that when we are away, classes will be a bit irregular, so we want to get you as far along as we can before we go. That does mean however, there will be half day classes all summer in the Hamptons." That was met by downright scowls. Ed and Ali were both already trying to figure out what they would do about that.

So, a few days later, there was another special train on the siding. There was a coach for some more of the Pinkertons who would be travelling east with them to Oakside. Mag was left with just a half dozen, and a couple dozen cowhands, armed to the teeth if needed. There were also a couple stock cars for some horses and Caleb's pony. He had steadfastly stated he was not going anywhere without it.

Deeds was remaining in Texas and had agreed to stay on the ranch, even with Carl away. He would make the commute in each day with Mag. Deeds and Carl exchanged firm handshakes and a brief hug. The two had been together almost constantly for the last few years and would genuinely miss each other.

Mel and Mag circulated through the group saying their goodbyes, each holding one of the new triplets. Rosa was there with the third. Les and Lou tore between the legs of all the adults, as four-year-olds were apt to. Carl snagged each of them and gave them long hugs. "We will see you two next summer in the Hamptons, if not before," he said. His hugs were heartfully returned.

Then the eight that were going boarded the train car and stood on the rear platform waving goodbye until the others were out of sight. They entered the car and sat in a tight grouping on a couple of sofas.

Caleb climbed on his father's lap, his head on his father's chest and his arms around Marcus' neck. "I know son, a whole bunch more change and you don't like that much, do you?" said Marcus gently as he held his son close. He was just rewarded with a tighter embrace around his neck in return.

Eventually the mood lightened and the four younger ones found things of interest out the windows as they passed by, going north then east. They went through some new areas for them, Arkansas, Kentucky, and South Virginia. They were deep in the old south and Carl was interested to see that many areas were still showing the devastation of the war many years after it had ended. The economy had clearly been ruined and nothing had grown up in its place to replace it. Their train passed through many stations on their way north, and it was clear the people were doing their best. Carl noted the people waiting on the platforms were often clad in what was their best clothes, often out dated and threadbare. He was a little embarrassed at the glances their private car got as it glided by.

During the trip Carl, Marcus, Dizzy and Captain Hayes spent many hours talking. Carl was impressed with Hayes, and had been right from the beginning. He was clearly intelligent and thoughtful, likely from the many hours he had spent alone on his voyages. The Captain could never allow too close a bond to develop between him and his crew. There must be no room for his orders to be questioned, even to the slightest degree.

For his part Captain Hayes enjoyed the days spent on the journey. He was getting a good view of something he had never had, a family of his own. He loved to watch the four younger ones and how they interacted. All were clearly very bright, although the Captain quickly saw that Ed and Ali were also rather sneaky. The boys were two sides of the same coin. Ed, although the younger, was definitely the leader of the two, and the spokesman when they were confronted over some thing or the other. They were constantly looking for the upper hand, any advantage over the other two, and they were determined to tell their father as little as they could get away with, about anything. Trouble seemed to be their middle name, so to speak. They had spirit, but needed a little self-discipline Hayes decided. He also saw that Carl saw this totally.

Tully was the opposite. He loved his father and his brothers, but he too saw that Ed and Ali were a bit secretive and deceitful. He accepted that; although he made sure not to be drawn into their little plots. Tully could be totally happy by himself and kept himself amused if he had to. He was level-headed and dependable, always eager to please. He was very bright and just seemed to be coming to terms with that. Carl often talked to him, and treated his as an adult; accepting what he had to say as he would have with any of his older sons. Tully relished those times. There clearly was a bond of steel between Carl and Tully, and they both knew it.

The Captain also closely watched Marcus with his son Caleb. He had gotten to know Marcus over the last few months, and respected him. He was a good sailor, and he had a good command of the men under him who respected him, and trusted him fully. Like Tully, Marcus had spent a great deal of time alone, and clearly thought over things carefully. He was clearly self-confident, and could be self-sufficient, if he had to be. There was another side which he displayed with his son Caleb.

Hayes had been more than a little surprised that day in Maine when Marcus had returned to the ship with a little boy in tow, who was introduced as his son. Hayes did the rapid calculations and quickly realized Marcus had been barely into his teens when the boy had been conceived. He had been what, fifteen or sixteen, when he had found out he was a father; but he had quickly accepted the responsibility. Now, seeing the two together, it was clear they adored each other. Marcus had spent so many years without any family at all, the little boy filled a deep need in him. Caleb had come to love and trust his father as he had no one else before. He was also clearly deeply attached to Tully as the brother he had never had. The three were often together, sometimes falling asleep at night over a book.

One day Captain Hayes was sitting alone in the lounge. Caleb came in carrying a book, clearly looking for someone. "What's the matter son, lose something?" said Hayes.

"Just looking for my dad, or Tully. I have this new book but it is still a little too hard for me."

"Bring it over, let me see. Maybe I can help."

Caleb slowly, and a bit reluctantly, crossed the room and presented Captain Hayes with the book. He was a bit afraid of the Captain, he was so stern looking and clearly in charge of something, everything.

The Captain looked down at the book and a smile crossed his face. "Well I'll be, a book on signal flags for kids. If there is anything in this world that I know something about, it is signal flags. We use them all the time on ships. Climb up on my lap and we will take a good look at this book."

When Marcus entered the lounge a little later, he was surprised to find Caleb sitting on Hayes' lap, his head on the Captain's shoulder, both enjoying the book.

"Now, that flag there, the yellow one, if you ever see a boat with that one on it, stay away. It means plague ship, sickness on board. You stay away because you don't want anyone on your ship to get sick too, might kill everyone on board." Caleb looked up at him, those blue eyes round at the idea of that.

Hayes looked down at that little face, the big blue eyes, and was immediately bewitched. For as long as he lived, Caleb would always have a friend, and sometimes, a needed refuge, in the Captain. Marcus saw it happen and thought to himself, "Way to go Caleb, another direct hit, right in the heart. You are amazing."

On the third day, just after noon, the train was shunted onto the spur at the landing. Carl got off the train with Captain Hayes and they stood for a few moments looking out at the village, the warehouses and the bay. "The village is called Oakside Landing. We built it to accommodate our security forces when we first came here but it is developing into a nice community. The men brought their families and many of them have started to transition back into their peacetime jobs as they are not needed. There is a butcher and a baker, no candlestick maker though, everything is electrified. We have a parson, a church, and a doctor, Stephen Fellers, you met him at the triple CCC. The population here now is just over a thousand and rising. There is another village on the estate by the factories of another thousand or so, people who work in the cigarette factories. We call that Factory Village, Factory for short. You know Hayes, after we do the voyage in the Three, you might like to retire here. I will build you a house just to keep you handy for any future voyages. We sort of think of you as family now you know."

"Let me think about it sir, it does look like a nice little place alright, and Stephen has already talked to me about it. I have to admit too, that I have grown quite fond of that little one, just in a few days."

Carl looked at him shrewdly, "Yes, Caleb does have that effect on people, doesn't he? He doesn't know the power he has. God help us when he discovers that, and then finds girls too."

Just then Captain Fassert and several of his men rode up. Fassert dismounted while his men continued along the shore checking the treeline carefully. Carl looked at the Captain, a question in his eyes, and he responded, "We have been having trouble lately."

"What? From the people at Oakville? I thought that was all settled when we left."

"No, not locals, not really. With all you have done, this part of the state is starting to prosper a bit. A group has moved in from downstate, mainly deserters, jayhawkers and thieves. They call themselves the Seventh Klavern of the Klan and they have settled on several of the deserted plantations. They ride at night, in the robes, raid outlying farms and estates. They take whatever fancies their eye. The people in the town are scared out of their wits they will be next. Their fool sheriff left town, moved to Georgia they say. The feds under that Captain Green seem unable to go outside their gates. We have reinstated perimeter patrols and upped the guards everywhere. The Pinkertons too. We have had some probing, but no direct confrontations yet. They are interested though and they will come. We have to be ready for raids, but there also is the chance they will try kidnapping. Or even both at the same time."

"Fer chrissakes, I was looking forward to a peaceful spring, not another goddamn war. Well, we have to have a meeting, everyone, but first we have to get this zoo moved over to the estate."

"When I heard the train coming in, I sent word to Oakside. There should be wagons and carriages here soon, and some people to help with all of this." In fact, that was true and soon there was a bustle as the train was unloaded and the people and stock moved over to the plantation. Carl let everyone have some time to get settled in, then assembled everyone in one of the lounges for a meeting. He invited the head of the Pinkerton detail, and Captains Fassert and Bevers from the Landing as well as the managers from the cigarette factories.

"Apparently, we have problems again and I want everyone to be aware of them and act accordingly. There is a group that calls itself the Seventh Klavern of the Klan, but who seem to me to be a bunch of thieves out to take advantage of the real locals. They use Klan regalia and tactics to terrorize the real locals who we have pretty much made peace with." He then turned to the head of the Pinkertons and said, "Max, when this meeting is over, I want you to wire New York and get two dozen more of your men out here. I will have a train at Grand Central, at ten. Your car will be paired with a baggage car, with some new ordinance. Issue some and let your men get acquainted with it on the way down. I trust the men at the landing all have modern weapons and are ready to go into action. Bevers, some of your sailors may have to work on land. Also, stay for a few minutes after this meeting, there is something else I have to talk to you about."

"Now, for the family members here. Fassert tells me we have to be prepared for a raid at any time, but also for an attempt to kidnap people to use as hostages. If you leave the house you do not go alone and you do not leave without guards, several of them. You always let us know where you are going and when you are due back. To make sure there are no more sniper incidents like with Tully, we are going to have several men in the woods overlooking the house at all times. You four younger ones are especially at risk and any attempt to not follow the rules will be dealt with harshly. Those of you with guns wear them whenever you leave the house, and have them handy inside it. Caleb, I know all these guns around are going to look quite tempting. You go within a foot of one and either your Dad or I are going to tan your hide royally, whichever of us get to you first. However, all is not lost. I will send out west for a set of pistols the right size for you, and your Dad and I will show you the proper way to use them. Ed and Ali learned at five and six. Fassert, I will leave it to you to set up proper procedures at the Landing, and to work with the managers at Factory to make sure they are all safe."

"Now Chuck, all the stock here will be a tempting target during any raids. Keep them in the close fields where we can look out for them, but not in one field where they will be too big a target, and too easy to take all at once. Make sure your men are armed at all times, but white men only. Armed black men down here only get themselves shot. I will telegraph the CCC to lend us a dozen or so armed cowboys for a while, to tend the horses."

"Jenn, fill me in on the school. What stage is it at, who is there, how many students?"

"The school is finished, ready for more students. Mom and Dad are staying there until I am ready to tend to it, after the baby. Des and I have been staying here, along with Dr. Fellers. We were afraid we might need him one night and not be able to get him. He feels I should deliver any day now. At the moment there are just three students, two boys and a girl. The plan is that as the number of students increases, we will get more staff."

"How secure does is seem to be?"

Captain Fassert cut in, "I checked it out sir. Remember how we designed it, everything opens to a central courtyard but solid walls on the four outside walls. A dozen well armed men could hold it forever, at least until we got help to them."

"Okay then, Max, up that order for Pinkertons from two dozen to three, we will station a dozen there until this all is over with. Chuck, take some men and tend to the stock, Des, Diz, and Marcus in the study with me and the Captains, Hayes, you too."

In the study Carl said, "Diz first set up the train for tomorrow morning, then help Max with his wire to the Pinkerton's Head Office in New York. Now Bevers, you are still single, aren't you?" At a nod, Carl went on. "The new yacht, the Sea Vista Three, gets here on the fifth of March. It has been built as an armed motor yacht, cannons, machine guns, room for twelve to twenty marines and two officers. I would like you to lead that party, select twelve men, and a second officer, from the group at the Landing. The Three will leave in the fall for a world cruise, likely from the Hamptons. Since it is a cruise for a year, I imagine single men would be better. Talk to

Fassert, and let him know the timing in case he feels he needs more men. We should have the current problem dealt with by then, but there will always be another it seems. Once we are at sea, your men can train up the rest of the crew, which we will bring up from the Montrose Shipping Line. Captain Hayes will help us choose them. Let him know the type of men you are looking for."

"Sir, where are you, I guess I mean we, going that you need firepower like that?"

"First, up the coast to Canada, across to Ireland and England, then Scotland and across to the Baltic, I want to see what is going on in Germany. Then, back around France and Spain, through Gibralter and into the Med. We will do much of North Africa, Italy and Egypt. We will take a new canal from the Med into the Red Sea and Arabia. That is where I expect you guys will earn you money. There are a lot of brigands in Africa and Arabia. Then we plan on India, Malaya and the South China Sea to the Philippines. Arabia is to see our oil interests, and Malaya mainly the rubber. We have holdings in all of that and I want to see whether we should expand them. I think that will be the real dangerous area. After the Philippines, we will do some of the Pacific islands over to Hawaii, and then to California. The Three will be used to go up and down the coast a bit then we will switch to a new rail car. The yacht will come back without us, around the tip of South America and back to Texas, where by then it will need a refit. The men from Oakside Landing will return to it by train. So, you see, for the marines, half the trip should be like a holiday but the rest…"

"Won't be," finished Bevers. "But, for a chance at a trip like that, I am sure there will be a dozen young men willing to take on the riskier parts."

Bevers and Fassert left to tend to what they needed to. Max told Carl the Pinkertons would be on the train the next day and he would set them up in the school. Until then the rest of his men would keep an eye on it, then he left. Chuck returned from having seen to the stock and the three boys sat with their father, serious looks on their faces.

Chuck said he was glad they all were there now. "I was a bit worried with just Des and I. Things were starting to sound serious."

"Now that there are a whole bunch of new men here, they will have to scope things out again before they try anything. That will buy us some time to get ready for them. We will use that time. Now Diz, the telegraph, to the

Whitehouse. Johnson isn't there any more but I know Grant quite well too. When you get through send the normal stuff then send this."

"Mr. President, I am again at Oakside, and again find myself tested by a gang of ex-reb cut-throats and thieves. I find they have been terrorizing the neighborhood, call themselves the Seventh Klavern of the Klan, but I doubt if the Klan would even have them. The local sheriff has fled for the hills and your local detachment of federal troops led by Captain Green seems afraid to leave their fort."

"Blackey, is it really too much to hope for a little peace here, the war has been over for years. I don't know how this country is supposed to get back to normal and prosper. Not everyone can afford their own army like I do, but I am getting mighty tired of it. From my costs here at Oakside alone I should get the next twenty years free of taxes. So, sir, can you do me, us, all a few favors. Put out federal warrants on all these members of the Seventh Klavern so my people can go after them legally. And, get that fool Green out of here and get someone in here who can lead these men and give us a hand. Sincerely, Carl."

Then the four sat and waited. It took about twenty minutes but there was a response. "Carl, so nice to hear from you. I remember fondly those many evenings at Oakside before the war, and our times at school, although we did get in a little trouble, didn't we? As to your problem, I directed that federal John Doe warrants be issued for all members of the Seventh Klavern of the Klan, that way you can deal with the issue freely and fill in the names later. I know I can trust you. As to Captain Green. We had been getting complaints from the locals at Oakville, and thought they were complaining because he was being too harsh on them. You have clued us in and he is receiving a wire right now transferring him to New Orleans, where there will be several people above him to keep him in line as they conduct an investigation of him. One of my own aides, Colonel Masters, has volunteered to go down for a year or so to get things in order. There will be a squad of my own cavalry going with him, give that unit in Oakville something to rebuild around. He is as good man, a family man, in fact I believe his wife's family was related to your wife's in Atlanta. He feels as we do that it is about time all this country got back on the road to prosperity. My railway people tell me there is already a train going to Oakside tomorrow, leaves New York just after ten in the morning. Would you mind if the train detoured to Washington to pick up the Colonel, his family, and staff, as well as some of the calvary? Then, you and your people could show them into town to take up his duties. Seems efficient. With all my best, U.S.Grant."

They all were reading over Diz' shoulder as he wrote the message on a pad and when they were done looked at their father with new respect. Des said, "Dad, you really do seem to know a lot of important people, just the right ones when you need them."

"Boys, there is something for you to learn here. Whatever world you operate in, it is beneficial to you to make relationships, foster them, with the important people in that world. Sometimes they will ask things of you, sometimes you of them, when you really need them. Now Diz, send this to the President; "Thankyou sir, I will instruct the railroad to stop in Washington, and will tell them to add three stock cars, a baggage car, and a coach for the cavalry unit. My private coach will be added for the use of the Colonel and his family. The train should get to D.C. about two P.M., then here about 4. And Blackey, we did have good times. Carl. "

"Then contact the railway to tell them of the changes, the new routing, and the fact they will have to pick up the coach here this afternoon to get it to New York in time. Also, contact Remington and ask them to add six more crates of those new guns, the army is a bit parsimonious with the equipping of their men. Also, alert Pinkertons about the changes."

Dinner that night was a joyous affair. Almost all the family was together again. Dr. Fellers was glad to see what he had come to regard as old friends. He renewed his acquaintance with everyone, including Caleb, who he found enchanting, drawn in by those big blue eyes. Carl was attentive to Jen and asked how she felt.

"Really, I am ready and I think it will be soon. I was sorta hoping you would get here in time, and you have. Just one comment. It better not be triplets, like Mag and Mel. I have a school to run."

"Even when they come you will not be able to do that for a while, will you?" Carl asked gently.

"No, that's why Mom and Dad have stayed for a while. But I can do a little work here and there on the administrative side, that is what I will be doing in the end anyway. As the school grows, we will hire the teaching staff. Right now, with only three, Mom and Dad are tending to them but we have other staff ready to come as soon as we need them. We set up a little nursery off what will be my office. The baby can sleep just as well there as it can here."

"Is the room ready for our three. Their tutors arrive the day after tomorrow?"

"Yes, fully equipped, all the supplies and books you will need, even a bit of a library for research. And then your company in Dallas, Montrose Publishing, has been sending four copies of everything they publish, texts and general interest."

"Yes, Marcus, Tully, and Caleb are the advisory committee. They see the first copies of everything before it goes into general production. It must be approved by them or it doesn't get printed for a full run. Now they will have lots of material for the bed time sessions, and in topics they are interested in. Maybe someday one of them might be interested in running it."

After dinner Carl and Dr. Fellers had a chance for a good talk. "You know Carl, she was determined to wait until you al got here. I am glad you are a bit early though, her time is near, very near. That is why I agreed to stay over here, at nights, so I would be handy."

That was an omniscient comment, as it turned out. That night again, well after everyone had gone to bed, there was again noise in the halls and the women of the house were sent for to help Dr. Fellers. This time there was only one, a girl, much to the distress of Des who had little experience with young girls, but knew quite well what older girls could get up to from the last summer in the Hamptons. As the house settled again afterward, Carl and Stephen shared a glass of Brandy before returning to bed. "You know Stephen, another successful delivery. You are becoming quite a valuable addition to the family you know."

"As it turns out, the boys at the Landing are much like yours. As they got their houses, they brought their families or girlfriends from home and well, they have been without them for so long. Bottom line, the parson had a whole bunch of weddings, and there are a whole bunch of new babies and more due momentarily."

"That's what I wanted, for the people at the Landing to put down roots. Sounds like they have started."

"Well, at least now they have something to fight for, other than money," said Stephen.

The next morning Carl and the boys tended to things around the horse barns and the house. Carl wanted them all re-acquainted with Oakside, and the people working on it. It would make it easier if trouble came. At lunch he said, "After lunch, we will go over to Factory, let you see the new ones, and about three we will head over to the Landing, to greet our new guests, they are expected about four."

They all found the visit to Factory Village interesting. Carl was glad to see that all of the new factory buildings were up and three were in operation with the other two soon to be. There were three new factory managers to be introduced to. Carl also saw there were several new houses completed, and many more started. "Des, you have done a wonderful job here with this. I didn't think things would be so far along."

"It wasn't like I was busy yet, no herds of legal clients at the door, and it kept me from worrying about the baby."

At three they left for the Landing. They went slowly since Caleb was along and was on his pony. Marcus rode beside him to keep an eye on his progress. Carl thought that all in all he was doing pretty well. About 3:30 they could see the smoke of the engine a couple of valleys over. Fassert, who was standing beside Carl, said, "Just another five minutes, ten at the most, depending on how heavy the train is."

A few minutes later they could hear gunfire, from the direction of the train, then, after a moment, strong return fire, from the train, Carl thought. Fassert said to his bugler, who was always standing nearby, "Sound assembly corporal."

They saw more smoke over the trees and heard the engine speed up. A few minutes later it burst from the trees and entered the clearing. It was in the pull mode, with the engine first. There was a cloud of steam and the engine came to a stop a little past him. Carl inspected the train as he went toward the end where the private car was. They passed several stock cars full of spooked horses, then the coaches with many of their windows shot out, and arrived at their car. It seemed to be full of bullet holes again, more than even the coaches. Carl and several of the boys rushed up the stairs and burst in, while the rest of the boys, and the Pinkertons took up defensive positions.

Inside they found the Colonel and his wife, along with two teenage daughters gathered around a small figure on the floor.

"Hey, I am Carl Montrose, looks like you had a casualty."

"Yes, my son Benjamin, he was by the window when the shooting started. He got it in the arm, and it is bleeding quite badly. My wife is applying pressure but I think we need a surgeon. I didn't bring one with me as I was told there was one here."

Yes, and a good one, delivers all my grandchildren, and tends to all our casualties. Des, have the landau brought over here, I will take the colonel, his wife, and the casualty over to Stephen's, he is working in his infirmary today. You see to the unloading. Fassert will see to the soldiers, Max, the Pinkertons, and Marcus, will you see to the two young ladies. The Masters will be our guests at Oakside for a couple days until we get the young man here sorted out."

Colonel Masters was talking to an aide, who had appeared shortly after the train halted. "They seem pretty well set up here. Unload the men and set up camp. Unload the stock and get them settled. If there are any other casualties, get them gathered in a wagon and we will take them to the infirmary the same time we do Benji. It looks like we will spend the night anyway, on the estate. Come up to the house with five or six men tomorrow about nine, and we will go into town and check out the new post."

Then he reached down and lifted his son, his wife remained close applying pressure to the wound. They went outside where the carriage had been drawn up close to the car. As he waited for them to get settled, Carl became aware Caleb was standing beside him, his little hand in his. At first thinking the boy was frightened, Carl leaned down and whispered, "It will be okay, I don't think he is badly wounded and Dr. Fellers will fix him up quickly. You don't have to be afraid."

"I am not afraid Grampa, it's just that when a boy our age is hurt, he sorta likes it when there is another boy the same age around to keep him company. I thought I should go with you, someone can take the pony back for me." The colonel and his wife had been listening to this exchange and they both smiled when Carl looked up at them.

Carl helped Caleb up the stairs and said, "Everyone, this is Caleb."

Caleb knelt on the floor beside Benji, and took his good hand as he said, "Hey Benji, I am Caleb and I just thought you could use a friend right now." Benji smiled back bravely and nodded.

The carriage, followed by a wagon with three or four slightly wounded men, quickly made its way to Dr. Fellers infirmary. When the party arrived at his door, Dr. Fellers checked them all over then said he would work on the boy first. Benji was placed on the table, his parents at his head, and Caleb and Carl at his good side.

The doctor examined the wound closely, then said, "It is a though and through wound, see, a hole on each side. Missed the bones, just got some muscle. Now son, I can give you some ether, but it will make you very sick afterwards, and everyone will have to leave; or, if you think you can handle the pain for a few minutes, I can do it without. I will let you and your parents decide." His parents were looking down at him as Benji said, "Without Doc, I don't want to be alone, and I don't want to be sick afterwards."

The doctor looked at his parents and they nodded. Stephen worked quickly and efficiently, but you could see Benji had to deal with a great deal of pain by the way he was biting his lip. Caleb leaned over and whispered in his ear, "Benji, tis okay, you can cry if you have ta. No one here cares, and I won't tell anyun."

That opened the floodgates, tears flowed and there was an occasional sob. Benji held Caleb's hand tightly. But, it was easier, and soon over. After Stephen bandaged the arm, and put it in a sling, he patted Benji on the head and said, "All done now, you were very brave. Now keep this sling on and keep quiet for three or four days to give the arm a chance to heal. I will see you on the fifth day, and let you know if you are ready to go back to normal. You can go now."

As the group came out of the room, Colonel Masters said, "You all go out and get in the carriage, I just want to check on the men."

A couple minutes later, after talking to the sergeant who was with the troopers, he joined them in the carriage with the comment, "They are okay, minor wounds, nothing they haven't had before. Good men, ready to go tomorrow." Then he looked at Carl expectantly."

Carl hollered out to the driver, "Back to the house CJ." Then he turned to the colonel and said, "Colonel, I expect you want to know what you have wandered into. I assume Blackey has told you about the Seventh Klavern we are about to tangle with. That likely was their first shot. I doubt if they even knew you were on the train. Probably thought it was us. They have been scoping us out, and I bet they knew there was an increase in my Pinkertons on the train too. I assume they were just trying to thin them out a bit, and maybe get me or one of my sons. They ran up against you. They also likely knew the leadership at the post in Oakville will be changed but expected that to take a while. Likely they wanted to move on us before that happened. Now they will have to re-evaluate everything before that can happen, will give us a couple more days to get ready."

"What do they want?"

"They use Klan tactics, terrorize the blacks. I think that is a cover though. They also terrorize the farmers and owners where they hit and take everything of value. I think they are deserters and thieves. The war brought out the worst of those types. If they can make a big enough hit, like here at Oakside, they likely will take all they can, split up, and head west. The local sheriff ran off when they appeared, and the local army unit seems to never leave their post. That is why I contacted the President. We have been friends, a long time, went to school together, spent summers."

"President Grant was quite emphatic, do everything I could to help, but that you had your own forces too."

"Yes, I have a large establishment here. There is the house and a horse breeding operation at the estate, Oakside. There is also a school for blind children there, close to the house. That, and the family, are largely guarded by Pinkertons. With those that came in on the train and what I brought from the west there are five dozen. God men but they don't do that well on horses. At the Landing, where the train stopped, there are about two dozen demobbed fed cavalry under Captain Fassert and about half that many marines under Captain Bevers. Most of the men have their families there, and houses in the village. We were well on the way to transitioning them back into civilian life. There is also another settlement, called Factory Village, or Factory, where the tobacco harvesting and production operation is centered." He reached in his pocket and produced a pack of Tulls. "These are ours and those particular ones support the school."

By that point they had reached the estate and were going down the grand avenue. As they topped the rise the house became visible. The colonel's wife gave out a sigh. "Mr. Montrose, it looks so beautiful. I was here before the war you know, as a girl. Your wife and I are both related, the Atlanta Turners, although they would rather not admit that now. How did you manage to bring this through the war like that."

"My wife died shortly before the war after giving birth to our fourth son. Before she died, she made me promise to get the boys out of the south before there was a war. I sold out, moved the family to Chicago, and invested. The estate was destroyed during the war but I bought it back and had it rebuilt using the old plans, with some modern upgrades in the areas of plumbing and electrification. Now, instead of cotton, which is dead, we do tobacco and breed horses."

As they got out of the carriage, they were mobbed by members of both families. His two older sisters made such a fuss over Benji he protested, "Take it easy willya, ya gotta let a guy breathe ya know."

Des said to Carl as they went in. "The girls are sharing a room, and we have Colonel and Mrs. Masters in the room across from yours. We were waiting to see how Benji was before we assigned him a room. Clarisa says dinner will be ready for six."

At that point, Caleb piped up, "Why don't you put Benji in with me, in my room. That way I can be there if he needs something at night. Dad and Tull will just have to bring story-time there at bedtime."

At dinner that night, Carl was instructed to call the Colonel Dean, and his wife Angela. It was also clear that the Colonel's two daughters, Leila and Louella, were the centers of attention for both Marcus and Dizzy. Marcus was absolutely captivated by Leila. Diz seemed pretty interested in her sister Louella. It was clear both girls were experienced in dealing with suitors and love-sick young men, they had been raised on army posts after all. But there was a spark of interest in their eyes too.

Carl saw this, as did Dean and Angela Masters. Benjamin had been banished to bed for his dinner, and Caleb had chosen to eat up there too, "To keep him company."

Conversation at dinner was wide-ranging and lively. The boys were interested in what life was like in the army and on army posts. The Masters were interested in life on Oakside. When they found out the family had also lived in Arizona and on a ranch in Texas, it was all even more interesting.

Over coffee after dinner, Angela said, "This was very pleasant, like the south was before the war. You are lucky you saved this bit of it. The sons that are married seem to have made good choices in wives and started families. They will enjoy life here."

"Chuck and Des will, they have chosen to live here at Oakside; Jenn to be with her school, and Nan has her father here. Marcus will lead the shipping company but he has not decided where to do that from, or who with yet. Now Diz is fascinated by communications, the telegraph and what will follow. Where he ends up is a bit of a mystery at this point, but he is the head of Montrose Communications."

Angela commented, "Marcus seems very close to Caleb, but he seems awfully young to have a son that age. Is it an adoption?"

Carl knew he was being worked, and likely why, but he had always thought the truth was always the way to go. He told the two Marcus' story and left nothing out. Dean was shocked speechless but Angela said, a slightly disapproving look on her face, "Well I'll be, for that as a start, he seems to be getting it all together. He must be a remarkable young man."

"He is, I trust him with my life, as I do all my sons. Marcus is going to captain our yacht next fall on a cruise around the world. I have full faith in him, and his abilities."

"So, he's not really your son, he's adopted?" asked Angela.

Carl said firmly, "There is no difference between my natural born sons and the adopted ones. I treat them all the same, value their input, and love them equally. They all get the same gifts at their weddings, and are treated the same in my will. There is no difference."

Both the Masters considered this for few minutes then the conversation turned to the next morning when the post in Oakville would meet their new commander. "You know Dean, that post seems to be to be rather undisciplined and rough at the edges, not at all like what you have experienced with Grant's army. Even the troops I saw out west seemed more together than these ones. I think there are gong to be some fireworks when you arrive. I wonder, should you leave Angela and the girls here the first morning, give you a chance to set things in order and scope out the Commandant's Quarters a bit before you bring the ladies? I have a feeling that will be a bit of a disappointment too."

Angela said, "Oh Carl, we would hate to impose any more than we already have."

"Don't be silly. There have been times in the past when this house has held fifty guests at one time. It really is no bother. Besides, I think there are a couple young men around here who would like to have you stay as long as possible. You are here, you are comfortable, enjoy it for a few days until Dean gets your new post in order, and while he does that, he won't have to worry about all of you, there are lots of armed men here to keep you safe." Dean saw the logic of the argument and agreed.

Angela had the last word though on the subject, as Carl expected she did on most topics. "Okay Dean, you can go off and set your world in order, and we will stay here for a few days while you do that. But, I want you to remember one thing. I have been an army wife for twenty years and there have been many a post that left much to be desired. I have made do, I could now. Oakside is a wonderful place and there is no reason not to enjoy it for a few days before I turn to the other."

The next morning just before nine one of the Colonel's staff officers appeared with a squad of troopers. At exactly 9:00 AM. Dean was ready and crisply said, "Okay men, let's go see what we have in store for us."

The group then rode away rapidly down the avenue and towards town. They arrived at the gates of the post at 9:30 and found them closed and locked, and unmanned. They waited a few moments then Colonel Masters sharply said, "Sarge, get off your horse and beat on that goddamn gate with the butt of your rifle until someone comes, and be loud about it!"

Finally, they heard from inside, "Cut it out! Everybody knows we don't start around here until ten, even with the Captain here, and he is away. Now, go away. Nothing around here is that important and nothing you rebs have to say needs us all to get up at the crack of dawn."

The men outside the gate glanced at their Colonel, and they all were glad they were outside the gate with him and not inside this fort. The Colonel sharply said, "Okay Sargeant Drew, beat on that gate again with the butt of your gun and continue until someone opens it."

The man beat on the gate at least a dozen more times before they heard the man return, swearing loudly, "What the eff is going on out there? Damnitalltohell. Does no one south of the Mason Dixon Line have a brain at all?" Then the gate was thrown open, and a large fat man, red faced, and dressed in a sergeant's uniform, stormed out the gate. He stopped, breathless, when he found himself confronted with a squad of prim and proper union soldiers and led by a very proper, and clearly very angry Colonel who glared at him. He snapped to attention and stood there wordlessly.

The Colonel said, "Sergeant Drew, this man in under arrest, dereliction of duty, improper dress, he is also demoted to a private, second class, remove his insignia. On the way to the guardhouse, stop and rouse the rest of his unit out to man their posts on the gate and the wall."

As the unit continued on Drew turned to the man beside him and said, "You really are lucky you know, during the war he would have shot you."

The group pulled up in front of the headquarters. By that point it was 10:00 AM. Colonel Masters ands his aide strode to the door as the rest of the men alit and stationed themselves across the front of the building. Upon entering, they found one man standing at a pot-bellied stove in the corner pouring himself a cup of coffee. His back was to the door as he said, "What the hell do you want this early in the morning? Even with the Captain here we never start before noon and he is away. Go away and come back this aftern..." He had finished filling his coffee cup and started to turn. When he saw who was there, he dropped his cup and snapped to attention. "Sor..., sorry sir, I think I am dead meat sir."

"Well son, I think that is the first thing I heard you say this morning that I agree with. Now, I am Colonel Masters, the new commandant of Fort Oakville. You have twenty minutes to get the rest of the H.Q. staff in here for our first staff meeting. I think I will check out my new office."

With that, he walked through the door marked Commandant. He was met by an example of total disorder and filth. It was clear that the old Commandant had lived in his office and the room was strewn with discarded clothing and remnants of old meals. Dean Masters bellowed out, "Sergeant Drew, come here!" When the man stood beside him, he said, "Drew, get a squad of men and clear out this swamp. All I want left is the office furniture and the maps on the wall. Ten minutes later it was done and Masters sat at his desk looking at the map on the wall. It was a good map of the area, had Oakside indicated on it. Oakside Landing and Factory Village had also been sketched on. Masters was also intrigued by the fact four or five small red X's had also been drawn on the map, scattered through the surrounding areas. By that point, it was time to meet his staff. Dean walked out into the outer office to be greeted by the sight of a surly group of ten or twelve men. Most were officers but the were a couple of sergeants too. The men all sprang to their feet as he entered, all of them saluting.

Colonel Masters stopped by one of the desks, returned the salutes, and then leaned against it saying, "At ease men. I am glad to see that you all have been schooled in military protocol, although I didn't see much proof of that on this post up until now. Men, this is a post of the United States Army, and despite the fact you seem to have forgotten, it is in enemy territory. I have a feeling your past commander never poked his head outside those gates and didn't care the least what happened out there. The people in the area liked that and did not bring any of their problems to him, preferring to be free to handle them themselves. Unfortunately, a group moved into the area that they could not handle alone, a group called he Seventh Klavern of the Klan. They have been terrorizing the out-lying farms and estates, gradually moving closer to the town, raiding, robbing, and murdering the locals with impunity. This all has come to the attention of the President in Washington and we have been tasked with solving the problem, along with some of the people from Oakside plantation."

"Surprised they are even letting us help. Never did before," muttered one of the officers.

"Yeah, that rich old goat out on Oakside looked after it all with his private army," muttered another.

"Well, for your information that old goat on the plantation is a bosum-buddy and childhood friend of the current president, Ulysses S. Grant, and the president was not pleased that there was a unit of his army right in he middle of things that was afraid to come out of its post. He told me to come down here and shoot each and every one of you for cowardice, if that was what I found. In case any of you are wondering where your Captain is, he is facing a court martial over that very matter in New Orleans. When a citizen who pays as much taxes as Mr. Montrose does, has to hire a private army to get his products to market when there is a unit of the American army stationed right on his doorstep, that is a scandal. Now trouble is brewing again and this post will not stand by and do nothing. Even more scandalous is that posts like this were placed in the South, not only to control the rebs after the war, but also to pacify the nation, establish a relationship with the citizens, get to know them, be their friends, help them, get them to trust the federal government again. There does not seem to have been any effort to do that here. You have stayed hidden behind your walls, grown fat and lazy, and no longer look or function like a part of the same army I do."

A Captain stood, "Sir, I am Captain Martin, second in command here, was, I guess. The Captain knew about the Klavern, knew where their main concentrations where, even had them marked on a map in the office, but he specifically ordered us to stay away from those places on the few patrols he let us send out. He also specifically told us to ignore the locals and what they were up to. There are a few or us here who do not like the way this post has gone, but I guess we sorta gave up."

As Martin sat, Colonel Masters said, "Men, all that is going to stop, right here, right now. I have one more item to attend to, and then I will leave for the day and return tomorrow at 9:30. I will then do a complete inspection of the post. That will give you and your men some time to get this place in order. I have a feeling if I were to inspect this place right now, there would not be a person here left over the rank of corporal and I would be doing court martials for the next two months. I warn you now, this will be a very difficult inspection. Dismissed."

The men stood and started to leave, but Colonel Masters summoned Captain Martin back. "You can help me with the one matter I have to see to today. The rest of my men, about two dozen more, and my family are out at Oakside. Our train was attacked by the Klavern on its way in yesterday and Oakside was the nearest port in a storm. I want you to make sure there are quarters ready for the men tomorrow, and I would like you to show me the quarters my family will be using."

"Oh sir, the quarters for the officers' families are totally unacceptable. All the officers took over one of the men's barracks for an officers' quarters. The Captain lived in his office, as I expect you saw. There are twelve of us officers who are entitled to have our families here, and none have chosen to do so. They are scattered all over the east. This was a CSA base before we got it, and I guess none of them had their families with them. The quarters are not even fit for animals, and not much can be done with them." The two men went and examined the quarters in question. Colonel Masters left with the same opinion as Captain Martin.

The group arrived back at Oakside just before lunch. Colonel Masters knew he would be grilled over the meal and did not look forward to what he would have to say. Angela opened the discussion with, "So, what time this afternoon are we going back?"

"Sorry dear, it won't be this afternoon. I got a look at the Married Officers' Quarters today, and they are worst than stables. None of the officers on the post have brought their families. Captain Green lived in his office. Disgusting. The whole post was. I already broke one sergeant to a private and threw him in the guardhouse. The rest have until tomorrow morning to get things in order before I do an inspection. I really do think there are still some good men there, Green just didn't let them develop. Carl, he even seems to have known about the Klavern, but if he did let his men off the post, he ordered them to stay away from the areas the Klavern were. Sheer incompetence, if not worse. I brought a copy of his map for you to see, and if what you know is the same as what is on the map."

Angela Masters stepped in firmly at that point. "Now, look here Dean. It is nice of Carl to let us stay here for a bit, but that is not a long-term solution. I demand that you figure something out immediately to solve this problem." To stress her point, she stood and stomped away to their room. Carl could only imagine what part two of this discussion would be like. Leila and Louella were pleased though, this would mean they had more time to get to know Dizzy and Marcus, who were both grinning from ear to ear.

That did not displease Carl either. He knew their mother liked the idea of the two girls making a match with the Montrose boys, she saw it as a way of regaining some of her former status as an Atlanta Turner, if such matches were to happen. The Montrose wealth was clearly evident, not that that would directly affect her, she was devoted to Dean and content with her life as an army wife. However, all mothers did like to see their daughters make a good match. Carl could accept that.

"You know Dean, I might have the solution for you. You know I have been expanding accommodations at both The Landing and The Factory Village. The contractors are still here. I can send them over to the post and in two weeks they can have the old units down and four, five flat units up in their place. Letting Angela work with them to design the new accommodations would keep her busy for the next two weeks or so, while you whipped the rest of the post into shape. Meantime, everybody is settled in here and things can just continue as they are."

Dean Masters looked at Carl. He knew what was brewing between the four younger ones, and he was pleased. It had to happen sometime, and these boys were better matches than any of the boys the girls would find on an army post. Keeping Angela diverted for a couple of weeks would be a blessing and allow him to tend to his duty at the post. But, he had one concern, "Carl, there is no way I can get an allocation from the army in that time period to pay for such improvements."

"Dean, don't worry about it. I will front the costs and you can pay back when you get it. I need that post up and running, and order restored here, before I can leave for the summer and the cruise next year. This is just part of the cost of setting that up. Besides, I might be able to drop a few words in a few ears here and there to speed up your allocations, and the other items that post might need to make it first-rate. Just give me a list." Dean Masters had no doubt Carl was speaking the truth in that area too.

Carl had a word with the contractors. "Do a top-notch job. The housing units are to be fully electrified, and with heating, running water, and proper sewers. Build a big enough power station to electrify the whole post and build some modern latrines for all the men, and the unmarried officers. The Colonel may need some other projects done, do whatever he asks for. Mrs. Masters will work with you on the design of the housing units, it will be easier to go along with her right from the start, in the end she will get what she wants, so spare yourself some aggravation." In the end, that was how matters went. The projects would take just under four weeks, but in the end, the result was a fully modernized and functional post, as good as any other in the U.S. Army; and better than most.

Dean Masters also worked on the men in the same time period. He made the men remember their training, and the pride in themselves they had once had. The post and the men rose from the ashes together, and the men came to value their new commander, and his methods.

During the weeks the post was coming up to speed, the Klavern continued to probe Oakside and observe happenings at the fort and in the town. It was clear the people on the estate were preparing for them, and the fort, which they had regarded as a minor inconvenience before, was starting to get itself together too. The Klansmen decided they had better act soon, before their opponents were up to full speed, but they were having trouble deciding where to strike. The Landing was well protected, as was the village by the factories. The estate and the mansion would offer the greatest rewards, but there was a private security force there too, and they looked tough.

"The school is the weak link. There are ten or so students there now, all blind, and four or so teachers, two, of whom are blind too. If we can get a half-dozen of those kids to use as hostages, they will have to give us whatever we want."

"But there are some of those fancy detectives there too," protested one of the other men.

"That just means we have to distract some of them long enough to get in the school. You saw how it was built. Once a few of us are in there, we can hold out forever. What we need is a feint, a fake attack, to draw some of them off, and distract the rest. The colored living area is in the woods behind the house. We could make it look like they were the target of an attack, and then once the defenders are fully involved there, launch the attack on the school and withdraw from the other. If we are lucky, we can be in before they realize it, and seal the place up, then negotiate for the real target, the money."

"How much money?" asked one of the others greedily.

"Look at that place, Montrose must have spent millions to get it back to the way it was before the war. I think we should come out of this with a million to split amongst us all."

One morning the family was spread throughout the house and over the estate. Marcus was upstairs with Louella and Leila Masters. They were in Caleb's room and he was showing them his pistols from his Grandpa Carl. "See, real, just a little smaller. And they are loaded, with more bullets in the holster belt. Even better, my Dad and the others have taken me out for lots of target practice." The girls were suitably impressed. Just then several shots rang out in the woods back of the house where the colored cabins were. Marcus rushed the three into a corner by the closets and pulled a heavy dresser in front of them. "Now you three get down in this corner and stay there until we see what is going on." Caleb started to protest and Marcus said, "Caleb, this is important and I am giving you a big job, look after Leila and Louella until we find out what is going on." Caleb nodded solemnly. Marcus then reached into the closet and brought three new repeater rifles down from the top shelf. He gave one to each of the girls and said softly, "You two do know how to use these?" They both nodded and Marcus thought to himself, "Army brats, should have known better than to ask." Marcus turned to go, then turned back, leaned in, and gave Leila a deep kiss. Then he was gone, rushing down the stairs to find the others.

Chuck and Nan were in one of the far barns looking at some new colts that Chuck was very proud of. "See Hon, they have the characteristics we are going for. Look at the legs, and the necks, and the bodies, muscular but sleek."

Nan was about to answer but just then the first shots sounded from behind the mansion. In just a few moments they were surrounded by six or so Pinkertons and forced back into the barn to one of the stalls where the walls were six inches thick. Nan started to protest, "But Chuck, the children?"

"Don't worry, by now Clarisa and the two nannies have them bedded down in that closet we had prepared in the nursery, and there are six or so Pinkertons around them. We will wait a bit and see what develops."

In the house, Carl and Des were in the law office and Diz was working the telegraph for them. The were communicating with Deeds back in Texas about some business matters when they heard the first shots from the workers settlement back in the woods. Carl said, "Diz, drop Deeds and wire Dean and Angela at the fort. Say, attack at Oakside, workers compound, then wire the landing and ask Fassert to get up here with as many men as he can manage, tell him workers' compound under attack."

Just then Jenn and some of the Pinkertons rushed in. She was carrying the baby and thrust it into Des' arms saying, "Here, you take Chrissy, I have to get over to the school."

"But Jenn, there is an attack out there and there are guards over there."

"Des, there are ten children there now, all blind, and of the four staff two are blind, my parents. They must be terrified. It is my duty, besides, all the action seems to be back in the woods, it will only take me a couple of minutes."

Carl looked at the Pinkertons and nodded. Jenn left with half a dozen of them surrounding her. They ran across the yard then among the trees on the avenue using them for shelter. At the school, they were just ready to start the attack when their leader saw Jenn's group coming and said to his men, "Wait, they will open the gates for them and we will attack just as they start in, take them by surprise and we will have our entry. Be quick and we will get the jump on them, get in and seal the doors behind us."

In the school Jenn's parents and the other two staff members had gathered the children in a cellar room that was safe from gunfire. The ten or so Pinkertons had sealed the gates and taken positions where they could watch the approaches. The fellow on the side closest to the house saw the party approaching with Jenn and yelled to the others. "Jenn and another six or so men coming from the house, get ready to let them in."

At the fort, when Colonel Masters got the message of the attack at Oakside, he yelled to his orderly, "Have the bugler call assembly, two-thirds of the men are to go with me, the rest man the walls in case this is a diversion." Within a few minutes Angela rushed in.

"Dean, what is this about an attack at Oakside, the girls are there. I am going with you, get me a horse."

Dean started with, "Ang, don't be silly, stay here where it is safe." But then he saw the look in her eyes and realized that was a lost cause, she was a mother, and her children were in danger, besides, she was one tough woman as she had repeatedly proven over the last twenty years. "Okay, sergeant, get her a horse, western saddle, as all the others are."

Ten minutes later, the men raced from the fort, Dean and Angela Masters at the head of the column. They were a smart looking force, ready for what they were heading to do, and the townsfolk were surprised, and a little frightened, at what they saw. They had been used to the way the soldiers had acted with their old commander. This was a whole new force to be dealt with.

As Jenn and her party approached the gates of the school, she heard the release of the lock inside and saw the gates start to swing open. She felt a sense of relief. This had been rather foolish on her part, but she had felt a sense of duty towards the school and the students there, as well as her parents. Then, there was a loud blast from the trees where the Klansmen were hidden and the fire was concentrated on the open gates. Jenn and her party were mowed down, as was the man who had opened the gate to let them in.

There was no opposition as about twenty of the attackers swept through the gates, sealed them after them, and then sought out the rest of the defenders, one by one. It really did not take long.

In the house, Carl and Des were both at front windows watching Jenn and her party approach the school. Carl had noticed a lessening of gunfire from the back of the house and assumed his men were regaining control. Really, it was just that the Klansmen had accomplished their goal and were starting to fall back.

Jenn had arrived at the gate and it started to open. Suddenly, there was a roar of guns and a huge cloud of smoke. Des cried out in anguish as he saw Jenn and the men fall. "Oh, my God, they killed her," and he collapsed on the floor, sobbing.

Carl groaned as he saw a couple dozen men storm from the trees and rush through the gate, then close it behind them. It was quiet now except for a few shots from inside the school. Carl assumed correctly they were despatching the guards. Then he turned and knelt by his son, holding him.

"Des, I am so sorry. From what we saw there is little chance Jenn survived. I know your loss, I lost my love too, and it will take years to get over this, in fact son, you never really do. You have to find comfort where I did, in the child she has left you. She will always be here, in that child." He continued to hold his son until the sobbing slowed, then stopped.

Finally, Des stood and said, "It's okay Dad, I am going to go and check on Chrissy."

Just then there was another outbreak of firing from deep back in the woods behind the workers' houses. It was very intense, but not very long. About ten minutes later Captain Fassert and some of his men approached the house from those woods. He came to Carl and said, "We caught them, trying to sneak out the back way, a little less than two dozen of them," he said simply. "What are the casualties here?"

"Six or seven of the workers wounded, they were not really out to kill them. It was a diversion. They got what they wanted, control of the school and some hostages. Jenn was going over with a half-dozen Pinkertons. When the gate was opened for them, the Klansmen attacked, swarmed the gate, and got in. The Pinkertons in the school have been eliminated, and Jenn and her party were slaughtered too."

"I am so sorry Carl, there has been a heavy price paid here today"

"And it is not over yet." That was the point when Dean and the column from the fort arrived, swept down the avenue, and pulled to a stop before the house. Carl quickly filled the Masters in on what had happened, and Angela alit and rushed into the house. "Dean, perhaps your men could lay siege to the school. When you have done that, I will go down and talk to them."

"You? Talk? Are you sure that is safe?"

"Dean, they got what they wanted, hostages, now they have to negotiate. Who better than me to do that? I will be safe enough."

It took Colonel Masters twenty minutes to get his men in place. There were even some cannon zeroed in on the school. Then he sent word to Carl, who walked down the avenue between the massive Oak trees. He would never again get the same joy from that walk as he had in the past. He would always think of the loss of Jenn. He was accompanied by a group of his detectives. He stopped in front of the school gates, the Pinkertons forming a protective screen around him with their bodies.

Carl yelled out, "Let me talk to whoever is in charge in there!"

In a few moments there was a response. They had been waiting, and watching, for someone to come and start negotiations. "Yeah, who are you and what do you want?"

"Cut the crap. You know what I am here for, to negotiate the release of the ten students and four teachers you have in there, and let me be clear on this, if anything happens to any one of them we will know you never meant to free them and the army will obliterate you with their guns, in fact they are itching to. Now, your whole purpose of taking the school was to get me to talk to you about releasing them. As for who, I am Carl Montrose. Before this goes any further though, bring the older male teacher up here. He has to assure me the children and staff are okay. They had better be, I lost family today, and I am not inclined to lose any more."

While Mr. Baxter was being brought up, the leader identified himself and said, "I am Sykes, I lead this group. You said you lost family? We didn't mean for that to happen. It makes negotiations harder. You were right. What we are after is money, a lot of it."

"Then keep control of your men. Any more losses and there will be no ransom paid." A few minutes later Mr. Baxter arrived and called out to identify himself.

"Hey, Carl? They said to let you know we are okay. We were all locked in that bunker in the basement when they arrived, said to open the door or they would shoot their way in and some of us might get hurt. I thought it was wiser to go along with them. I hope I did the right thing."

"You did sir, they will look after you now, give you food and water. They will do that because they are bargaining with me now for your release and I have told them if anything happens to any one of you, that will be the end of negotiations. Sir, that is what they were after from the start of this. Now, sir, there is something I must tell you, and it breaks my heart to do so. I would want to know as quickly as possible though if it were me. Jenn is dead. She was trying to get over to you, had a half dozen of the detectives to protect her. The Klansmen let her get to the gate and when it started to open, they wiped her party out, stormed the gate, and finished the rest of the men off that were in there to protect you. They used your daughter to get their goal, control of the school." There was a cry of anguish as Baxter gained a full understanding of what had happened.

A few moments later, after Mr. Baxter had been led away, Sykes said, "You didn't have to do that you know, you could have left it until they all got out."

"Sykes, I believe in facing facts fully, and as soon as you know them. There are a few facts you better face, fully and now. We are going to gather our people now, and take them up to the house where they will be tended to and buried in our graveyard. We are also going to retrieve the two dozen or so dead Klansmen from the woods behind the house. We will gather them in a mass grave in the woods, and give them a Christian burial, with a pastor, because that is the right thing to do. That will give you a few facts to face, the main one being you are on your own now. The only support you will get will be from the men you have in there with you. That will take us a few hours. When I come back, I want your exact demands, in writing. We will be exact in this, no misunderstandings. Got it?"

"Got it. The loss of the men is no big deal, we have more than enough left, and besides, it just means a split among twenty, not forty."

"Your men will be so pleased to see how much you care about them," Carl said sarcastically. "Be back in three or four hours."

It was a busy four hours. The bodies were returned to the house. The Pinkertons were laid out in the second parlor were their associates could tend to them and visit with them a bit. Pinkertons' New York office was contacted by telegraph, told of the casualties, and asked if the families wished to have the bodies returned to New York or wanted them buried in Virginia, in the family graveyard, that day. There really only were families for three of them. An engine was ordered for the rail car and those three bodies were taken into Roanoke first for an embalmer, and then to New York.

Carl went and talked to Des to see if he wanted a full embalming, or whether he wanted Jenn buried immediately.

"Gee dad, I never, we never discussed that. Shouldn't we wait until her parents can come?"

"Son, given the situation, that may never happen. In any case, I have a feeling negotiations are going to be long and difficult. Whatever you decide they will understand. I have asked the pastor from the Landing to come over, as well as Nan's father. The pastor will tend to the Klansmen, and then he will be free for us if we want him to. He will also see to the Pinkertons who are being buried here. There are fifteen. I am having a little private cemetery being prepared beside ours right now."

"Dad, I have never been much for embalming, what they do. I would rather have her laid to rest as soon as we can, beside Mom. Right now, I am going to go up and spend some time with her. I have no interest in the Klansmen's funeral, but when it is time for the Pinkertons, come and get me. They have always done their best for us and I want to be there."

The pastor arrived, in a bit of a fluster, having been told what was expected of him. He held a short ceremony out in the woods, accompanied by a couple of the detectives. Admittedly, it was short and to the point, the pastor not sympathetic to the lot. Then he attended to the Pinkertons. All of the remaining detectives attended, along with some of the soldiers from the Landing and all of the family. All felt the same way, these were good men, who gave their lives trying to protect Jenn. They deserved a good funeral. The cemetery that had been prepared for them was idyllic, just a little off to the side of the family one, under a big oak tree and beside a small stream.

Jenn's funeral was last. Everyone attended, the family, all the remaining detectives, all the household staff, and many from the Landing. Jenn had spent considerable time there and helped them set up their own school for the village. She had made a positive impression on everyone. Stephen Fellers thought of her as another daughter and found the ceremony especially difficult. Colonel and Mrs. Masters were there with their two daughters.

Carl spoke for the family. "My daughter, Jenn, was a special person. All who met her knew that. She came to us in a time of extreme need, and as soon as she got here, we all knew Tully would be okay. She did her job well and I know the new school would have been a wonderful place for those children attending it. She would have settled for nothing less. When a relationship between her and Des developed, I was ecstatic. I was despairing that any woman would be able to bring him to heel, but she did, after a little fireworks. They were just starting on their wonderful journey through life, and their own family. We have all learned, at least those of us who have been around a while; life is not always fair, often unkind, and most of the time unfathomable. This is one of those times when we just cannot understand why, we can just do our best to carry on as best we can. That is what Jenn would have done, and what she would have expected of us. We must not disappoint her."

When the others were heading back to the house, Carl stayed to walk with Des, but he said, "Go on Dad, I am okay, I just want to sit here a while, with her, this last time. I will be up shortly." When he got back to the house, Carl found that the others were subdued. Deeds had arrived from Texas and he went to comfort Carl. When he asked where Des was, Carl said he was sitting out by the graveside. Deeds said he would go out and sit with him, "After all, he is my partner."

Finally, Carl decided it was time. He rounded up Colonel Dean, and Captain Fassert, along with several of his detective as a bodyguard, and they walked back down to the school. It was mainly dark, but there were some lights on in the rooms above the gate. As they stopped where they had stood before, Carl heard, "Well, about time. Here are our terms." A rock with a paper tied to it, landed at Carl's feet, thrown from the window above him. He leaned and detached the sheet of paper, then opened it. Fassert held a lantern up so he could read it, since it was starting to get dark. Carl read slowly, then he reread it.

"I cannot say that all of you will be allowed to go free forever. I will agree, that as long as you leave the hostages behind, and that they are all okay, we will let you leave unmolested. What happens in the future, I cannot say. Your people are trouble magnets, and this money will not change that. I am not responsible for what happens in the future. As far as the figure mentioned here, seven million, the answer is no. That is a ridiculous sum. I will come back in the morning for a more reasonable offer. Goodnight."

"But..., but..., you are supposed to negotiate," stammered Sykes.

"Sykes, that is not how I negotiate, bargaining like an old woman in a flea market. You present me with an offer I find reasonable, I will accept, and the deal is done. Just remember, whatever we agree to will take a little while to get together and I will have to send to New York for it. Don't waste time, and look after my people. Everything depends on my getting them back in the same shape they were when you got them." Then he turned and walked away with his men.

In the room above the gate there was some disagreement. "See, I told you that you were asking for too much. He would never go for it. You better get us that million to split like you promised us. What we took from all the others was nothing, they had nothing."

"Well, this one has more, lots more, but he is tough, that is the reason he has what he has. I admit, I misread him. I thought we would have to haggle back and forth until we got there. I see now he doesn't like that. Tells you something though, he is a man of his word. We will get our money, we will ride out of here. What happens then is up to each of us. We have committed a lot of crimes here. If we let the money go to our heads someone will notice us and we will be arrested. That is why when we leave here we scatter like the birds, do not contact each other, and make new quiet lives. Tomorrow, I will hit him with what we really want, the million. I think he will go for it, and there are only twenty of us now."

After most of the men left, Sykes was left with his two main lieutenants. Whispering, he said, "This is working out as I had hoped. During the time we have, let's whittle down our numbers bit by bit. There are twenty of us now; with a million that will be $50 000 each. If we can get our numbers down to ten, that will be $100 000 for each of us. Find excuses to send little groups, one or two at a time, outside the wall. Let the army deal with them.

The next day, just before noon, Carl returned. "Sykes threw out another stone and yelled, "You took your time, didn't you? You said morning."

"It is before noon, it is morning. Now let me read this." A few minutes later, "Okay Sykes, this is still a lot, a million, and in tens and twenties. But, that word is magic and I guess you have sold your men on it. This will take three or four days. I will telegraph New York and my bankers today. My train and some of my men will leave tomorrow to go there and get it. Then, another day for them to get back. This has to be done carefully or we might attract other thieves. Then, it will take us the better part of a morning to count and double count it, then load it in the twenty saddle bags as you requested. By noon on the fourth day, you will all be on your way, that is if we have all of our hostage back, nice and healthy."

"Speaking of nice and healthy, we lost three men last night. Those soldiers out there would not know anything about that, would they?"

"Look Sykes, you are lucky those soldiers are not in there tearing you to pieces, they want to. Our agreement only holds for those of you in the school and when you leave, I will ensure you getaway safely, that is all. If any of your men are foolish enough to go outside the walls before that, they are responsible for their fate. I cannot control that. Now, we will get started on the arrangements. You will not see me until the fourth day, unless there are problems. Every morning some of the staff from the house will bring you down some fresh food, to do you and the hostages for the day. There will be no beer, wine, or liquor. This is not the time to have anyone lose control of themselves, is it."

On the way back up the drive to Oakside, Dean Masters said, "My men did have a fire fight last night with three men near the edge of the property. What do you think it means?"

"Likely some of the men just got tired of drinking water, and were looking for some moonshine. If they were at the edge or the property they got too far, tighten your men up. What it means is that Sykes is thinning the herd. A million split twenty ways is a lot less than a million split ten or twelve ways. I think we can expect several more of these encounters, warn your men. They can get killed just as easily as the men in the school."

Dizzy was quite busy for the rest of the day passing messages between Carl, Deeds, Mag and Charles Birch. The lines between Texas, Laramie, and Oakside were red hot. Finally, the money was arranged and trains were ordered as required. Deeds would lead the group going to New York, accompanied by the necessary Pinkertons. The head office of the detective agency in New York was alerted as they would provide extra manpower in the city.

At Oakside, people were trying to come to terms with what had happened. Marcus found Tully and Caleb sitting alone one day in a dark corner of the second storey hallway and sat beside him. "Boys, you seem to be deep in thought. Can I help?"

Tully started. "We both miss Jenn, she was good to us. Things were looking so hopeful with Des. She, neither one of them, deserved what happened."

"I know boys, it was all so unexpected, and so unfair. Life is like that. All I can suggest is try to think of the good times you had with Jenn, and the good life she was having with Des. She would never have wanted to give any of that away to avoid what happened. She had a lot of joy in her life. Be happy for her for that."

Then they all were quiet for several minutes but neither of the younger ones made any effort to move. Marcus knew there was still something else they were thinking about but that they were both reluctant to bring it up. He thought he knew what it was, but he waited.

At last Caleb gave a sigh and said, "Dad, we see what is happening between you and that Colonel's daughter, Leila, and we don't, I don't, like it. The three of us have become close. I waited a long time for a family, and a Dad; and Tull here is like a brother to me, and another son to you. I, we, like all that. Now here she is, a girl, and she will change everything. Don't forget where I lived. I know what guys want girls for and how crazy they get about that. Dad, I, we, are afraid you won't love us, me, anymore; if this goes on the way it is."

Marcus was silent for a few moments then said, "Boys, let me be clear to both of you. The closeness we all have will be there forever. You both have a big place in my heart and nothing will replace that. For a long time,

I was alone. I didn't think I needed anyone else. Then the Montroses found me and made me a part of their family. I liked that, it opened up a new part of me I didn't know there was. Then I found out about you, Caleb. At first you scared me, then I gradually saw what it was to be a father, and I liked it. Then Marcus found a new place with us, as a brother to you. I found I liked that and how a new relationship developed between the three of us. All of that will never change. As far as Leila, if that ever develops into anything, which is far from certain at this point, it will not take anything away from the two of you. Another part will open up in my heart for the two of us, totally different from the part for the three of us. You shouldn't see that as a threat, in fact, the two of you might get to like her too, and develop a relationship with her. In any case, at some point, the two of you will start to develop relationships of your own, with girls, Tull far sooner than Caleb, I hope. I will have to learn to accept that too. It is all part of maturing, growing up."

The two boys had been listening intently. Finally, Tully nodded and Caleb said, "Well Dad, if that is how things are, we are gonna make sure we use our share of your time. I want my share of loving before Leila uses up the rest. You have to remember, there were quite a few years there when I had no one to love, Tull either." Then the two jumped on Marcus and wrestled him to the floor, all of them laughing together.

When the money arrived from New York, all the people were surprised at how much there was. A million dollars in tens and twenties was a lot of bills. The bank in New York had assembled the currency, but they had not sorted it into the fifty thousand-dollar packages that would be required. All the adults in the house were pressed into that procedure. The money had been brought into the second parlor, and was carefully watched there by a team of Pinkertons. It was too tempting a target not to do that, even though it was in the home. A couple dozen new saddle bags were brought from town and gradually they were filled with the required amounts, after the totals had been checked and rechecked. By the fourth day the task was completed and the saddle bags were sitting on two dozen horses in front of the mansion. One dozen troopers each held the bridles of a pair of the horses, watched by a team of detectives lest one of the troopers succumb to a fit of avarice and bolt. Accompanied by Colonel Masters, Captain Fassert, and Deeds, Carl led the group down the Grand Avenue to the school. Once they were gathered there, Carl yelled up, "Okay Sykes, we are here with the money, in the manner you requested. Let's get this over with. Send the hostages out."

"How do we know you will keep your word. Those saddle bags might be empty. When you get the hostage and we come out, we might all be shot."

"As far as the money, send someone out to get any two of the bags and then take them in and count them yourself. You will see they are right on. We will wait." They stood silent as a nervous teen came out the gate and to the horses. He took two of the bags and disappeared inside. Carl and his group waited about twenty minutes.

From the room above the gate, "Okay, looks like the money is right. We need you to rearrange the saddle bags though, there are only ten of us left. The others had accidents, or, whatever." Carl smiled at Dean Masters with that I told you so look.

"We are still a bit concerned about being shot when we come out there."

"Look Sykes, I have kept my word, and I assume you have too. We will do this bit by bit. The saddle bags have been moved and the troopers with the extra horses will move back to form a circle to the left of the gate. You send one of your men out to take a pair of the horses, and that trooper will move to the circle too. Then send out a couple of hostages and they will go inside the circle. Keep on that way, a couple men then a couple of hostages, until you all have your money and we have all the hostages. The deal will be done, and you will leave. You will not be bothered. I am sure that you have all decided to go in different directions and even if we do send out a squad or two after you, they cannot chase twenty rabbits, rather ten, in all different directions."

That process was followed, and soon the hostages were all safe, and the thieves secure on their horses. Sykes said, "Okay Montrose, you have kept your word in all this, and we will too, see ya." Then the remaining Klansmen were off in a cloud of dust. Colonel Masters turned to Carl and said, "Do you want us to go after them? We might catch a few."

"No Dean, it is useless. They will resurface though, that kind can't keep a low profile with that kind of money. The Pinkertons have their net out and we will deal with them."

The hostages were taken up to the house and made comfortable. Jenn's parents spent some time with Des and Chrissy, then Carl took them out to the graveyard where he left them alone for a while to sit by Jenn's grave.

When he came back for them, they were at peace. Jenn's Dad had a few comments. "Carl, with al that has happened, we want to go back to our school in New York. The children should go home for a while anyway. This has been hard on them, the other staff too. For the fall we will see that it is staffed properly and the children, along with any others that have turned up, can return. We will run it as a subsidiary of the school in New York, this school is totally ready to go, with up to about fifty students. We do have one request though. Could the name be changed to the Jennifer Baxter School for the Blind? Jenn had high hopes for the school and it would be nice to see it continue in her name." Carl agreed and in a couple of days all the former hostages had gone.

Then Oakside started to return to normal. Chuck concentrated on the horse breeding program. Des, Carl and Deeds busied themselves with the cigarette factories, and their marketing arrangements, as well as the law practice. Des was a bit distracted, but it was good for him to have something to bend his mind to. The whole family watched with amusement as Marcus and Dizzy continued their pursuit of the Masters girls. Leila and Louella handled the two artfully, raising hopes one day and dashing them the next. The boys had no idea of, or control over, what was going on.

One day Carl, and Captain Hayes, who was watching the goings on with amusement too, had a discussion of the matter. "You know Carl, this is pitiful watching this, the way those girls have so much control over those boys. Soon Marcus will be in command of fifty men and a multi million-dollar vessel, and I have no doubt he can handle the job. But, right now, with that girl, he is lucky he even knows his own name. She has him totally bewitched. Both girls have. It is bad to see two young men like that, reduced to bowls of pudding; bad for the reputations of all manhood."

"I know Cap, this is totally out of character for Marcus, and I think soon he will realize it. He is not the type to let other people see him make a fool of himself. I think he is sort of caught in the moment, as it were."

"The sooner the better, as far as I am concerned," sniffed Captain Hayes. "The new ship is supposed to arrive next week and then there won't be any time for any more of this nonsense."

During the first few weeks after the hostages were freed, the Pinkertons had their ears out and gradually they began to pick up hints from all over the Old South of young men who seemed to have become recently wealthy spendthrifts. They followed up all leads, as directed by Carl, and when they were sure, they involved the local lawmen. Carl had posted a reward of ten percent of all monies recovered and that bounty incentivized the local law to co-operate with the Pinkertons. In the end, very few of the men were arrested, choosing to go out instead in a blaze of bullets. The Pinkertons and the local lawmen were only too happy to oblige them. They had brought dishonor to the South.

As this process was drawing to an end, Des came to Carl one day and asked, "Dad, is it okay if I take the railcar for a few days. I want to stop in on Mag, and there are several clients a little further west I would like to confer with before we make the move to the Hamptons?"

"Sure, I was gonna send Deeds home in it anyway, then you can use it. Just make sure you take some of the Pinkertons. There are still a few of our "friends" left out there and those that are left are a little miffed their friends have been caught."

Two days later the rail car left and headed west, with Des, Deeds, and a dozen or so Pinkertons on board. Des and Deeds discussed several legal matters that were pending but Deeds could see that Des was distracted. The arrival in Texas at the CCC was joyful, and the two brothers greeted each other warmly. After dinner that evening Des said, "Now that the two of you are here together, there is something I wish to ask you Mag. If something were to happen to me in the next, say, ten years, would you and Mel be willing to take on Chrissy? She is a girl, and I want her to be raised as one. Other than here, everything else looks like an all-male household. I specify the ten years, because by then it will be too late, she will be a hopeless tom-boy and you wouldn't be able to change her." Mag was shocked and Deeds a little surprised.

"Des, you are my brother and you know we will do whatever you ask, and I know this is a bad time for you, but things will get better, you might find someone else, have more children, maybe even girls."

Des laughed then said, "Then you will have nothing to worry about, will you? Mag, what took Jenn came out of nowhere. People never know. I just want to know that Chrissy would be okay." Then he looked at Deeds. "Lionel, would you write up a codicil to the will, tonight, and I will sign it. That is the only pressing change. We can tidy up all the rest with a new will later."

That was when Deeds knew exactly what Des was up to, but he bit his tongue and said nothing. This was Des' business, and considering what had happened to Jenn, he deserved to be allowed to deal with it as he saw fit. For the rest of the evening the three discussed general Montrose matters. Des said that he would be leaving the next morning to see his clients out west, but might stop in again on his way home. Deeds bit his tongue again at that. After all, Des' clients were Deeds' clients, and Deeds knew there were no unresolved clients out west.

The next morning when the engine arrived, Des and his Pinkertons boarded the train. They all shared the private car. Des and the leader of his unit, Jeff Drew, sat in a corner of the car talking. "Jeff, have they been watching him, and has anything changed?"

"We contacted the local marshal, name is Bennet, and he has been keeping an eye on our target, from a distance so as not to alert him. He has been keeping a low profile, hardly goes out, but Marshal Bennet is sure the man is Sykes. His habits are irregular, but he does go down to a local restaurant each day for dinner at six."

It took a day for the train to get to Kansas, and it pulled into the Wichita terminal about two in the afternoon. Des ordered his Pinkertons to stay on the train, and he and Drew went to see Marshal Bennet. "That man killed my wife. I want to be the one to kill him. I want you there. I will challenge him, he will have his gun, and he will draw first. It will be self-defence. I do not want you to interfere. The reward however will be all yours, you can even say you killed him if you want. Only I have to know that I settled the score for Jenn."

"What happens if he beats you. Frankly, you look a little too Eastern, too rich for this type of thing."

Des motioned to Drew, who produced a set of pistols from the briefcase he was carrying. Des stood and put them on under the jacket he was wearing. "Marshall, I grew up with these, fought off murdering Apache for a month on a trail drive, and I have kept my skills up. But, there is always a chance he is better. If I lose, I still want him brought to justice, you have the warrants and Drew here will help you if need be. We have calculated that man has personally killed over twenty men, after the war. You don't want him here spoiling your nice little town."

"Son, I shouldn't let you do this, but frankly, I am a bit intrigued by how good you are with those guns of yours. But, to be sure there are no problems after for anyone, I am going to deputize you and your man here. This is going to be legal. You will have your chance, and if you fail, we will get him. I read about that raid on your school in Virginia.

The two were sworn in, and then everyone checked their guns. About 4:30 they all went and checked the route Sykes would have to follow to get to dinner, chose a spot in a barn where they could watch and not be seen, and waited. Precisely at six, they saw their quarry leave his house and walk down the street towards the center of town. Des could see that Sykes was vigilant, constantly scanning the street before him so he waited until he had passed and then stepped out behind him. "Sykes, it is time. Stop, then slowly turn around and face me."

Sykes slowly turned, but he held his hands out at his side, away from his body. "Who are you, I don't know you."

"Maybe not, but you killed my wife at that school raid on Oakside, in Virginia. I am here to make that right."

"Don't get me wrong here, but you are rather young, wouldn't you say, barely twenty, if that. And, you look rather bookish. Are you sure you want to do this?"

"Granted, I am a little young, but I grew up in Arizona where each year is worth two or three back east, and I am a lawyer now. That just puts the odds in your favor, I guess." Des elbowed his jacket out of the way revealing his twin Colts. For the first time there was a flicker of doubt on Sykes' face.

"You look like you know how to use those, but I don't think you are faster than me, can't be, never was anyone faster." With that, Sykes went for his guns, he was wearing twin holsters too. However, he barely got his guns out when there were two shots from Des'. A look of surprise on his face, Sykes sank to the dusty street. "How, how did you do that? So young, and a lawyer yet?"

"As I said, you grow up fast in the west, and I shot my first injun before I was thirteen, many more after that. And Sykes, you deserved what you got, Jenn was such a good person. I really really wanted to do this."

A few seconds later Sykes closed his eyes for the last time. Drew and Bennet emerged from the barn. Bennet slapped Des on his shoulder. "He was right. I really didn't know if you had this in you. You were really fast though, you could make a living at this sort of thing you know. Say, you are going back east aren't you, soon like?"

"Yes marshal, I am, just as I told you. I am a lawyer now, besides, I have a daughter to raise. From what I know about girls, I think that is going to be dangerous enough."

A couple days later the private car was shunted in to the siding at the landing. The men borrowed a wagon there and proceeded home to Oakside. Des sent the wagon back with a couple of the hands and entered the mansion. He met his father in the hall. "Hey Dad, home now. Going up to see Chrissy." Just from the manner he said it, Carl was suspicious. He had raised too many sons to not know when they were being evasive. The fact that the Pinkertons filed past him, and none of them looked him in the eyes, confirmed it. Someone was hiding something.

Carl waited a couple of days for someone to say something, but no one did. Finally, he summoned Jeff Drew to his office. When he entered, Carl waved him to a chair. There was a long pause while the two men stared at each other, then Carl said, "Okay Jeff, out with it."

Jeff waited a bit, then he told the whole story of what had happened on the trip west. His last sentence was, "So, I guess I am fired then?"

"No Jeff, you aren't. But this has brought something home to me. Til now all you Pinkertons have been mine, loyal to me. Clearly, you have developed a loyalty to, and the trust of, Des. I want you to get say six other men and you will become Des' security detail, for him and his family. Des had to do this, I understand that, but you make sure there are no more shootouts in dusty streets. That is your job."

At first Des was uncomfortable being trailed all the time by a group of men, but he got used to it. Afterall, he only had half of them, the others sharing duty outside Chrissy's nursery. That made Des feel good. One evening Des and his father were sitting by a fire in the parlor. For once they were totally alone and Carl took the opportunity to bring the matter up. "Des, you do know I know?"

"Yes Dad, I thought you did. I appreciate your not going on at me about it."

"Des, you are a man, and at times men have to do things in order to feel right about themselves. I understand that. I just want to be certain you know those times are rare, very rare. Most of the time we let our Pinkertons see to things like that. But this, with Jenn, I understand getting Sykes for her was the only way to bring that chapter to a close."

"By the way, thank you for setting me up with my own Pinkerton detail. It really is better, you get to know them and trust them."

"I left Mag his own detail at the CCC, and when the rest of the others start to get settled with homes and families of their own, they will get their own details too. For now, though, all the rest are going abroad with us in the fall and the big unit can look after all of us."

"You know Dad, about that, Chrissy and I might go on the first part of that trip with you, Europe and the Med. We can catch a steamer home from Egypt. I talked to Deeds and he is willing to work from here while I am away, keep an eye on things for us, Oakside, the law practice, and Mag will be in Texas."

"Sure, I always hoped you would change your mind. You don't have the same connection to the school as Jenn had. This might be good for you, a new outlook. As far as Oakside, as long as there is someone people can go to, it will be okay. Glad to have you along. I guess we have to start thinking of that, the Three should be ready to go in a few weeks."

The yacht, Sea View Three had arrived from the shipbuilder the week before. The whole family had gone to the landing to see her, but just from the dock. Carl had said, "We can just look from here. Captain Hayes says the crew from Galveston will start arriving tomorrow, but it will take a bit for them to get it ready for us. Much of the furniture still have their wrappings, and none of the linens have been unpacked, same with the glassware, table ware, and kitchen ware. We want the first time you go aboard to allow you to see her at her best. The crew have to get to know her too. We will wait a week and that first day we will take a little day cruise along the bay. Give everyone a chance to get her ready and used to her."

That evening Carl was in one of the parlors, talking to Captain Hayes. The Masters were in another corner talking quietly. The accommodations at the fort were almost ready and they were discussing their move over to it. Marcus walked in and over to Leila, then said in a rather commanding tone, as he held his hand out to her, "Leila, we have to talk, can we take a walk, now."

Hayes looked at Carl and said, "Well, the Captain is back, about time."

The two were walking along the Grand Avenue, among the huge oaks, when Marcus pulled Leila over to a bench under one of the trees. "Leila, we have to either finish this, or take it to the next step. I have let you run me silly the last few weeks, because I love you, and it was fun being in love. At some point that had to end, and that time is now. The Three has arrived, and I have to go back to being a man, a captain of a ship and all its crew, and stop being a silly love struck teenager."

"I want us to have a future together, but if we are gonna do that, I want to be sure we are both on the same page as far as expectations. You look around here, at Oakside, and it is a grand house. We are not grand. I think Carl just bought it back, and built all this, to remember his wife, and maybe his family, it was his family house. If you get to see the cottage in the Hamptons, it is very grand but it is not us either. Carl just bought it to complete his business transactions and repay his social obligations there."

"The closest to what we are is the CCC, the ranch in Texas. It is a big house for a ranch, but it is a ranch. We live rather plainly there and everyone goes into Dallas to work every weekday. I work there, I run Montrose Shipping. I will spend a year with the cruise, but that is what I do. I don't want you taken in by any of the frippery. Your mother was an Atlanta Turner, so was Carl's wife. She gave it up to move here and marry Carl. Your mother gave it up and married your father. The bonds were broken completely when both ended up on the wrong side during the war, your Dad in the Union Army, and Carl a Northern Industrialist."

"You are taking an awful long time to get to the point, if there is one," said Leila gently.

"The point is, I want you to marry me, but I want you with no delusions about who I am. I was adopted into all this. It is not really me. I am a plain man, a working man, a serious man. My wife will have to be all that too. I am a father, my wife will have to be a mother. I work five days out of seven normally, my wife will be alone a lot, or somehow become a part of that. Leila, I want you to marry me, but you must understand what I have said, and accept it. Can you? Will you marry me?"

"These last few weeks, and all the nonsense, I was just waiting to see you assert yourself. I knew most of what you said. My mother may have a few delusions about the Atlanta Turners, I don't. My mother made her choice and became an army wife, and I have made mine, you. I am sure that, despite what you say, we will have a wonderful life."

Marcus' face broke into a wide grin and they embraced for a long while. When they broke apart, he said, "I guess we had better go tell the folks."

"Yes, we should, but I suspect they already know."

When they came back into the parlor, there was something about the way they walked. Marcus led, and walked with a purpose. Leila followed, happily. The adults looked at each other knowingly. The Masters were sitting with Carl and Captain Hayes, which was convenient, thought Marcus, he only had to do this once. The two stopped in front of the four.

"Everyone, we have an announcement, we want to get married. When the Three takes her shake-down day cruise for the family, I want to have the wedding aboard her. Then we will bring everyone back here, drop them off, and if you agree Dad, take her out for about a week along the coast. That will let Captain Hayes and the boys get to know her, and me and Leila really get to know one another."

"Now that is an excellent idea," said Hayes. "I will move into the Captain's cabin for the week, and you two take a cabin on the owner's deck. You will be all alone, no other passengers, very private," he said pointedly. The Masters were more concerned about their daughter having a happy marriage then than they were about the schedule of some ship. They liked Marcus and had come to see his unusual youth as less of a detriment and more of a hardening of the steel of Marcus' character. They knew Leila would be safe with him, and with the evident wealth of the Montroses, more than comfortable. They had also seen enough of life at Oakside, and with Carl and his family, to know that no-one in the family would be allowed to waste their life in the useless ways of the rich. They approved of the plan and bought into the idea of a ceremony on the ship a week or so later.

Marcus and Hayes had a quick meeting and Hayes took on the job of preparing the yacht for the trial cruise. Crewmen were arriving daily from Texas and were immediately pressed into service. One of them had been purser on one of the liners in his youth, and his experience was vital. Clarisa volunteered house staff to work on the yacht, at least until after the honeymoon cruise, and she led a group to man the galley. After all, the staff on the Three was already over two dozen, and no cooks had arrived yet. All the crew had to be fed and tended to.

Bevers even approached Carl to see when he wanted him to start the security detail on the ship. "I have myself, two sergeants, and a detail of eighteen men who have volunteered for this. They see it as a bit of an adventure, and there are no wives to answer to."

"That sounds good but make it clear to them, they may have to really work on the cruise. This family seems to attract trouble. It is not likely to be a pleasure cruise. You might as well start them now though, drill with the weapons, and get to know how to work with the Pinkertons. Everyone will go with us to the Hamptons for the summer, and early in the fall we all will be off."

So, one sunny Saturday early in May the yacht, Sea View Three, set off on her shake-down cruise. All of the Montroses were aboard, Mag and Nan had come up from Texas with Deeds. The Masters were there with some assorted aunts, uncles and cousins they were able to round up at short notice. From the Landing were the parson and his wife, Dr. Fellers, and Captain Fassert with Lieutenant Bevers. Clarisa, CJ and DJ were there from Oakside.

The guests were in awe of the Three. The boat knifed through the water at eleven knots, silently, and without any vibrations. The guests and family marvelled at what was aboard. The ship was totally electrified, from the lights to the meat lockers in the galley. There were calling tubes systems all over the ship if you needed assistance. The lounges and parlors were huge, and full of luxurious furniture in red velvet and gold trim, as well as a good assortment of leather furniture, so the ship was not too feminine. There was crystal for the tables, and for the lighting fixtures. The cabins on the owner's deck were at the same level, but in a subdued way. The Three was much larger than the Too, with three decks below, rather than one, many more cabins for the staff, and a crew of almost fifty when you took the security people into account. As the men soon found out, it had its own cannons, armory, and private army. That caused some discussions among the males on board.

"Christ, do you see all this? What is Dad thinking? I thought this was just a little cruise, not an invasion."

"You know Dad, and how trouble always seems to find us, where-ever we are."

"He has been right in the past, making sure we had what we needed."

"Then I think if he feels we may need all this at some point, we likely will."

At three in the afternoon all the guests were called together in the largest lounge for the ceremony. The Colonel gave his daughter away to a very nervous, but very determined Marcus. She had her sister as her maid of honor, but Marcus had chosen Caleb as his best man. Caleb was adorable, although he didn't think so, in a blue velvet suit with short pants.

His Aunt Nan had absolutely scrubbed him in his bath and his long blond hair glowed as a result. When the ceremony progressed to the point where he had to produce the rings, his eyes glowed with mischief as he produced one with a large spider on it and handed it to his father. Luckily, Marcus looked down at it then whispered to his son, "If you want to make it to your next birthday, your sixth, you better be able to fix this. There are lots of hungry sharks out there."

Caleb feigned confusion for a few seconds, then said, "Uh, sorry Dad, that is one of mine. Yours are in the other pocket...Here."

Leila had caught the interaction, but she was smiling as she saw a wedding ring of diamonds slip on her finger, the match to her engagement ring. After the ceremony she received congratulations from all of those present, but when she had a moment she snuck up behind Caleb and hugged him whispering into the closest ear, "You know hon, you are very cute today, like a little angel, and I liked the bit with the ring, but you are my son now, and my son gets two kisses a day, from me." Then she proceeded to do just that, two big kisses on his face, despite his protests. Afterwards though, Caleb could not help but think to himself, "That felt nice. It felt good, having a mother again, and Leila ain't all that bad."

Then the party progressed for the rest of the day. Carl had hired a string quartet that played in the main lounge, during the meal and into the evening. It was a good Montrose family day. As the yacht pulled up to the dock in the late evening Marcus met on the bridge with Carl and Captain Hayes. "Cap, after all the guests have disembarked, take us out into the bay and find us a nice place to anchor. Post an anchor watch, and have security post a watch too. We would make a nice plum target out there at anchor. Tomorrow, into the ocean and along the coast, wherever the weather looks good. Put her through her paces, if there is anything wrong, we want to know now, not out in the middle of the Indian Ocean. Tell Bevers to train his men too, on all their weapons. The ordinance is aboard now. Dad, when we get back in about a week, we will know where we stand, as far as the Three being ready for a world-wide trip."

"Try not to worry about that Marcus, after all, this is your honeymoon, the time for you and Leila to get to know one another. I checked, there is even one of those talking tubes from the owner's suite to the kitchen. You can even have your meals delivered to the rooms. Let the boys play with the boat and the big guns. They will figure it all out in the end."

The next week on the Three was very busy. Bevers' men delighted in their new "Toys". Everything was of the latest design and top quality, that was the only way Carl would have it. The four cannons and the new machine guns were a hit. "Much improved over the old Gatling guns", was the consensus. The rest of the Three's crew put her through her paces and they too were pleased. She was a good ship, quick to obey orders from her helm, and very fast.

When the ship returned eight days later, Carl went on board and came across Captain Hayes and Lieutenant Bevers on the bridge. Bevers was the first to comment, "Mr. Montrose, just want to tell you, from my standpoint, she is a wonderful ship. The four cannons and the nine repeating guns are well placed and they all work perfectly." He blushed a bit then went on. "Everybody was so enthused we used up a lot of the ordinance on board just practicing, I am afraid you will have to re-order. Proved one thing though, what you had would only have lasted fifteen or twenty minutes. In a pitched battle with a determined enemy, you will need four times that at least, and then there will be times we cannot replenish, out in the middle of nowhere. We have to have much more aboard before you sail into dangerous waters."

"Okay Bevers, I am glad you and your men gave the weapons a good workout. Prepare a list of what we need at the level you suggest, and we will reorder immediately."

Bevers was quickly off to attend to his task, and Carl turned to Hayes.

"Sir, the Three is almost perfect. She handles all seas, and answers to the helm perfectly. A nicer small ship I never saw. When you need it she can sustain fifteen knots. There is not much out there that can catch her. But, there is one problem, a tremor in the port engine shaft. On an old ship you would let it go, but this is not an old ship. She needs to go back to…"

"We should contact Newport and have the shaft replaced," finished Carl. "All right, I will telegraph them, and say you will be there next Wednesday. For what I paid for it, the Three should be absolutely perfect."

Just then Marcus joined the two. "You told him then?" he said to Hayes. "Dad, I could feel the vibration anytime they went to high speed, not at cruising, but at full speed. This is not just a matter of tuning. She will have to go into drydock and that shaft should be replaced. You make that clear to them, nothing less."

"Hell, I am going with you to ensure that, but will that intrude on you and Leila?"

"I am not taking Leila, this is my job, and she will have to get used to the fact there are times when I have to go away. I had a feeling you might want to go. How about we tale Caleb and Tully? They were good all week, weren't they?"

"Son, they are boys and they are never perfect, but they were definitely good enough to merit this little trip."

So, the next week, with Hayes and the other mates, a striped down crew of five, six Pinkertons, and the family group of Marcus, Carl, Caleb and Tully; the Three set off for Newport News, and the shipyard. It was a leisurely cruise and there was lots of time for Marcus and Carl to spend with their sons. Carl was surprised when he asked Tull how he was looking forward to the summer in the Hamptons, he got an enthusiastic response, "This year I am really looking forward to it. This is the first year I am really looking forward to the social side of it, you know, the girls and the parties. Ed and Ali had a bit of that last summer, and they are sure ready for more. You know Dad, I think you better have a talk with them. They seem to have some questions and they keep pumping Caleb about what went on in the house, you know, where he lived until Marcus got him. They want to know what he saw, and I mean exactly. Caleb keeps saying he saw nothing, but I think he knows a lot more than he admits. He's a smart kid, and if it happened, he saw it, all of it. Whatever it was, Ed and Ali intend to do it this summer, and as much as they can." Carl just groaned and felt a headache start to develop.

"What about you? Are you ready for all that yet?" asked Carl.

"I don't know Dad. I think I have grown up enough to spend some time with girls, parties and stuff. That is just part of growing up, isn't it? This other stuff that Ed and Ali are so eager for, I want to enjoy the rest first. I have some idea of what the other is about, although not exactly. We grew up on farms and ranches. The stuff in between, the meeting the girls, what real love is, finding the right girl, that is what I am looking forward to. When I get through all that, I think you and I need some talks then, about the last part."

"That is very wise Tull, you always surprise me how mature you have become. When you start to get into areas you feel you have to talk about, you come and see me right away, okay?"

At about the same time, Marcus was talking to Caleb. "You know Caleb, our time here at Oakside, for this year at least, will be over soon, and then we will move on to the "cottage" in the Hamptons; then in the fall we will start the World cruise. You are going to be quite a world traveller before you are seven. You know Caleb, I want to talk to you a bit before we get to the Hamptons. The house there is very grand, grander than all the others."

"More than this, Oakside?" asked Caleb in awe.

"Yes, more than even this, but you have to remember something, it is really not very real. Really, the whole way of life there is a bit fake. Grandpa Carl just has it so that he can conduct business there. Some people seem to expect it with the kind of money Grandpa has. Just try to enjoy it, but keep your feet on the ground. The kids there are much different too, act older, are interested in different things. We are not going to live that way. I will not allow it. You watch out for Ed and Ali, they will buy into all this and play it for all it's worth. They have their own goals for the summer I think, and I would rather not have you involved in any part of that, it can only end badly."

"I know, when boys become 12 or 13 they change, they become bigger, down there too, and they get hair, a start of a beard, down there too. And they want only one thing, a girl to... Well, like the girls at the house. They want it so bad they act sorta crazy most of the time. You know, back at the CCC, we used the swimming hole together. Marcus is not showing any of those changes yet, but his voice is starting to change a bit. Ed and Ali though, they are. I think they are going to get into, and cause, a lot of trouble this summer."

"See what I mean, and I want to keep you, and Marcus if we can, away from that."

"Yeah, we should try to save Marcus, he has been good to me, a good brother. They haven't done much for me except ask questions about how people acted there and who did what."

"You haven't..."

"What? Told them? Nah, I know what they want to hear but like you told me, I am gonna grow up proper, and a gentleman, and there are some things gentlemen don't talk about, right Dad?"

"Right Caleb, sometimes I forget how mature you are becoming." Caleb glowed with pride.

Marcus tried to spend as much time as he could on the trip with Caleb and Tully. He even took them up on the bridge with him when he was there. Both boys seemed interested in everything. The helmsman even let them steer a bit when there was no traffic. Marcus showed them the charts and how to navigate and plot positions on them, and was surprised at how well they caught on, especially Caleb, who was not yet six. He thought to himself that maybe there were a couple more family members for Montrose shipping.

When they got to the shipyard, the plan was that Carl and Marcus would check into a local hotel while Captain Hayes would stay on the ship with the striped down crew. When the shipyard found out, they protested, but Carl cut them short with, "You know, us yacht owners do talk to each other. I have heard many stories of perfectly good boats going in for some work and then having to have their carpets or furnishing replaced afterwards because of shipyard workers taking tours with oily boots. My people will ensure your workers confine themselves to the engine room, warn them. Warn your people, this is a new boat and will remain that way or you people will be paying a lot of money."

When they went out for a trial cruise with the Newport people, they tried to convince him it really was not a problem. "After all, the tremor only appears at very high speed, 14 or 15 knots and you can't afford to cruise at that speed so how often will you feel it?"

Carl would have none of that. "This is a new ship, there should be no problems. I have been advised that I could return the ship to you, and sue for non-performance of contract. Demand all my money back with interest. Do you have any idea what the interest on almost three million dollars is for a year? I am giving you a chance to right the problem, you should feel lucky."

The shipyard people conferred and decided they were indeed lucky, given the alternatives. The Three was pulled into an empty dry-dock for the new shaft to be installed. The Montroses left the ship in the hands of the crew and checked into a local hotel. By the third day they got word the boat was ready and they could leave. During the two days they had with them, both Tully and Caleb enjoyed the time with their fathers, as did their fathers.

The four went for a walk through the town of Newport, which was very different than Texas or Virginia. The streets were paved, the sidewalks concrete, and the people all seemed to be in a hurry. There were kids selling newspapers, vendors with sausages, popcorn, corn on the cob and apples.

They saw a bookstore and Caleb insisted they go in. Both boys were ecstatic to find copies of some of the first Montrose Publishing books for sale on the shelves. There were well over a dozen. Carl was a bit surprised too.

When they left, they went further down the street to find a library, which the boys insisted they also enter. They found the children's section and again searched the shelves. They found a total of eighteen books their company had issued. They also found the librarian in charge of the children's department who sat with them for several minutes.

Caleb started, "That company. Montrose, is owned by our family. We two help them chose the books to print, and have even suggested some of the topics to try to find."

"Nothing gets published until we see it and approve it," said Tully proudly.

"That explains it then. I could see there was something different about that company. The children love the books and always look for new ones whenever they come. They can understand them and are interested. I don't know why other companies don't involve children in the books they publish, right at the start. After all, they are the ones that will choose the books, the adults just pay the bill."

When they left, the two boys walked down the street excitedly talking about other books they should recommend. Carl and Marcus followed behind with Carl saying, "That was interesting, wasn't it? I didn't know getting you guys involved right at the beginning would be so successful. The idea of getting the end users of a product involved right at the beginning of its design is a good one and can be used in lots of areas. We should for example ask our customers what they want in the future with the tobacco products. Have to get the guy we hired for marketing thinking more that way. It wouldn't be so hit and miss with new products, as it is now. Find out what the people want first, then make it."

One afternoon they found a livery stable, and once assured by the owner that he had horses suitable for all of them, rented horses and went for a ride outside of the town. They found a road along the shoreline and followed it for miles. The countryside was so different from Texas or Arizona, quite lush. It was even different from Virginia with its miles on miles of cultivated fields. There were many miles of forests and grasslands. When the road returned to following the beaches, they took the horses down there and rode in the surf, something none of them had done before.

When they stopped for a rest in a deserted cove, the sat looking at the beach and the ocean. Tully blurted out, "Dad, that looks so good, can Caleb and I go for a swim?"

"But, your suits are back in the hotel," said Carl.

"Come on Dad, a little skinny won't hurt anyone, and we are out here in the middle of nowhere, there is nobody to see us," replied Tully.

"Yeah," said Caleb.

"Oh, all right, but not too deep, remember Caleb is just learning to swim and he is not very tall, just to his waist deep."

Carl and Marcus watched the two frolic in the surf, then finally Marcus stood and started stripping off his clothes. "They are having too much fun out there, I am going in too. You should think about it Dad."

"Me, I am a titan of industry, an industrialist. What would my colleagues say if they saw me frolicking in the waves indecently."

"Not likely, but even if they did, what are they gonna do, take away the mines, railways, and property? Dad, live your life when the chance appears, enjoy." Then he ran naked into the waves and joined the others, who were a bit surprised, but glad to welcome him nevertheless.

Carl considered what had been said for a few moments, then stood muttering, "I oughta have my head read, doing something like this, but this does look like fun, and I should enjoy stuff like this while I still can." He then entered the water, not totally nude, but almost; he still had on his under-alls. The four played in the water for a good hour and a half, enjoying themselves and totally occupied. None of them noticed the lone figure slink from the undergrowth to the pile of clothes and rifle through the pockets of the adult clothes, he didn't bother with the kids' stuff, not expecting much of use in them. He grabbed the two sets of adult clothes and scurried of into the brush. He went through the pockets again as he hurried away. The one set, the younger and smaller set, had not yielded much of interest, just thirty or forty dollars. The other set though, a gold mine that almost stopped him in his tracks. There was a nice gold fountain pen, two gold watches, five nice cigars, the expensive ones, a set of eyeglasses, some matches, some loose cash, about a hundred, and a billfold. The billfold was what shocked him, it contained ten or fifteen business cards, but he didn't know how to read, and over twenty thousand, almost thirty, dollars. He wondered what sort of people walked around with money like that, no one he knew for sure. He stopped and sat on a log at the side of the road. He wondered what he could do with the money. If he started to spend money like that around there, people would notice, and wonder how he got it. There was no legal way. He would have to go away, far away, but there was enough there he could buy a little place of his own and manage on his own from the rest for ten or fifteen years, if he was careful. "Whoever you are, you silly bastard, you changed my life. Thankyou."

When the four came out of the water, they sat on the beach for a bit to dry in the sun. Marcus was the first to notice something. "Dad, did you do something with the clothes, Caleb's and Tull's are here, but where are ours?"

The other three rushed over to the little pile of clothing then they took inventory. Carl pronounced the verdict. "Well, Caleb and Tully are okay, all their clothes are here, get dressed you two. I have just the under-alls, and they don't hide much. But Marcus, you're….."

"I know, I know. Everything to hide, and nothing to do it with."

"Here Dad, take my shirt, I have a sweater. You can tie it around your waist. It's not very big but at least it will hide the, you know."

"Thanks Caleb, and I will take you up on that."

We are going to have to find some neighbors nearby and try to get them to help us, lend us some clothes, all on trust, since all the real money is gone. I have more in the safe at the hotel, but we have to get there, which we won't dressed like this. The group went up to the road, which still was blessedly free from traffic, and turned further away from town, as they already knew there was not much settlement between there and the city. They went a couple of miles further and came upon a small but well-kept farm. There was a lady hanging clothes on a line in a side yard, and two boys sitting on a bench on a verandah by the front door. The four entered the yard but stopped half way to the lady in the yard. Carl sent Tully and Caleb forward to explain the situation and ask for help. "Be polite Tull, we do not want to frighten her."

Tully and Caleb edged forward and Tully spoke, "Sorry to bother you ma'am, but we need some help. We were swimming down the road on the beach a while back, and someone stole our Dad's clothes and money. He wondered if they could borrow some clothes." The lady listened intently, then glanced at the other two on their horses.

She reached in her clothes basket and came up with a revolver. Holding it lightly, she advanced on the two men on the horses. "It's not too often two men as near naked as you two show up on my doorstep asking to borrow some clothing. Now I daresay, you two really do need those clothes, especially the young one there with that tiny shirt around his waist that really doesn't hide much. My husband died a year or so back but there are still some of his things around that might do, go around to the barn and I will send this one out with what I have. You can change there, then come back around to the front porch where I will give you a glass of lemonade before you head on your way. You two older ones are looking a mite sunburned."

Ten minutes later, two very embarrassed men, and two very amused Montrose children were sitting on the front porch in rockers with the lady of the house and her children. She commented, "Well, you two look better, a bit like farmers, but better. Now I can see the two younger ones going skinny dipping, but you other two? Have to admit for the younger one though, that would sure be a way to attract a lot of girls."

"Married ma'am, just a week ago," said a blushing Marcus.

"Carl Montrose Ma'am, my son Marcus, his son Caleb is the younger one and my son Tully, the elder. We can't thank you enough for rescuing us. I should never have let myself be talked into this, but as you age you sometimes let the younger ones talk you into things, just to get a bit of that youth back."

"Mr. Montrose, you are not all that old. My name is Agatha Harrison. My husband was Colonel Roger Harrison, of the union army. These are my two sons, Drew is the elder and Sam the younger. We bought this place just after the war and did fairly well with it. But, since my husband died, I have struggled. Too much for a single woman. This is our last week here, that Roland Fidelity bank in town will take over next week. I will come out of it with enough to rent a little place on the side of the city. My father always said that was where I would end up when I left to marry Roger, and that was before the war. A lot of us have seen their fortunes changed by that war, haven't they, even the high and mighty Atlanta Turners? They would have turned over in their graves knowing I was teaching high school, before the children were born."

"The Atlanta Turners? My wife was one of them. We married before the war too, and her dying wish was that I get our three sons of the time out of the South before it started, save them. We sold Oakside and moved to Chicago, then out west. I got Oakside back and rebuilt it. Reminds me of her."

"Your wife was Mary Turner then? We were cousins, first cousins, I was at Oakside a couple times before the war, with Roger. Beautiful house, beautiful area."

"Mary loved to have parties. There were so many, and so many people, I am afraid I don't remember. Sorry. But, you mentioned you were a teacher. Near Oakside, there are two new growing villages and there is a new middle school, soon to be a high school. Would you like me to put your name forward, I am sure you could get a job there, with my recommendation. There are free houses for newcomers and you said you already like the area and have to move anyway."

"I am afraid I couldn't, much as I would like to. You see, when I was teaching before, I had to quit when Drew was born, he is blind and I had to stay home to look after him, and teach him what I could."

"Drew? Blind?" Both Carl and Marcus were looking at Drew closely. "There is a new school opening right on the estate in the fall, the Jennifer Baxter School for the Blind. It will be totally modern, first rate, perhaps even one of the best in the country, and it is free, sponsored by one of our cigarette brands, Tulls. You see Tully here was blind for a while and we established the school for him. Now Drew can take his place, we will see to it. You can take one of the new houses in the village, Oakside Landing, teach at the school and have Drew home for the weekends."

"That all sounds so perfect."

Carl went on, "I don't have any of my cards, they were in my suit, but before we leave I will get you the name of who to contact there, so count on moving there for the fall, a new job, and a school for Drew. Now, we had better get into town and get ourselves sorted out there. Thankyou again for the clothes, I will get them back to you."

As they rode back to town, Marcus said to Carl, "Funny isn't it, how something brought us to this point at this time, to people who need our help. Without the events at the beach, we would have just ridden by."

"Yes," said Carl, "But I still should not have gone swimming near naked. The results could have been quite embarrassing, more than they were."

At the Livery, the owner was quite surprised to have his horses returned to him by two farmers, when he had rented them to two business men. At the hotel, the desk clerk glanced up when they entered, and said, "Deliveries to the kitchen are made to the back, not here in the lobby."

"Oh stop it you fool. I am Carl Montrose, and I want the keys to my rooms." As he was leaving Carl turned and said, "Have your head laundry person come and see me in an hour, and also, have the head of the Roland Fidelity Bank come and see me here, at his earliest opportunity."

When the bank manager, a Cecil Dawson, arrived, Carl said, "We both know that you offered a ridiculously low price to Agatha Harrison for her farm, taking advantage of her situation." Carl handed the man a draft. "When you complete arrangements next week you will increase your offer by that amount. Tell her you were examining your portfolio and realized your mistake and corrected the matter. Say you were sorry for the mistake. In case you are wondering who I am, giving you orders like this, check with your bank head office. You will see that I bought your bank. Dawson, I never expect to hear your name again, if it is concerning anything shady like this, you will be discharged and likely jailed. You have made the one mistake you are allowed, to work for me. Now, get out of here, and do as I instructed."

Marcus was called to the shipyard the next morning, and telegraphed back to Carl that the Three was ready, they could leave the next day. Carl, Caleb and Marcus rented a carriage and driver from the livery that afternoon and drove out to the Harrison farm. Agatha had been thinking about the day before and come to the conclusion it was all too good to be true. Therefore, she was surprised when a large carriage pulled into her yard and Carl Montrose got out with the two boys.

The four boys gathered on one end of the porch and talked. Carl and Agatha sat at the other end and chatted quietly.

"You know, I almost convinced myself that you were a dream, that nothing that day really happened."

"Me? A dream? Not likely. But I did come to believe that maybe Mary had something to do with it, as an angel up there. This school will be good for Drew and I think you will come to love it there at the Landing. It was meant to be." He passed her a card. "This is the card of a trusted friend and advisor, Lionel Deeds. Most of the family is going abroad, starting in a few days. Deeds will be staying at Oakside while we are away and tend to affairs there. I have already telegraphed him and filled him in. The school will begin its intake August 15th and Drew is already enrolled. Deeds says he will have the deed to a new house by the school where you will be working, ready for August 1st. When you get down there early in August, look him up at Oakside. He will get you settled and see that things go well."

The Three left the next morning for Virginia. It was a quick quiet trip and the boat performed flawlessly, no sign of the tremor. The evening after it arrived at Oakside, at dinner, Carl made his announcement.

"Since everything here is in hand, Diz is finished with the horses, the factories are running like swiss watches under their new managers, Des has legal matters ready to turn over to Deeds; we shall leave the day after tomorrow to start our adventures. The Hamptons first, then abroad in the fall. Mrs. Langley has been alerted to our imminent arrival. You have one day to gather all you want to take with you and move it to your cabins on the Three. New nannies and tutors have been engaged and they will meet us in the Hamptons. Then, God Help Us, in the fall, we are off."

There was quiet at the table. All present were thinking of the year ahead and the trip around the world. Most were wondering what they would see and who they would meet, perhaps what they would gain from the trip. Caleb was gloomily thinking of the changes that would occur, he didn't like change. Ed and Ali were thinking of the one goal they had, first with the girls in the Hamptons, and then hopefully with others as they travelled. They were very eager to get started. Carl looked at them, knew what they were thinking, and immediately felt a headache start that he was sure would last for a year and a half.

The Montroses would be going abroad, and Carl was not sure the world was ready for them.